The Secret of the Prince Bishops

Wayne Robson

authorHOUSE®

AuthorHouse™ UK Ltd.
500 Avebury Boulevard
Central Milton Keynes, MK9 2BE
www.authorhouse.co.uk
Phone: 08001974150

First published by AuthorHouse 5/21/2009

ISBN: 978-1-4389-7420-0 (sc)

This book is printed on acid-free paper.

CHAPTER ONE

THE NORTH AFRICAN DESERT.

The body had been cleansed and purified. The scent of herb potions made his head swim, feeling light as if floating in the clouds. Were there any clouds?

For three days he had fasted, he felt weak but his mind was talking to him.

Why are you here?

Why did you come?

He stared at three walls of rock, only a candle flame flickering in the darkness showed him a doorway or porch way or entrance.

Entrance to what?

With his companions he had ridden hard over the desert to this place.

Why? Only his mind told him he had to be here.

He'd heard the voices many weeks ago.

Who were they?

What did they want of him?

A figure appeared in the entrance, staring into the tomb-like interior.

"You will follow me now, you are prepared," the voice seemed like a phantom, dressed in a white toga-like robe.

The man rose, dressed only with a piece of linen around his waist. Unsteady on his feet, the figure held out his arm and steadied the visitor. They walked through what seemed like a myriad of catacombs, passages hewn out of the solid rock.

The figure stopped.

"You will go straight ahead, do not deviate," the voice seemed to drift away and then it was gone.

He walked on and entered a vast chamber lit by hundreds of candles but the scent was burning his mind.

A voice spoke but it was more like the hiss of a python.

"Sit in the centre and we shall disclose the reasons for you coming."

The voice seemed as if it was in a trance.

"Why did you come?" the voice spoke.

"My mind was telling me, I seem to have been brought here, I could do no other," the visitor said.

"Very well, that is how it should be." A ghost-like figure emerged from behind what seemed to be an altar.

"Who are you and what do you want of me?" the visitor enquired trying to see the figure appearing before him through tired and squinting eyes.

The figure spoke.

"I have much to impart to you, listen and remember well. We are the servants of the ancient ones who lived many lifetimes before. Those ancients travelled the world and held the secrets of the universe. After great chaos they split into many groups helping mankind, instructing them and giving some the secrets.

Many of your kind were endowed with secrets but

only to help mankind live and prosper. Many of your kind used those secrets and power to destroy only for the benefit of themselves.

You have been chosen to right that wrong.

We signalled your mind to come to this place so we could tell you what must be done.

There is no deviation from this. We are not asking you, we are telling you what must be done and you will be able to do it."

"Why have you chosen me for this purpose?" the visitor asked wondering what the future could hold.

"You are the chosen one, the one who will lead victorious armies," the voice trembled.

"But you must pay the price with immortality if you succeed."

"Immortality," the visitor replied shocked. "I will become one with the immortals?"

"Only if you follow our directions, any deviation in course will be fatal," the voice moved closer.

"Are you willing to follow the chosen path?" the voice changed tone not enquiring but suggesting.

"I am," the visitor replied thinking only of greatness, immortality and being the chosen one.

"Listen well and remember. Many ages past, a great gift of power was bestowed on the Persian Empire from the ancients in the East. This power has become corrupt and cannot be allowed to go on.

It was given as a symbol of hope and faith to increase the ability of man to cope with the future. Now it is used to destroy mankind and it must cease. You are the chosen one to carry out our commands," the voice drifted back to a hissing as if sickened by what mankind had done.

"I will obey your commands mighty one," the visitor bowed.

"You will on pain of death," hissed the voice.

The visitor bowed and replied, "I will."

"Then listen well and remember. What you seek is inlaid in a carrying box carved with the visions of the Gods.

What is inside does not concern you.

You will never know for you must not look.

If you see or try to use this power, it will be upon pain of death.

You will take this source of power and hide it for all eternity so that no man shall ever again try to misuse it.

You will be watched by the Gods in your endeavours and you shall triumph only if you keep to the path you have today sworn by."

The visitor stood erect, "what is the path you have chosen for me?"

"Very well, you are the chosen one to create a New World and a New World order.

Speak of this to none. You will retrieve the secret of the Persian Fire and hide it forever. It must never again be used against humanity. Seek the box only, now go and do not return." The snake-like apparition seemed to dissolve back into the darkness.

"I cannot fight the Persian Fire, it is used to destroy armies, it is the lightning of the Gods," shouted the visitor.

A voice from the air said, "Fear not, you will succeed."

The visitor turned, a light now seemed to appear from one of the tunnels.

He walked towards the source of the light. Stumbling, he stopped, his eyes hit by shafts of sunlight. He sank to his knees until his eyes once again beheld the light of day and the warmth of the sun spread over his body.

His companions saw him.

Running over to the porch way, they helped him walk over the burning sand to the camp.

The man stood erect and shouted, "bring me my armour and water."

He dressed, threw water over his body and drank. Looking up he said,

"Now I am prepared to become the King of Kings, the Master of this World."

The companions all drew their swords and in unison shouted,

"Hail our King, Hail Alexander."

Alexander gathered his horse and mounted.

"Now let us away from this Oracle, I have work to do," Alexander issued the order.

"We must ride from here at Siwa and destroy the Persians."

Then they were gone, riding like the wind throwing up clouds of sand as if making offerings to the Gods, heading straight for the Persian Army.

YEAR 330 BC

Alexander's army marched ruthlessly onward.

Nearly three years had passed and King Darius had been defeated at Issus and two years later at Gaugamela, the king had fled Eastward.

Alexander issued the order.

"Find Darius, bring him, his followers and belongings to me. I want him alive. I need to talk to him. Tell him I am merciful."

Several of Alexander's top commanders had tracked Darius in the East of his country.

Eventually they came upon a caravan where they were shown his body, brutally murdered by one of his provincial governors.

Alexander had given orders to take him alive. The penalty for governor Bessus was not the friendship of the Greeks but death.

The soldiers took what remained of the caravan back to the Greek camp.

Alexander viewed the murdered body.

"This is no way for this man to die, build a funeral pyre and bury him with respect," he ordered.

"Put all of his belongings in my tent," Alexander said, he had already seen a carved box, which he knew, was the reason he was there.

"Leave no guards around, I need to give praise to the Gods for our victory. Take all the precious stones and silks. The gold and silver is to be shared among the army, leave everything else, touch nothing or we may offend the Gods."

Alexander left, leaving the commanders of his army to give praise and bury Darius.

Alexander stared at the box. It seemed fairly ordinary about two arms long and half an arm wide. The inscriptions and signs carved into the wood were icons of the Gods but nothing seemed as if it was dangerous or harmful.

Was this indeed the secret of the Persian Fire? It

hardly seemed possible, whatever was inside could help destroy or rule the World.

He looked at the lock, only a metal bolt secured the top, thinking why not look at the secret of the Ancient Ones?

He suddenly remembered the Oracle's words. "Look not inside," or were they the words? It seemed many years since he undertook the quest. He had fulfilled all that had been asked of him and the secret was in his hands.

Drawing back from the box, he walked to the tent entrance.

"Ptolemy," he shouted for his second-in-command.

The commander entered, bowed and saluted.

"My Lord," he said, "What is your command?"

Alexander put an arm around his shoulder, "I need to speak with you good friend. I have a mission for you and it must be done without question or deviation."

"As always My Lord, whatever you wish, it will be done," Ptolemy replied.

Alexander spoke, his voice trembling, "you will take this box to Byzantium, there you will make it disappear. No one must ever find this box again. Inside are messages from the Gods that should never be read by mortals. That is why you will hide this away forever. Do not look inside for certain death will be upon you. On your return, you will go to Alexandria. There you will rule and govern Upper Egypt in my place. May the Gods be with you."

"Your wishes are my commands mighty king, may the Gods smile on you," replied Ptolemy.

"You leave at first light and I will take the army to Babylon." Alexander breathed a sigh as if a heavy weight had been lifted from his shoulders.

Alexander's sleep that night was broken, thoughts of the Oracle still swilled in his head. How could such a small thing be so mighty? What was it that could rain down terror on the mightiest of armies?

He rose from his bed, walked to the box and ran his hands over it. He was ruler of the World, he was immortal and no one could harm him.

He slid back the bolt and opened the lid.

Resting on silken cloth were three pieces of a strange metal but staring up at him was a golden claw as if copied from some mythical bird, as large a man's hand and lying beside was the largest red ruby he had ever seen. This was nearly as long as the claw and seemed to have been shaped in some strange geometrical design.

As he picked up the claw, white dust particles blew around from the box. Alexander tried to wipe them from his body. He suddenly remembered the Oracle's warning, "Do not look inside, certain death." Alexander smiled returning everything. His mind raced thinking it cannot be certain death, everything is here and it will be lost for eternity.

Ptolemy took his section of the Army and set off for Byzantium the following morning. He would return to Egypt to rule. Alexander later entered Babylon.

That night it seemed that Zeus himself was throwing thunderbolts. Alexander stared out at the sky from his Babylonian palace. It seemed to his followers that a nearby thunderbolt had illuminated Alexander, a blue glow appeared all over his body. He convulsed and fell dead. The Oracle's words were true.

CHAPTER TWO

LINDISFARNE 793 AD

In this year terrible portents appeared over Northumbria which sorely affrighted the inhabitants. There were exceptional flashes of lightening and fiery dragons were seen flying through the air.

On the 8th June in that year of the Lord, the heathens came and destroyed Gods church here with raping and slaughter.

They did not come by all the treasures there. Some of the monks escaped taking with them their Gospels. Their fellow monks were killed or enslaved and the monastery put to the torch.

On the mainland the remaining monks wandered for many years, fearing to stay in one place too long because of the raiding parties of the Norsemen.

Over the years, many Vikings had settled and from their stronghold at York, the Kingdom of Northumbria was born.

CONSTANTINOPLE CIRCA. 900 AD.

Everyone feared the Varangian Guard.

Vicious Norse mercenaries who fought for Gold and plundered everything that their employer's directed them to do. They kept the Sultan in power and destroyed all that threatened that power.

The Bloodaxe was no different.

He and his followers had fought for many years in these hot lands. The cold of their homeland was just a fading memory.

His name was Eric but Bloodaxe was added by his enemies because the double-headed axe he carried had seen so much action and spilt so much blood, that the might of his reputation carried all before him.

Something was troubling Eric. He had received messages from his homeland that he was now the rightful heir to the Kingdom of Northumbria and was to be crowned in Viking York.

Eric summoned his senior officers.

He had never wanted to live in any of the palaces there, perhaps, he thought it would make them as soft as his employers. So a tented village was always enough.

As the officers arrived Eric spoke of the messages, though they were really a summons.

"I am to become King in the land of Northumbria, so our time here is at an end. We will take what is ours, as much as we can carry and leave this land," Eric spoke with absolute command.

There was no need to tell the Sultan why or when, the command was Eric's and no one stood in his way. Over the next few days, horses and carts were duly assembled and the Guards exercised their right to Palace Plunder. This meant that they could indeed take whatever they wanted as long as they could carry it.

However, Eric was an honourable man.

His message for an audience with the Sultan had been granted and he now stood in the throne hall of the palace. The palace guards were standing to attention but knew they could not and dare not stop Eric and his small army of heathen hordes.

"Your Majesty, I and my men will leave shortly. There are enough warriors to see that you will be kept safe in your lands. We will return to ours. It is my intention to take our plunder with us and at this moment we are loading our wagons," Eric bowed, turned and walked away from a glorious campaign, still alive and rich.

The next morning Eric and his main commanders were checking the wagons.

Gold and Silver plate, jewels, precious silks and perfumes.

"My Lord," said Gudrun, commander of the wagons.

"We will encounter much hardship on this trip. The mountains will be difficult with the wagons but we will be halted by none if they wish to live.

I fear though we must not tempt fate with bad omens.

This box hidden in the crypt was never touched, the stories of its magical power say no one must go near it."

Eric laughed, "I'm near it now, and I'm still here. Do not be afraid of stories."

CIRCA 935 AD

Eric the Bloodaxe and his followers had no problems in the long haul home and now had been crowned Viking King at York.

He was troubled. He had many visions in his dreams. The seers could not foretell the reasons for this.

This last night, Eric was travelling in the countryside, sleeping in a tented village.

The dream came over him but this time a figure appeared to speak.

"The box of the Gods must have safe passage to the people who will come to the Dun Holme. Seek them out, for they will keep the gift of the Gods safe," the voice was disappearing almost with a hissing sound.

Eric woke with a start. What was the meaning of this dream? Who are the people to come to the Dun Holme? What Gods?

Eric summoned his advisors to the tent. "I have been told in a dream to seek for the people of the Dun Holme. Who are they? They speak of Gods." Eric sank onto his bed. "Find the people and the meaning. I don't understand what is needed of me," he drifted off into a deep sleep.

"It was not difficult to interpret the dream," spoke the seer later. "The gift of the Gods must be returned to the God-Like people. The wandering monks. They reside at Chester-Le-Street."

Eric gave his orders, "take the box and give it to those monks, tell them not to open it for the wrath of the Gods will come and devour them all. Death follows the box. This was foretold by the ancients."

The morning broke with menacing clouds over the Stain Moor. Eric always wondered how such a relic could hold so much fear for mankind.

A box carved by the Gods with a metal bolt, surely it cannot be evil. The box would lie with the monks alongside the remains of St. Cuthbert. There it would be safe.

Eric slid the bolt and opened the box.

Inside lying on a bed of silk were three metal rods.

Then he saw the claw of gold. He picked it up to marvel at the carving of this mythical looking bird's claw. White dust powder fell over his clothes.

He looked at the precious stone, a ruby of enormous size.

What did all this mean?

He closed the box, he knew nothing was to be disturbed.

He knew it was against the commandment to open and look in the box but nothing happened, he was safe.

Outside the thunder roared. Odin was angry. Thor was firing lightening bolts.

Eric shouted for his first commander.

He entered running, nearly out of breath. "My Lord, the cart is prepared, let me take the box."

He picked it up, walked out of the tent and placed it on the cart.

"Guard that with your life," Eric shouted, "and make sure the monks know all the tales about it, they probably enjoy a good story."

The cart rumbled off across the Stain Moor.

Eric put on a large cloak, nothing could keep this rain out.

He walked a few steps from his tent and stopped.

The lightening crashed all around.

One bolt seemed to strike the earth close to him.

The soldiers looked in amazement and fear.

Eric's body seemed to have a blue glow all around, the soldiers cowed. Was this some mighty portent from the Gods?

Eric clutched at his heart and fell dead.

995 AD

The community of monks finally moved to the Hill Island or using its old name, the Dun Holme. It was safe here from Viking raids. It was defendable and almost inaccessible from three sides in the massive bend of the river.

It would be here that the foundation stones of a great cathedral would be laid.

It was here that the sacred remains of St. Cuthbert would finally come to rest.

It was here that the great gospel book would reside along with the treasures that had accumulated.

It was well known in tales of the Ancients, that in the region of Scythia dwelled Griffins which defended great treasure troves of gold.

Here, in this, the Lord's house the treasure and secrets would remain.

The Ancients had found the resting-place, guarded by pious and trustworthy mankind.

All would now be safe, hidden from view and revered.

And so it was for more than 300 years.

CHAPTER THREE

IN THE YEAR OF OUR LORD, 1346.

The commanders, Percy and Neville had mustered the English Army at the Prince Bishop's Palace at Bishop Auckland.

The Scottish King, David Bruce, son of Robert, with the aid of the French, had sacked the Northumbria town of Hexham and his army was moving toward Durham.

Lord Percy spoke to one of his Captains, "this palace is pretty good for a church man eh!"

Captain Welsh replied, "the Lord does move in mysterious ways. I could not afford this if I battled all my life."

Percy spoke, "we have a problem. The Scottish Army is camped near the Bear Park and we fear Durham might fall. I want you to take a squad of battle hardened soldiers and get to the Cathedral. The relics and treasures of our Lord must not fall into Scottish hands or especially the French.

I have written this letter which you will present to the Prince Bishop. It explains everything. He will see that what we are doing is prudent for the moment.

Bring everything back here for safe keeping."

The Captain replied, "no problem Sir but as I do not know the area may I take some of the local squadrons who know the terrain?"

"Of course," said Percy, "check with Lord Neville, he will know the best men."

Welsh saluted, turned and sought out the Lord Neville.

"I have a duty for the Lord Percy to get to the Cathedral before the Scots and he suggested that you could tell me which local men I could use, as they know the area," said Welsh.

Lord Neville knew what was required.

"I'll give the orders for William De Hertburn and his squad to accompany you. Take my seal and get him to come here," Neville spoke quietly but with a commanding tone.

Each squad was being arranged in their battle groups so it was not difficult to locate De Hertburn. On seeing the seal of Neville, he followed Welsh to his Lordship.

"Welcome De Hertburn," said Neville, "I want you to take your troops with Welsh and get to the Cathedral, bring back the relics and make it fast or the Scots will be upon you. You know the area well don't you?"

"I do indeed Sir, my men know every road, ditch and gully between Stockton and Durham. After all my family came from Stockton and exchanged Hertburn for the Old Hall."

"Of course," said Neville, "my apologies, my friend. I forgot that your family took the name of the Hall. Now go all of you, and God speed. May the Lord bless our endeavours today. Good luck Captain Welsh and to you Wessyngton."

The forward sentries had reported the Scots camping down and not even sending raiding parties out. The squadron of Wessyngton had no problems reaching the Cathedral and loading the treasures onto their carts.

The Bishop seemed to be uneasy when the Gospel Book was loaded but he looked relieved when the relics of St. Cuthbert were loaded with the carved box.

The soldiers knew of the tales of the relics.

In the Rites of Durham, it said that there was at Cuthbert's shrine, part of the Rod of Moses and a Griffin claw with a precious stone said to be worth a King's ransom.

The soldiers, being superstitious, kept well clear of the relics.

The party moved off, heading toward the palace at Bishop Auckland.

Some three miles south of Durham, stands the great Whin Sill.

This outcrop of rock wanders for miles along the high point of Durham.

The squadron hauled the horses and carts to the top of the Sill and turned west keeping the Kirk always in their sights.

There seemed to be a lot of army activity along the Sill.

A large squadron of mounted cavalry was spreading along the ridge.

"It looks like they're getting ready to attack," De Hertburn said to Welsh.

Welsh had observed down on the level what appeared to be numerous Scots infantrymen, seemingly totally oblivious to the English cavalry.

De Hertburn looked down the plain, "do you fancy joining them and having a first go at the Scots?" he said with a sly grin.

"Why not?" replied Welsh "but we have to make safe this cargo first."

"We'll leave it under guard at the Kirk," said De Hertburn.

The horses pulled the cart for several hundred yards until they found some level ground outside the Kirk.

Welsh said, "if we're leaving this here, even guarded, we need to make a list of what we've got, so we can check it when we get back. These soldiers are good but I wouldn't trust them as far as I can spit."

De Hertburn walked to the main door of the Kirk and saw the local priest.

"Father," he said, "can you write?"

"Of course my son, what is it you require?" said the priest.

"The Cathedral goods are in those carts and we need to off-load them here, make a check list and go and fight the Scots," said De Hertburn.

The soldiers lifted the boxes and put them in the Kirk. They mounted their horses and charged off after the main cavalry. The Scots still seemed unaware of the English presence and shortly after mustering for the charge down the Sill and along the plain, hundreds of Scots were lying dead from the Sill to the river.

De Hertburn shouted to Welsh, "round up our men and let's get back or the Lord Neville will string us up."

Welsh replied wiping sweat away, "that was one hell of a Race down there, we certainly butchered those Scots."

The main part of the army was coming down from Auckland off the Sill, making camp around Hett, a mile South of the river. Everyone knew the big battle would come tomorrow but with God's help the English would prevail.

De Hertburn and Welsh with their troop, or what was left of them, cantered toward the Sill and along to the Kirk.

"We need to get the carts loaded and to Auckland before getting to camp," said Welsh.

"Find the priest and get the list so I can check to see that these thieving swines haven't helped themselves," said De Hertburn.

Welsh came out of the Kirk, the men had already loaded most of the boxes and books onto the carts.

"Here's the priests list," said Welsh.

De Hertburn took the script. "Where the hell did this paper come from?" yelled De Hertburn.

"I think the priest just wrote it on a page from one of the books," said Welsh.

"Sweet Jesus, if Neville or Percy find out some of the Cathedral goods have been defaced, we'll swing for it," said De Hertburn.

Welsh looked horrified, "just make sure all is correct and say nothing. You just don't known what happens in the heat of battle," said Welsh.

"All right," said De Hertburn, "I'll dispose of the list, get the carts to Auckland and get back to Hett. After the battle tomorrow, we can go our separate ways and forget this."

The carts were driven off to Auckland, the boxes wrapped in cloth, all the books carefully stacked and covered.

Back at the Kirk the priest was praying. "Who knows what will happen tomorrow, the Scots cannot be allowed to rob us of these relics," the priest said, kneeling before the altar. He knew many places to hide just in case but before him and behind the altar was a long box wrapped in cloth. It should have been on the carts but these relics were too precious for ordinary man. The priest had took it upon himself to take it back to the Cathedral when the countryside was quiet again, for now he would keep it hidden from men's eyes.

He had written in one of the books on the carts what had happened and that the sacred relics would be returned. He knew that because of untrustworthy people, he had written in the book some lines in a form of code that only he and the three could decipher. He had recognised lines already written by the Prince Bishop. He thought that this was the best way to keep the relics safe. He was going to make sure these Cathedral relics were returned to the Prince Bishop, after all he was a man of God.

The following day, the armies met in a bloody battle. The Lords Percy and Neville were victorious. It took several days to capture and rout the stragglers of the Scots Army. These invaders from North of the border would never take the Dun Holme, its castle or cathedral.

The battle had taken its toll on both sides.

Even the intervention of the French, mostly Knights Templar, had not turned the tide.

It was said that it was their appearance at Bannockburn that had won the day for the Scots.

They had been living there, in exile since that fateful Friday 13th when most of their comrades had been rounded up by the Inquisition.

The day after the battle, the Lords Percy, Neville and their commanders, gave thanks for their victory in the Cathedral.

The treasures of the cathedral were returned, several days later, accompanied by the priest of the Kirk.

Inside the great nave, he saw a man he knew well, having served him for many years.

"Greetings my Lord Bishop," he said bowing his head.

"Its good to see you again, old friend," replied the Bishop.

The old Bishop was instructing the Master Masons on exactly how he wanted his tomb area built. He was going back and forward across the Palace Green to check on restoration and additions to an area of the Castle.

"All the relics as you instructed, are present my Lord. They are outside, what is your wish for them?" inquired the priest. " I kept the box wrapped separate but I had to make a list for the soldiers and there were no writing materials, so I had to use."

The Bishop stopped him, "never fear Father, I know, needs must when it's the Lord's duty. Bring the relics in," the Bishop giving instructions on where they were to be placed.

All were replaced, except the engraved box.

"This is the famous Box of the Gods, is it not my Lord?" asked the priest.

"Yes," replied the Bishop, "this has caused many problems for the Prince Bishops.

Let me tell you Father, you have always served me well, therefore what I say to you now you will never repeat. Word has been given from one Bishop to the next about this relic for over three hundred years. I think it is about time that this stupidity ceased. I have plans for this."

"How may that be done?" asked the priest.

"That which was hidden from man's eyes should forever more never be seen," the Bishop said looking sad but relieved. "We must ensure that this never again gives us any cause for concern or worry. Leave this here with me. I shall deal with this. Let not this box or its contents give man concern again. Only when man is ready to receive once again the word of God, should this be revealed."

The priest bowed, kissed the Bishops hand, and left.

De Hertburn returned home to his Hall in Wessyngton and never uttered a word. He kept the priest's list hidden. Welsh had fallen from his horse and was killed by a Scottish sword during the battle.

There was a strange story about some English soldiers, a couple of weeks later, trying to loot a Kirk and accidentally had killed a priest trying to stop them. Lord Neville had had them hung.

On the 31st December 1540, the Cathedral and its contents were surrendered to the Crown. The rod of Moses, griffin claw of gold and precious stones were never found.

CHAPTER FOUR

The English Colonies.

It was the 6th of June 1768. The work had finally stopped.

Despite the attentions of mosquitoes, rattlesnakes and the local Indian tribes, it was finished.

A total of 1,737 days in the field.

This meticulous survey had taken nearly five years of his life.

He sat on a stone and his mind wandered back while drawing sketches on his note pad.

Not bad for a simple Geordie lad, he thought.

He had always found mathematics and astronomy easy. Perhaps that was why the Royal Society had heard of him.

Founded in 1660, the Society was the National Academy of Sciences supporting and encouraging research into both pure and applied sciences. Fellowship of the society was, of course, strictly limited.

He had been selected by the Royal Society to travel to Sumatra to plot the transit of the planet Venus but that expedition had fallen foul of a French man-of-war. So ultimately he had ended up at the Cape of Good Hope and then St. Helena, drawing maps and collecting tidal data.

Back home, he had been called to Kiplin Hall, near Richmond, the home of Lord Baltimore.

It was then that he had been informed about the long running boundary dispute over the possession of land in the developing provinces of America.

Why he and Charles had been chosen seemed a mystery but on the 15th November 1763, they had arrived here to begin their commission.

The work was really to provide the boundary lines between the lands belonging to Baltimore and Penn. East to West separating Pennsylvania from Maryland and part of West Virginia and North to South between Maryland and Delaware.

As far as they could, every fifth mile stone marker had on one side the coat of arms of Baltimore and on the other Penn.

This last marker had been shaped as an obelisk, only about 4 feet high, with the coats of arms engraved, along with the completion date.

This last marker would have to be used for something else.

Jeremiah was 35 years old, at the completion.

On the last day, one of his helpers came to him with a question.

He was nearly as old as Jeremiah, being 31 at the time.

"How are you today?" Tom enquired politely, "I see

you're drawing again."

"Just thinking about building up my house back home, now that I've finished here," said Jeremiah.

Tom looked at his sketches.

"That's an interesting concept you've got there," said Tom.

Jeremiah looked down at his rough drawings.

"There's a few things I thought I would change. I never liked wide staircases, so I'm going to build them narrower. Corners always seemed such a waste of space, so I thought a pentagon or octagon shape for the rooms and I've always fancied a dome on the roof to let more light in," Jeremiah sighed, "maybe one day I'll have the time."

"Those are brilliant ideas," said Tom, "I don't know why anyone hasn't thought of them before. I trained as an architect but never got taught anything like that. Maybe someday I might get around to designing such buildings."

"Who knows what the future holds," said Jeremiah.

Young Tom, as he called him, had come with a simple problem.

"Now we have completed this work, can I bring my friend to see you? He has something he'd like to show you and I believe it is to do with where you come from. I have studied what it says and I am good with puzzles but this is nothing to do with my country, so I thought you might understand it better," Tom asked.

Jeremiah replied, "Of course, I'll have a look at it."

And that's where the problem began.

The next day Tom arrived with his pal who he

introduced as George. He was about eight years older than Tom.

He handed Jeremiah what looked like a piece of parchment.

As Jeremiah unfolded the paper, his eyes lit up.

It was a list.

A list that said the contents belonged to the Prince Bishop.

The contents being books, silver, gold, precious stones, altar goods and the Gospels.

There was also a mention of the "Fire of the Gods."

A smaller inscription near the bottom of the page appeared to give some chronology of that time but it also said that the resting-place of a "Box of the Gods" was foretold in the "Gospels."

This writing looked different from the rest. Could it have been added later or had someone else written it?

What did that mean?

The words in old English were still easily read. What Gospels?

They certainly seemed a puzzle. Jeremiah looked at the inscription.

"From the Saint by Galilee, over the marble where only Man shall tread, to the Saint with the Nine. The highest in Christendom shall guard the Fire of the Gods for Eternity. Look to the Gospels for salvation."

"Where did this come from?" enquired Jeremiah.

George replied, "it has been handed down the generations of my family for over 400 years. I thought that you being a righteous man and coming from my family's homelands, could take this back and maybe see if there is any mystery about it, or whether it is just a list of Church property. Every generation of my family thought it may have some historical meaning, some of my ancestors fought battles for the English and I think the time is coming when we may be fighting against them."

"This has to be kept safe, I don't know what it's all about but it could be important," said Jeremiah. "It definitely mentions the Prince Bishops and they are from my homeland of Durham, in England."

He looked around the immediate area.

"There is the last stone to go into place. Will you two lads bring that obelisk to me," said Jeremiah.

Jeremiah showed the lads, at the base of the obelisk was a ground out long hole.

"This is an example of proper Masons working. Masons left hollow pillars to insert their working tools and plans. If we put the paper in here and seal the base, it will be safe on its journey," said Jeremiah.

George said, "I know about Masonic tools, from my lodge. I've been trying to get Tom here to join for ages, maybe he will someday."

Jeremiah rolled the paper and placed it in the recess, then he sealed it airtight with a cement mixture. He engraved a mark in the cement.

Jeremiah said, "well lads, I'll let you know what I find out, although it may take a while."

"That's alright," said George, "a few more months or years won't matter, its been lying around our house long enough."

"Well," said Jeremiah, "I'll do my best to let you

know but in the meantime, I can predict good progress in the future for you two.

You are bright lads and I'm sure you will go far in you chosen careers. Good luck to you Tom Jefferson and to you George Washington."

Jefferson spoke, "the work you have completed here will go down in history. It will for centuries be spoken of as the line drawn by Mason and Dixon, you never know, there may even be a song written about it."

With that they left.

Both surveyors remained in America for a while carrying out observational work for the Royal Society.

By the time Jeremiah Dixon left America, with all his instruments and tools carefully stowed, he already could feel the wind of change in the colonies. Only 10 years later, revolution.

Arriving back home in Cockfield in January 1769, he found that he was required by the Royal Society to travel to Hammerfest in Northern Norway, to again try to observe another transit of Venus.

Mason and Dixon would never work together again.

The obelisk dutifully brought back to England was kept with the tools of his trade and his equipment in a building at home.

His return from Norway was his last trip outside the country.

In his last few years before passing away at only 45 years old, he completed a Plan of the Park and Demesnes at Auckland Castle, just down the road from his home.

The border stones for the park had been quarried locally and the masons working on the plan had been given permission to use any of his tools and instruments.

The sculptured obelisk had been removed to be used as a marker in the grounds of the park. It was fitting that this object was used in the Bishop's Palace. Long forgotten was the plastered base and long forgotten in America was the piece of paper.

Two more years and the British would be defeated and Washington and Jefferson would have other things on their minds.

CHAPTER FIVE

THE PRESENT DAY.

Jim Hendry had a good reputation as a green keeper. At five foot ten and 160 pounds, he was as strong as an ox. Years in the military and then civilian work for various governments had kept him fit. His black hair and brown eyes complemented his outdoor tan. His muscular physique was still apparent, rippling underneath his shirt. He had never lost his expertise but that was in the electronics of warfare. He had learned his skills firstly in the Royal Electrical and Mechanical Engineers and honed them further with the Ordnance Corps, before joining Special Forces Operations.

People on both sides of the Atlantic had used his skills many times.

Under his supervision, the Golf Course was one of the best in the county.

The time had come for some repairs and alterations, purely to retain its Championship status. In the far reaches of the turning point, around the holes 8, 9, 10 and 11, some serious rebuilding was necessary. Maybe it wasn't as good as Amen Corner but Jim took immense pride in designing this course.

He was riding with Fred Reed on the JCB digger, when they pulled up along the ninth fairway.

This fairway swept down on the left into a massive gully, which bordered Auckland Park.

They both climbed off the digger and walked down the slope to the bottom of the gully, Jim already calculating his new design.

"The first thing I want to do, is to clear all those large stones and rubble for about 50 yards, then level the bottom of this ditch. When that's done, we can start the contours of the new fairway," said Jim.

"I can see just one problem," said Fred, "most of those stones are from the old wall of the Park. They have been here for years probably since that part of it collapsed and fell down into the gully."

"OK," said Jim, "what we have to do is to take out the lower stones and build them into the wall up there. A bit of dry stonewalling won't do any harm and that makes it safer for the golfers.

After all, we'll probably find hundreds of golf balls in here, so we can sell them back to our shop."

Fred replied, "I'll have to clear all the long grass and broken branches first, so we'll need a skip."

"Just pile it all up at the far end of the gully and I'll get a skip in later," said Jim.

Fred began taking all the rubbish in the scoop and piling it all up. "We could burn most of this," he said, "and spread the ashes around, give the soil underneath a bit more fertility."

"Maybe later," said Jim, "I want the area clear so I get a better picture of the contours for the design."

Later that day, Jim and Fred started moving some of the wall stones up to the far side of the gully, so that they could build up the collapsed wall. Dead on five, they packed in for the day.

The next day Fred started up the engine on the digger.

"What I want you to do now is to clear at least 6 inches of topsoil and heap it up, so that we can bring in good quality soil for under the turf," Jim shouted over the roar of the engine.

Fred took the digger down into the gully and began the painfully slow excavation. It had to be slow so that no mistakes were made.

Jim was looking carefully at the area Fred had cleared at the rear of the digger. Now and again removing stones and roots from the site.

Jim ran up to the digger and waved at Fred to stop the engine.

"I need you to reverse back about twenty yards, the soil still has too many stones and roots in, they need to come out," said Jim.

Fred reversed the digger and started taking a few more inches off the soil surface.

Jim gave the thumbs up sign so Fred knew all was OK.

It was then that Jim saw something in the ground. He thought it was another stone, a thin one about 4 feet long.

He called Fred to stop.

"Can you give me a hand with this one?" said Jim, "I can't get it out. Fetch the shovels off the digger."

They took alternate sides of the stone and dug in the

shovels.

Jim said " if you can get right underneath it, it should come out when we both lever."

"I think I'm under it now," said Fred.

"Lever it now," said Jim.

As the stone came out of the ground, both looked surprised. Jim began removing dirt and soil from the stone.

"That is a strange shape for a stone," said Fred.

"It's not a wall stone," said Jim, "its an obelisk marker, probably from the grounds of Auckland Castle. It must have been here for hundreds of years, maybe, since the land slip that brought that wall down into our gully."

"Is it worth anything?" asked Fred.

"That's all you think about," said Jim, "if it is worth anything it's only because of the history factor."

"So how much is history worth then?" said Fred.

"How the hell do I know?" said Jim, "it has to go to some one or some place that can tell what it is."

"You're probably right," said Fred, "if we take it to a museum, that's the last we'll hear of it."

"Well in that case," said Jim, "there's only one place and one person we can take it to."

"No, No, No" said Fred, "I know who you're thinking about, he may be your cousin but he's a rogue."

"He might be a rogue to some folks," said Jim, "but he's the only person I'd trust. Just think about this. Who do we know who's a scientist, biochemist, medically and military trained and knows ancient history and archaeology?"

"I thought he was retired now," said Fred.

"He is, supposedly," said Jim "but he still has his

fingers in plenty of pies and when he sticks his finger in, he always comes out with a plum. If he doesn't know what to make of this, he has plenty of contacts that will. Just wrap this stone up in a blanket and take it to the car park.

Put it in my boot and lock it."

"I've seem some of his contacts, Al Capone would run from them," said Fred.

"He's not as bad as that, we need him, he's just a little eccentric," said Jim.

"Eccentric's not the word I would use," said Fred.

"You may be right but let's get this thing to him and see what he makes of it."

"Fine," said Fred, "Where's he at now then?"

"Don't know really, he comes down to the Pub at times but he lives in Hett Village," said Jim, "I'll take it up there tomorrow and leave it with him. He'll sort it out and if it is important we'll find out."

"Great," said Fred, "I'm telling you though, whatever he does there's always trouble following close behind."

"He does seem to attract it," said Jim "but just put it down to being outspoken and a bit controversial."

"OK then, leave it with him and we'll hope for the best," said Fred.

"Now all we have to do," said Jim "is to find him, after all everyone knows Colburn Lord."

CHAPTER SIX

The sun was angled about 45 degrees casting shadows of the arches of the Great North Road Bridge across the River Wear at Croxdale.

It carried the A167 now, further upstream, only about 80 yards, was the original A1 Road Bridge.

Plenty of traffic passed above but at river level it was hardly noticeable.

There had been ample rain on the hills a couple of days ago and fresh floodwater had come down.

It was never a problem for this great river but its tributary, the Browney, could easily overflow and cover the road and flood into the Honest Lawyer.

What a name for a motel, there's not such a thing, is there? The people who owned it allowed their overflow car park to be used by the local angling club.

The river was running off now, only about 3 inches above normal and the colour was just right looking like a cup of tea, no milk of course.

There was no apparent rising of the trout, perhaps it wasn't quite warm enough but still they have to eat.

Could be worms, larvae or nymphs, who knows?

Beneath these arches, the river flowed fairly fast its contoured course swinging the main stream to the South bank, then back to the centre before swinging into the North bank. All between 2 and 4 feet of water. Ideal trout water.

There was no use for dry flies.

Why do they call them that? They are never dry and they are half submerged anyway. It's easy to dry them off if you know about Amadou, a fungus that grows on decaying Silver Birch trees.

Chop it up, destroy any parasites or bugs with Saltpetre and this stuff is one of the most water absorbent materials known.

So in these conditions, you use wet flies. Those on a short leader floating just below or a few inches below the river surface.

Flicking across the river surface was a size 12 down eyed, micro barb hook, body of purple, hackle of Partridge, or was it Snipe?

It was followed after two feet of line with a Blue Wing Olive and then an Iron Blue Dun as the top dropper.

Looking back along the monofilament 6 pound breaking strain line, to the semi-sinking fly line, back to the 9ft. Carbon fibre rod, down to the left arm of its owner.

Colburn Lord liked nothing better than to park up in the motel, walk back along the road and field to fish the stream.

He had caught many good trout here but always returned them.

Catch and release was the best way to preserve stocks.

Many people knew him and had seen him often fly fishing the Wear.

He was of the old school of fishing.

Not for him 10 or 12 feet of rod with one shop bought fly on the end of some of the most expensive fly line you could buy.

Dressed in waders, only on the legs, not chest and looking like he needed a new jacket. His had been bought in Cabellas, Nashville, many years ago but most of all he loved his hat.

The famous Tilley hat worn all over the world. It made a great fishing hat.

At six foot 2 inches and 180 pounds, with a perfectly toned muscular physique, he still looked good for his age. Getting into the middle forties and still having a six pack was something most men didn't have. His light brown hair was showing a little silver in places and his blue eyes and swarthy skin, hid years of exposure in foreign climates.

He had served her Majesty with distinction, setting up the lethal combination with his cousin. They had been through some nightmare situations but thanks to Jim's electronic expertise and Colburn's strength and tenacity they had survived. Then just as retirement loomed, the Civil Service beckoned. Not the pinstripe suit brigade but sorting out problems for Governments, problems that had to be dealt with quietly and efficiently with no-one knowing you were there, or who you were. Colburn was an excellent negotiator and closer. If he could not negotiate a peaceful conclusion then his orders were to close it, permanently.

Now official retirement meant peace and quiet.

As the line swam around with the stream, that ever so sweet music to his ears began. The ratchet on the reel.

This meant that the fish had taken one of the flies and was bending the rod over. It was a good one.

It always gave him satisfaction to think that he sat upstairs tying artificial flies and they were good enough to make trout think they were real.

Playing this trout wasn't difficult. Once he had the head upstream out of the water, it was easy to slide the landing net underneath and bring the fish to the bank. Carefully releasing the hook, he took a photo of it on his digital camera and slowly stroked the fish as he put it back in the water.

Fly-fishing was a Gentleman's sport.

He examined the fly the fish had just taken, it was OK, chewed up a bit but flies are like humans, there are always some imperfections in them.

He sat on the riverbank. There was no point in going back in straight away. Give the trout some time to settle and get over the disturbance made by catching the last fish.

Then, his mobile in the top zippered pocket went off.

Pressing the green telephone button he said, "Lord, have mercy, who is this?"

Very few people had Lord's mobile number and most of those knew not to disturb him while fishing.

"Colburn, its Jim," the voice said.

"How did you get this number?" Colburn asked.

"I'm up your house right now, your wife said it would be all right," said Jim.

"Well its bloody not all right," said Colburn, "just leave me in peace, I'll see you later."

Jim replied, "I have something of interest Colburn

and I think it will be worth your while to look at it now."

"It had better be good," said Colburn "the trout are feeding well today."

Jim said with urgency, "this needs your special attention."

"I see," said Colburn, "is it a problem to fix?"

"No," said Jim, "I don't want to talk about it over the phone, can you come back now?"

"Give me 15 minutes and I'll be back," Colburn said, switched off the phone and started walking back to his car.

CHAPTER SEVEN

It was still a fine sunny day, only a few white cumulus clouds dotted the sky.

Lord was still annoyed at being dragged away from his favourite sport.

He put his gear away carefully in the boot of his car, no need being annoyed with the fishing gear, that was precious to him.

He started the car, an eight year old Ford Focus Estate 1800cc diesel.

It had served him well but was getting past its prime.

He pulled out of the motel car park, just below the "mad mile" of dual carriageway from what used to be the "Cock of the North" pub, now just another little housing estate.

He drove over the River Bridge, up the bank past part of Croxdale.

Just over another mile, he turned left at the "Coach and Horses" pub.

Reminiscing, just how good that place was when it was a drinking pub and not an eating house.

From there the sign says, Hett, one mile and a half.

Lord smiled, the distance was only one mile.

It was those small things in life that were important.

Driving home, the village was in Lord's words, "like living in Brigadoon."

He often said that the only difference between Hett and Brigadoon was that Brigadoon came alive for one day every hundred years.

Living here suited his "retirement."

Turning into the Green, then round the back of the houses, he pulled up onto his parking place, next to his garage.

He got out of his car and locked it. He trusted no one. Then walked up past his small garden and through the back door.

He did not have to shout, "I'm home," his wife was always there making the tea. It seemed as if she had a sixth sense of when he was returning but this time she knew exactly.

"Hi love," said Lord, "what's the rush with this one then?"

"Your Jim is in there," nodding to the main lounge, "he's got something big this time," said Val.

Val had met Colburn while both were at university. They married young and prospered, even though both a civilian and military career had, at times, taken toll of the marriage, neither of them would swop each other for the world.

Val was the sort of women that all men looked at, a young forty-five.

Only being five three, up to five five with heels, still a size 10 figure, long brown hair, blue eyes and quite muscular.

She had played lots of sports and used to be a demon on the Netball court, so consequently, didn't wear skirts that often, unless they were long, because they showed powerful thighs and calf muscles.

Usually it was trousers but you could still see a hell of a figure in them.

Nobody bothered her in this village though. You didn't get on the bad side of Colburn Lord.

Colburn walked into the lounge, fishing jacket still on, dressed in a dark green plain shirt and similar coloured combat trousers. He was wearing slippers. After taking his waders off at the car, the slippers went on. He had a habit of driving in slippers.

"Hi Jim, what's up now pal?" Colburn asked.

Jim stood up, "need you to take a look at something, found it when we were digging up a bit of the Golf Course, I think it could be valuable."

"That's what I like to hear," said Colburn, "where is it?"

"You walked past it, it's on the bench, in the extension," said Jim.

They both turned to walk back out through the kitchen.

"Pick up your tea lads," shouted Val, who had come through to sit down in the lounge and finish the Daily Express crossword.

Jim and Colburn walked into the extension.

"That's it on the bench," said Jim.

Wrapped in a dirty bit of towelling was a thin mound about four feet long.

Colburn started to unwrap the towelling.

"Well I can see it's made of rock, you could have

washed it down first. If Val sees this mess we're in bother," said Colburn. "Take it outside on the patio and wash it down with the garden hose."

Turning on the hose, muck, dirt and mud all came away from the obelisk.

Colburn dried it down outside, before he dared bring it back in.

Maybe no one bothered him but he didn't want to upset his wife.

He stood it upright on the bench.

"It's a good piece of masonry, beautifully carved," said Colburn.

"But is it worth anything? asked Jim.

"Depends on what it is or what it was," said Colburn.

He went to a kitchen draw and took out a magnifying glass.

He always kept one there because Val was always looking for the expiry dates on the food and the print was always that small. It was easier to magnify it.

"Well," said Colburn, "it looks like engravings of Coats of Arms on opposite sides of the column and there is a date here. I can't quite make out the exact number but the year is 1768, hang about, the date says June 6th."

"Great," said Jim, "now all we need to find out is what it was made for."

"Easier said than done Jim," said Colburn.

"Why?" asked Jim.

"Well I'll tell you dipstick," said Colburn, "If this was made for something specific and with those Coats of Arms, made probably for some of the so-called nobility, if we spread the word around;

They might want it back – for nothing.

We get jail time for thieving.

The owners might not be around now, unless they're 250 years old.

You can't keep treasure trove – officially.

So if I make any enquiries, it has to be done on the quiet, see?"

Colburn shouted through the house, "Val where's the digital camera?"

"Try with your fishing gear, darling," Val replied jokingly.

He always had one with him, to record the fish he caught. Just in case there was "a big one," then he could prove it.

Colburn got the camera and photographed the engravings of the Coats of Arms.

"Now Jim, finish your tea and we'll see what this is."

CHAPTER EIGHT

Colburn switched on his lab-top.

"Marvellous thing, the Internet," he said.

Jim remarked, "see that icon in the bottom right, it means you have no security on it, anyone could hack into this."

"I don't use this one for anything important. This one only gets used by Val sending e-mails to her friends and family and if some one wants a copy of those, they can have them," said Colburn.

The images were downloaded from the Olympus camera to a photo programme.

"I'll get the best image we can, then search for comparisons on the web," Colburn mumbled under his breath, "if this came from Auckland Park, I don't want the Bishop of Durham knocking on my door asking for his obelisk back."

Two decent images came up from the Coat of Arms.

"I'll save this on the desktop for easy reference," said Colburn.

"Now double click on the Google icon, type in Coat of Arms and away we go," said Colburn.

"Now pick one to do with Heraldry," Colburn said as the list of preferences appeared.

"Click on that one," said Jim, "it looks as if it has something to do with royalty and the nobility."

"Bloody great," said Lord, "we'll be here all day, look how many there are. It looks like every family in England has a Coat of Arms."

"You have to search specific areas," said Jim, "type in 1768."

Dozens of heraldic symbols came up on the screen.

"OK, lets start at the beginning with A," said Colburn.

It was only a few minutes at the end of the "A"s, that Colburn saw a virtually identical Coat of Arms, under the name Baltimore.

"That's definitely one of them," shouted Jim.

Val got up and glanced over their shoulders.

"I don't know how you two ever survived without women," said Val.

"If one side is Baltimore, then try Penn for the other."

"Why is that?" said Jim.

He shouldn't have asked.

Val always went to the local quiz night in the village hall.

It was still called the Hett Arms Quiz, from the days it was in the pub. She was good at quizzes. In fact, when the local pub team was in an area quiz league, she played as part of a four-person team, virtually unbeatable.

"Penn and Baltimore, argued for ages over their land boundaries," said Val. "Come on now, you know who sorted them out."

Colburn stood up in amazement, "of course the Mason Dixie Line, Charles Mason and Jeremiah Dixon. Dixon came from Cockfield.

This has got to be one of the marker stones from the borders. I thought souvenir hunters stole most of these. This one obviously escaped, I wonder why?"

Jim said, "it obviously wasn't needed, so he brought it home."

"Then why was it on the Auckland estate?" said Val.

"I know from the history of this area, that he did a job at Auckland Castle, before he died. This must have mistakenly been used by those working on that job," said Colburn.

"Well, now we know it is of historic value, it must be valuable," said Jim.

"Type in Penn, Baltimore then Marker Stones, see what comes up."

As the screen cleared, horrified looks appeared on all their faces.

There was the marker stone staring right back at them.

Only the words under it sent shivers down their spines.

**"Stolen from the American government, should this be found, contact the nearest Embassy.
Anyone finding and keeping this obelisk will be prosecuted under Federal Law."**

"No way," said Colburn, "someone knows something we don't and I don't like that. Hang on a minute, that date says 1768, there wasn't any American government then. We still owned the place. So something doesn't add up here."

Suddenly a haze came over the screen and it went blank.

"I told you," said Jim, "it's a virus, close it down now. Either that virus was in your computer, or it was attached to the screen you were searching. Someone, somewhere knows we're looking."

"Well, this creates a little problem, obviously someone wants to get their hands on that obelisk. I wonder why? There has to be more to that obelisk than we have found. Let's have another look at it," said Colburn already realising that trouble may just be round the corner.

CHAPTER NINE

Somewhere from Grosvenor Square to the Embankment, Civil Servants were rushing around.

In one large office decked with years of military regalia sat Colonel Stewart. Long past his distinguished military career but in charge of Anglo-American operations.

He heard the knock on the door.

"Enter," he barked out as if it were an order.

Simon White entered and said, "we have just received notification from the Americans that the Obelisk project has been accessed and they have asked for our help."

Stewart smiled, "about time, let's see if we can have some fun with this, only let them know what I tell you, it could be pay-back time for the porkies about Iraq. Everything comes through me, understand?"

White replied, "surely we have to inform the P.M. don't we?"

Stewart smiled again, "politicians think they run this country, let's not upset them. They don't realise that they may try to run it but it's people like you and me that's in charge. Let them be happy in their own little world, ignorance is bliss.

What information have the Americans given us?"

White put a folder on Stewart's desk.

"So far everything they know is in there," said White.

"Good, keep it that way. Get me a cup of coffee will you, this may be a long read," said Stewart.

He sat and opened the folder, it wasn't a long read.

Just stated that the programme had been accessed and a virus sent after identification of the computer and its owner.

It was then that Stewart's face contorted.

He threw his cup across the room, breaking on a bust of Wellington.

He was ranting and raving when White rushed back in.

"Sir, is there any problem?" White appeared worried.

"Problem, problem, there's bloody well going to be a problem. Do you know who accessed that programme?" raged Stewart.

"I did look in the folder but it meant nothing to me," said White.

"Never heard of Colburn Lord then, have you?" said Stewart.

"No, who is he?" said White.

"If you can imagine all your bloody nightmares coming in one dream, then that's Lord," said Stewart.

"You don't mess with him and come first, you might not even come last. With him you won't even finish the race. I was still serving when he was around. Every dirty job that needed doing, he did it and came out smelling of roses. He was the man you got if there was trouble with people, chemicals or bacteria. He knew how to handle it. He could break into Porton Down and be out of there before those technicians were back from the toilet and they didn't even know anyone had broken in. Anywhere in the world was that man's oyster. You know the codes you have for the North Korean missiles, well Lord travelled to Seoul arriving on a Tuesday, up to the North, flew back Thursday in time to have Good Friday and Easter with his family and they don't even know we have them.

He was good, damn good. His eye and hand co-ordinations were the fastest ever recorded in the forces.

Luckily for us there's always an Achilles Heel."

"And you know what it is, Sir?" said White.

"I sure do," said Stewart, "the man is just plain honest, wouldn't have anything to do with us. The Yanks haven't got a clue what they are letting themselves in for. We will just feed them a little and watch the fireworks, then clean up the mess."

White said, "will there be a mess?"

"Sure will if I know Colburn, luckily there's only one man better than he is and that's the one that trained him," said Stewart.

"Who's that then?" said White.

Stewart smiled breaking into a grin and said, "Me."

CHAPTER TEN

Val shouted from the lounge, " put some paper down on that bench, I don't want the worktops scratched."

Colburn did as he was told no need to upset the wife.

Laying down the obelisk on its side, then turning it all around, he examined it with a magnifying glass.

"There's not a mark on it anywhere," exclaimed Colburn.

Jim replied, "so what does that mean?"

"I haven't got a clue," said Colburn, "but someone knows and I'm going to find out."

Only the base of the obelisk was rough, obviously where it had been cemented to something else.

Colburn opened a nearby cupboard and took out a pallet knife that they used for wallpaper scraping.

"I'm going to try and remove some of the excess cement and see if there's any clue on the base," said Colburn.

Scraping slowly at the cement base, he suddenly stopped and smiled.

"There you go," he said, "what did I tell you?"

Jim looked and said, "fine, what are you looking at?"

"Look at that mark etched into the base," said Colburn.

"Yes, I can see it, but what is it?" said Jim.

"It's a Mark Mason sign. Whoever finished this obelisk, put his mark there for recognition," said Colburn.

"It just looks like a little triangle and lines," said Jim, "what do you think it means then?"

Colburn grinned and said, "Masons sometimes used pillars and obelisks that were hollow. They supposedly put their tools or drawings inside them."

"So there could be something inside this then," said Jim.

"Get me my drill," said Colburn, "I'll drill slowly into the base and see what happens."

Fixing a Number four-drill bit into the Black and Decker, he slowly started drilling into the cement. After about two inches of drilling, the drill head shot straight through into an open space.

Colburn drilled ten more holes and the bulk of the cement filling fell away.

Clearing the rest away from the base with the pallet knife, Colburn shone a torch light inside the obelisk.

"Well, well, well," he said, "is this what we shouldn't find?"

Colburn picked up a pair of long Spencer Wells forceps and as they practically disappeared inside the obelisk, he pulled them out slowly, bringing with them a roll of paper, wrapped in cloth.

He laid the roll on the workbench and carefully removed the cloth from the paper.

When the roll of paper was exposed, he carefully opened the roll, putting a glass candleholder on one side and a salt and pepper pot on the other.

Colburn and Jim just stared blankly at the paper.

"OK," said Colburn, "somehow this has got to be important enough to land us in a Federal jail."

Jim said, "I'm reading down this and it just looks like a list of all sorts, papers, boxes, jewels, Gospels."

"Where does it say jewels and Gospels?" said Colburn.

He looked further down and it became apparent that this was some sort of inventory belonging to the Prince Bishops from Durham Cathedral.

"I don't know," said Colburn, "if this is a list of belongings from Durham Cathedral, what do the Yanks want it for?"

Colburn shouted into the lounge.

"Val, can you come here a minute?"

Val came through to the extension, "what do you want now, another cup of tea?" she said.

"Didn't you do private history tours around Durham at one time?" said Colburn.

"Yes," she replied, "the last one was for a group of Lady Lions. You should remember we both got an invite to the Lions dinner that night."

"Yeah, I remember now," said Colburn, "it was a good meal."

"What do you want anyway?" said Val.

"If I was to reel off a list of belongings from Durham Cathedral, as if they had been taken away from there, could you think of any reason why that would be?" asked Colburn.

Val replied, "anything of importance belonging to the Cathedral would only be moved in a time of extreme emergency."

"OK," said Colburn, "what would constitute an emergency?"

"Fire, flood, earthquake, war," said Val, "something along those lines.

Hang on a bit, there's nothing officially been removed for about 700 years, since the Scots were coming down here and getting pushed back."

"So, when do you think was the last time it happened?" said Colburn.

"I'd have to check," said Val, "but not since Neville's time, the Battle of Nevilles Cross. I remember reading somewhere that a lot of the treasures were removed by the English, just in case the Scots attacked Durham. I also read that they were returned."

"Were all of them returned?" said Colburn.

"I suppose so," said Val, "why did you ask that question?"

Jim stood all this time looking in amazement, and then he spotted a small piece of the paper that seemed to have a coloured piece of picture on it.

"See that," Jim said, "this looks as if it has been torn out of a book."

"Roger that," said Colburn, "any idea what this writing means, what the hell is the Fire of Eternity?

OK, lets re-cap on this. We have a piece of paper, or what looks like old parchment. Written on it is a list of belongings from Durham Cathedral. Then we have this bit of a puzzle."

"Why is it a puzzle?" said Jim.

Colburn looked up with a half smile and said, "how the hell did a list of the treasures of Durham Cathedral, get over to America and why is it so damn important to them. We need to solve that riddle?"

Val took another look at the parchment and a wicked smile came across her face.

"You know, you might have been rough, tough soldiers and good at history but you know diddly squat about your local area. I'm going to put the kettle on, you two go and sit in there and I'll give you a history lesson."

Colburn and Jim walked through to the lounge, Colburn shouted, "have you seen something I haven't?"

"No," said Val; "I've just remembered something about the Battle of Nevilles Cross. After all, we're living on part of that history. I'll get the tea made, I don't think it's the list that is the important part, it's that paper stuff its written on and the riddle."

CHAPTER ELEVEN

Colonel Stewart shouted for White, who rushed in as usual.

"I want you to locate Jock Strane for me. I don't care if he's in prison, get him out,"

said Stewart.

White enquired, "have you any idea where I should start looking?"

Stewart grinned and said, "anywhere in the world that shit is happening. Try through military records first, we might be lucky. We're going to need him if the Yanks think they're going to win this one."

White, with a puzzled look asked, "why are the Americans so secretive about this. It looks as if this has been going on for years?"

Stewart smiled, "It's all to do with the little black book, listen in, this is for your ears only. This book has little bits of information, secrets, about anything that America or anyone else, was up to. No one saw it bar Presidents, they handed it down one to another. No one is supposed to have seen, or even know about the book. It officially doesn't exist."

White replied looking puzzled, "so how do we know about it then?"

Stewart smiled, "Anglo-American relations of course, plus we have better agents. We've known its contents for years. This obelisk was mentioned in the very first draft."

"You mean from the first President?" said White.

"Sure do," said Stewart, "his family came from here you know, but we don't know why the obelisk is important. It's obviously not what's engraved on it, so something must be inside it that the Yanks want badly. So if they want it, I want it first. Now find me Strane."

It wasn't difficult to locate Strane.

Customs and Immigration had him in detention for coming back to the United Kingdom without a passport. He said he had to leave Angola fast. It was probably true.

He had worked as a mercenary, been in the British Army, could never settle down, so hired out his "talents" to anyone who could pay.

White had him released.

He enjoyed the ride to London in a limo.

Arriving at White's Headquarters, he recognised the building.

"So someone wants my help then?" Strane asked.

White replied, "it's not my job to acquaint you with the facts."

"Whose job is it then?" enquired Strane, as they walked along the first floor of the building. "I might have known," he said as he opened a door without knocking.

"Good morning Colonel," said Strane, walking into the room.

"How's it going Jock?" said Stewart.

Strane grinned, "if I'm here, what crap is going on?"

Stewart replied, "I'd like you to do a little job for me Jock, just following and watching and reporting only to me."

"Nothing's that easy if you're asking me to do it," said Strane, "who am I following and watching?"

Stewart grimaced a little, "I want you to watch and report, that's all. I need to get some information before other interested parties."

"OK, wipe my slate clean and you're on," said Strane.

"Who am I watching and who else is interested?"

"There are some people from various departments in America who would like this information first," said Stewart. "We need to let the people who are searching find out whatever they can. Then you get that info. and give it to me. That's simple enough isn't it?"

Strane smiled, "the Yanks are no problem at all, now who am I watching?"

Stewart walked to a window and stared out to the street. "The person I want you to watch and follow and I don't care how you get the information, is Colburn Lord."

Strane stood up and replied slowly, "You bastard, you couldn't lick his boots. So I clean up your mess. This one's gonna cost you."

CHAPTER TWELVE

Val Lord made the tea. Three mugs, skimmed milk and two sugars. She put them by Jim and Colburn and sat on her recliner.

"First things first," she said, "before any more history, you better fix that double socket in the kitchen. I'm sick of getting a static shock from it and the plug every time I use it. I want it fixed, OK?"

Colburn begrudgingly grunted something under his breath.

"Don't you moan about it, you never make the tea," said Val.

" Now, here are the history facts.

When the Scots under David Bruce attacked England, our army under Neville and Percy formed up at Auckland Palace.

It's believed that some of the Advance guard came along the old Roman Way to Merrington and then to Ferryhill.

At some time, they must have spotted some of the Scots, because they charged down off the hill, along to Thinford and Past the Coach and Horses, down to the river, slaughtering the Scots. The main body of the

Scottish army had camped at Bear Park and later that day the bulk of the English army camped down here in Hett.

The day after was the big battle of Nevilles Cross and we kicked the Scots back north.

Now it's probable that before the Battle of Butcher's Race from Thinford to the river, any valuables were removed from the Cathedral, to be looked after by the English. So it's what was taken out and presumably returned that's important as well as the riddle."

"Right, OK, I follow you so far," said Jim, "so why is the paper and riddle so important?"

Val heaved a sigh, thinking are these that thick?

"Look, I think that the important word here is Gospels," said Val. "What Gospels were kept at Durham?"

Colburn smiled, "of course, there was only one that would be irreplaceable."

"Christ," said Jim, "you don't mean what I think you mean?"

Val smiled, "there's only one gospels that are that important, the Lindisfarne Gospels and I think that paper, is paper from those gospels that someone tore out and wrote on. When they were returned, it was obviously not noticed.

You would have to check the Gospels to see if the pages matched."

"No problem," said Jim, "we just go to Durham and check."

Don't be so stupid," said Colburn, "they aren't there anymore, are they Val?"

"It's been a sore point around here for many years,"

said Val. "Probably at the time of the Dissolution of the Monasteries, all the churches were literally robbed of their wealth by the state. To cut a long story short, the Gospels are now in the British Library in London, you can peruse them on line. Durham has been asking for their return for ages.

However, to get back to this obelisk, it seems obvious that something that was returned was hidden. What it was, God knows."

"He's probably the only one that does," said Jim.

Val continued, "this riddle gives an exact place for something, what, I don't know.

The saint by Galilee is not Galilee in Israel, it's the Galilee church in the Cathedral and the saint by that is Saint Bede. If you look across the cathedral from that point, at the far wall is the Tomb of Saint Cuthbert by the Chapel of the Nine Pillars, simple see?"

Colburn finished his tea.

"Well you've sorted that out. I told you she was good, isn't she Jim? Now if we can sort the rest out, we've cracked it," said Colburn.

"If you let me finish," said Val, "you're always butting in."

"Soooory," said Colburn, "carry on, if you've got more."

Val started again, "it has to be in the Cathedral because close to the Galilee Chapel going towards the other side, is a line made of marble in the floor, where it's said that no women can go past, so only man can do it. So it has to be inside Durham Cathedral."

"OK," said Colburn, "if you look down from the Galilee to the Nine Pillars area, what do you see?"

Jim replied, "I've been in there, you look past the font, to the throne on the right of the Nine Pillars area."

"That's exactly it," said Colburn, "if you go past Cosin's Font, on the right is Hatfield's Tomb, with the throne above. It is said to be the highest throne in Christendom. There you go, cracked it."

"Fine" said Jim, "now what the hell does it all mean?"

Val sat up with a look of realisation, "of course," she said, "I remember reading a history of Mason and Dixon and I am positive that they met Washington and Jefferson over there, so I think that's the Yankee connection. Also there was a relative of Washington that fought at the Battle of Nevilles Cross. You never know, he may have got to hear about all this, wrote it down, and passed it down the generations."

"She's a little marvel, isn't she Jim?" said Colburn. "All those hours studying trivial pursuit comes in useful sometimes."

Val said indignantly, "cheeky sod, so what now?"

"Well," said Colburn, "if the throne guards the Fire of the Gods, we need to know what the hell that is. Then if we have to look to the Gospels for salvation, then that's what we'll do. It seems that someone wants us to look to the Gospels and we need to find out who."

Jim stood up, walked to the window and looked out over the village green.

"What concerns me," said Jim, "is using the word salvation. Do you think we're going to hit problems solving this puzzle?"

"Who knows," said Colburn, "looks like we'll have to do some travelling."

"Travelling where?" said Val.

"Listen, this is they way I see it. There's obviously something important to the Yanks about this, otherwise they wouldn't threaten Federal action. Also it says, that throne guards the fire, what that means at the moment, I haven't a clue. Then look to the gospels, surely means there's something in those Gospels that is vital as a clue.

"I agree," said Jim.

"I'm in on this one," said Val.

Colburn stood up, "well folks, it seems to me we only have to do two things."

"And what are they?" said Jim.

Colburn smiled, remembering old times, "we have to go to London and check the Lindisfarne Gospels and check out Hatfield's tomb."

"That doesn't sound too bad," said Jim.

Val stirred from her chair, "you must be joking Jim, I know what he has in mind and it is bad. They won't just let us thumb through the Lindisfarne Gospels and you can't go tinkering with a tomb in Durham," she said.

Colburn smiled.

"Oh God, I've seen that look before," Val said with slight horror.

Colburn spoke, he had a mischievous look, "what we have to do is quite simple, we have to probably desecrate one of the most important Heritage sites in the world and break into the British Library, simple as that."

CHAPTER THIRTEEN

Val Lord drove their Ford out of the village, stopping at the Coach and Horses on the main A167 and waited until there was a gap in the traffic. Going practically straight on, she drove into Spennymoor and parked up in the local ASDA car park.

She parked by the taxi ranks because there was always someone around to keep an eye on the car.

She hadn't noticed the blue Mondeo that followed her out of the village. It had pulled out from the dirt track by the telephone kiosk.

Val needed a few supplies for their trips, so the shopping was necessary.

The driver of the Mondeo watched her enter the store. He slowly got out of his car and walked to the adjacent doctor's surgery. After all, most people going to that doctor's surgery used this car park. He made sure no one appeared to notice him, just another shopper.

He returned after a few minutes, walking past Val's car. As he was passing, he swiftly

bent down and his hand quickly went under the rear wheel hub. It was as easy as that to attach a homing device.

Perhaps if he had chosen the other wheel hub, he might have noticed that a device was already there.

Jock Strane worked fast.

He had telephoned an old army pal at Catterick for a favour.

It was only 30 minutes drive to Hett and finding the right car was easy.

He did not use a magnetic device, they could come away on bumpy roads. Super glue was better.

Now two different sets of people were monitoring the car. Wherever it went, they would know and the Lords would have no reason to suspect anything.

Jock had booked in at a local motel, The Honest Lawyer.

He didn't know this was where Colburn Lord parked when fishing the river Wear.

In his room he monitored the signal from the car, wondering what the hell all this was about.

He thumbed through Lord's file, still marked special operations.

Civilian career, army times, everything was here, and he read;

Colburn Lord, the date of birth made him 45.

6feet 2inches, medium bone structure, probably some of the 6 pack was hopefully turning to fat.

Reading on he saw what had made Colburn special among the specials.

Reaction time well above normal, to the point of being unbelievable.

This purely meant that anytime someone tried to better him, his superior reactions won the day. He could out-gun or out-draw any cowboy.

Strane thought they must be slower by now. It's physically impossible for his pathology not to have lessened over the years. After all he was retired!

The blinking on his monitor told him that the car was heading back to Hett but occasionally his monitor gave a double beep. That could only be interference from some other close source of electrical instrumentation.

Strane sat back and thought, someone else has an interest!

The monitor in the Mondeo was also double blinking at times, the driver knew someone else was in this game.

Val parked up at the rear of her house and picked up the shopping from the back seat.

She thought, just look at those views across the Wear valley.

At least living here you can tell what weather is coming, if you can see the hills, it's going to rain and if you can't see them, it is raining.

She dumped the shopping on the benches in the extension.

Colburn had made some quick drying cement, put a few inches of it in the obelisk and marked it with a triangle and lines to imitate Dixon's initials.

"That's how we found it," he said.

"So what are you going to do with it?" enquired Val.

"These treasures have been around for hundreds of years, a few more days won't matter," said Colburn, "Jim and I are driving to Edinburgh."

"Fine," said Val, "Why?"

"We'll leave it, as instructed, for the American Embassy. Just dump it on them, then see what they make of it," said Colburn. "They will send it over the water, and find it empty. That should give us enough days head start to see where the information we have now leads us. It's only 3 hours drive, we'll be there and back in a day."

Val said jokingly, "I suppose you want a flask of tea and a couple of pork pies."

"That will do nicely, darling," said Colburn with a smile.

"Have you got any idea where to start?" said Val.

"Jim's worked it all out, he's away getting some gear for our trips," said Colburn.

Colburn thought that this enterprise would take more brain than brawn. Between him and Jim they had brain and plenty of brawn but he felt that this time Val's super computer brain would be the key to success.

He wondered what success meant. Chasing after ancient relics was fun but not if Federal agents are on your tail. He knew how to slip those easily and being a veteran of running around the Hereford hills, he had enough experience to beat any agent. What was bothering him, nagging away, was he felt something was not quite right. Something not apparent now. He felt that he had covered all the bases. It was time to start.

When Jim returned they would head for Scotland and get rid of the obelisk. It was a pity he thought, it would look nice in the front garden.

The drive took them out of Hett and onto the A1M motorway.

Passing Durham on the left, to the Angel of the North. The rust bucket as the locals called it. Then off that road past Newcastle International airport and onward over the hills.

After Otterburn, where the famous battle of Chevy Chase took place, they climbed up to Carter Bar and the border. They both wondered that if Scotland became independent, would there be passport control here, why not?

Down the other side, round the hairpin bends and watching for the speed cameras.

There was only one from Newcastle to the border but at least 14 after that to the outskirts of Edinburgh.

It was easier after Dalkeith, not to take the ring road but cut straight into the heart of the city.

Eventually passing the Commonwealth Pool, where the swimming events in the 1986 Commonwealth Games were held, they headed for Holyrood area.

Double-parking by the Embassy, Colburn jumped out and shouted for one of the guards.

"Give us a hand with this, its addressed for the Embassy," said Colburn.

"What is it?" said a guard, standing to order in a neatly pressed uniform.

"How the hell do I know," said Colburn, "I just deliver stuff."

The guard picked up the packaged obelisk and took it inside, to be scanned by the x-ray machine.

Jim and Colburn drove away and retraced their northward drive, back south.

"We'll be back by 4," said Jim, "fancy a pint then?"

"Sure," said Colburn laughing, "our pub's always open, belongs to that group, lockey inn. Always open for residents."

The drive back was enjoyable and gratefully uneventful.

Two people sat at their monitors.

Even they couldn't figure out what was going on but they reported back, on one round trip to Edinburgh.

It was time to sit back, monitor and let it happen, whatever it was.

Strane thought to himself, if Colburn Lord is mixed up with this, then there's more to it than I know. It was obvious that Stewart hadn't told him everything but it could only be of military or medical importance.

The American knew more than he did, but he too had surmised that his government was not telling him all the facts. They were only interested in something that would benefit America. Patriotic he may be but the pieces of the puzzle just didn't fit.

Why chase this Englishman, what did he know?
It was nearly time for them both to start unravelling the mystery.

CHAPTER FOURTEEN

Jock sat in his room occasionally glancing at the small screen of his monitor.

It was just like following satellite navigation, only sitting still.

The bleep showed the car parked up for the night.

They wouldn't make a run in the night, he thought, there's no reason to suspect anything.

The same double-bleep was sounding, just like before. He knew that the interference was another monitor. It was happening more often and that was annoying. He could use it to locate the second instrument, but there again, so could the other user.

So as long as both instruments were switched on, they could be used to locate each other.

Jock felt something was wrong.

A knock on the motel door stirred him into motion.

"Yes," shouted Jock.

"House keeping," a voice replied, "I have some clean towels for the bathroom, Sir."

The voice sounded male, slight accent.

Jock thought unusual to have male housekeepers, he opened the door slowly.

In England, he didn't carry weapons.

"I might have known it was you," laughed Jock.

"You're getting too easy to find my son," said the visitor, "I think we need to talk."

"Come in Doug," said Jock, "you still posing as an American tourist?"

"Around here, it's the best way," said Doug, "we all blend in perfectly."

Doug Kaminsky was of German extraction, living in Texas, in the Fort Worth Metroplex area.

About 5 foot 11 inches, of solid muscle.

Ex American Special Forces, he'd left the army to work as a civilian contractor.

The government used him at times on operations that required more brain than firepower and this seemed one of them.

"Fancy a cup of tea?" said Jock.

"Coffee please, just can't get used to that taste," said Doug.

"I'm not surprised, that Gnats piss you have over there and you dare to call it tea," joked Jock.

"OK, jokes over," said Doug, "let's get straight to it, we both know we're following the same people, we've worked together before."

"And I remember you shafting me and running back to your lot," said Jock, "that ain't happening."

"Orders are orders," said Doug, "I'll tell what I know and maybe we can come up with a compromise."

Jock looked at Doug with a wicked grin, "let's face it, neither of us trusts each other, so why should we work together. In the end both our governments want information."

"That's right," said Doug, "but it's up to us what information we give them. This time it seems this job is a stroll in the park. So why call us in? We are just two men employed by our governments to do a job. On the quiet, of course."

"That's the problem," said Jock, "it's not governments is it? It's some little covert operation that hardly anyone knows about and for what?"

"Well, let me lay this one on you," said Doug. "All I know is for a couple of hundred years, someone high up has known about this."

"So, what the hell is this, then?" said Jock.

Doug drank his coffee and started with his Texan drawl.

"It seems that a hell of a lot of years ago, some writing turned up that may or may not indicate a weapon of mass destruction."

Jock laughed, "like shit," he said, "not that crock again. They weren't there last time, were they?"

"Haven't got a clue what it is. Just someone high up thinks there may be," said Doug.

Jock looked totally puzzled, "you mean to say that, years ago, someone saw some writing that may indicate a weapon?"

"That's about it," said Doug.

"No way," said Jock, "there's got to be more to it than that."

"I agree," said Doug, "so do you know anything that could help us?"

"Just like you," replied Jock, "I've got instructions to monitor and follow Colburn Lord."

Doug smiled, "when I was first told to follow him, I thought, not him again. I think we've both had enough of him in the past."

"Well," said Jock, quietly strumming his fingers on a table, "I was told that whatever he finds out, I have to know and report in. No questions are to be asked on how this is done or what the end product of Lord may be."

"I've got similar instructions," said Doug.

"Well then," said Jock, "lets agree some rules here. How about whatever is going on, we share and report back whatever we want to. Then if weapons are involved, we may know where we can get a better offer from than our present employers. It's up to you what you do, or should we just wait and see? Are you carrying?"

"Not in England," said Doug, "didn't think it was necessary on this one."

"It shouldn't be," said Jock, "I just can't see what this is really all about. Someone knows, or thinks they know, that some crap is going to happen. Surely if the military is involved, we've got better weapons now than two hundred years ago. So this has to be big."

Doug replied, he was puzzled. "If some joker found some note a couple of hundred years ago. That note was obviously kept by someone in high authority. Then suddenly, we get called in to watch Colburn Lord. It seems obvious that Lord has this note, why don't we just take it from him?"

Jock smiled, "my sentiments exactly but our powers that be obviously don't want the note."

"Why not?" said Doug.

"You know, you were never the brightest button on the uniform. It's what the note says, that's important. Maybe instructions, I don't know. Lord will follow whatever is written down, find anything there is to find, then we take it off him," laughed Jock. "Then we decide what to do with whatever it is."

"Sounds good to me," said Doug, "can we shake on that?"

Doug held out his right hand, force of habit pressed the thumb between Jock's knuckles. To his surprise, he felt Jock's hand reciprocate.

He smiled, "well brother, I see you've been on the square. How old is your grandmother? Does this make us brethren in arms?"

Jock recognised the allegory.

"For now," said Jock, "I will treat you like a fellow brother. When this is over, what I will promise you now, as a man of honour, we will discuss the outcome, not fight. Welcome to England, Brother."

"Your lodge would be proud of you," said Doug, "it makes you wonder how much of this problem has been talked about, with handshakes over the years."

Jock replied, "in both our countries, what we call civil servants rule, and there's a hell of a lot of handshakes going on. Just think on this. If we are after some form of weapon and its powerful enough to outgun our modern weapons, then maybe the Great Architect of the Universe had something to do with it."

Doug bowed his head slightly, "So mote it be," he replied, "all we need to figure out is what Lord is up to."

"OK," said Jock, "you can figure it out first."

"What do you mean by that?" said Doug.

"Its easy, I'm going to get my head down, you take first watch on the monitor.

Wake me in four hours, partner."

CHAPTER FIFTEEN

When organising any trip, you have to start somewhere.

Val Lord was checking through drawers in one of the rear bedrooms to see if her walking gear was washed and clean. She walked to the window and stared out over the Wear valley to the hills opposite.

Silently she thought to herself.

To really understand history you have to envisage what the place was like at the time.

Not the ploughed fields and houses but open meadow and forest.

She looked left up to the ridge of the Whin Sill at Ferryhill.

Perhaps the old Roman road had made its way over that ridge and down to the river, after all, the road there used to be the Great North Road until the A1M was built.

The grassed and planted contour just off the ridge used to be the local pit heap.

That's all gone now, but the soldiers would have charged straight off the ridge and down the valley.

Charging up to the Thinford area, down past the Coach and Horses to the river.

Just think of the archaeology that would have been along that site. Pity when they built the Black and Decker factory and Rothmans, they didn't check for finds.

Now they're building a new Fire Station opposite the Coach. I bet there was no-one metal detecting, pity, no one really cares any more, just plough history into the ground.

She put thick socks into a small rucksack and came downstairs.

"You OK Val?" said Colburn, "you look a bit down."

Val replied, "No, I was just thinking of all the history from around here that even the locals don't know about, or care."

"Like what?" said Colburn trying to joke about it.

"For example," Val said, "how many people would know that there was a large English army camped here once. They would probably say, I hope they didn't drink from the duck pond without realising that the pond was there at the time but not with the filth you get from those ducks and geese. They were never there then, the water would have been pure. Or they could have got the water from the underground spring, just down that public footpath. Most villagers don't even know that's there."

"Well," said Colburn, "unfortunately we're not here to educate them, we have a bit of searching to do."

"Have you worked out your plan of action then?" said Val.

Colburn got out of his recliner chair and went to a small marble-topped table in the lounge. He put the paper he'd been scribbling on, down on the surface.

He started to relate his assessment of the situation.

"When our Jim gets back here, I'm sure we should go to the Cathedral first. There has to be something at, in or around that tomb that will lead us somewhere. We'll just go and have a look with the rest of the tourists for now. We dress like tourists; jeans and scruff order."

Val sat on her chair, "you know, the more I think about that inscription, the more I worry," said Val.

"What's to be worried about?" said Colburn going over and giving her a hug.

Val looked up, "you know as well as me that others are in on this and we don't know what this is all about," she said rubbing Colburn's hand.

He replied softly, "the way I see it is this. I've tried to apply logic to this. If other folks know about the obelisk, that's fine. They didn't know we had it until we dropped it off at the Embassy in Edinburgh. I don't know if someone thinks there's something inside it, that unfortunately seems probable but they don't know what, I think."

"You mean, you hope," said Val.

Colburn continued, "it seems probable that way back, maybe to the middle seventeen hundreds, someone had seen that writing but didn't know what it meant. Neither do I.

It also seems possible, that because others know of our connection with the obelisk, we probably will be watched. I don't look on that as a problem, we can easily slip them, especially in Durham and London. The only problem I can foresee, is what happens if we do find anything. Then it could all hit the fan."

Val smiled at him, he always made things sound so simple.

"I'll tell you what, if we do find anything, it's obviously something that's important to the Yanks and if it's important to them, the Brits won't be far behind. The thing is, without another lead from Bishop Hatfield, we could look in those Gospels all day and find nothing."

"I agree entirely," said Colburn, "I think we have to expect British and American involvement in this and if I'm right, remember who is in charge of Anglo-American military co-operation, that little cretin Stewart. I'll deal with him in due course but I'll guarantee he's already got someone on it. When you sum it all up, we know nothing and someone expects us to find something. Then they'll try and take it away.

That's when the fun begins. So only at the end of this can we expect bother. Someone needs us to do their work for them. So be it."

Val sighed reluctantly, "you're probably right but I wish you wouldn't enjoy it so much. I agree with Jim on one thing. I don't think there's any Fire of the Gods in Durham Cathedral that would be sacrilege. It's looking to the Gospels for salvation that worries me. I rather find my own salvation than someone give it to me."

Colburn laughed, "come on love, when have I let you down?" he said.

"Never," said Val, "I just would, at some time, like a lifestyle that's looked on as ordinary."

"Boring you mean," said Colburn.

Val turned to him, still with a loving look and said, "no surprises and safe."

"That's what I said," he replied, "boring."

About eleven in the morning that day, Jim arrived back with the gear Colburn wanted.

He walked up the garden path taking a couple of hard glances at the car parked on the driveway.

He shouted, "It's just me," as he came in through the extension into the kitchen, then into the lounge.

Colburn enquired, "have any problems getting everything?"

"Everything's there," said Jim.

He turned and looked at Val.

"How long is it since that car was washed?" he said.

"Why look at me, I don't use it that much," said Val, " is there a problem?"

Jim looked at Colburn, "unless you paid someone to clean it, there's some strange marks on the rear wings. Looks like someone brushed against it, or you've had a scrape."

Colburn stood up and went into a kitchen drawer for his binoculars and gave them to Jim.

"Jim, you go upstairs and check out the landscape, I'll just walk down the path and have a glance at it."

Jim came back down after a few minutes and Colburn came in from the garden.

"The areas clean," said Jim.

"Val," shouted Colburn, "go and put the car in the garage will you? Then I can nip down and check it over."

Val went out grabbing the car keys from a tag in the kitchen. A perfect three-point turn put the car away in the garage. Then she returned.

Colburn explained, "if anyone was watching, the car is in the garage and they can't see what I'm doing."

He went out to the garage, looked at the car.

All this seemed familiar, he'd seen it all before.

He knelt down and felt under the wing. Sure enough, a transmitter.

He always double-checked everything. Being thorough had saved his bacon a few times. Checking all round the car, another transmitter, glued in this time.

He left everything in place and went back in his house.

"Everything OK?" said Jim.

"Of course," said Colburn, "not only have we a magnetic transmitter on there, another one is glued in place. So that simply means, two people have us bugged. Looks like we were right, Anglo-American co-operation."

"What now?" said Jim.

Colburn smiled again, "we just leave them there for now, let them follow. When we tag who it is, we'll take them off. For now, I've got an idea for Durham. Let them follow our car, it's only going as far as the Graduate's Society, then we'll ride the bus."

Val smiled and thought, he's done it again, come up with a beauty.

Let them follow into the outskirts of Durham and then we take the Park and Ride,

Bloody brilliant!

"Jim, will you bring in the equipment? I'll need to check it over," said Colburm.

The equipment, in a rucksack, looked like a miniature B & Q electrical department.

Jim had seen most of it before, apart from what looked like small sonar and a hand-held computer with a small trident.

"What's these two for?" asked Jim.

He was right about sonar.

"I thought we could use this to determine the density of the rock," said Colburn.

"Just like looking for a submarine, it sends a signal out and bounces one back if it hits anything. What should happen, if it's solid, the signal will just return immediately or we should see no return because it's overlapping the outgoing one. If there's a gap or hollow somewhere, this will find it."

Val looked at the both of them, "I suppose you've thought about the inside of the Cathedral, very sedate and quiet. I don't think the officials there would appreciate the ping of a sonar resonating around the place."

"Very probable," replied Colburn, "then we go to plan two and use this instrument that we use in archaeology for mapping the ground. This will give us a two-way plan of the area and see if there are any anomalies. In simple terms, if there are any faults, holes, dug-out areas or solid rock, we will see it on the map that we can make."

Jim looked puzzled, "that's fine," he said, "just, for example, say we find some hidden hole near the tomb, what then? Even we can't go and move a tomb, can we?"

Colburn used his logic again, "if Hatfield wanted to hide something, if I was him, I wouldn't wait until I'm dead. It seems logical that he would conceal it before his tomb was in place, so it may be under it, to the side, over it, I don't know, yet. What does seem apparent, is that these instructions, if we call them that, were written for someone to follow. So whatever may or may not be hidden, was at some point in time going to be found. I think we can rule out, inside the coffin, I hope so anyway."

Val looked at him and laughed, "hell, I was just beginning to see myself as Lara Croft. I don't fancy raiding that tomb though."

"Well, if it comes to it, we will," said Colburn, "but the available evidence does suggest that Hatfield did something to leave us a clue."

"Of course he did," said Val, "I think he, or someone, added to that list of the Cathedral relics, or added words I should say. Anyone that had served as a priest under the Prince Bishops would know the layout of the Cathedral. Now if you closely examine that list again, someone who knew something was going to be hidden would only have written those last words. I think that even before the relics were taken out of the Cathedral, the Bishop knew what he was going to do. I think there was a problem, don't know what, but Hatfield saw an opportunity to solve it. There lies the riddle. The highest throne in Christendom is guarding the Fire of the Gods, for eternity. I don't think so, that's why he's referred to the Gospels, those two clues must be connected."

"So we carry on as before," said Jim, "now we know someone is following, we can watch our backs better. When do we go?"

"No time like the present, I'll get the car back out. Jim, you get the equipment. Val you just look pretty as always," said Colburn.

"Flattery just might get you everywhere," said Val, "but don't get your hopes up, let's go."

Doug was miles away in his thoughts, he'd woken Jock up for his watch.

Jock was in the bathroom, washing and shaving when

a text message came through on Doug's phone. He read it.

"Cheeky bastard," Doug shouted, "Lord's dumped the obelisk off at the American Embassy in Edinburgh."

Jock came out of the bathroom, "what bloody obelisk," he shouted angrily, "you holding out on me?"

"Christ, Jock I thought you had been told about it," Doug said almost apologetically.

"So tell me now," Jock was annoyed.

Doug pulled out a copy of a drawing from his coat pocket.

"That's it," said Doug.

"So why is this so all-damned important?" asked Jock.

Doug sat on a chair, "let me tell you a story," he said. "It appears it happened way back at the time of our first president, Washington. He had come across a scroll that had belonged to his family and it must have been handed down the generations. Well, it seems he showed this to an Englishman who he hoped could help decipher it. His pal at that time was Jefferson, he was good with puzzles but even he couldn't understand it. He gave it to this Englishman, and when he came home, he was supposed to help with it. Along came the Independence War and all must have been forgotten. This drawing has been in presidential possession all this time."

"So what's with the obelisk?" said Jock.

Doug carried on, "it seems that the Englishman, put the scroll inside the obelisk and sealed it. Safekeeping I suppose. Then that was that, it's been on our records for nearly three hundred years."

Jock looked amazed, "and you Yanks have just been waiting for it to surface all this time?

"Seems like it," said Doug.

"Of all the obelisks in the world, the one you want turns up with Colburn Lord," said Jock. "Now that's bloody amazing."

"What's really amazing, is that it is the right obelisk he had," said Doug, "he dropped it off in Edinburgh. Its already been verified as genuine. However, when they put it through the x-ray machine, sure enough, there was a hollow centre but nothing was inside."

"OK," said Jock, "so what's so all fired important about an old scroll that's hundreds of years old. If you lot think it's about a weapon, you must be crackers."

Doug smiled and said, "that's why we're here, to find out."

Jock was sitting on the bed, he turned to Doug and said, "if you think about it, can there really be a weapon from hundreds of years ago that's better than something we have now. I can't really believe that but if Colburn Lord is involved, then there's definitely more to this than anyone really knows."

"Shit," shouted Doug.

"What's up now?" said Jock.

Doug grabbed his coat, "get your coat and keys, Lord's on the move right now."

CHAPTER SIXTEEN

As the car headed out of the village, stopping at the main road junction at the Coach and Horses, it seemed the best time to check the forward planning.

The car turned onto the A167 and headed towards Durham.

That piece of road was still known as Butcher's Race where the forward army of the Scots was soundly beaten.

As the car travelled down the bank and over the river, Colburn took a sneaky glance at the river. He always liked to keep the state of the river in his mind, merely to determine the next time he would go fishing.

Passing the hotel, no one noticed the car slipping across the road behind them coming out of the hotel car park.

At the end of the dual carriageway they turned right going towards Durham.

After the Girl's School, the crematorium and St. Oswald's Golf Course, the car turned right into the new car park built by the council.

The student apartment blocks were still under construction, Colburn thought it would have been great to live in those when he was there.

There were always plenty of spaces to park.

Jim and Val got out, Colburn popped the boot.

Taking a rucksack each, they headed to the bus stand, locking the car first.

The county council buses ran frequently, at least every 15 minutes, so usually there was always one waiting.

They got on a bus, paying one pound seventy pence each. This gave them all day riding and free parking.

They sat at the back of the bus. From here you could observe everything and everyone. They had no need to speak, they knew exactly what to do.

After a few minutes, the bus pulled away.

Out onto South Road, Colburn looked to his left at Van Mildert College. His mind raced back to the building of the student's block. Looking at the decorative pond, or small lake, in front of them. He remembered the floodwater coming off the Golf Course and down towards the building. The lake just formed, so the builders left it there and used it for decoration. How many students knew that? On past Collingwood and Grey on the right and Trevelyan and St. Mary's on the left. Between those was the Japanese University.

Colburn mused in his mind, a sign of the times. The Japanese invest so much around here, they even built their own university.

With the Science site on the right, the bus halted at the New Inn cross roads.

This was one of the first places where the Cathedral area can be seen in all its glory.

The bus carried on down Anchorage Street and Church Street into New Elvet passing the famous balcony of the Royal County hotel.

All seemed to be thinking of the great Big Meeting days or to call it correctly the Durham Miner's Gala.

Hundreds of banners of the different mining lodges were paraded that day. Sadly now there are no mines left in the area so the gala day now is not what it used to be.

All the major Labour leaders, since the 1930's had been on that balcony.

What fun it used to be.

The shop windows all boarded up and the bars open all day, there were always fights. Nothing major and Jim and Colburn were usually in the thick of it.

Turning left over Milburngate Bridge, the bus pulled round to the Milburngate Shopping Centre. It seemed everything was Prince's or Bishops. Even Colburn's old Golf Club at Sedgefield has the Prince's Course and the Bishop's Course.

Colburn nodded at Jim and lightly touched Val on the leg, quietly saying, "off here."

Picking up their kit, looking like tourists, they got off the bus.

They walked up to North Road and turned left into Silver Street and across Framwelgate Bridge.

Val stopped momentarily in the centre of the bridge and looked up at the castle and cathedral. "No matter how many times I come here, I still marvel at the beauty of that view," she said and carried on walking.

Silver Street rose up a slight incline into the Market Place.

Jim in his usual reminiscing way said, "remember what it used to be like. The world famous dome-topped police box over there, directing the traffic. How the hell did that copper do that job? It must have been a nightmare with the traffic from Silver Street, Saddler Street, Elvet and Claypath."

Val piped up, "it all finished in 1975. Now we've got traffic control with entry charges."

Colburn slowed a little, "come on then, think of your trivia, what's important in the centre of this market place?"

"You're never gonna catch me like that," said Val. "You're thinking of the statue of Charles William Vane Stewart, the 3rd Marquess of Londonderry, Old Fighting Charlie. Well the sculptor Raffaelo Monti did it, made of plaster and electroplated with copper. Very forward thinking at the time and it was said to be perfect. Then a blind man feeling with his hands found that the horse had no tongue. Is that enough for you?"

"Always the clever one, that's why I love you," Colburn smiled at her.

The market place as usual, was teeming with people.

Some were local shoppers, rushing around so that they would spend the least money in the pay and display car parks. Most were students, obviously not in lectures, or skipping them, sitting on the benches chewing Big Macs. Others were plainly tourists, easily spotted as they normally had a camera hanging around their neck. At one time you could spot them by their language. Nowadays all nationalities came to Durham to work.

They all walked up the slight incline of Saddler Street, giving thanks for now there was less traffic up here, due to the congestion charge. People were still criss-crossing the road, looking in the quaint shops dotted about.

At the top of the street, it turned into the North Bailey

and the first sight in total of the magnificent structure of the Cathedral.

They all strolled on with the flow of people, hardly noticing the castle on their right hand side, past Hatfield College and the Heritage Centre along the side of the Palace Green.

This green was like a Bowling Green, perfectly manicured befitting such a World Heritage Site.

The trail of people led like a snake towards the great North Door, which is the main entrance to the cathedral with the famous sanctuary knocker.

Colburn hesitated here, standing with a few tourists busy clicking their cameras.

"All this history right on your doorstep and most local people don't even bother to come here," he said rather sadly. "They don't even know about sanctuary."

Val interrupted, "sanctuary was not just at this door. The boundaries would probably have been from about Nevilles Cross and Gilesgate. It can be traced back to about AD597, the reign of King Ethelbert. Later on the Saxons laws continued the practice.

When a fugitive knocked on the door, he was admitted. He couldn't carry any weapons and a watcher looked him after.

The Palatine coroner heard his confession and he had to promise to leave for a port and the country in 40 days or return to sanctuary. They had to wear a black gown with the yellow cross of St. Cuthbert on the left shoulder. He could wander about here as he wanted and attend the cathedral services."

Jim said, "we could do with a bit of that right now, wandering all over with no-one stopping us."

"Unfortunately," said Val, "sanctuary was abolished by King James the First."

"Pity," grunted Jim.

"Well," continued Val, "when they left here to go a port, they only wore a sackcloth and carried a white wooden cross. This protected them by law, when they were travelling to their port of exit. You'd look good wearing sackcloth around here now."

Val half laughed under her breath, "that sanctuary knocker is world famous as well. It's not the original but it's supposed to be an exact copy with the lion's head, mane spread out and empty eye sockets. They probably contained ceramics."

"OK folks," said Colburn, "now it's time to test the water, let's get inside."

They had no reason to believe they had been followed, it didn't matter anyway. They weren't bothered, just visiting the cathedral, being religious.

Back in the park and ride, the following car had parked and left.

The occupants couldn't get on the same bus, they might be recognised.

They couldn't just stay in the car park without riding the bus. The car would be clamped, so they drove out back south, stopping in a lay-by near the crematorium.

After all they knew eventually, Lord and the others would return to pick up their car and they would be waiting. Trying to find them around Durham wasn't an option.

The area wasn't very large for a city, so waiting was the

obvious choice. They knew eventually their time would come and Lord's would be up.

CHAPTER SEVENTEEN

Durham Cathedral is absolutely unique.

It is probably the finest example of Early Norman architecture in England and its massive grandeur is only enhanced by the magnificence of the site.

It was the Cathedral of the Prince Bishops of Durham who, until 1836, exercised virtually regal jurisdiction.

Without parallel in historical association, it was the church of a great Benedictine monastery. Most of all it was the shrine of St. Cuthbert, the most famous saint in the North Country.

It is, by any standards, an architectural masterpiece, a tribute to those that conceived and built it. Knowing full well that they would probably never live to see the fruits of their labours.

Even though Jim, Val and Colburn had been here many times in their lives, the sight of this awesome and beautiful cathedral was unforgettable. The sensation they felt on entering never diminished, the sheer size enhanced by not being surrounded by other buildings.

The three walked in, quietly with heads slightly bowed.

Colburn whispered, "turn right first, we need to check out everything so we know what was written on that parchment, is correct."

They all walked slowly towards the Galilee Chapel, stopped and turned by St. Bede's tomb.

Looking down the great nave, practically in front of them was the black marble slab.

Women were not allowed to the east of this, so only man could go. All fitted so far.

The saint by Galilee and only man can pass.

Colburn nodded onward.

They walked slowly, looking around like the tourists, along the nave. Wandering past the intersection of the north and south transept. Onwards past the choir to the Chapel of the Nine Altars and the tomb of St. Cuthbert.

They all turned around.

"OK," said Colburn, "it does all fit, let's go."

Standing with the Neville screen at their backs, to their left was Hatfield's tomb with the Bishop's throne above it.

Val was quiet, as if the religious ambience of this place was overcoming, then she spoke quietly and with reverence. "The first thing to bear in mind is that Hatfield had this area constructed during his lifetime. His coffin wasn't put in there until 1381. The throne was already built. So he knew about this part of the cathedral.

Before we do anything, I think we have to remember the history of that time. If there had been any secrets, it is most likely that they were handed down from Bishop to Bishop.

There had always been rumours to that effect.

In fact the rumours were said only to have started in Elizabethan times.

She was a Protestant when she came to the throne

and allegedly some Roman Catholic monks broke into St. Cuthbert's tomb and removed his body.

It was supposedly hidden by three of them in another part of the Cathedral.

When one of the three died, the other two entrusted the secret to a new third man and it was passed on like that to this present day.

This supposedly occurred about two hundred years after Hatfield but even to this day, some people still believe the story.

Now what I am saying is that it is possible that the Bishops did the same.

It would be of no advantage to keep any secrets themselves, because they could die suddenly without having the opportunity to pass the information on.

Therefore it would seem prudent that the Bishops entrusted information to at least a couple of their most reliable priests, who would have been with them at some time in this Cathedral.

So we have to think of what may, or may not have happened."

Colburn leaned a little against one of the pillars of the vaulted ceiling.

"I think I might be able to shed some light on that. I have read a lot about the Prince Bishops and there were some great builders and then there were some right idiots.

If Hatfield had any idea of who would come after him as Bishop, I think any secrets would stop with him."

"Why is that?" said Jim.

"Well it is documented," said Colburn, "let me continue. After Hatfield there was a Bishop called

John Fordham. He had been secretary to the King and Prebendary of York and Lincoln. He was judged to be the worst of the Durham Bishops. He's been described as a traitor, slanderer and downright wicked person.

When the English nobles tired of Richard the Second's shortcomings as monarch, they marched on London and demanded he remove his favourites from office.

Fordham was removed because the Barons wanted a more trustworthy person.

They got Walter Skirlaw who turned out to be a great builder Bishop."

Jim moved so he could talk quietly in Colburn's ear, "so what you're saying, is that Hatfield couldn't trust any secrets down the line."

"That's what I think," said Colburn, "how about you Val?"

Val replied, "I totally agree, if there was anything he would hide it for eternity.

However, I do think that there would be a trail to follow. These people were pious and trustworthy and I think that they may, or again may not, have wanted these secrets to be given to mankind, if they were worthy, at some time in the future."

"Great," said Jim, "no time like the present."

"Do you think you're pious and worthy, Jim?" enquired Val.

Jim replied, "of course, I'm vegetarian and C of E, does that count?"

Val looked at Jim as if he was a cretin.

"You know I was just joking Val," laughed Jim, "I've read Sir Walter Scott. If I remember right it was a poem of sorts called "Marmion".

Val and Colburn had quite a shocked look on their faces.

Val said, "Jim you're full of surprises."

Jim took a seat on one of the nearby pews, "instead of being full of something else I suppose. I know more than that, how about;

> There deep in Durham's gothic shade
> His relics are in secret laid
> But none may know the place
> Save his holiest servants three
> Deep sworn to solemn secrecy
> Who share that wondrous grave."

"That's lovely," said Val, quite amazed, "now how about the quote on Prebends Bridge."

"Don't know it off by heart," replied Jim, "but it's words to the effect of, that Durham with its castle and cathedral was a mighty fortification and the Scots marauders never ever captured it."

"Jim, I've now seen you in a new light," remarked Val, "I never thought you were deep and understanding."

"Does this mean I get to play on your quiz team?" asked Jim.

"In your dreams," Val said jokingly.

Colburn was looking at the countless number of visitors, slowly ambling around the place, most in quiet meditation. This place did that to you.

The three moved off, slowly in unison as if they had practised the moves time and time again.

They stopped, just like many of the visitors, in front of the Episcopal throne, which surmounts Bishop Hatfield's Altar tomb.

It was indeed a magnificent sight.

To those people who have never seen this area, it has almost indescribable beauty.

It was obvious that some of the plasterwork and paintwork had been touched up or replaced over the years but the absolute details of this tomb area were outstanding.

Too many visitors were walking up and down, the task before them seemed impossible but Colburn always seemed to have a way out. Military training had taught him one thing. If others can't do it, then find a way.

His spoke to Val, "get your drawing pad and pencil out, make it look as if you're drawing this area."

Jim piped up, "we can't take soundings with all these folks milling about, we'll get thrown out. I know we've been throw out of plenty of places but I'm not going to get into a fight with priests."

Colburn was looking around, obviously his brain was working overtime, "no need for that," he said, "we'll be able to do geophysics, a little bit at a time. We'll make it look as if we want to copy it all on paper."

Hatfield's tomb was recessed in an archway.

To the right were a couple of painted and engraved wooden columns, mirrored on the left. However, on the left there were six columns. On these columns were copies of what appeared to be coats of arms.

Farther to the left were six marble steps, with a small wooden but elaborately carved gate, leading up to the throne. The carvings of the palisade were perfect medieval designs.

In between the six columns were plastered and painted icons, looking in need of repair. In these spaces from the ground level, to just past the centre line of the fifth space, were what appeared to be stone half bowls. These again had intricate carvings but what seemed strange was that these half bowls had their tops covered and sealed.

Colburn looked at Val's drawings of the coats of arms. Something caught his eye as he turned to observe the tomb area.

"We know that this tomb area was open until 1381 when Hatfield died," Colburn twisted his mouth as he thought aloud. "It just doesn't seem likely that he put anything in those three walls at the side and behind the coffin. They would have been exposed all that time to anyone who wanted to look and I don't fancy trying to move that stone and look behind it. It also seems unlikely that he wrote any inscription around here before he died. There would have been too many around to see it.

So possibly it has something to do with the woodcarvings and insignia.

Now Hatfield's Great Seal was basically a knight on horseback, with helmet and plume and a shield with one inverted chevron. I think there may have been three lions as well.

Look at those carvings. It just seems that the vast majority of them are blue, with lions and inverted chevron; Hatfield's.

So I think the old devil put those there to tell people, if you think I'm hiding anything, try these. Let's get the other images to see if they make any sense."

Val said, "I've already taken a sneaky picture with the digital. I'll go through it with a fine toothcomb, back home."

"Naughty, naughty," said Colburn, "well done, I didn't

even notice the flash. We have to get the ultrasound and geophysics on that area. It's obvious we can't do it with all these folks around, so there's only one thing to do."

"OK," said Jim, "what now?"

Colburn grinned, "looks like we're doing nightshift."

Jim groaned, "so how are we going to break into here then?"

Colburn stared impassively at the carvings, "we're not breaking in, the plan is to break out. We'll stay here.

Val, you go back on the bus now and study the drawings and photo. Here's the car keys, and by the way spend a bit it Marks and Spencers."

Val looked puzzled, "why?" she asked.

"Get a few carrier bags worth of clothes and food and put them on the back shelf of the car, then no-one sees in. Everyone has Marks and Spencer's bags, it's just like everyone wants a Harrods bag when they're in London.

I'll put my phone on buzzer, ring if you find anything.

We'll see you sometime in the morning."

Val didn't seem surprised, she knew Colburn too well. He'd been in too many precarious situations before and always came up smelling of roses.

"Look after him, Jim," she said, "and don't get into any trouble."

Val made her way back to the main door, quite happy to go shopping, especially in Marks and Spencers.

Jim moved edgily toward Colburn, they were both standing in front of the tomb.

"I agree with you, it has to be some sort of message in those shields."

"I hope so," said Colburn, "it would make life

easier. Hatfield wouldn't have made it impossible, just difficult."

"OK," said Jim, "are we kipping in the cloisters?"

"Too many folks out there and they stay late," said Colburn.

"How's that?" said Jim, looking puzzled.

"Quite simple," Colburn remarked, "it's where they filmed a lot of the Harry Potter films. All the foreigners want to see that part of the cathedral. We are going to a quieter part after we've been to the café for something to eat and a cup of tea."

"I thought it was always quiet in here," said Jim, "so where can we doss down for a few hours?"

"Just up there before the south transept, is the Durham Light Infantry Memorial Chapel. That's where we'll stay until everything is closed. I suggest we work about two in the morning."

"Is there no security?" enquired Jim.

"This is a House of God," exclaimed Colburn, "look around, we're just getting sanctuary. No one is expected to break out, everyone wanted to get in. If the Galilee bell tolls, then someone is getting sanctuary."

"And if it doesn't ring?" said Jim.

Colburn grinned, "then they haven't found us. Now where's that café?"

CHAPTER EIGHTEEN

Colburn and Jim both ordered tea.

At least it was Tetley's, even if it was a drawstring tea bag.

The blueberry muffins looked good today, so two of those and two rounds of tomato and cheese on white bread. All were added to the tray.

They sat the farthest away from the door.

It was as if both were pondering and waiting for the dark to descend.

"The sandwiches are for supper and we'll buy some bottled water before we leave," said Colburn.

Jim jokingly replied in a whisper, "can we not get a couple of cans of brown ale for later?"

Colburn looked at him as if he wasn't there and answered in disdain, "sometimes I worry about you Jim, you know there's more to this than we know already and still you joke."

"Well if you can't laugh at life, what can you laugh at?" replied Jim.

Colburn sipped his tea, it was hot, "we need to see that area again in the light before we sleep tonight. Remember your army training. Every time we did an exercise, they always dropped us somewhere before dark, and then we had time to plot the area in the light. When it got dark, it looked entirely different and you had to march on compass bearings."

"There's plenty of time," said Jim, "thirty minutes to closing at six. I've checked all the gear and it's working fine. I'll get the geophysics of that area pretty quick."

"Fine," said Colburn, "I hope we're right about this, Val will text about ten. I hope she can come up with something."

Val had done her shopping.

Buying food in Marks and Spencers was always a treat. You could always guarantee the quality. Along with a couple of blouses and a new pair of trousers, she had four carrier bags to haul back on the council bus.

When she arrived back at the Park and Ride, she quickly found her car and placed all the bags on the rear shelf. She couldn't use her rear mirror well but it was necessary for the play-acting. She knew somewhere before home, someone would be tracking her movements.

She started the car and drove carefully out of the car park turning left towards Spennymoor. As she passed the crematorium of her left and Mount Oswalds golf course on the right, she did notice a car pull out of a lay-by.

She couldn't tell if this was important, it didn't matter anyway. She was just going home.

Turning left on the dual carriageway at what used to be the Cock of the North Public House, she drove back over the rivers Browney and Wear. Up through part of Croxdale and turned into Hett. Home sweet home, she thought.

As she pulled in to their parking area, she thought,

I'll try the clothes on first, then have a look at the photos. Must get the priorities right.

Back in her bedroom she tried the clothes on. Of course they fitted. She could have done this in the shop but she always had confidence in Marks' clothes. Putting them all away on hangers in a wardrobe, she put on comfortable slacks and a sweater shirt. Then she came downstairs and switched on her computer.

After attaching the scanner to a USB port, she downloaded the photo of Hatfield's tomb area from the Olympus camera.

When the picture was up on the screen, she clicked on best photo and started to stare at it.

She used the photo options to scan it from all angles.

Nothing stuck out as abnormal. This wasn't going to be easy.

Put yourself in Hatfield's position, she thought.

If you were going to leave clues in the fourteenth century, surely it couldn't be that hard to crack the code.

The photo just showed an area of plastered stone. In some places the plaster was missing. Covering a lot of the area were coats of arms, mostly Bishop Hatfield's.

It was certainly a beautiful sight, but nothing seemed abnormal.

It had to be outside the tomb area, she thought, the tomb was put in later and she was sure the Bishop wouldn't want someone moving his tomb, even many years in the future.

So it had to be around the plastered areas and coats of arms.

She already had spent over an hour staring at the photo.

Well she thought, enough is enough, there's nothing like a good cup of tea to stir the brain. She walked into the kitchen, half filled the electric kettle and put an Earl Grey tea bag in a cup with two sweeteners. She always thought, keep the sugar calories down and have a Marks and Spencers pork pie. I won't count those calories.

Biting into the pie gave her a feeling of ecstasy, the best on the market. Sipping slowly the Earl Grey tea, she looked again at the photo.

Then it struck her!

Why were those half bowls or half fonts, not in a geometric progression?

Masons were always particular with angles but why not there?

She printed off a copy of the photo and took a ruler.

Starting from the floor font, numbers one, two and three appeared to be in line.

Numbers three, four and five seemed to be in line.

Number three was out of line! Or was it number four?

She drew a line connecting all five covered fonts.

Sure enough it was a parabola.

She knew she could describe it to Colburn as he had drawn many of these during his work in Sports Medicine, plotting lines of Lactic Acid intensity, for Army recruit evaluations of fitness.

The coats of arms must be in some sort of sequence, she thought.

Even allowing for those that are missing, there seemed no apparent logic in the placement of the plaques.

There were a few of the plaques that seemed out of place.

First column top, double red chevrons.

Second column centre, black and yellow stripes, like a bumblebee.

Fifth column about centre, red shield, white cross.

Sixth column, two up from ground level, red shield with black stripe.

Did that mean that the family of that shield was persona non grata?

It wasn't much to go on but it was all there seemed to be.

It was getting late now, she thought I'll text Colburn about eleven and the rest is up to them.

The car following Val had gone past the turning to Hett and turned full circle at the Thinford roundabout.

They could see from the blip on their monitors, that the car was parked up back at Lord's home. It had been impossible to see into car from the rear because of the shopping.

So reluctantly they returned to the motel.

Watch and wait, that was their job.

Colburn and Jim finished their teas and buns and just like the rest of the tourists, picked up their bags and backpacks and returned to the main part of the cathedral.

It was getting close to six.

They wandered back past the South Transept and central tower, to the choir area and Hatfield's tomb. They were both used to scanning areas in daylight, then returning in the dark. Army training was excellent.

"I hope Val comes up with something," said Jim, "I can't see where to start."

Colburn always had a reply, "where there's a will, there's a way. If something was here to be found, then god willing, it will be. There's no point hanging around here. Let's get to the Chapel. It's going to be a long night."

Castell's clock nearly told the exact time Colburn thought glancing at his Tag watch He opened the door of the chapel.

There was memorabilia of the regiment everywhere but both scouted for places to rest, hide and not be found. There were plenty of cushions on the pews, at least they would be comfortable.

They couldn't hear the tourists leaving, everything seemed still, just like a graveyard. There were of course plenty of tombs in the cathedral, so being like a graveyard seemed apt. The only sound they heard was someone opening the door of the chapel, walking inside, checking for visitors and leaving.

It was quite permissible in this chapel to sit and contemplate. Many tourists did just that remembering the lives this regiment had lost during many years of futile wars but at closing time, they were out.

No one looked behind or under altars, it would be sacrilege to be there without permission.

Colburn and Jim waited until it appeared all was quiet, and then they took some cushions, made a rough bed on the floor and rested up.

Army training had taught them, sleep when you can, any time of the day or night. You never knew when you were needed for action.

Both seemed to rest with half an eye open. It seemed

like an eternity in the stillness of the chapel, eerily quiet, and then Colburn's phone buzzed. A text message from Val.

Reading the text with a pen flashlight, Colburn nudged Jim.

"Val has apparently found a geometrical error in the placement of those stones that look like half fonts. She says it's like a lactate curve," he said in a whisper.

"Fine," said Jim, "do we need the aerobic threshold point then?"

"Don't know," said Colburn, "she's also found something strange about the positioning of some of the coats of arms. At least she's given us some points of reference to make a start. I think we will still check the lot with the geophysics though. Better be safe than sorry. So now we wait, two in the morning it is. See you then Jim, goodnight."

They both lay down having set their phone alarms for two, on the buzzer.

At two, on the dot, the phones went off, both stirred.

They poured some water onto tissue and wiped their eyes. It was time to start but first things first.

The cheese and tomato sandwiches came out of the backpacks and were demolished in no time, washed down with a few sips of water.

"Can't go to work on an empty stomach," said Colburn.

Jim nodded as he munched into his sandwich.

After eating and clearing up the rubbish, they went to the door of the chapel. Turning the latch silently they peered out into the blackness. They waited a couple of minutes for their eyes to become accustomed to the dark. No need to rush.

Trained in stealth techniques, they both quietly made their way towards the tomb.

Now the work would start. Nobody should interrupt them, after all this was a church.

Jim removed some equipment from his pack. It looked like a small trident, like a gardening fork with a battery run computer on the handle.

Jim whispered to Colburn, "you hold the pen torch and I'll take readings of this whole area."

Placing the forks every few inches took time. Up and down all the columns and inside on the plastered marble. "Time flies when you're having fun," Jim joked.

"How much longer?" enquired Colburn.

"Be finished in a couple of minutes, then what?" said Jim.

"We go back to the chapel and check the read-out," said Colburn.

Nothing stirred in the whole of the building. From the Nine altars past the choir, under the central tower up the nave to the Galilee, everything seemed still. It was an uneasy stillness. From the height of the massive vaulted ceilings came a wind sound as if every ghost was trying to fly around at once. Of course, there are not supposed to be spirits in this cathedral but who really knows. The thing was, plain and simple, very little worried Colburn on active duty.

"That's it done," said Jim, putting the recorder back into his backpack, "now let's see if the readings tell us anything."

The two made their way quietly back to the Memorial Chapel, opened the door and entered. Nothing but blackness was observed. To the public it would have been a frightening experience.

Using the pen torch, their only source of light was shining on the recorder side of Jim's trident sounder. Pressing the display buttons, Jim saw it first.

"Got it," whispered Jim, "look at that display."

Every section of the plastered marble walls and pillars, showed no resonance. They just appeared to be solid rock, totally black on the screen.

Except one part.

A thin grey line appeared from the left of the fifth column and appeared to just drop down to nothing after a few inches.

Jim pulled out a photo of the tomb area.

"What did Val say about the coats of arms?"

Colburn replied in a whisper, "there appeared to be some that were placed in positions that were not logical."

"No one in those days knew anything about logic," Jim said staring hard at the screen trying to mate the photo with the anomaly.

"The way I see this, is quite simple. See that shield with the red background half way up the fifth column."

Colburn stared at the photo, then the screen, "I agree, that's got to be the spot."

Jim smiled, in the dark of the chapel, "sure is, X marks the spot, a big white cross. Let's go."

Going back out into the main cathedral was no less daunting than before.

With a slight north wind outside, the vaulted rafters

seemed to creak in unison and then in sequence. It was as if some unearthly spirit was unhappy that they were looking for the secret.

Jim held the torch while Colburn carefully tried to dissect the outside of the coat of arms with a small scalpel. Val had been right in her diagnosis. Now would they see what else could be found?

Colburn was scraping quietly around the edge of the shield when suddenly it sprang off the pillar and landed. Crashing onto the floor.

The noise just didn't reverberate, it echoed throughout the whole building.

"Jesus Christ," said Jim, "who's going to hear that? I'm telling you Colburn, if any of the priests come, I'm not going to hit them, not priests. I draw the line somewhere."

"It's OK," said Colburn, "unless any are sleepwalking, I don't think they'll come looking for intruders, would you?"

"No," said Jim, "but I'd dial 999 and let someone else do the job. So can we speed up a bit?"

Colburn looked with dismay at the place the shield had fallen from. Even looking at sophisticated sonar type readings, he knew one thing. Behind the shield was nothing but solid marble.

They both just collapsed on the floor, looking at each other.

"The readings are right, something has to be here," said Jim, nearly resigned to the fact that this mission was already a failure. "I just don't believe I went wrong in my readings, there's definitely something there. I picked up the anomaly."

At that moment both jumped back and froze at a seemingly distant noise.

"What the hell is that?" said Jim.

"It's my bloody cell phone in my pack," Colburn said speedily getting it out. "It's another text.

Message reads hope you are still up. Looked at pictures again. It's not the white cross shield. Look for blue cross or chevron on the side. Luv Val."

Taking the torch Colburn looked at the side of the pillar by the white cross. Sure enough, vaguely, but just visible appeared a blue cross. It was also obvious that this was an area that had been repaired, plastered over.

Colburn took the scalpel blade and slowly started scraping the surface. Quite large pieces of plaster fell away.

"Would you believe it, look at this Jim, a mark of a mason. This has to be it," said Colburn.

Scraping around the mark, a rectangular groove appeared.

Colburn scraped further into the groove and then found that he could remove the small stone with a little coaxing using a chisel as a lever.

What was behind the stone?

Colburn stared in with the torch but all he could see was what appeared to be a metal ring.

"Now what?" said Jim.

"I think we're meant to pull the ring," said Colburn. "Now if my hand was two inches wide, I could do it."

"Maybe you can't but Spencer Wells can." Jim brought out a pair of long Spencer Wells forceps from his pack. "You're not the only one who goes fishing."

Colburn inserted the forceps into the hole, grasping the finger-holds of the forceps tightly, he gripped the metal ring and pulled.

Nothing, it didn't move.

"Try it again," said Jim, "it's probably just stuck, rusted up over the years."

This time Colburn gripped the ring and locked the overlapping lower part of the forceps fast.

With his feet levered against the side of the pillar, he pulled again.

Something moved.

"What was that noise?" Colburn whispered.

"I don't know," replied Jim, "it seemed to come from behind you."

Colburn pulled on the forceps again.

There was the sound again but in the darkness behind him, nothing could be seen.

"Flash that light around Jim, see if you can spot anything."

Jim peered all around the wall, then his face lit up.

"Behind you, on that fourth font thing. The lid's moved."

Colburn turned to see what Jim was talking about.

Sure enough, there had been movement of the top small slab.

With ease Colburn prised the lid a little more using a small chisel for leverage.

The top moved to one side.

Colburn put his arm around Jim, "and the prize is?"

He lifted out a piece of cloth, rolled up.

Laying the cloth on the floor, he carefully unrolled it.

Inside the cloth was a piece of paper, rolled up.

Opening it slowly under the torchlight, he could make out some words.

"That's it," he said, "we'll read this better at home, in the morning. Now let's get all this back in place."

Sliding the stone back across the half font top, they replaced the rectangular stone from the column. Then they cleaned up as much plaster as they could find.

"It's a good thing, forward planning," said Colburn, "I thought we may have to do some scraping around."

Jim smiled in the darkness, "are you going to tell the Bishop of Durham that some of Hatfield's tomb is held together with a squeeze of No More Nails."

"It does the job," said Colburn, finally replacing the coat of arms. "Looks like it's been there for centuries."

The two of them took the paper scroll and slowly made their way back to their chapel sleeping quarters. After gently closing the door, they went back to their cushions and lay down. They would leave in the morning when the first tourists entered.

"Are we going to have a look at what Hatfield left?" enquired Jim.

"Why not?" said Colburn.

Jim held the torch and Colburn carefully unrolled the paper. Surprisingly it was not too brittle. Jim kept hold of one end. Colburn scanned the paper with the torch.

"I can read this," said Colburn, "but I don't entirely understand it. I think we need Val's brain on this."

"Come on, what's it say then?" said Jim impatiently.

"It doesn't say a lot, just a few words," said Colburn.

"The essential bit seems to say;

"Aldred will show the way to the Fire."

"And who the hell is Aldred?" asked Jim.

Colburn replied sleepily, "haven't got a clue, We can wait until tomorrow, it's been there seven hundred years, another day won't matter."

With that both lay down to rest. It would soon be morning and the priests would start their work.

They would easily slip out with the crowds.

Colburn would ring Val to pick them up and then they could see where the next trail led.

CHAPTER NINETEEN

It was around seven thirty in the morning when Jim and Colburn started to stir.

No one had bothered them in the chapel as they expected, but people were moving about the cathedral.

Picking up their gear and backpacks, they walked toward the door and very quietly and slowly, turned the knob.

Colburn opened it a few inches and carefully looked out. It seemed like visitors were already viewing the magnificence of the surroundings.

They both slipped out and slowly walked through the nave to the sanctuary knocker door. Both looked around, pointing, behaving just like tourists and straight out of the door onto Palace Green.

It was a beautiful sunny morning.

"Just in case anyone is watching or following, I'll ring Val and tell her to stay at home and we'll walk. It's only four miles and we can track up the back roads to home and anyone will think we've just got up," said Colburn, speed dialling his mobile.

Val answered and Colburn said they were walking back.

"Any success?" asked Val.

"Is the pope catholic?" answered Colburn, "see you in about an hour."

It was a pleasant walk home. Colburn and Jim were quite used to long walks.

This time they didn't have to trek through jungle or desert, chopping creepers every stride or kick sand for miles.

Retracing the bus route out of Durham, past the New Inn and up to the roundabout, and down the dual carriageway. After passing the motel and crossing the Wear, they turned left into Sunderland Bridge and the back road into Hett.

Very little traffic used this road because it was so narrow with lots of bends, although during the famous "rat run" from about 4 o' clock until 5.30, cars flew down this road, trying to avoid the congestion at the Thinford roundabout. Colburn thought, "that should stop, it's dangerous."

Practically dead on the one-hour mark, Colburn and Jim arrived back.

Val already had the kettle on, the smell of bacon in the air.

Val said, "sit down lads, an English breakfast coming up."

Both their mouths watered just at the thought of a full English breakfast.

It seemed incredible that you could actually get this in a tin but there's nothing like the real thing.

Both washed. Val wouldn't have them sitting down covered in overnight dirt.

Then they tucked into breakfast and big mugs of sweet tea. Heaven.

Only when the plates were clean, wiping them with the fried bread, did Val speak.

"I'll put these in the dishwasher, then we'll sit down and see what you have found."

She was dying to see whatever they found but she knew the old saying, "only mistakes are made in a hurry," so a few minutes more wouldn't matter.

Sitting around the table, Colburn took the wrapped cloth from a side pocket in his backpack. Opening the cloth and unrolling the paper inside.

Colburn read out the words, "Aldred will show the way to the Fire."

"So all we have to do is to find Aldred and he'll show us the way," said Jim, "but who the hell is Aldred?"

Val smiled as usual, "once again it's up to me to teach you history. Listen in and I'll tell you a story.

Are you sitting comfortably?

We worked it out before that the Gospels mentioned in that first paper were probably the Lindisfarne Gospels.

Well, this proves we're right."

Colburn and Jim sat with looks of admiration on their faces, she was good.

"What you have to remember, or know, is that these Gospels have a uniquely important place in the culture and heritage of this area.

This book represents the pinnacle of achievement of Anglo-Saxon Northumbrian artwork at the end of the 7th Century. It draws together all the different influences that shaped Christian art at that time.

It is a masterpiece of early medieval book painting.

It's said that Eadfrith, the Bishop of the Lindisfarne church, originally wrote and illustrated the book around the year 700 AD, plus or minus a few years and it's adorned with gold, jewels and silver gilt.

Not to bore you with too much history, this is what we need to know.

Just like many medieval manuscripts, the Lindisfarne Gospels were written in Latin.

However, round about the year 970 AD, they were owned by the Minster of Chester-Le-Street. The Provost there at that time was a man called Aldred.

What he did, which was quite amazing at that time, was to add an Anglo-Saxon translation to the Latin text. Actually he wrote in red ink underneath each Latin word and this makes it the oldest surviving version of the Gospels in any form of English."

Jim looked puzzled, "OK Val, I understand all that but how does a Latin translation of the Gospels help us?"

Colburn leaned back in his chair, "I think I know where this is going, the translation has nothing to do with this, does it Val?"

"You're getting faster in your old age," said Val, "the important fact that we have to know is this.

Aldred added some notes at the end of the book.

It is usually called "Aldred's page."

That's how we found out about Eadfrith and his followers.

Aldred wrote it down at the back of the book. So it's something he wrote, or is on his page. That has to be the clue to the fire."

Colburn interrupted, "the only problem with that, is that page has been on show for over a thousand years and plenty people have seen it.

The only thing that seems to follow logically is that Bishop Hatfield added something to that page. It was in Durham for a couple of centuries after that, although it was only used for ceremonial occasions. Then at the Dissolution of the Monasteries, it disappeared, ending up, surprise surprise, in the library of Sir Robert Cotton. His family later donated it to the Cotton collection of the British Museum Library, which became the British Library in 1973."

"I think you two will need another cup of tea," said Val, "I can see where this is leading."

Colburn leaned over to Jim, "you better get some clothes and kit together, we need to make a trip down to London."

"Fine," said Jim, "but we can't just look at the page, can we?"

"Unfortunately not," replied Colburn, "we'll have to remove it for a close inspection."

"Steal it, you mean," said Jim.

Colburn smiled at him, "we're not going to steal it, just borrow it for a while. It's going to mean another nightshift, with security this time."

"Bloody great," said Jim, "what about our tails?"

"I think we can work out an interesting route for them," Colburn looked up and smiled, "we've got rid of plenty of them in the past."

Val interrupted, "you know, we could all end up in the Tower for this but there's one thing we haven't seemed to mention."

"What's that?" said Jim.

"If Hatfield did write something on that page, how has it not been seen by now?" Val hesitated, "unless you can't see it at all."

Colburn stood up, "that's probably it, you cannot see it, it's hidden somehow. Let's get packed. Jim, we'll pick you up at your house in our bugged car. It looks like we're going to need a place to quietly examine this book page. We may need a powerful microscope and maybe a few chemicals."

Val looked inquisitively, "and where may that be, I wonder?"

She saw the grin on Colburn's face, "I think I know exactly where, the Lord moves in mysterious ways,"

It didn't take long to throw a few clothes into a bag, put them in the car with a few tools of the trade, especially the Swiss Army Knife. That usually came in handy.

Driving off out of the village, down to Low Spennymoor to pick up Jim, they didn't even notice they were being trailed. It didn't matter though, Colburn had plans for whoever was tailing them.

After picking Jim up, they headed South past Aycliffe and joined the A1M.

It should take five hours driving, with a stop.

CHAPTER TWENTY

The A1M, for most times on the Northern end is a dual carriageway road, with nothing to make driving easy or interesting. A few sections of three lanes, sorted out the heavy goods vehicles and driving seemed easier then.

Colburn drove past Scotch Corner and onwards past the old Catterick Camp airfield. Now full of army trucks. Past Leeming Bar and onto the new three-lane section where the A19 traffic joined. At Wetherby the new A1 became the M1 the road veering to the right.

He always drove South on the old A1. It seemed faster and shorter in miles. He knew every bend of the road all the way to London.

It was nice he thought, to see the reverse side of the Ferrybridge Power station, after years of driving on the other. Some new roads had been beneficial to drivers.

Coming up to Barnsdale Bar services, he pulled the car into the car park.

"What are you driving around for?" said Jim.

Colburn replied, "look for a car with kids in that may be going on holiday."

Jim spotted a Focus C-Max.

"That one there looks full of luggage and there are toys in it."

"That'll do nicely," said Colburn. He parked next to it. "We'll just hang on here a bit. Let's see who is in the car."

After about ten minutes, a family came out of the services.

One male, one female and two boys, probably about six and eight.

As they neared their car, Colburn, Jim and Val got out of theirs.

Val smiled at the other women, "nice day, going on your holidays?"

The women replied, "Yes, down East Anglia, if we ever get there."

"I know," said Val, "the traffic is murder, gets worse every week."

Colburn and Jim already had small tubes of super glue in their hands, quickly feeling for the electrical sensors under their rear wings.

Pulling them off and applying the glue to them, they walked slowly around the rear of the holidaymaker's car and fixed the sensors to it.

This car would probably make the Lincoln turn off and eventually head towards Norwich.

That will give the followers something to do.

Colburn smiled, winked at Jim, got back in their car and drove out of the services heading South.

Eventually the holidaymakers turned onto roads heading for East Anglia and Jock with Doug in attendance duly obliged and followed.

"That should give us a time break," said Colburn, "but if they're good at their jobs and I bet they are, they'll be back."

After Peterborough, the road widened again.

Devouring cheese sandwiches, sausage rolls and a flask of tea, made the journey tolerable.

Ignoring the M25 turn-off, they continued straight towards central London.

Signs for Mill Hill and Finchley appeared. Colburn looked for the signs that said Mill Hill East. The underground station loomed up but he turned onto the road towards the barracks of the Postal Engineers. He knew there was ample parking on that camp and both he and Jim had their Army Officer ID cards with them.

Locating the guardhouse, because of courtesy and he didn't want his car blown up, he reported in. Using the story about visiting officer friends and asking where they could park.

There was no problem after the guardhouse sergeant with two pickets examined the car thoroughly.

Being a weekend he knew security would be tight.

They would be leaving Sunday afternoon anyway.

After parking, they picked up all their gear and clothes walked through the married quarters and back to the Tube Station.

Mill Hill East is a branch line of the Northern, joining at Finchley.

They needed to go to King's Cross. First they travelled on to Waterloo and booked two rooms for the night in the Union Jack Club, only for Forces personnel, past and present.

Val was staying alone at the Club, she didn't mind that. A Saturday night in London could be fun. She wished she was twenty years younger but she thought, a nice meal, a few drinks at the bar and an early night. That's best.

She knew the bar in the Club well. No doubt some half-drunken squaddie would try it on but when she flashed her officer ID, they'd crawl up in a ball and apologise.

They were nice like that.

Colburn and Jim were heading back on the tube to King's Cross, and right next door was St. Pancras. It is easy to navigate the underground, all you have to know is which line you want and whether you want to travel North, South, East or West.

The stations were full of the usual travellers. All nationalities and creeds, most with backpacks or cases. Colburn and Jim fitted in well.

Getting off at Kings Cross, they slowly walked with the crowds to the escalators, heading for the main rail station.

Then they went outside and turned right, they were on Euston Road.

Past the St. Pancras rail entrance and there at number 96 was the imposing piazza of the British Library.

They both strolled across the piazza to the main entrance. It was an imposing new building built in brick. It did seem to fit in with the new look London was trying to create.

The entrance loomed ahead.

As expected, because of the ongoing security concerns, bag searches were being conducted on all visitors using the St. Pancras entrance.

Waiting patiently in the line to be searched, Colburn and Jim slipped off their backpacks and handed them to one of the security men.

They knew they had far more experience in security than the Library staff. If you hand someone your bag, you know well they won't bother too much, you have nothing to hide.

Jim was being patted down when his security man felt something.

"Can I see that?" he said.

"Of course," said Jim, taking out a tin of rolling tobacco.

"You can't smoke in here."

"I know that but I'll need one after I've been here a few hours," said Jim.

The security man smiled, Jim knew he was OK.

Colburn went through with no bother.

Slinging their packs back on, Colburn said "wouldn't mind being patted down by her," as he glanced back at the security woman checking the females.

"Don't let Val hear you say something like that," Jim said sounding surprised.

Colburn replied, "Val always says to me, when you stop looking, I know you're getting old. After all, you can still look but don't touch. How about a cup of tea and a sandwich? We need to keep the calorie levels up. See that sign, upper ground floor is a café or first floor restaurant."

"Café's good for me," said Jim.

Sitting with a small tea pot of supposedly tea, made with a tea bag that was manufactured years ago and a couple of pork pies that made British Rail catering taste like Chef of the Year. They overlooked the King's Library in the rear of the entrance hall.

Colburn looked around just checking for anything

abnormal, then leaned over the table towards Jim. "In the lower ground floor, there's lockers and storage, we could leave our kit there, until close to closing. I might have a look at the postage stamp display while we're here. Take the chance when you can.

On the next floor are the restaurant, Rare Books and Business Centre.

The next is manuscripts reading room and another business centre.

Then on the third floor are the Map's Reading Room, Reader's Terrace, Asian and African and Voila! The Cotton Room.

Remember him? He's the one that gave the Gospels to this Library.

Nice of him to give away something that didn't belong to him. Let's say our work here is his Nemesis.

After tea we'll just wander around and recce that area in particular."

"Roger that," said Jim, wondering what they would find and how the hell were they going to get out of there.

"What's the escape plan then?"

"Haven't got a clue," replied Colburn, "seems like we have to go back through the front door."

"Carrying a big parcel?" said Jim.

"You only see, what's in front of your eyes. If you're distracted, you notice nothing." Colburn grinned, "I've got some semblance of a plan, I just hope the timing is correct."

"What if it isn't?" asked Jim.

"Then Val's probably right, we'll end up in the Tower," replied Colburn.

"Bloody great," moaned Jim, "are we making a move then?"

"I want to have a look at the stamps, I've got a couple of Australia kangaroo stamps back home, they might be worth a few quid," Colburn joked as they started ambling around.

First they went to the lower ground floor and dropped their packs off in the cloakroom lockers. Both thought at least we'll get our pound coins back.

Eventually, after strolling around the other floors looking intensely at the books and objects on display just like the other visitors, they ended up on the third floor.

It was nice to see that the Gospels held a place of honour.

A display case on metal legs holding up what appeared to be a large plastic case, with the book opened.

"Isn't that beautiful," said Colburn, "no wonder Durham wants it back. It's theirs anyway but this place won't release it. Although they did let it come home, or at least to Newcastle, a few years ago, to be exhibited in some gallery. Good of them wasn't it?

That case looks pretty solid plastic, not bullet proof. They must think the Bishop of Durham might come down here and take it home. Trusting souls aren't they?"

Jim joked, "it would be easy to smash it open and run."

Colburn grinned, "then all hell would break loose, see those sensors round the hinges, the alarm bells would be ringing all over. Then no way out. Down three floors, no way. We have to walk out with the visitors and tourists. We can't use heat, that'll set them off, we have to find a way into that and not from the top."

"OK," said Jim, "do we cut it from the bottom and let it drop out?"

"Nice thought," Colburn leaned down to check his shoelaces. There were more sensors around the base, inside the case. "Well, that scuppers that idea."

Looking from the side he thought, where's the electric supply coming from? The sensors may be motion activated but if there's no internal battery, there must be a source of power. Nothing was plainly obvious at first. They both scanned the area still trying to look like visitors in awe of the manuscript.

Jim noticed the bolts keeping the legs in place.

"I can check for a power supply later," sad Jim, "but I'm sure the power comes through one of those legs, one has to be hollow. If the supply is cut, the sensors won't work."

Colburn mused over the idea. "It may be that if the supply is cut, an alarm will sound in central security. So we by-pass it, no problem."

Jim said, "we need to check the security patrol times. See those boxes on the wall over there, they're used by the patrols. They insert a key into them and a time is logged on their little machine. It proves they've been there.

They may patrol every half hour or hour at least."

Colburn nodded to Jim, "it's nearly four, we'll wander a bit more and get our kit. Security on a Saturday night means listening to Capital Radio and drinking tea. They won't be expecting any problems. Trouble is, there are very few places to lose ourselves and I don't want to be on the ground floor, evading security up all the floors. The only place up here are the toilets."

"That's fairly obvious," said Jim, "they're sure to check in there."

"Of course they should but will they. If it was you, how would you do it?"

"I'd kick every stall open," said Jim.

"Yes, you would but this is the British Library. I think they'll bend down and check. So all stalls have to be left open."

"Fine," said Jim, "so now what?"

Colburn walked over to another small door. He opened it, looking around to check no one was watching. Inside were the tools of the trade of the cleaning staff.

"This will do nicely," said Colburn observing a few bottles of liquid polish and a bucket and mop. "Fancy not having a vacuum cleaner or a floor polisher, they need a bit of army training. We can stay in here after cleaning, if there is any tonight, it's a perfect place. We need to get our kit out of the locker and get the flask filled up. Fancy another cup of tea?"

They wandered slowly back down the stairs. There were still plenty of visitors around.

Retrieving their packs from the locker on the lower ground floor, they made their way up to the area of the information desk.

"You go and get the teas in Jim, I need some information," said Colburn.

Jim made his way back to the café and Colburn wandered over to the information desk. Waiting patiently in line, he spoke to an attractive young lady, who looked of Asian extraction.

"Could you help me please?" asked Colburn, "what time are you closing tonight?"

The young lady replied, "six, as usual."

"Thank you," Colburn turned to leave and stopped. Turning back to the desk, "so I still have time to finish my study in the Reader's Room then. I don't want to be chased out by the cleaners."

"That's fine Sir, our cleaners work early morning before opening. You still have time, security will let you know."

"You've been a great help, a credit to this Library," said Colburn.

The girl blushed and said, "thank you, it's nice to be appreciated."

"You're welcome," said Colburn, walking away to the stairs towards the café.

Jim was sitting at the same table, observing movements when Colburn arrived.

"Got your information, then?" asked Jim.

"Everything's set, let's enjoy tea and then get back," said Colburn.

The crowds were beginning to thin It was close to quarter to six.

Colburn and Jim drank the last of their tea, stuck a sandwich in their packs and made their way up the stairs. Most people were now coming down. The floor was practically deserted. They looked around as if observing the exhibits and when the last person left, they opened the closet door and both stepped inside.

"Jim, have you got your special key set handy?"

"Sure have," replied Jim.

"Then lock this door from the inside. If security tries it, all the better."

Jim used his special tool, which looked like a set of

feeler gauges. Once inside a lock they spread out to fit the internal shape perfectly. Now it was locked.

Colburn thought, now we only have to check the security patrol timings for the first few hours, then the fun begins.

They sat on the floor, using the pen torch they assembled the gear they should need.

Both thought it was just as well no one opened up packets of biscuits or chocolates. The amount of tools and electrical wiring hidden in them, as well as latex gloves, tape, you name it, it was there. Forward planning was everything, what could go wrong?

CHAPTER TWENTY-ONE

When you're in a situation that requires quiet and thought, the best course of action is to sleep when you can. Never mind the time of day. The circadian rhythm of the biochemical clock can be trained and Army training is the best for that. You learn to sleep when and where you can and awake fighting fit.

Jim carefully checked that all his equipment had the correct batteries that had been fully charged previously. He knew he would need just two things, speed and stealth. The rest he would leave up to Colburn. Working as a pair, one always watched each other's backs.

Colburn sat on the floor of the cupboard, eyes closed but his mind was still racing checking over and over the forward planning.

Opening his eyes he whispered to Jim, "over the next couple of hours we'll check the timings of the security staff but it will probably only give us a maximum of one hour to complete the job. Luckily the security box for the guard's key is on this wall, so we'll easily hear him. Then we decide at what time to go for it. I'm thinking three or four in the morning, probably four. The staff will be tiring by then and hopefully not paying too much attention to duty. I'm expecting them by then, just to walk straight to the box, turn the key and walk out. If I wasn't expecting anything, that's what I would do.

The only problem is how not to get noticed during that hour."

"Why should anyone notice us?" enquired Jim.

"Because they have television screens in security and the camera for this floor is right above the entrance," Colburn replied, "so we have to devise some way to incapacitate the camera but not the monitor."

Jim rubbed his chin, Colburn knew this was his way of pondering a problem.

"The way I see it is this. The camera is not infra red, just plain old black and white. It's not scanning the room, it's taking a static picture, probably with a wide-angle lens so it can cover most of the room. So it's absolutely certain that it's covering our book area. Now I need to work around that area for less than one hour, without it showing up on the screen. Have I covered everything?" said Jim.

"Covered is the exact word Jim," exclaimed Colburn, "sometimes you come up with brilliant ideas."

"I know I do," said Jim, "but just this time, can you tell me what I said?"

Colburn shifted his position, "we can't stop the camera show, even making a static picture on it will alert the guards."

"I agree," said Jim, "so how can we stop the camera seeing us."

"We don't," said Colburn, "we will be there all the time."

"Right, fine," said Jim, still with puzzlement in his voice, "so how do we make ourselves invisible?"

"Just like you said, we will be covered," said Colburn, " covered under those dust sheets on that shelf."

Jim's face had the look of not following a word Colburn said. He couldn't fathom out how they could just take a large sheet, put it over the bookcase and hope no one would notice. Then he spoke, "surely the security guard might notice a big dust sheet that wasn't there before?"

"That's just the point, it will have been there and on several others. They will assume that something is going on as regards cleaning or renovation and if it's seen a few times during the night, then it will become natural and expected. Remember, you only see what's there.

Now we have enough sheets in here to cover several displays, just keep the biggest one to work under.

We have to get these on the displays and over the Gospels now before the first patrol. Open the door and let's go."

Colburn and Jim stood up and grabbed all the covers from the shelves. Jim opened the door.

"What if someone is monitoring the screens now?" said Jim.

Colburn thought a couple of seconds, "strip down to your shirt, they will probably think we're part of some cleaning staff and by the time they get up here to look, we're gone. Locked in the cupboard and everything is safe with the displays. Even if they check them, all will be present and correct. Now go."

It only took a few minutes to rush out and cover several display items.

The largest sheet was left to cover the Gospels. It was perfect, not just right down to the ground, it trailed a few feet over, all around the exhibit.

Jim and Colburn were tucked back into their cupboard getting comfortable for the night, when they heard the first security guard. He walked over to the timing clock, inserted the key and turned it. That time was stamped on his tape. Looking around, he couldn't help notice the dustsheets over some of the exhibits. He reached for his radio.

"Hello control, this is Security Four, Over."

"Hello Four, this is Control, Over."

"Control, do you know anything about dustsheets over the exhibits on this floor? Over."

"Hello Four not a clue, must be something to do with cleaning, check everything is in order and carry on, Over."

"Roger, Wilco. Out."

The security guard was diligent, he lifted most of the covers and everything appeared, as it should be. Colburn and Jim heard the guard try the doorknob, it was locked.

The guard slowly walked from the room, checking around the walls and ceiling with his flashlight. They heard the door close. Both breathed a sigh of relief.

Part one of the plan was successful.

Jim whispered again to Colburn, "it's just like old times isn't it?"

Colburn replied, "I hope it doesn't turn out like some of the old times, get some shut eye and we'll go for four o' clock. Goodnight."

Both of them settled down. They knew they wouldn't sleep heavily, they would check they guard's timing for the first few hours and then be good to go.

Jock's phone buzzed, it amused him as it played the entrance of the Emperor from Star Wars. He pressed the little green telephone.

"Strane speaking," he said.

"Where the Hell are you?" the voice asked.

"Hi Colonel, I've got them covered. Don't worry, they're parked up outside a hotel in Wymondham, near Norwich," Strane replied.

"I know where Wymondham is cretin," said the Colonel, "you know Strane, I would rather have you on a job than Rambo."

"Well I appreciate that Colonel," said Strane.

The Colonel continued, "but if you had one less brain cell it would be lonely."

"What's the problem?" asked Strane.

"Have you checked the car you're following?" enquired the Colonel, sounding even polite.

"Well no, but it's on my screen. I know exactly where it is," said Strane.

"Oh, do you now?" replied the Colonel, "then how come it's logged in on the military computers at Mill Hill Barracks?"

Strane didn't reply for a few seconds. He thought all the money and expertise of the British and American secret service and we've been following someone going on holiday to Norfolk. He quietly smiled, thinking, I might have known Lord wouldn't make it this easy.

"OK, so what now?" replied Strane.

"I don't really care what you do, just get to Mill Hill and don't lose him again," the Colonel slammed his phone down.

"Problems?" asked Doug.

"Not at all Doug. It seems we're following a car, probably going on holiday to the Norfolk Broads," Strane replied with a smile. "Lord's car is parked up in the Postal Engineers depot at Mill Hill."

Doug had a resigned look on his face, "He's a crafty little beggar, ain't he?

At least I've seen some nice countryside. I'd better radio in to my people where we're going. Best keep them informed. Just enough to keep them off my back, I still wish I knew what this was all about, someone's not telling it all."

Strane looked over at Doug, "you know very well in this game, it's all need to know and we don't need to know. I'll head back to the A1M, then it's a straight run down to London."

Doug turned his head and thought, "I wonder what he's up to in London?"

Strane started the engine and headed back the way they came.

"I'll tell you something," he said, "Lord won't be in London to visit old pals. He's up to something. All we are supposed to do is find the car and follow it. Park up at Mill Hill, wait of him returning and probably follow him all the way home. Exciting isn't it?"

Doug replied, "if that's what it takes, then that's what happens. There's plenty of time for us to find out what the hell is going on and when we do. It's our game."

CHAPTER TWENTY-TWO

When the British Army has trained you, there's hardly any equal in the World.

You can sleep on a sixpence and still know what's going on around you.

How many people get on the London Underground, fall asleep and still wake up when it's their stop. It's exactly the same, you're asleep but you're not asleep.

The people that go past their stop wouldn't be acceptable for Army life.

Colburn and Jim both heard practically to the hour, the guard walking in and turning his time key. They automatically checked their watches for any slight deviation from the normal pattern. There wasn't.

When you think of how the eye and brain look and compute things, it is always conceivable that if you look at something long enough, that sight will become normal.

If you walked past a building every day, covered with scaffolding, all you would think of is cleaning or repairs. Day by day you would expect to see scaffolding. The only time you would notice any difference was if the scaffolding wasn't there.

And so it was with dustsheets.

The guard just walked past everything on each

occasion turned his key, proving he'd been there at the time stated on his tape and walked out.

At a couple of minutes after four, the guard returned, inserted his key in the box, turned it, the time was stamped on his tape, then he walked out.

Jim nudged Colburn with his foot, "party time," he whispered and put his feeler type gauge into the lock and opened it. Just a little.

The room was still lit but with diffuse lighting. Probably to save on the electricity bill.

Who could blame them, the cost of it was rocketing.

Colburn quietly leaned toward Jim, "I'll be on the floor under the camera so I can check you can't be seen. Leave your mobile on in your pocket on vibrate, just in case I need to get you. I'll do the same. Now you get under that cover and start work. A quick dash should do it. Under this lighting any television screen will be grainy and as long as nothing moves afterwards, there should be no problems. If there is, I'll deal with them at the door.

After three it's go, one, two, go."

Colburn skirted the walls avoiding the bulk of the camera lens.

Jim slid out, crawling fast with his kit and was under the sheet in less than five seconds. He ripped open a small packet of talcum powder, rubbed it all over his hands and put on a pair of surgical gloves.

Under the sheet there was ample room to work, between the legs of the stand.

Jim reached into his kit and felt for his micrometer.

This was used in many industrial places to determine the thickness of plastic or paint coatings but mainly it gave a reading if something was solid all the way through, or not.

He shone the torch on the dial face as he pressed the meter against the first leg. His phone vibrated in his pocket. He answered it.

"What's up?" Jim whispered.

"You're lit up like Blackpool Illuminations, keep the light hidden," said Colburn.

"OK," said Jim, "let me know if there's any more problems."

He carried on. The first leg showed off the scale readings, it was solid.

So were the second and the third.

Jim smiled when he saw the last reading. Just as he thought, it was hollow.

Putting the meter away, he glanced at his watch. Only seven minutes gone.

Now he had to saw away at two places on that leg.

Colburn heard the small hacksaw blade cutting into the metal. He thought, just as well the camera didn't pick up sound.

It didn't take Jim long to cut half way across the leg in two places.

Then he changed the angle of the blade and started to saw downwards from the top cut to the bottom one.

Colburn sat mesmerised at the sound but he was listening intently for any movement outside. He hoped that security were getting tired by now and probably had their own television on or listening to Capital Radio.

Jim put the saw away and felt for the pliers.

He inserted one of the blades into the cut and gripped tight on the handles.

With a slow levering motion, the cut section rose up revealing the electric cable.

Taking out forceps, he gripped the cable and pulled very gently, to determine how much play or slack there was. Sometimes everything goes to plan. There were at least five inches of spare cable.

Leaving the forceps in place hanging on the cable, Jim took a small scalpel and started to strip the wires. Not an easy job. Going straight through them and the alarm would sound but he'd done this before. The electric had to be cut to the display without alerting the security staff. So the power had to be diverted somewhere else.

Out of his sack he pulled the electric screwdriver and its small charger.

Surprise, surprise, the charger needed mains electricity to charge the screwdriver and he would need it fully charged later.

He quickly took the plug off the charger and fitted the three leads into a block.

He had stripped the leg cables in three places.

On the bottom three leads, he attached the metal clips and using the bypass device, attached the clips to the top ones.

Wiping away the sweat on his brow he cut the middle leads.

Nothing happened.

He inserted the bottom three cables into the block charging up the screwdriver.

At the moment, the current was still going to the bookcase, using the bypass.

He unclipped the top three.

The power was running straight to the screwdriver. The heart rate started to attain normality.

His phone vibrated again.

"Forty five minutes gone," whispered Colburn.

Jim replied, "I'm OK for using the screwdriver, sit tight."

Jim looked up at the six Phillips screw heads and thought, I hope none of them are stripped.

There were one at each corner and one at the top and bottom. Leave the bottom one until last. The bottom of the case should come down and the book should slide out.

Each side screw came out. Thank God thought Jim.

He positioned himself so his shoulders would take the weight of the base and the book. He unscrewed the top one. The base moved a little but Jim's shoulders took the weight.

Now for the bottom screw. His arm was angled but he managed to fit in the driver head and reversed screwed.

Suddenly it all came away, the base fell.

Jim fell onto his back and caught the falling base and the book.

His phone vibrated.

He reached into his pocket and pressed to reply.

Colburn's voice whispered, "we've got a problem."

Jim replied quietly, "you might not believe it, but so have I, the base and book are on my chest."

"Keep quiet, the guard is coming on his rounds," said Colburn, "keep still and don't move, lights out."

Jim shut down his phone. Keep still and don't move I couldn't if I wanted to, he thought.

Colburn crawled under the nearest dustsheet and waited.

It would be easy to incapacitate the guard but that would create too many problems.

The guard entered and went straight to the security port, turned his key and looked around. He stood still. Was there something going on?

"Control, this is Four, Over.

"Four, this is Control, Over."

"Control I need you to check something for me, Over."

Both Jim and Colburn sweated. They both knew they could take care of the guard but that wasn't the plan.

"Four, this is Control, what's the problem, Over."

The guard walked slowly back to the door and turned to face into the room.

"Control, can you knock off the alarm to floor three fire door, I need a smoke, Over."

"Four, it's done, don't be long and report in when you've finished, Over."

"Cheers Control, Out."

The guard opened the doors and walked to the end of the corridor.

Jim and Colburn heard the fire door open.

Colburn crawled out from under the sheet and belly crawled over to Jim under the sheet.

"Better get this lot cleaned up fast," said Colburn.

He closed the Gospel book and moved it to one side.

"Let's get the base back in place," he said.

Colburn held the base, Jim quickly putting the screws back in.

"Trouble is, with the wires cut, I'll have to leave the screwdriver as it is," said Jim.

"Wipe it all down for prints and then we'll get back in our little cupboard nest," said Colburn.

They both quickly cleaned up, leaving the screwdriver and it's attachments underneath the cover. Then quickly picking up the book, they returned to the cupboard.

Nothing appeared changed, on the surface anyway.

Colburn thought, three more security visits would take them past eight o' clock and by nine the place would be open. Then they could leave.

Jim thought how the hell do we get that book out of here.

Colburn had placed it in a large Harrods bag but you just can't walk out, can you?

"When the cleaner's come in, they will think the dustsheets are for something else and they won't touch them, they'll Hoover around them.

Visitors will be coming in, so security will be looking at people coming in, not going out," Colburn said in a hopeful manner.

Jim and Colburn settled down to wait out the next couple of hours.

As usual, security was on the hour, every hour, very diligent.

All they had to do now was leave this place with a large book in a Harrods plastic bag. They couldn't stay in the cupboard until that time, the cleaners would want to be in for their cleaning equipment.

All that was left were the rest rooms on that floor. They would go in there after the eight o' clock security guard and wait.

Colburn always had something up his sleeve, Jim hoped.

The eight o' clock guard came in just like clockwork. Straight to the key and turned it to stamp the time on his tape. The guards would change at nine.

Jim and Colburn heard the guard leave, looking through the keyhole to check. All seemed still and quiet. After a few more minutes, they checked that their kit was all safely packed in their rucksacks. Slinging them onto their backs, Colburn picked up the Harrods bag.

"Time to make a move," Colburn said, "open the lock up."

Jim opened the lock quietly.

"Now, what we have to do is slip out of here and head to the nearest restrooms out in the corridor. The camera basically does not cover the outside walls, so keep close into the sides and we'll meet under the camera by the door."

"Roger that," replied Jim.

Both moved quickly out of the door and raced round the walls using opposite sides and met at the door. Colburn eased the main doors open and looked carefully and cautiously out into the corridor.

It was all clear.

With no cameras apparent in the corridor, they just walked fast to the restrooms, found the males and went in.

Jim spoke after regaining his breath, "if the cleaners start at half past, they'll get their kit first before looking around where to start cleaning. What if they lift those sheets?"

"They won't," said Colburn, "contract cleaners just clean where they can see, after all they are not supposed to touch the exhibits."

"Let's hope you're right," said Jim.

Colburn whispered under his breath, "Have faith."

Time always seem to drag when you're waiting but eventually everything comes around. About eight forty-five, they heard voices outside in the corridor.

"Right on time," said Colburn, "now if we can hang on another twenty five minutes, the first visitors will be in. On a Sunday it's mostly university students studying the reference books. It's the quietest time for them to do it."

Suddenly the restroom door was flung open and a cleaning cart came flying in.

They both looked up, shock and horror on their faces.

There behind the cart stood an enormous figure, practically seven foot, well-muscled and ebony skin.

He looked as surprised as Jim and Colburn.

Jim bent down under one of the sinks and rattled the pipework.

"Morning," said Jim, "do you need to clean in here now? We have to fix some plumbing in here but we can do it later."

The big man mumbled something that sounded like OK.

Colburn and Jim picked up their gear and bag.

"You clean here first, we'll come back later," said Jim.

Then they slowly walked out.

"Thank God for cheap labour, he'll get on with it and say nothing," said Jim.

Outside in the corridor, Colburn looked at his watch.

"It's a bit early but needs must, some of the students will be in and the others will be on their way."

Colburn flipped open his phone and speed dialled, someone answered.

"Now" said Colburn and rang off.

Val had had a restful night at the Union Jack Club. She had decided that a kebab from the greasy chippy round the corner was enough and then had a couple of Gin and Tonics before retiring. There was no problem with the young soldiers in the bar. She thought she might be losing her appeal. Setting the alarm for seven, she was up and out by half eight, dropping the keys in the slot at the front desk.

She decided to walk over Waterloo Bridge and along the Embankment. There was plenty of time and it was a nice morning. The sun was just breaking through an early morning mist.

She could see the Houses of Parliament when her phone rang.

On answering she only heard one word, then she dialled a number Colburn had given her.

A voice answered, "Security."

All security heard was a voice saying;

"The will of Allah must be heard, this is your fifteen minute warning, before the words of the Infidel will be exploded. A bomb has been planted in your building."

Val closed her phone.

The security staff at the library consisted of many moonlighting soldiers who knew the drill.

Then all Hell broke lose.

Jim and Colburn were still on the third floor when the fire alarms sounded.

"There you go, right on time," said Colburn, "use the stairs, the lifts should be in lock down."

They walked briskly to the staircase and started down passing the second floor, onto the first.

A security guard came rushing up the steps.

"What the hell are you two doing?" he shouted angrily, "get down and out, the place is being evacuated."

"Is there a fire?" enquired Jim.

"Just get out now," the guard replied.

On the ground floor it was bedlam.

Everyone was being herded out of the building. Sirens could be heard droning in the morning air.

There were plenty of students to mix in with. No one was noticing what people were carrying. The order was to get them out.

Colburn and Jim were virtually pushed out of the main doors onto the plaza outside.

Police cars and vans were parked up. Teams of armed officers were pouring into the building.

Army Ordnance Corps transport was pulling in, the noise was deafening.

"That's it, we're out," said Jim, "now what?"

"Now we meet up with the urban terrorist that made that call."

"Then what?" enquired Jim, as they both drew in excess oxygen.

"We get the underground from here to Victoria," said Colburn. "We'll get off there, I fancy a stroll down Vauxhall Bridge Road. Let's take it nice and easy and then,

In Arduis Fidelis."

Jim smiled, "I thought as much, Steadfast in Adversity."

Then they turned left and headed for the Underground.

CHAPTER TWENTY THREE

The underground was pleasantly quiet for a change. Colburn and Jim descended into the station, got a ticket for Victoria and followed the signs to the platform.

The trains were at irregular intervals but it was only about five minutes wait before the electric overhead sign said two minutes.

As the train pulled alongside the platform, they carefully noted that the few people on the train and their platform appeared to be the usual travellers you would expect.

A few obviously working that day but most were carrying cases and packages just like them. They fitted in, no problem.

It didn't take long for the train to arrive at Victoria.

There were a lot of passengers getting off, maybe heading to the main line station or the bus depot. They merged in with the crowd, heading up the escalators and out into the daylight.

It was a pleasant stroll down Vauxhall Bridge Road, not many people about and thankfully not much traffic.

They walked on, not speaking, until they reached the main road to go across Vauxhall Bridge. Turning left, they wandered along Millbank.

Going straight past their intended destination, they came to the Tate Gallery.

"I remember this well," said Jim, "best cup of tea and bacon sandwich in London on a Sunday morning."

"Sure was," replied Colburn, "and there's my lovely little terrorist, waiting on the steps.

Hi darling, had a good night?"

"Lovely thanks," said Val, "I see you've been borrowing books."

"Let's go," said Colburn.

They all turned round and walked down the side of the gallery. Turning left, they approached a military guardhouse.

"Just remember to flash your military I.D. These are civilians manning this one," said Colburn.

As the three turned into the barrack square, they filed through the gate opening, holding up their I.D's for inspection.

They walked straight across the square, toward the imposing façade of the Royal Army Medical College.

As they walked across, Colburn said quietly, "these doors should be locked but there will be a Corporal on duty. Flash your I.D's and leave the talking to me."

Colburn pressed the buzzer on the side of one of the columns. From inside they saw a man emerging, in full uniform. They held up their I.D's to a pane of glass in the door.

The Corporal opened the door.

"Good morning Sir," said the Corporal, "you do know that the officer's entrance is on the main street."

"We apologise for disturbing you but we need to use the Library to carry out some reference work," said

Colburn, "may I sign out the Library key and we may need to use the Biochemistry teaching laboratory."

"That's fine," answered the Corporal, being surprised that an officer had apologised to a junior rank, "just come to the office window and sign for the key. How long will you need it for?"

"Only about a couple of hours," replied Colburn.

"OK," answered the Corporal, "if I'm not here, just leave the key on the counter, I'll be just doing my rounds."

"Thanks for your help Corporal," said Colburn.

They all smiled and went left up a few steps, then right up a few more and turned around to go up the steps to the second floor and the Library.

Colburn opened the double doors of the Library.

Inside it was a typical private Library. The bookshelves around the room, apart from the large window to the North, were full of books, new, old and even rare manuscripts neatly displayed on the seven shelves.

Colburn placed the Harrods bag on the centre table.

"This place, what was it really?" enquired Val.

"If I tell you that, I'll have to kill you," Colburn replied jokingly.

"All this place is, or supposed to be, is a centre for Pathology testing that couldn't be done in any of the Tri-Service Hospitals. So the samples are sent here.

On this floor is Parasitology, grew big cockroaches and Histology, the bacon slicers.

On the first floor, where we came in, are just offices and underneath us is the Biochemistry Department and lecture theatres.

Now on the ground floor there's Virology, the Electron Microscope and Bacteriology. That's about it, this place has a close liaison with Porton Down as well. That covers the lot, or that's all I'm saying.

Now let's have a look at the Gospels."

Colburn slipped the book out of the bag carefully onto the table.

Opening it at the first page, they gasped as they observed the intricate handwork and artistry of the writer. Seeing it up this close was the only way you could really appreciate the magnificence of the manuscript.

"Now," said Colburn, "what did you mean by Aldred's page?"

They all put on white gloves from their rucksacks, already making out the English translation between the lines.

Turning the pages over carefully, they soon came to the final pages.

There seemed to be a couple of pages missing and a couple of blank ones.

"Where the hell is the message?" said Jim, "it must be hidden somewhere."

They all sank back into the chairs, Colburn muttering aloud, going over the clues.

"I know these Gospels were re-bound about 1852 but it seems nothing was touched. So we can assume that if a message is here, it's still here," said Colburn.

"We can only assume that if there is some writing here, it's hidden."

"Invisible writing?" said Val, "or just faded over the years?"

"Jim, nip downstairs into the Biochemistry. In the

bench cupboards there are microscopes. Bring one up," said Colburn, "Oh, bring up some Norit as well."

"What's that?" said Val.

"Activated charcoal," said Colburn, "old fashioned stuff, used to use it in a test for vitamin C, years ago."

It didn't take Jim long to return with a bottle of charcoal in his pocket and a microscope in his arms, and an old Gillett and Sibert up to eight hundred times magnification. He plugged it in a nearby socket.

"You're not using oil immersion on the page, are you?" asked Jim.

"No" replied Colburn, "we should only need four hundred magnification to check for indentations in the paper. I'm pretty certain it's this last page we need."

Colburn turned the book carefully with Jim holding the bulk of the weight, they slid the page under the light of the microscope. He started scanning up and down until it appeared in the correct focus.

"Move the book over a bit at a time," said Colburn.

Jim gently pushed the page through and past the lens.

"Stop," sad Colburn, "now go up."

Jim pushed the book in an upward direction.

"I can see indentations in the page, it's not faded," said Colburn, "hand me that charcoal."

He gently tipped the charcoal over the part he was scanning. It was an extremely fine powder and it just seemed to obliterate the section of page. Gently running his finger with his glove over the area, he blew on the powder. They could all see indentations where the charcoal had remained. He re-positioned the page under the microscope lens and re-focussed.

"Looks like we've hit the mother lode," said Colburn, "there are a few lines of writing. This was never meant to be seen by the naked eye."

"Can you read it though?" said Jim.

Val took a Biro and paper from her rucksack, "You read, I'll write."

Colburn moved the lens to a position where it seemed the writing began.

"This is all I can make out, write this," said Colburn.

*"The fire asleep, the wall South.
Above we fill the mouth."*

Colburn scanned, repeatedly focussing. "There's nothing else. I'm sure of it," he said. "Better get all this cleaned up."

Suddenly the library door banged open. All three jumped up but in readiness.

"Sorry about that." The Corporal stood in the doorway. "Have you everything you need?"

Jim replied first, "Thanks Corporal, we're fine. Any problems?"

"Sure is Sir, just had an emergency phone call," said the Corporal.

"Anything we have to do then?" enquired Val.

"Not at all Ma'am. Just someone from across the river rang up and said our flag on the tower was flying upside down," said the Corporal, "and I'll have to reverse it now."

Val smiled at the soldier, "we'll be finished here soon. You go to your duties. Wouldn't want anyone to think we're in distress here."

"No Ma'am, whoever put the flag up this morning, is in for a rocket. Upside down is a sign of distress and there's plenty of old soldiers who like to tell us we've got it wrong," said the corporal, "have a good day and don't forget to drop the key back."

Then he went on his way along the corridor into the officer's mess, to climb the tower.

Jim and Val were already tidying up.

Leaving the microscope on the floor in a corner and the charcoal behind some books on a shelf.

Using his white gloves, Colburn brushed the charcoal off the paper so it looked as if it had never been touched. Jim and Val used their gloves to brush any charcoal onto the floor. They knew the cleaners would vacuum it up in the morning.

Colburn closed the Gospel book.

"I know it's a pity but we can't take this with us. I would like it to be returned to Durham, maybe someday." Colburn said reluctantly.

He walked over and placed it carefully on a shelf with other rare books and manuscripts.

"Let's go," he said. They all picked up their rucksacks, left the library, locked the door and dropped the key into the office before exiting the College.

They all walked out of the compound, waving at the civilian guards and walked out towards Vauxhall Bridge Road.

"What's the plan now?" said Jim, as they walked up the road towards Victoria.

"Well, we get back to the car and drive home." replied Colburm.

"Is that it, then?" said Jim.

Colburn smiled as he looked at Val.

"Any thoughts on history Val? We need to decipher Hatfield's note."

"Well I can come up with some thoughts. Where do we fill the mouth?" asked Val.

Jim joked, "I'm supposing he meant food. From a plate, in the kitchen."

"That's exactly it," said Val, "they ate in the Great Hall. He wouldn't have taken any object far. Wouldn't have disposed of it, like ditching it in the river. My guess is he hid it so no-one would find it but left a clue on that book."

"Seems logical," said Colburn, "seeing as he says the fire is asleep. It could well mean the fire is buried and hidden forever."

"I think I know where he means," said Val.

"At the time he was supervising his throne area, he was also involved in renovations of the Castle across Palace Green. Under Hatfield's design the Great Hall proper, occupied the whole of the block on the West Side of the castle. In fact, you can still see some of the wall of Hatfield's Hall from the courtyard on the South side wall.

So that text could refer to the South Wall of the Castle. Possibly where it meets the Great Hall but there's a problem."

"Isn't there always?" said Jim.

Val continued as they walked, "sometime around the end of the fifteenth century, the southern end of the Hall was converted to nearly what it is to this day. I think this is the area that Bishop Hatfield is pointing us to.

Unfortunately, Bishop Fox converted this area into a staircase and four storeys of rooms."

"So what's the problem?" asked Colburn.

"I think it's reasonable to assume that Hatfield hid whatever underground when he was overseeing the building. That area now, the upper floors are residential accommodation, the first and second floors house the College library and the basement, where we might have to go, is a wine cellar."

Colburn stopped in the street and looked at the other two, "so it's decided, we head home for a rest and a shower. Then we'll decide how we're going to look into the basement area of the Castle"

"I love this game," said Jim, "we rob the British Library, bring most of London to a halt with a bomb threat and now we're going to storm a castle."

"Only the wine cellar," said Val, "and don't come back empty handed."

"What would we look for?" said Jim.

"I'm sure Hatfield will have left some sign," said Val.

"Let's hope so," said Colburn, "now I need to make one more call but from a payphone."

There were a few payphones down on the first level of Victoria underground.

Val and Jim got their tickets to Mill Hill.

Colburn dialled the British Library.

"Security," said the voice that answered.

"Tape this message," said Colburn, "I want no mistakes. By now you have seen the confusion we can create, there never was any bomb. However you should be aware by now of the missing Lindisfarne Gospels, taken illegally from Durham Cathedral.

As a token of our good faith, we have left them in the Library of the Royal Army Medical College, Millbank. We are the United Front for the Restitution of the Gospels. You will hear from us again." Colburn rang off, "fifty four seconds, good no trace."

They all boarded the tube and changed to the Northern Line at Kings Cross, back to Mill Hill East.

They could all imagine the surprise and shock on the Corporal's face when Police and Army converged on the College. He may have some explaining to do but the names on the signing in register were false. It was not a court martial offence.

Alighting the underground they walked back to the barracks flashed their I.D. and shouted to the gatehouse they were taking their car out now.

After loading their kit in the boot, Colburn drove out.

The Orderly Sergeant Major on duty, took note of the numberplate, then picked up his phone. He dialled the number he'd be given the previous day and spoke, "that car is leaving now, is that all you need?"

A voice replied, "that's fine."

Doug and Jock pulled away.

"We're not losing them again," said Jock, "keep close this time."

There was no need to wonder if they were being followed, they were heading straight home. Four hours of easy driving and they would be there.

The only conversation in the car, was different ways of breaking into the wine cellar of the Castle.

Then Jim came up with a beauty, "don't they do tours around the Castle?"

Val replied, "yes, I don't know the timings but the tourist office will know."

Jim continued, "then why don't we join an organised tour. At least we can see the place legally, before we tear it to bits."

Colburn didn't look up from the road ahead, "let's hope it doesn't come to that but it gets us in officially. That's a go."

Jim put his head back on the seat and was asleep in a few minutes.

Val had said she would stop awake and keep Colburn alert but she was out for the count before they reached Staples Corner.

Colburn smiled to himself, "just like old times but I think I'm getting too old for this, next time we fly down."

CHAPTER TWENTY-FOUR

Driving from London to the North isn't fun. It is easier using the old A1, even though most of the road after Peterborough is just two lanes. The scenery is more pleasant, far better than the monotony of the M1 and M18.

Passing under the M18 leaves about thirty miles to Wetherby and then one more hour home.

Colburn was beginning to get tired as Val and Jim began to stir.

"Thanks for the company," Colburn said with a laugh, "it's been like driving two corpses. Luckily the snoring kept me awake."

"Where abouts are we?" said Val with a yawn.

"Just coming up to Scotch Corner," answered Colburn, "about forty minutes and we'll be home."

Jim and Val stretched out, rubbing their eyes, trying to stay awake.

"Notice any tail?" said Jim.

"Hard to tell," replied Colburn, "I've noticed a couple of cars that have been with us all the way but it really doesn't matter. By now, someone will have realised it was us at the Library and the College but they don't know why. I think we should expect a visit soon. Someone will want to know what we know."

Jim looked puzzled, "I just can't believe the Americans have a hand in this. What's in it for them? They never do anything without an ulterior motive."

Val said, "It's logical to assume some connection with Washington but it's difficult to tie down an exact reason. We can assume that the American side of it only knows a fraction of the story from History. They seem to think that this is about some magical force."

Colburn interrupted, "trouble is Val, I think it is about some sort of firepower and if that's right, we need to find it first and then decide what to do with it."

Val continued, "we can assume that the message in the obelisk came from America and we found it here. Also it's safe to say, that message or some form of it had been in the Washington family for generations but they never knew what it meant. Now that it has surfaced, someone wants to know."

"Well," said Jim, "if they had cared to study old English history and from around here in particular, they may have understood it a bit better."

"Unfortunately, that's true. Most Americans look on Washington as the father of the nation and some even know he has English roots but that's the sum of most of their knowledge," replied Val.

"The name Washington comes from old Anglo Saxon. HWAES means a Saxon chieftain, INGA means, the family of and TUN an estate of the Hwaes family.

Put it all together and you have Hweas-Inga-Tun.

That's how it all started. You can trace the family roots back to the Ancient Kingdom of Northumbria. In fact the earliest of the family were descended from Conan the

Thane, King of the Cumbrians and the Ancient Earls of Northumberland, from about 1000 AD."

Jim said jokingly, "so if the Americans knew that Washington was descended from Conan, they might pick Schwarzenegger for the next president."

"Just typical of you, take it serious for once, it's important," said Val. "The original Washington estate was situated on a tract of land between the river Tyne and Wear. It was a centre of learning and the cradle of the Christian community, at that time. When you think that here was written the first ever book, other than the Bible, penned by the Venerable Bede. It was called "An Ecclesiastical History of the English Speaking Peoples" and from there the English language and Christianity was spread to the Americas and around the World.

Now the first ancestor of George Washington to live at Washington Hall was William Fitz Patric. He moved to Hertburn, near Stockton and became known as William de Hertburn. Then later the family moved to Wessyngton Hall, taking the name William de Wessyngton.

It was Sir William de Wessyngton the Fourth, that fought at the Battle of Nevilles Cross and it has to be that connection to the Cathedral treasures. The manor house continued in the possession of Washington descendants until it was sold to the Bishop of Durham in 1613. The same year, Captain Samuel Argall, a stepson of the Washington's, went out to Jamestown to trade with the Potomac. It was he who kidnapped Pocahontas from the tribe and took her to Jamestown, where she met John Rolfe and converted to Christianity. He went on to be the Deputy Governor of Virginia in 1617 and the rest, as they say, is History.

One interesting fact is that while the family moved to different places in England, the grandmother of George Washington, the first President, is buried at Whitehaven, over in Cumbria. Just for you Jim, the word Hwaes is still used to this day."

"OK, I give in," said Jim, "you're the History expert, or is this a joke?"

"No joke Jim, we still shout Hwaes the Lads at the Football," said Val.

"Well the next time I'm out on the toon, I'll be sure to get that into the conversation," said Jim. "I'm sure the average Newcastle football supporter is just waiting to be told that."

Val went on, "I think there's more to this. There's no way a list of Cathedral treasures could be looked on as that important. The Americans can't have them anyway. I think that someone else in the family knows something about this and left some other record. Someone in that ancestry knew something else. I'm positive about that."

Colburn said, "I'm sure all will be revealed in due course."

Val continued, "it seems logical to assume that a list of Cathedral artefacts was written down on a piece of manuscript that probably came from one of the books, if not the Gospels themselves. Then to talk about some form of Fire of the Gods, seems to me that someone has seen or has known about this Fire. Therefore, I'm thinking, that someone else wrote some of those words on the manuscript from the obelisk."

Colburn never turned his head when he was driving, looking straightforward he said, "That is quite logical. It's apparent that the manuscript paper was in the Washington family for centuries. It could well have been added to. So what we all need now, is to re-assess all the clues to make sure we've missed nothing. Try and put some sort of time line on the clues and most of all Val, we're home. So will you put the kettle on and I'll garage the car. If anyone followed, they only know we're home."

Val and Jim went inside. Colburn put the car in the garage. Most people in the village left their cars out but Colburn didn't take any chances, with anyone.

Val filled the kettle and plugged it in. A static spark jumped at her.

"I'm sick of asking him to look at that plug, we'll all go up in a blue light," said Val.

Colburn came in from the garage, got his tea and sat in his recliner in the lounge.

"I'm getting too old for that driving, my back's killing me," said Colburn.

Jim replied, "never mind about your back, Val's moaning about that plug again."

Colburn turned his head and smiled at Val, "I'll fix it," he said.

Val smiled back, "when I see pigs flying, I'll know it's fixed," she said.

"Don't be like that, I'll do it," said Colburn.

He relaxed in the chair, "now let's get some semblance of order to this problem, get around the table, we need a think tank." Colburn stood up and they all sat around the table.

"Now" said Colburn, "we know a lot of the history but we need to try and sort out all these individual clues. So let's start at the beginning or the beginning as far as we know it.

We know it all started for us when Jim found that obelisk and we located that parchment in its base. That led us to the cathedral and we found Hatfield's message about the Gospels. Then looking at that page in the Gospels, it pointed us to a section of the Castle. That it appears is where we are at this moment in time."

Val leaned forward on the table, "I think that covers everything we've done but it's obviously not the whole story. There could be many combinations and permutations of this story but my gut feeling is it goes further back in time.

We know the Washington's had their parchment in the family for about four hundred years. Eventually taking it to America when part of the family went over there.

George obviously showed it to Dixon, who brought it back. Possibly he sealed it in the obelisk for safe keeping, before it was used inadvertently as a boundary marker for Auckland Castle estates."

"I agree with that logic," said Jim, "but how did it get into their hands and what the hell is all this about anyway. We don't know and probably anyone else is only guessing, about the power, fire and Gods connection."

Colburn rubbed his chin, staring into space, thought and turmoil going through his mind.

"I agree, there's something we're not seeing. Our intelligence and the Americans would only follow up something like this, if there were money in it, or power. Or they are just guessing like us.

If there was something of interest to them in the Cathedral treasures, then they must have some idea about it.

Cathedral treasures came about from visiting royalty or people of that status but there's no reference to that sort of gift before the Crown robbed the Cathedral.

Therefore it may have been in their possession when the original monks came to Durham."

Jim butted in, "most of the treasures or artefacts from that time were given by the Norsemen. They just about ruled everything around here."

Colburn mused over that thought, "Jim, that's an interesting line of deduction. The Norse really didn't have much treasure themselves, certainly nothing of value from their own area. They usually carried anything precious with them at all times. From this we could deduce that anything of value came from outside the Norse area."

At this Val stirred, "the only place I can think of where Norsemen obtained treasure from, at that time in history, was Eastern Europe. There were thousands of them over the years, worked, or raided out of Constantinople. They came home with the part of any treasure they stole for the Caliph, as payment for their work. So if this treasure was obtained from over there, I'm afraid we just couldn't guess at where it originated or what it was."

Colburn's mind was stirring now, wondering about the origin of whatever they were looking for.

Jim spoke, "it's alright guessing about all this but how does it help us in the future?"

Colburn said, "remember your Army training. Learn as much as you can about the opposition. Only then can you plan any future campaign.

It seems to me that much of the treasure in the East was built up from the Roman and Persian times. I remember particularly in the accounts of early Persian battles, comments about Persian Fire."

"I remember," said Jim, "wasn't it supposed to be like Greek Fire?"

Val sat upright, "No it wasn't. Greek fire was based on Naphtha and that even burns on water. That couldn't have been thought of as treasure or power.

Now, whatever the Persians used, I suppose could be construed as some form of power."

Jim said, "but eventually they got beat, finally by Alexander. So the great power didn't help them there."

Val replied, "that's true but what if they hadn't got it by then. Who knows what could go wrong. All I can think of is that wherever this power originally came from, they might have taken it back. Who knows?"

Colburn was listening intently to the arguments and hypotheses, eventually he said, "if we are to continue the search, then we need to look into the Washington family history to see if there is any connection or mention of this power. I don't want to go blindfold, looking for some power and it blow up in my face."

Val replied, "it's easy to search his ancestry, nearly everything is on the web."

Colburn smiled, "history yes, but not everything will be there. Anything of real importance would have been given by family word of mouth or written down secretly. It stands to reason that's what would happen. So is there anything that we know of, or has been written, that could connect the ancestral line with any sort of power?"

Val was an expert on the History of Durham. It wasn't just an interest, it was a passion. If anyone could piece it together, it was she.

"I've been racking my brains about this," said Val, "but there's only one mention I can think of during the time before part of the family emigrated to America.

After Hatfield died in 1381, as we know, he was a great one for building. The Cathedral and Castle went through a long period of neglect.

In 1416, Prior John of Wessyngton was appointed to oversee repairs. He may have been part of the clergy because he wasn't the first born and couldn't inherit the estate.

I know that the family continued to live at Washington until 1399, when the estate went to another William but he was the last of that name to own the Manor. It continued in the possession of Washington descendants, like the Tempests, Mallory's and Blakestons, until it was sold in 1613 to the Bishop of Durham.

The interesting fact about Prior John, is the mention in chronicles that he did not, or could not, repair the main bell tower.

The story goes that it was supposed to have been set on fire by lightning, on the eve of Corpus Christie, 1429 and just got patched up. It wasn't entirely rebuilt until 1470 by Bishop Lawrence Booth."

Jim mumbled, "well there's some power then, takes a lot of electricity from a lightening bolt to destroy a tower."

Colburn's eyes lit up, "it does seem strange that something that can break and burn, has the power to bring down a bell tower. It makes you wonder that in doing all the repairs, digging and building that he found something. I wonder.

If he had been repairing for example, the Great Hall on the West Side of the courtyard, might he have come across Hatfield's secret?"

Trouble is, there was a lot of alterations to that area

over those years. Remember Bishop Fox converted that area and Bishop Cosin even had the moat filled. Mind you that was about two hundred years after Wessyngton."

Jim smiled, "can you imagine a moat around most of that Castle. How the hell did they get the water up there to fill it? Must be the best part of two hundred feet above the river."

Colburn laughed, "would take a lot of buckets, or the Archimedes Screw. All we can do is go and take a look. I think we can agree from the verse in the Gospels, that Hatfield put whatever, somewhere in the lower ground of the Great Hall towards the South Wall. So we do need to have a look in the wine cellars. Those walls are too thick for imaging, so we may have to do a little plaster reconstruction ourselves. Hammers and Chisels everyone, let's be Mark Master Masons."

Val replied, "OK, we can chip away at the plaster but what are we really looking for?"

Colburn replied, "once again we have to assume that some mark or indication has been left at the place where Hatfield intended his secret to stay. It could be Hatfield's Coat of Arms, could be a Mason ensignia or even Wessynton's Heraldry. I know their Coat of Arms changed over the years but the latest has to be Argent, Two bars and Three Molets in Chief Gules.

Jim replied, "how wonderful, now what does all that mean?"

Colburn looked at Jim, "you know I love you like a brother but you were never the brightest button on the coat. Believe me, you'll know it if you see it. It's different from Hatfield's. Any Masonic mark we'll soon pick up. What do you think, Val?"

Val replied, "I think we have to join a tour of the castle, with our cameras and go from there. We will be able to look all around most places during the day. If we get into the wine cellar, fine. If not we can look ourselves but I do suggest that this enterprise and by that I mean any digging, should be done during the early evening."

"What makes you say that Val?" asked Jim.

"Quite simple, there's still students around. What time of the day would they be occupied with work or more likely, play? Early to late evening," said Val. "Only thing that concerns me is that the bulk of the students in the Castle are studying Theology."

Colburn smiled again, "I think we can assume that these would-be priests, still like a pint or two. So some will be in, others will be out. It's not a problem.

We just need to get in and do some checking."

With that Jim got up, "everything set then. I'm off home now, be back early in the morning with some mining equipment."

Val interrupted, "just bear in mind that things are usually never what they seem."

"Now what do you have in mind?" said Colburn.

"Only that we should expect the unexpected," said Val.

"Like what?" said Jim.

Val carried on, "remember the pomegranates carved at Rosslyn. No one had seen those until a hundred years later. So how did the masons that built it know about them?

Could it be that the story of one of their ancestors had actually gone and returned from America, a hundred years before Columbus.

That brings me to another point about History. When Columbus was in Portugal, at the court of King John the Second, Martin Behaim was there at the same time. Now I'm not saying they spoke to each other but it is possible.

Columbus wanted to sail to the West and was looking for sponsors and ships. Behaim was also a navigator and geographer and had constructed his own globe in 1492. It can still be seen in the Nuremberg National Museum. It was only about 51 centimetres in diameter but it showed land or continents to the West. So what I am saying, Columbus might have known where he was headed all the time. Written history is not always correct, so be prepared. It wasn't only Columbus that knew the World was round. So we should not look all the time for the obvious. "X" does not always mark the spot."

Colburn stretched his arms and said, "after that history lesson, where can we go wrong?" He grinned to himself. "See you in the morning Jim, be ready to do the Durham tourist trail. First stop, tourist information then the Castle tour."

Jim left and drove home. Colburn's eyes were nearly shutting.

"Time for me to hit the sack Val, I'm shattered," said Colburn, "maybe the years are taking their toll."

"I could do with a good night's sleep," said Val as they both climbed the stairs, "but I was thinking that we should go over tomorrow's plan again."

Colburn turned to her and smiled and said, "if I had my time over again, I'd still pick you."

"I love you too," said Val, "just how shattered are you?"

"If you promise to let me fall asleep," said Colburn.

"When?" said Val.

Colburn walked into the bedroom holding Val's hand, "afterwards," he said, lying her down on the bed.

Jock and Doug had arrived back at the Motel down the road from Hett. Sitting down in Jock's room, Doug was the first to speak.

"Great waste of time that was. Here to London and back, for what?"

"Everything comes to them that wait," replied Jock. "Report in and let them know where we are and what the Lords are doing."

Doug replied, "we don't know what they're doing, do we?"

Jock said, "there's still a trace on his cousin's car, when he moves, we'll know and follow as per instructions."

"Then what?" asked Doug.

"Then at some point, we'll have to come face to face with Colburn Lord," said Jock.

Doug smiled, "I'll look forward to that," he said.

Jock looked at him and smiled, "I wouldn't be in any hurry if I was you. He used to be better than both of us put together. You only want to hope he's mellowed with age. We would be better off trying to come up with a way to negotiate."

Doug enquired, "and what if he doesn't want that?"

Jock grimaced, "then all hell will break loose."

CHAPTER TWENTY-FIVE

Val was always out of bed first. This was her time to relax, have a cup of tea and read a few chapters of her latest book from the library.

Usually, about forty minutes later, Colburn would wake up. He was used to seeing no one beside him. He never knew whether Val had got out of bed because she had woken up, or whether he was going to be in trouble again for snoring.

After lying for a few minutes, stretching on his back, Colburn got out of bed and dressed. He went into the bathroom for a wash and to clean his teeth. He also always knew that the sound of footsteps upstairs was the signal for Val to put the kettle on.

He came downstairs dressed in jeans, T-shirt and a cardigan with a zipper.

His normal greeting on a morning sounded more like a grunt but Val knew it meant, "good morning."

Colburn went into the kitchen and picked up his usual mug of tea. This was always the best taste of the day.

Re-entering the lounge, he threw a baseball cap onto his chair, the cap read, "Durham Sport."

"Thought this might be useful today, we might blend

in better with the tourists," he said as he sat down to drink his tea.

"I've had a few thoughts about today," Colburn mused over his tea, "just in case, I'll rig some of the old identification cards for Jim and myself."

All he had to do was change the photographs in one and stick them in another and what Colburn had was dozens of fakes.

Identification cards from BT, Northern Water, Electric and Gas companies were easy to copy, once you had an original. Colburn's previous occupations for the military and government meant he had an inexhaustible supply of fake documents.

"We should only need the Water Company ones today," said Colburn, "so I'll fix those for Jim and myself. You might have to stand guard."

Val replied, "I've already checked the tour times. If we get a move on we can catch the ten o' clock one. We'll need to go to the tourist information shop first."

Jim was already pulling in on their driveway.

Val heard his car.

"I'll make another pot of tea then, ok?" she said as she went into the kitchen.

Jim came in.

"Morning Val, Colburn up yet?"

Val smiled at Jim, "only just, he'll be pulled round after the next mug of tea."

Jim laughed, "nice to see nothing changes, morning Colburn."

He looked at the apparition in the chair, "now there's a face only a mother could love."

Val shouted out, "leave him alone Jim, he's already got today planned."

"OK," said Jim, "what's the plan then?"

Colburn looked up at Jim, "good morning to you, cheeky sod. We all join a normal tour of the castle and judge it from there. The best plans are always the simple ones."

Val came in with two mugs of tea.

"Now, talking about simple ones, are you two going to leave the castle in one piece. None of the Scottish Armies ever got near that place. Not one stone was out of place and I'd like to think it stayed that way."

Colburn replied, "We only need to look for some form of sign. I'm sure Hatfield or the Prior would have left a clue."

"That's great," said Jim, "because at the moment I'm getting a bit clueless about what's going on."

"Never fear," said Val, "I'm sure his mind is seven steps ahead already."

Colburn got up, "I'll fix up a couple of Water Board ID's for us Jim, just in case. Have you got the mallets and chisels?"

"Yes I have," replied Jim, "but why are we going to be the Water Board?"

Colburn replied, "I thought just in case we have to dig, we need a cover."

Jim looked puzzled, "why not, we'll just dig up the moat until we hit water."

"It's something like that," Colburn laughed at that thought.

They all finished their tea and put the mugs in the sink.

Colburn and Jim were carrying backpacks, Val just a handbag.

Jim looked at her, "are you not bringing any tools then?" he asked.

"No way," said Val, "I'll be needing proper money to pay for the tour."

Jim startled, replied, "you mean we have to pay to see something that's been there for 900 hundred years?"

Val replied, "Jim you can't always beg, borrow or steal everything in life."

Jim had a wicked grin on his face, "you've forgotten one Val."

Val looked at Jim, "no I haven't, you can't blow it up either. I'm coming along this time, just to see you don't damage the place. I love that place and you two are going to be careful, right?"

Colburn and Jim looked at each other and burst out laughing, "if it can withstand a Scottish invasion, it will stand after we're finished."

Val replied, "all I'm saying is, don't you dare damage the castle."

Colburn opened the back door. He walked with Jim down to his car.

"Are we taking mine today?" asked Jim.

"Sure are," replied Colburn, "you seen the price of diesel?"

They drove out of the village heading for Durham City.

Turning right at the roundabout, once again past the Golf Course, Jim turned left after the new traffic lights and towards Van Mildert College. On the right he pulled into a car park.

"Why are we parking here Jim?" asked Val.

"Two reasons," said Jim, "One, it's not far to walk. It's a nice day and if anyone is following it will make their job harder."

"And the second reason?" said Val.

Jim smiled and said, "it's free."

They all got out. Jim locked the car. Slinging their backpacks on their shoulders, they set off past the Japanese University down to the crossroads at the New Inn.

All past the Inn, cars were parked with inches to spare between them. Students seem to have that sort of money these days thought Colburn.

They didn't speak much strolling down past the Student Union, turning left at the Royal County Hotel, towards the Market Place.

Crossing Elvet Bridge, Val noted, "where can you see a more magnificent sight? There's no sight like that anywhere else in all these lands."

Val was right, the castle on the rock was a majestic and imposing sight.

Tucked away in the far corner of the Market Place was the Tourist Information shop.

Val went in, Jim and Colburn stayed outside, their eyes scanning the multitude of people wandering back and forth, sitting, eating and shopping. Looking for anything out of the ordinary.

The people following were good as well.

Val came out, "I've just spent twelve pounds on these tickets, I want that back from you when we get home."

"Did you get a receipt, then?" asked Colburn.

Val looked at him and smiled, "if you want my help, then you pay."

They set off up the hill. Walking up Owengate and along the side of the Palace Green.

The tour began at ten, from the Gatehouse.

There in front of the Gatehouse was a small, smartly dressed man, probably in his fifties with a massive badge on his jacket that said, "Guide."

"This must be it then," said Jim, as Val went up to him with the tour tickets.

"Good Morning," said the guide, "if you would step inside the gatehouse area, there are several others on this tour. I shall be starting in two minutes."

Sure enough, in two minutes the guide joined the group, which was actually about twenty people, seemingly all several nationalities but predominantly, Japanese.

The guide spoke, "my name is Keith and I'm your guide on this morning's tour of this famous castle. I will be speaking quite a lot and at great length. At the end of the tour you will be free to re-visit any of the places we have been to and I will be more than happy to answer any questions at the end. If you will just follow me, we shall begin the tour."

Colburn smiled and nudged Jim, "that's when we give him a tip and get rid of him."

Jim nodded.

The guide began his speech, "before any wandering around this castle, let me give you a very brief history of this castle high up on the peninsula.

The original stonework was, of course, built as fortifications as the Prince Bishop's combined important judicial, administrative and military functions.

The present Castle follows the typical Motte and

Bailey plan of a Norman Fortress, with the Keep on a Motte or mound and a walled inner Bailey or courtyard containing other buildings.

Unfortunately, except for the Norman Chapel and the Undercroft of the present Great Hall, not much survives of the first building."

Colburn nudged Jim again and whispered, "the Great Hall it is then."

Jim winked at him.

Keith continued, "a lot remains of the large hall built on the north side of the courtyard by Bishop Puiset 1153 to 1195, although it has been added to and altered over the centuries. Most of the original architecture, you will still see in the Norman and Tunstall Galleries. A century or more after Le Puiset, Bishop Bek began to build the present Great Hall on the west of the courtyard and this was later extended by Bishop Hatfield. He also re-built the octagonal Keep on the mound to the east.

During the many wars between England and Scotland, this fortress seems to have done its job well as there is no record of this castle ever been taken by force.

Now, it is virtually impossible to set the date when this castle's military function ended and it became more residential. The Halls of Le Puiset and Bek were obvious signs that Medieval Bishops intended to live comfortably, if not lavishly.

By the time of Bishops Fox and Tunstall, in the early fifteen hundreds, there was the desire to see this castle as a residence rather than a fortress. The length of the Great Hall was reduced and offices and kitchens were installed.

The military significance of the castle, vanished with the Union of the Crowns under James the First and Seventh. Much of the property went into disrepair and eventually under Bishop van Mildert it became a college and then part of the university.

The castle still houses more than eighty students and members of the teaching staff and provides the dining hall, common rooms, library and administrative offices of the college. The Norman   Undercroft of the Great Hall now serves as the Junior Common Room.

Apart from its normal occupants, the castle has seen many visitors over the centuries.

For example, Edward the Third, Queen Margaret Tudor of Scotland, James the First and Second, Charles the First and of course, our present Queen, Elizabeth the Second.

Now let me start with the Gatehouse.

This driveway to the castle from Palace Green follows the site of the former Barbican and across a dry moat, which was filled in by Bishop Cosin, to this Gatehouse. You can still see evidence of Norman work in the outer archway of the Gateway and the passage through has a vaulted roof. The great gates probably date back to the early sixteenth century.

Now follow me through, please.

From this inner arch of the Gatehouse, you will observe a range of buildings surrounding three sides of the courtyard, which we presume, corresponds to the inner bailey of the old Norman fortress.

There is a mixture of architectural styles clearly indicating additions by different builders over the centuries but the work of individual Bishops may be identified by the coats of arms placed at various points on the walls. Each of these shields carries the arms of the Bishopric on the left and the personal arms of the Bishop, on the right.

To the left of the gatehouse and connected by a curtain wall, is the Fellow's private garden. This three-storey building called the Garden Stairs now houses various administrative and domestic offices. Just like other parts of this building, it carries over its doorway, the arms of Bishop Cosin, whose heraldic device of a fret resembles a criss-cross trelliswork.

The principal building on the West Side, to your left in the courtyard, is the Great Hall. Built during the thirteenth and fourteenth centuries by Bishop's Bek and Hatfield.

Under Hatfield's design, the hall occupied all of that large block but the southern end, nearest the gatehouse, was converted to its present form as a staircase with four storeys of rooms, by Bishop Fox at the end of the fifteenth century.

The upper floors contain residential elements, the first floor is the college library and the basement is the wine cellar. No tasting today, I'm sorry.

However, the original framework of the tall windows of Hatfield's era, can still be seen from the courtyard on the south wall of the building."

Val muttered under her breath, "thank God nothing's changed."

Colburn leaned in to her, "makes it easy, doesn't it but does Keith ever stop for breath though?"

Keith continued, "the eastern wall of the Great Hall was changed by Bishop Cosin, adding the present buttresses and entrance porch. You can see his coat of arms over it.

Directly opposite, if you follow my arm, on the north side of the courtyard, next to Cosin's Staircase, is the late twelfth century building of Bishop le Puiset. Bishop Trevor restored the upper part of that building in the eighteenth century. The original round-headed Norman windows took on their present shape then. The Gallery built against it conceals the lower part. Bishop Tunstall built this in the sixteenth century and his Bell Tower and Chapel link it to the Great Hall.

Bishops Cosin and Crewe near the end of the seventeenth century extended Tunstall's Chapel, in the north east corner, over there, to the east.

Beneath the Chapel at courtyard level is a modern doorway opened in 1952. This now gives a better access to the stairs leading to the keep. The present keep, standing on that high mound on the East Side of the courtyard, was designed by Anthony Salvin in 1840 to provide residential accommodation for the then new university. This unfortunately, is not open to the public and while built following the original shape and ground plan, has little historic interest.

Now let's walk over to the main entrance."

As the tour group ambled over, Jim mumbled to Val, "how long is this tour?"

Val replied, "about two hours."

Jim twisted his face, "hope I can stay awake that long."

Colburn put his hand on Jim's shoulder and said, "we'll learn some history and observe everyone's movements. Just go with the flow."

Jim nodded and yawned.

Arriving at the entrance, Keith started again. "Cosin's Porch, which encloses much of the old Gothic doorway, leads to the Great Hall. From there, separated by a wooden screen and double doors, is the access to the Buttery and great Kitchen.

Around this part of the castle, you can observe the handiwork of Bishop Fox, who shortened the Great Hall. You can see his emblem there, showing a pelican piercing her breast to feed her young with her own blood. The screens, together with his motto, date from around 1499.

Bishop Fox probably adapted the twelfth century building to serve as his kitchen. The roof, brickwork, windows and three fireplaces, have remained unchanged and undamaged for nearly five centuries."

Jim looked at Colburn and Val mingling with the group and thought, "undamaged until today?"

"You can still see many implements and cooking vessels on the walls, the meals for about three hundred College members, are still made here every day."

Keith smiled at his group, "we do use modern equipment now for the meals."

Most grinned and half-laughed at his comment.

They walked on into the Great Hall.

Keith shouted to the rear of the group, "please keep up, there's ample time for taking pictures at the end.

Now this hall is the dining room for the University College. We think it's the largest and certainly the most impressive in the country. It measures one hundred feet long and forty-five feet high, however, the present appearance of this interior, can only be traced back to the 1830's and the foundation of the university.

Having said that, those two shorter windows on the West Side and the beams of the roof, survive from the original hall and those two pulpits on either side date back to the time of Bishop Fox.

As you can see, the walls are adorned with many military trophies. These include a set of Cromwellian helmets and breastplates. Various rifles and flags, especially of the Wallsend volunteers from the Napoleonic Wars.

Those portrayed around the walls include three of our Bishops, namely Barrington, Van Mildert and Maltby but let me point out Canon Wellesley, whose brother was perhaps the more famous Duke of Wellington.

You can return here after the tour to browse at your leisure but for now let's carry on.

The older houses in Durham City contain many fine staircases but the grandest of them all is Bishop Cosin's Black Staircase. As you can see, it stands at an angle between the Great Hall and Le Puiset's building, built around 1660. It is mostly made from oak, with the exception of the carved side panels. Originally it was free standing but because of structural defects, it was found necessary to insert those cylindrical support columns at each angle of the stairs.

If you would follow me on to the first landing, where now you can see the carved wooden screening with double doors, bearing Cosin's coat of arms. This leads to Tunstall's Gallery.

Please follow me through."

The tour shuffled their way into the gallery.

"This stands directly opposite the gatehouse and was probably approached under a canopy by a flight of steps from the courtyard. This archway is generally said to be, one of the best examples of late Norman stone carving in the whole of England. Most of the items on display here are military, from the castle armoury. However may I bring your attention to the exhibit of Maundy money, which the present Queen Elizabeth, distributed in the Cathedral in 1967.

Carrying further on, this gallery passes the head of the staircase in Tunstall's Tower, built around 1540 and was extended eastwards in the late seventeenth century by Bishops Cosin and Crewe. Both their sets of Arms may be seen several times in the roof.

Much of the present woodwork, the altar, panelling and some of seats, were installed since the castle passed into university hands. Bishop Tunstall brought some of the seats and stalls from Auckland Castle. On the south wall of the Chapel is a good early copy by the fifteenth century Flemish artist Van der Goes, showing Christ's body being taken from the cross.

Please follow me and we will visit the State Rooms."

Jim and Colburn were getting a little tired, perhaps bored but Val took everything in enthusiastically.

Jim tugged Colburn's arm and said, "I can't see anyone following us, if they were, they would have died from boredom."

Colburn replied, "hang in there, not much more now, then we can take photos and explore."

"Bloody wonderful," said Jim, "wake me up when its time to go."

The tourists followed Keith like sheep, most hanging onto his every word, he carried on with his monologue, "this Norman archway in this Gallery leads to the lower part of le Puiset's hall, which contain the State Rooms, which were created mostly during the eighteenth century. The first you will see is the Senate Room, until recently, was occupied by the Judges of the Assize on their visits to Durham. This room stands to the east of le Puiset's building, over the Norman Chapel and behind Tunstall's Chapel. Its name is derived from the fact that the University Senate used to meet in here during the nineteenth century. Please take time to observe the magnificent seventeenth century overmantel of the fireplace, which bears the arms of James the First and Sixth and of Bishop James, 1606 to 1617."

Jim joked to Val in a whispered voice; "he didn't live long then."

Val glared at him replying, "those were his years in office here, dipstick."

Jim was taken a little aback, "I was only joking, Val."

Val smiled at him, "just listen and learn," she said.

Keith never seemed to stop, continuing, "note the Flemish tapestries from the mid seventeenth century, depicting the story of Moses."

They wandered on next to the Bishop's Dining Room.

They could tell the guide was nearing his favourite area, as his voice suddenly got slightly louder, stressing more points of observation and enthusiasm swelling.

"This is now the Senior Common Room of the University College and in my opinion, the most impressive of the State Rooms. The ceiling and windows are decorated in what was then extremely fashionable,

Strawberry Hill Gothic, mainly for Bishop Butler 1750 to 1752. The most notable pictures in here are of George the Second and his consort, Caroline of Anspach and of course, the world famous view of Durham City from around 1850."

Colburn put his arm around Val, "it's a lot different from when I was at university. Nice to eat off that table. All set with silver service must be worth a bit. I was lucky to scrape up the money for fish and chips after a few pints."

Val looked at Colburn, "have you seen the price of fish and chips recently, they probably order them in, and eat them out of the paper."

Jim butted in, "always tasted better that way."

Keith continued, "the Bishop's Rooms are entered from this second landing of the Black Staircase. Their name is derived from the fact that the Bishop of Durham always reserved this suite for his own use, after it was taken over by the university.

You will observe that the sitting room is hung with tapestries like those in the Senate Room and also contains a fine set of eighteenth century dining chairs, while the bedroom has a magnificent four-post bed from about 1760.

Let me just refresh your memory so that you all don't get disoriented. Like Tunstal's Gallery, this Black Staircase is built against the south wall of le Puiset's hall and on the third landing you can see some of the original external appearance of the old Norman building. To the right of the archway leading from this staircase are two round-headed windows, which look down over the courtyard.

Inside this upper floor, once called the Constable's

Hall, is what is now known as the Norman Gallery where a great deal of Norman architecture can be seen.

You can also see evidence of major subsidence here, from the line of the south wall overlooking the courtyard, the wall bulges outwards and is also several degrees out of the perpendicular. This upper hall was originally one large room but some was eventually sectioned off for servants quarters and these in turn were converted into undergraduate rooms.

If you would all kindly follow me down the stone spiral staircase at the East End of this Gallery, it will lead us down to the ground floor of Tunstal's Gallery and to the present entrance of the Norman Chapel."

Keith even continued talking while descending the steps.

"This building is the oldest part of the Castle, dating from about 1080."

A few of the foreign tourists muttered amongst themselves. Probably to them, like Americans that come here, thought that ancient meant pre-second world war.

"The six columns here show some early Norman sculpture. Some of the carvings represent foliage, some of animals and some appear as quite grotesque masks.

The north west column shows a sequence of a hunter leading a horse and following hounds in pursuit of a deer.

This chapel was unused from Tunstal's time and it was altered in the early days of the university so that access could be gained from the courtyard through the east wall to the staircase of the re-built Keep.

Now with the opening of this present route under Tunstal's Chapel from the courtyard to the Keep stairs in

1952, the former function and appearance of this Chapel was restored.

So, this magnificent building, virtually being the oldest in Durham City, is now again used regularly for its original purpose after nine hundred years.

That, ladies and gentlemen, concludes your tour today. Please feel free to ask questions and you may re-visit any of the sites you have been through this morning and take your time to enjoy the splendour and magnificence of this castle.

Thank you all for being so attentive."

The group seemingly in unison applauded the guide. It had been thorough and informative.

Val fiddled with her handbag and walked up to the guide.

She shook his hand and said, "thank you Keith. I wish there were more people like you with the knowledge and enthusiasm, so that these buildings can be really appreciated."

"Well thank you," said Keith, "it's not only a pleasure to walk around here, it's a privilege."

With that she withdrew her hand, leaving a crisp twenty-pound note there.

"Please," said Keith, "there's really no need."

Val looked at him and said, "the more you spread the word of this place, the more people will come and when they see the grandeur and beauty of this castle and cathedral, it will give them something to remember all their lives."

With that she turned around and walked off. Jim and Colburn ambled after her.

Outside, they looked around at the great structure,

they were near the base of the Keep, across the courtyard from where they needed to be.

Colburn took Val's arm, "let's just wander back around past Cosin's staircase, in front of the Great Hall and get to the Garden staircase We should be able to enter the library area and get down to the cellar. Remember Jim, take photos everywhere, just like the Japanese tourists."

There were dozens of people milling around the courtyard area. Some on other tours, some working, others just enjoying the serenity of the courtyard.

The three reached the South West corner, still taking pictures but now just hidden from any full view of the Gatehouse.

Colburn looked around, "Jim, I need you to find the lower level of the wine cellar. You can just slip away, no one will notice. Val and I will stay here taking pictures, go now."

Jim slipped away.

Val said, "what if Jim bumps into anyone down there?"

Colburn replied, "he's just a tourist looking around, with a camera. Someone will point out where he can and can't go."

"Surely the cellar will be off limits," said Val.

"I sincerely hope so. You wouldn't want people wandering in there stealing the Bishop's wine," replied Colburn.

"What are we looking for when we get in," said Val.

Colburn smiled at her; "I haven't got a clue that's the fun of this. One thing seems to lead to another, it may never end."

Jim had easily found the College library.

Knowing there had to be a staircase down, he found a locked door on the South wall.

It was the only apparent entry or exit point.

Luckily it had modern locks.

Yale had always been a place of great learning, but to Jim Yale meant using his modified Swiss Army knife, with attachments that would open any lock.

There had only been a couple of people perusing books, probably students, Jim thought, judging by their age. It was easy to appear to be searching the racks for a book and slip the knife tools into the lock.

A faint click gave Jim the sound that the door was open.

With no one really observing who was in the library, Jim quickly opened the door, went through and pulled it nearly closed behind him.

Descending the stairs, his eyes bulged at what he saw.

He thought, if this was the wine cellar for the university, then I'm going back there.

There were racks to the roof filling the cellar.

Quickly working out the dimensions, the cellar seemed no more than twenty feet by twenty feet, racks all against every wall and lined up in regimental fashion down the centre. There could have been a few thousand bottles on display.

Nothing was apparent, as expected.

Jim examined all the walls of the cellar.

It appeared that the original walls had been plastered.

"Great," thought Jim.

With nothing really to report, Jim returned up the

stairs and slipped back into the library. Pulling the door nearly closed by slipping a piece of thin cardboard over the lock. Even if someone noticed it, they may think someone is in the cellar to get wine or take an inventory.

Jim exited by the entrance of the Great Hall and walked back to Colburn and Val.

"Any problems?" asked Colburn.

"Entrance is through the library. Doors open now at the rear. The cellar is packed with wine racks, you can get to the walls behind them but they're all plastered.

I'll need time to do some echo soundings for gaps or holes but we might have to chip off all the plaster," Jim reported.

"OK, so what your assessment is, we need time, correct?" asked Colburn.

Jim replied, "without any luck, two hours."

"So," said Colburn, "we need somehow to buy us a couple of hours of time. Were there many folks about?"

Jim said, "a few using the library. I think we have to expect people coming and going all the time."

"Right," Colburn thought, " I reckoned that we may need some excuse to have a look around. Looks like the College there, has a potential flood risk."

Jim laughed, "so the Water Board needs to check out the plumbing."

"Precisely," answered Colburn.

He looked at Val, "fancy doing some sketches of this castle?"

Val replied, "OK, what do you want me to do?"

Colburn looked around still checking the few dozen people walking about, "go and ask the security man in the gatehouse if it is permissible to sit a do a few sketches and don't bother noticing when Jim and I come to talk to him."

Colburn pulled the two identification badges out, "put this on Jim and follow my lead."

Val walked over to the gatehouse. There appeared to be just one security man checking tickets. Waiting until a lull in proceedings she approached the gatehouse.

"Excuse me," said Val, "could you tell me if it's alright to sit and do a few sketches of the castle?"

The security man looked at her. He seemed a pleasant chap. Elderly, the sort that gets a job in B and Q to stop getting bored at home.

"That's no problem, dear lady. We close at five though. Please enjoy the surroundings," said the security man.

"Thank you," said Val, "it's always a pleasure to be here."

At that moment an arm came over her waving a plastic badge.

"Are you in charge here?" said a voice, it was Colburn.

"Yes, I suppose so, but could you wait until I've finished with this lady?" said the security man.

He continued, "please take as long as you like, dear lady."

"Thank you," said Val.

"Now what can I help you gentlemen with?"

Colburn and Jim flashed their badges. The security was efficient, checking the entire wording and the photos. Just as well Colburn had done a professional job on them.

"Water Board," said the security man, "is there a problem?"

Colburn began his story, "it seems that several pipes around this area are leaking and we need to use sounding equipment to locate the leaks. Unfortunately, according to our charts, you have one main pipe that comes under the Palace Green and into that corner of the castle."

Colburn pointed out the South West area.

"We don't know exactly where and we don't think any of the castle area is at risk but we have to check. Can we gain access to that area but in particular, we will need to be at ground level and below."

The security man looked puzzled; "the only place below ground area over there is the wine cellar."

Colburn looked at him, "the wine cellar, OK, we'll check that first."

Looking horrified he said, "I can't let you in there, it's out of bounds to most people."

Colburn replied, "it may be out of bounds now but you could be swimming in there soon. I'll tell you what, how about you come with us so you can watch what we're doing."

"Sorry Sir, I can't leave my post," he replied.

Colburn rubbed his chin as if thinking, "how about a compromise then? We go and do our job, it will take up to two hours. Then you come and quickly check the cellar for damage and search us before we leave?"

The security man thought for a while, "that seems perfectly acceptable, the door is through the library but you will have to sign for the key."

He reached under the desk, opened one of the doors and lifted out a key.

"Please sign this and put down the time and reason for taking it."

Colburn signed the name on the badge. His writings were scrutinised by the security man, as he handed over the key.

"Right now, which way is it?" said Colburn.

The man pointed out the entrance.

"We'll be as quick as possible, thanks for your help. I'll make sure the Dean knows of your speedy co-operation."

Colburn and Jim walked off, noticing the queue of people waiting to get in. Both thought, just as well his mind is on work. They noticed Val sitting on a bench in the corner, she pointed to her hand. Colburn noticed it was her two-way radio, he switched his receiver on as they walked up the steps.

Going through the library, only about four people were busy studying.

Jim said, "I needn't have bothered opening that door now we have a key."

"You need to keep in practice," replied Colburn.

Nobody looked up as they opened the door and went through, Jim retrieved his bit of cardboard. Walking down the cellar steps, Colburn got his first look at the wine racks.

"I see what you meant about this place. There are a few folks I know that would be happy to get locked in here. Now where to start?"

Colburn and Jim looked at the situation, walking up and down the racks.

Colburn began, "Now put yourself in the Prior's position, wanting to hide something.

It's unlikely to be on the outside walls, remember this was once, one long hall.

He may have been working on the foundations of that hall, so logically, put something deep underground. So we are left with two walls of plaster and I think it would be unlikely that he put anything above head height, so we need to check those two half walls for soundings."

Jim was looking for his micrometer in his backpack when Colburn said, "it's going to take too long, get the hammer and chisels, the plaster should not be bonded to the walls."

With sharp enough chisels, the top layer of plaster just broke away. Chipping away, the sound covered by the depth they were at, most of the plaster broke free dropping behind the racks lined closest to the walls.

"How much of this are we doing?" asked Jim.

"Chip it all off, then we'll have a closer look," replied Colburn.

In less than half an hour, all the plaster from the lower part of the two walls was off.

"Now use the strong torch beam and the brushes and look for anything at all," said Colburn.

Brushing dust away with one hand and examining the wall with the bright light, they covered the bare stonework very quickly.

Jim had only dusted away half the North-facing wall when his fingers felt grooves in the stone work.

"I think we've hit pay dirt," said Jim.

Colburn pushed himself up from his squatting position behind the racks of the East wall and came over to where Jim was furious brushing the stone.

"Pour some water over it," said Colburn

Jim took out a bottle of mineral water from his bag and splashed it over the wall, most of it running down and over the floor.

"Told you there was a leak in here," joked Colburn.

They both peered at the grooves; Colburn ran his fingers over them.

He smiled, "I think you're right, it's shaped like a shield, on the left there seems to be four lions around a cross and the right looks like lattice work. Hang on a minute."

Colburn pressed the speak button on his radio and whispered, "Val, you there?"

The reply came, "everything OK down there?"

"Val what's the significance of four lions in a cross and some latticework on the opposite side of a shield?" asked Colburn.

Val whispered into her radio, "if both of you had paid more attention on the tour, you would know, those are the insignia of Bishop Cosin."

"Thanks Val, over and out."

Colburn turned to Jim, "I reckon the Prior must have told the Bishops about this and eventually one of them decided to try and lose whatever it is for good."

Jim said, "then why leave clues?"

"Maybe they thought in hundreds of years to come whatever it is or was, would be safe in our hands, who knows?

What we need is to dig away the cement stuff around this block and see what's behind it."

Jim started chipping around the cemented area. The soft cement soon fell away. He had dug in about four inches all around the stone when he drew back the chisel and hammered it into the bottom corner and levered. Eventually after trying all corners, the stone came loose and with a little leverage from two chisels simultaneously, the stone began to inch forward.

Colburn grabbed the stone as Jim levered it out and placed it on the floor. Taking his flashlight he looked into the hole.

"What's there?" asked Jim excitedly.

"Seems like nothing," replied Colburn.

"No way," said Jim, "stick your arm in."

As Colburn's hand reached what appeared to be a dead end, he felt a short, tubular object.

"There's something here," said Colburn, grabbing the object and drawing out his hand.

As it appeared into the light, it appeared to be a fairly cylindrical piece of horn bone.

Using the flashlight, he examined it closely.

Both ends seemed to be blocked with wax.

Taking a knife from his pack, he gently scraped away the wax from one end.

"Give me some tweezers Jim," requested Colburn.

"What makes you think I carry tweezers with me, do you want to pluck your eyebrows? Will forceps do?" said Jim.

He handed Colburn his forceps. Colburn inserted them into the bone horn and gently pulled out a roll of parchment type paper.

Carefully putting down the bone, he unfurled the paper.

Colburn held it open while Jim shone his light on it.

There was writing, still legible.

"What does it say?" asked Jim.

"I can't make it all out in this light, I can read some of it," said Colburn.

"So, what can you make out?" said Jim.

Colburn squinted in the light.

"I can make out the words, Our Hand in the Meadow. We need to get this back home."

"So, have you any idea what this is about?" asked Jim.

"Not a clue," replied Colburn, "but that's what it must be, a clue. Val might be able to work on it. Let's get back."

Jim and Colburn surveyed the plaster mess. Both stood up.

"Put that block back in and then we're out of here," said Colburn.

Jim forced the stone back in with the help of his boot.

Colburn put the script in his backpack, packing up their tools, they both left.

Back up the stairs, locking the door, through the library and outside.

They strolled past Val, still sitting enjoying the late sunshine of the day.

As they went past, she got up to follow.

Colburn walked up to the gatehouse, still with a queue of people.

He shouted to the security man, "here's the key back, you'll need to check us out."

Probably flustered after a day's crowds, he replied, "you're OK, no need for that, is everything fine with the water supply?"

"Everything is fixed now, don't expect any more problems, thanks for your help," said Colburn.

Val walked past Jim and Colburn and out onto the Palace Green road.

They caught up with her walking down Owengate.

"Did everything go according to plan?" asked Val.

"No problem," answered Jim.

"Well there may be one problem," said Colburn, "we appear to have come across another clue but we need to get home and sort it out. I'm tired."

They strolled back retracing their morning route to the car park.

Getting in to Jim's car Val said, "what sort of clue is it?"

Colburn replied, "seems to be some more text, I couldn't make it all out down there."

Jim drove them back. Going down the dual carriageway, Jim said, "I'm sure I've seen that car before, two cars back, it's definitely following us."

The car turned off into the Motel after the end of the two-lane road.

"Maybe I'm wrong, it's turned off," said Jim.

"You're not usually wrong Jim. Let's assume we're still being watched I'm sure we'll find out sooner or later."

Jim eventually pulled into their parking space at the rear of the house.

As Colburn was getting out he said, "now let's see if we can work this one out."

They all went into the house.

Val, as usual, put the kettle on. There was nothing like a good cup of tea after a day out. Using the drawstring tea bags, three cups were made within a couple of minutes.

Colburn carefully took the paper from his backpack and began to unroll it.

Using the usual salt and pepper mills as paperweights on each of the curled ends of the paper, he began to examine the print.

"This wording is mostly too faint to see. I can make out those words we saw but there's something before and after that," said Colburn.

He wandered around for a while trying to think of what to do. He could always come up with a plan but there was little in the house that could help.

His eyes seemed to sparkle, "I know what we can try, some electrophoresis."

Jim looked at him, "we haven't got the facilities of a pathology laboratory. Are we going to break into Dryburn Hospital?"

Val shouted over, "it's not Dryburn any more, it's the University Hospital at Durham."

Jim replied with a bit of disgust, "yes, I forgot, when the new buildings went up around the old ones, they changed the name. I suppose the government could say they built a new hospital, what a farce."

Colburn said, "there's always things in the house you can use."

He went to a drawer and pulled out a nine-volt battery. Then to one of Val's kitchen drawers and took out a roll of baking foil.

Walking away upstairs, he returned with a large roll of copper wire that he used for the bodies of some of his trout flies and a bottle of "Dry Light"

Putting it all down on the kitchen bench, he ripped off a section of the tin foil.

Gently laying it down on the bench, he placed the paper over the top, weighted down.

Then using cling film to cover the paper and keep it flat, he used sticky tape to fasten a length of copper wire to either side of the bottom of the tin foil.

The two loose ends of the copper wire were inserted into the positive and negative poles of the battery.

"That's it," he said, "in theory that should be sending a nine volt current through there. We'll just leave it for a while and let the electrons flow and finish our tea. Then if we take off the cling film, keep the paper flat and use the Dry Light. Any indentations due to protein residue should become apparent."

Jim looked puzzled, "that Dry Light you use on your sea trout flies, how is it going to work on here?"

Colburn explained, "this stuff is purely a fine, luminescent powder and yes it's mixed with varnish or resin to make the flies glow but you can use it just like you've seen on CSI for fingerprints. Seeing as we haven't got any dye for staining like pathology, this should stick in any grooves in the paper, if we dust it like looking for fingerprints. I've got a few colours but I think the red one will do the trick."

They all finished their tea.

Colburn carefully removed the cling film and kept the roll weighted down and flat.

He sprinkled the luminescent powder over the paper and using a pastry brush, starting to gently brush the powder over the surface of the paper.

Words began to appear.

After he had finished brushing, the battery was disconnected and he lifted the paper up. Taking it over to the sink, he let the excess powder fall off and the gently blew on the rest.

He laid the paper down and weighted each end.

Jim looked amazed, "how the hell do you come up with ideas like that?"

Colburn replied, "age and experience. There's no substitute for it. The young kids nowadays think they know it all. I'll fetch down my fly tying magnifying light."

He went back upstairs and returned carrying his fly tying lamp.

Inserting the plug into a socket, he switched it on and pulled the magnifying light over the paper.

"Now let's see what you have to say."

They all bent over the large magnifying lens.

The words could be seen as clear as day.

Colburn said, "you read them out Val, I'll write them down."

Val positioned herself over the centre of the lens.

"My God," she said, "this is amazing."

Jim retorted, "just give us the words Val, please."

Val started to read the words.

"*The Three shall keep safe the power.*
Destroyeth the Tower.
Hidden in the shadow
Given by our hand in the Meadow.
Keep safe by the Dragon"

"That's all," said Val, "nothing else has come up."

They all sat back and thought.

Colburn said, "OK, now we have to work this one out."

Jim piped up, "it is another clue, isn't it?"

Val answered, "it's definitely another clue."

They all walked into the sitting room and sat down.

Jim was the first to speak, "it seems to me that each of those lines must mean something."

They all agreed.

Colburn said, "OK, let's take it one at a time. First line, The three shall keep safe the power."

Val interrupted, "that has to be a reference to the triumvirate. It was always supposed that there were three persons with the knowledge of the Cathedral's secrets. That's if there were any secrets. When one died, another was recruited. We thought that this had ended with Hatfield but obviously it continued. So I believe that line to mean that three people at the time this note was written, knew what was going on. It must have carried on until at least Cosin's time, when he put his mark on the stone. It might still be happening today, who knows?"

Colburn said, "that would appear logical to presume, so we agree that three people knew what was going on."

Jim laughed, "I wish to hell I was one of them."

"So do I," replied Colburn, "life would be a lot simpler."

Val continued, "the next line, Destroyeth the Tower. This must mean when the Bell Tower of the Cathedral was destroyed. I think the good prior got his hands on whatever we seem to be looking for and somehow, something went wrong and the Tower was destroyed. The official explanation is that it was destroyed by lightening."

Colburn interrupted, "there were obviously spin doctors in those days putting a different point of view. Nothing has changed much."

Val said, "I'm not sure what the line, Hidden in the Shadow means. It could refer to a dark place, unlit."

Jim said, "or if there's another bit of paper to find, surely it means it's hiding place, out of sight."

"Or," Colburn noted, "it could simply mean it's not on that page."

Jim replied, "like another book."

"Possibly," thought Colburn, "or on the side that's not in the light, on the reverse side. We'll just have to see when we find it."

"You mean if we find it," said Jim.

"Have faith Jim," said Colburn.

Val continued, "I'm sure I've seen the words, Given by our Hand in the Meadow, before. It rings a bell but I just can't place it."

"Don't worry, it will come to you," said Colburn.

Suddenly Val spoke, a look of shock on her face, "Oh my God, I've just remembered where I've seen those words. I believe the full quotation is;

Given by our hand in the Meadow, which is called Runnymede, between Windsor and Staines on the fifteenth day of June in the seventeenth year of our reign."

"Jesus," said Colburn, "the year 1215, he's talking about the Magna Carta. So are we to assume that the next message or clue, is written on the Magna Carta."

Val replied with authority, "I believe that's correct but once again, there's a problem."

Jim groaned, "well, when is there not a problem."

Val continued, "As far as I know and we can check of course, there were four original copies of the Magna Carta in England. The four documents are held in the British Library, who has two and one each in Lincoln and Salisbury Cathedrals."

Jim looked puzzled, "I thought King John signed only one."

Colburn answered, "Probably that's right. Whether he signed it or not, his Seal was stuck on them. I believe a lot of copies of that document were made each time it was issued, so that all the people present could have one. I believe one used to be at Durham. Or they may just have a copy.

Jim said, "two in the British Library, if we had known, we could have had them as well."

Val said, "I'm not sure that would have mattered. Those documents and as a matter of interest, also known as the Articles of the Barons, came from different sources.

One was found in Dover Castle about 1630. I remember that one was damaged by fire about one hundred years later. The other came from our old friend Sir Robert Cotton and is in the Cotton collection.

According to historical accounts the copies were given to Bishops, Sheriffs and others but the exact number is really not known. They were all sent out from the Royal Chancery."

Jim was puzzled again, "so if there's so many copies, which one do we want?"

Val replied, "the trouble is, the original copies have been shown all over the World.

It's quite possible that they were mixed up years ago. People claim to have original copies in private collections."

Colburn was stewing over all the facts, "We can only go and see those that are available. The one in Lincoln should be OK. I remember the Bishop of Lincoln was one of the original signatories. Salisbury should be OK, because Elias of Dereham, who was present at Runnymede, distributed some of the copies but later became a Canon of Salisbury and supervised the construction of Salisbury Cathedral. So I reckon he kept an original. It's possible that one of them down in London is an original but I think we'll leave those until last."

Jim said, "they won't be expecting another break in so soon."

Colburn replied, "I don't think it will come to that, just yet Jim."

Val interrupted, "I can see another problem."

Colburn and Jim looked over, Jim groaned.

"There's also one in Washington, in the National Archives. This one is supposed to be a 1297 copy or original being conferred by Edward the First and entered on the English statute rolls. It was purchased by the Ross Perot Foundation and is on indefinite loan to the Archives. Well they bought London Bridge didn't they? The thing is, this one came originally from the Earls of Cardigan, from Wales, the land of the Dragon. So it may have been kept safe there."

Jim asked, "why would the Americans want a copy of that?"

Val continued, "the Magna Carta Jim, helped shape the United States Constitution. It is said that it was a springboard for Jefferson's Declaration of Independence. In particular it means the concept of Law is supreme, above Kings, or Queens and James Madison drafted this into the constitution. So the Magna Carta is important to the American people.

Also there is a connection between America and Lincoln in England.

Certainly from around 1607, Lincoln adventurers

sailed to the New World and took with them the Magna Carta principles.

You remember Captain John Smith, he was a Lincoln Man, set up the colony at Jamestown, on the James River."

Colburn said, "what about that American one?"

Val replied, "we need to look at that one first, coming from the land of the Dragon."

Jim looked around, "great, I could do with a bit of a holiday. Then what, we break into the National Archives and steal their copy?"

Colburn replied, "we only need a look at it, to check it out. Or check the back of it."

Val stood up, "anyone for another cup? Then how about we book a flight and hotel. I've always fancied going to Washington."

Colburn muttered, "right, we'll go but bear in mind there is some tentative American connection with this puzzle. They aren't so easy to fool. Their security is better now and they'll be watching us."

Jim replied with delight, "they can look but they won't see. Nothing is as obvious as what is right under your nose. We will all go for a weekend break, come back next Monday or Tuesday".

Val laughed, "right, that's if you're both not in San Quentin."

Colburn stretched out, "Washington it is then."

CHAPTER TWENTY-SIX

It's remarkable how easy it is to switch on your broadband, surf a site like Expedia, check flights to Washington DC and book a hotel.

Everything was done for the Thursday flight from Manchester. A Holiday Inn at Wimslow for the Wednesday night and the Holiday Inn Central in Washington, for four nights with a Monday evening flight back.

As Colburn always used to say, "what could go wrong?"

Jim had gone back home for a while to rest and pack clothes and equipment.

This time the equipment would have to be quite selective.

It would be frowned upon if you tried to take saws, drills and hammers on a plane. In fact security would drag you away and that's before you got to duty free.

He had to make sure all his mini-instruments were fully charged and working.

Colburn had asked, in particular, for the pen flashlight to be able to convert white light into the spectrum colours and have filters to use single or multiple wavelengths.

If there were any more writing to observe, it would

have to be done using these wavelengths from infrared to ultraviolet.

Jim had fashioned a pen torch to operate from an internal battery. The light emitted went through a small crystal of ruby and then came out more like a laser beam.

With a glass cutting diamond and multipurpose screwdriver, everything was set.

The cutter, screwdriver and suction pad would have to go in the hold. Jim knew those would never go through the carry on baggage x-ray equipment.

Packing the minimum of clothes into a holdall type bag, he was ready.

Just up to the village, pick up Colburn and Val and away to Manchester.

His tourist clothes only consisted of jeans, one pair of good slacks for evening dinners, four Wrangler shirts, four T-shirts of differing designs, four pairs of socks and a variety of St. Michael underwear.

America was the only place he used a cut-throat razor. He couldn't be bothered to take adapters.

Final check toothpaste, shaving cream, antibiotics, cortisone cream and band aids. You never know what may happen and hospital treatment for foreigners was extremely expensive. Insurance companies would always argue whether to pay anyway.

He remembered to put in a sewing kit, good for stitches.

Now all was set.

He put on his plain dark blue jacket and checked for his passport, money and credit cards. Picked up his bag and car keys, locked the door, checked it and went to his car.

He drove from Low Spennymoor, up the by-pass to the Thinford roundabout, turning left heading towards Durham. After about one mile, he turned onto the Hett road at the Coach and Horses pub. Another mile of winding road and he was in the village.

Driving through and turning right into the line of houses that was The Green.

He pulled round the rear road and onto the parking place.

He could see Val in the kitchen, "tea must be on," he thought.

"Hi all," he shouted as he came in.

Val replied, "we're nearly ready, tea first though. You can't get a good cup of tea where we're going."

Colburn said, "we need to be at the hotel by half three, four at the latest. Most guests won't arrive until five or after, so we can book first on the courtesy hotel shuttle bus for the morning. It only takes six at a time and the luggage."

Colburn was dressed in a pale blue shirt with matching dark blue slacks. Jim seemed quite amazed because he knew Colburn's sense of dress was abysmal. Val must have packed for him, he thought. He still wore trainers.

Val, quite the opposite wore a white crinkle blouse that just tantalisingly gave a hint of a bra and heel length flower patterned skirt. She looked extremely smart.

Two small suitcases were on the floor of the extension.

"These for the car then?" asked Jim.

Val replied, "yes thanks, just put them on the back seat."

"OK," said Jim, picking up the cases and carrying them out to the car.

When he returned, the tea was ready.

Val and Jim went into the lounge with Colburn.

Val spoke, "I've got the e-tickets for both flights. Make sure you two have your credit cards, passports and money."

Jim spoke up, "we're doing some shopping then?"

Val replied, "naturally, with the dollar at nearly two to the pound, everything is cheaper over there and it will help keep our cover."

Colburn smiled, "who needs the Intelligence Corps, when you have a wife like mine?"

"Why, thank you," replied Val, "not often I get compliments."

Colburn looked at her and smiled, "what would you think if I was giving compliments all the time?"

"Quite simple," replied Val, "I'd know you had been up to something."

Jim said, "the thing is Val, compliments should only be given when they mean something and most times you're a mean something."

Val looked at Jim, she knew he was joking, or he'd better be.

"Jim," she said, "you know we love you lots but if you had one less brain cell, it would be lonely."

Jim laughed, he knew he wasn't the brightest button on the shirt but he knew his job. No one could match him with electronics and explosives.

They finished their tea, washed the cups and put them in the dishwasher.

Time for a last visit to the toilet, flush, switch off the

mains water, check all windows are locked, lock the back door and go.

As Jim was driving off Val said, reminding them, "check now, tickets, passport, money, we're not going back."

Colburn and Jim re-checked everything.

Now for a two and a half-hours drive to the hotel.

Jim and Colburn had done this drive many times before. It had been their usual way to join the M6 and then M5 south.

Their only variation was in summertime with a detour through Barnard Castle. Picking up the cross Pennine route at Bowes, through Kirby Stephen and onto the M6, was more scenic but half and hour longer. You could often see the low-flying harrier jets along that road, practising bombing techniques.

Jim had the road mapped out in his mind.

Down the A167, past Aycliffe, pick up the A1M and head South.

Once on the A1, there would be no deviations until past Wetherby, when he would pick up the M1 before turning onto the M62.

It was a boring drive, Colburn seated next to him was asleep before they hit the motorway. Val sat in the back next to the cases, reading a book.

There was nothing fantastic about the scenery. Odd houses, farms and miles of fields filled with rape oil seed. The landscape looked as if it had a yellow carpet. Jim thought of all the people he knew with allergies. So much for human concern, only maximise the profit. It was a sign of the times. No longer fields of Barley or Wheat, hardly a pea, bean, turnip or potato in sight. No wonder we had to import so much putting up prices, as long as biotechnology wasn't affected.

It's said that seed helps to make cheaper fuel, cheaper for whom?

After bypassing Leeds, Halifax and Huddersfield, the M62 traverses the infamous Saddleworth Moor. Tragic reminders of the Moors Murders.

Passing the highest point of the motorway and the highest in England at 1221 feet, they descended for miles past Rochdale, the M60 road and round to the M56.

Another ten minutes driving found the junction that would take them out toward Cheshire.

Passing the Airport junction, Jim turned at the next one and stopped at traffic lights.

"You can all wake up now, we're here," said Jim.

On the green light, Jim turned right and drove down under the new runway and into the Holiday Inn car park.

Jim got out and stretched.

Colburn went into reception, returning saying, "I said we'd be back in four days and so they said we could leave the car here. No need to put it in the hotel's long term car park."

They each grabbed their luggage and went inside the hotel.

The receptionist was a young girl of about twenty. Short, with dark hair and brown eyes, but with a pale complexion. A badge on her lapel said June.

Colburn leaned on the reception desk, "reservation for two rooms plus four days parking, name of Lord."

June quickly typed out the name on her computer.

"Here it is Mr. Lord, one double and one single for one night and four days parking."

A confirmation came out of the printer.

"If you would just sign at the bottom and put your nationality and car registration in those blocks," she said pointing to the blocks with her pen.

Colburn scribbled his name, put the registration in and then wrote English under nationality. This really got to him at times. He never felt British or United Kingdom, he was a North Eastern man, born and bred.

June handed over two electronic keys cards.

"Thank you," said Colburn, "may I book three seats on the six thirty minibus in the morning?"

"No problem, that's it booked for your party," replied June, "how will you be paying?"

Colburn took out a credit card and put it in the machine.

June said, "can you enter your pin number please?"

Colburn tapped out the four-digit code, looked at the small screen that said pin OK and removed it. He handed Jim one of the cards.

"Thanks for your help," said Jim as he took the single room card from Colburn.

The room numbers were consecutive; Most hotels gave single travellers a double room anyway. The numbers on the hotel walls indicated the rooms were just around the corner from reception, up five steps. More like a mezzanine level.

"What time do you want to meet at the bar?" said Val.

Colburn thought for a while, smiled and said, "strip, shower and dress, one hour Jim."

Jim replied, "fine by me," looking at his watch, "see you at five."

A few minutes after five Colburn and Val entered the bar area of the hotel. It was just around the corner from reception. Jim, as expected, was already there.

"Pint of John Smiths?" asked Jim. Colburn nodded. "Gin and Tonic, Val?

"Thanks Jim," she replied.

Colburn picked up a bar menu, perusing the limited options.

"Looks like it's curry all round," he said replacing the menu card in a rack on the bar.

They picked up their drinks and sat down around a nearby table.

Jim asked, "room OK?"

Colburn replied, "same thing as usual. Nothing spectacular."

These hotels were nearly always used in transit. There were people coming and going at all times of the day and night. So all that was required was a bit of comfort and clean sheets.

"All agreed for curry then?" asked Colburn.

Val and Jim agreed.

He stood up and went to the bar, ordering three curry dinners from the barman paying in cash.

Returning to the table he started to go over an action plan.

"When we arrive, I think we have to assume our data will have been forwarded and there may be a reception committee. We just have to play the tourist. We're there for a long weekend break to see the sites of their wonderful capitol. I can't see any reason for them to stop us, but I think they'll try."

Jim took a mouthful of beer, "they will assume we're up to something, so I think we'll get followed."

"Well, we'll just let them follow us around the tourist areas. I think we'd better not lose them straightaway. If we do they will send for reinforcements and that may make the job a bit harder," said Colburn.

"Look," said Val, "can we not just have a quiet night. A few drinks and a meal, without worrying what may or may not happen."

"Fine with me," said Colburn, "another round everyone?"

After finishing three rounds and a very palatable curry with tasty naan bread, the time was creeping to eight o' clock.

Val said, "I know it's early but we'll be up around four, to get ready and down here for the minibus. We will need plenty of rest for the next few days."

"I agree," said Jim, "it will be ten before I'm asleep, that's only six hours."

Colburn looked at Val with a slight smile, "might take us a couple of hours to get to sleep Val," he said with his cheeky grin.

Val looked across the table, "well we are on holiday aren't we?"

Colburn looked a bit surprised, "is that OK then Val?"

Val smiled back, "only in your dreams."

They all got up and walked back to their rooms. There were no sounds from them until radio alarms signalled four in the morning.

Colburn thought as he was getting up and dressing, "I thought people said as you got older, you need less sleep. What a load of crap!"

Val put the electric kettle on, "however did you manage doing government business, looking like you do on a morning? It takes you an hour to pull round,"

"Easy answer Val. Most times I had Jim with me, playing Batman," said Colburn.

After a cup of insipid tea, Colburn felt a little better, washed and shaved.

Bags were re-packed, labels checked and locked.

Down to reception for six.

Jim was already there, sitting in an armchair reading the courtesy newspapers that were strewn around.

"Morning all," he said looking at Colburn, "God you still look like a bag of crap on a morning."

"I love you too Jim," grunted Colburn in reply.

The minibus was on time.

Bags were loaded in the rear and the three took their seats. There were no other travellers on this run.

The driver asked, "which terminal?"

Jim replied, "British Airways."

It only took about ten minutes at that time on a morning to cut through some of the back roads to the airport. Pulling up in front of departures, the driver offloaded the bags. Val pressed a five-pound note into his hand.

"Thank you Ma'am," he said.

"Just make sure when we arrive back, you're on time ok?" said Val.

"No problem," replied the driver.

For that kind of tip, he would even check arrival times.

They all picked their bags up and wheeled them into the departure lounge.

Now all they had to do was to manage the queues and questions of the airways and their staff, without erupting into a rage.

Not easy in international airports.

The file of people twisted around steel posts and plastic tape, like a snake coiling around its victim. Each movement of two feet at a time was greeted with relief.

Eventually a hand beckoned from behind one of the desks and the three crawled over dragging the luggage.

"E-Ticket," said Val, "name of Lord."

The three slapped their passports on the desk.

Jim was thinking, "those counters are made to accommodate people who are over six foot six. There's a poor woman over there, must only be five foot, can hardly reach the counter."

You always get the same questions, over and over.

"Have you packed your own bags?"

"Could anyone have tampered with them?"

"Are you carrying any of the objects on this card?"

Jim thought as he heard the questions, "does anyone ever say yes to the last questions?" He doubted it.

The woman behind the counter was busy tapping her computer.

"Put your bags on the scales please," she said.

All three were loaded in turn, getting a sticky paper strip for the destination airport put around the handles.

Then they disappeared behind her and into the oblivion, that was the realm of the baggage handlers.

She handed back the three passports, each containing a boarding card, visa waiver form and customs declaration.

"Just look at the electronic boards for the gate call," she said, "have a good flight."

Colburn replied, "thank you," but wondering all the time if they would ever see the luggage again.

They all wandered off to the gap in the counters that said "Departure Gates."

Once through, everyone was again snaking round aisles of tape, before the dreaded x-ray machines.

Eventually they were beckoned forward, removing shoes, belts, watches, money and anything metallic. Putting their jackets in a plastic bin for the machine to explore.

Val walked first through the metal detector, no buzz.

Colburn next, no buzz.

Jim went last, buzzers sounded.

He was waved over to a security man.

"Arms out please," he said.

"I know," said Jim, "assume the position."

Some people find it embarrassing when this happens. Jim didn't.

A hand held detector was waived all around his body and a thorough search took place.

The detector bleeped in front of Jim's chest.

"Sorry, I forgot this," he said opening his shirt to reveal a large St. Christopher medallion. "Patron saint of travellers you know."

The security man waived him on.

Val and Colburn had already re-dressed and put away their passports and boarding cards. Jim soon followed.

The end of the conveyor belt looked like a clothing shop. People re-dressing, putting on shoes, belts, checking their money and heading for duty free.

Colburn was not in the mood for shopping. Going straight to the nearest café with Jim, he ordered two "all day breakfasts."

Val bought some toast and croissants with jam.

Two large pots of English Breakfast Tea came with it.

Val looked at Colburn's plate, "I still don't know how you two eat something like that

this early on a morning."

Jim replied, "remember Val, breakfast is a regimental parade, miss it and you're on a charge."

"So that's the excuse for a thousand calories in every mouthful?" she enquired.

Jim said, "charges you up with energy food."

Colburn smiled as he stuffed down the sausage. "You know it's a fallacy to think you burn fats for energy. As soon as you wake up, you use your carbohydrate system for making molecules of Adenosine Tri-Phosphate. If you use fats, you're working that slow, you're not moving. The only time fats are more important is when you're in a coma or you are hibernating for the winter."

Val replied, "so if that's your story and you're sticking to it, why do you eat it?"

Colburn munched his way through the bacon, "simple answer, I like it."

After gorging themselves, Jim and Colburn sat and drank their tea while Val went to look at the shops.

She returned after only ten minutes with a couple of newspapers and a new Clive Cussler book.

"Didn't you want any perfume love?" asked Colburn.

"Yes," replied Val, "but when I checked the price I realised that I can buy it cheaper in the supermarkets. So much for duty paid and duty free."

"Never mind, you might get some in Washington," said Jim.

Colburn and Jim took the newspapers and began to read.

Time eventually passes, even if you only observe all the other travellers.

Businessmen, wearing their suits and ties, knowing full well how uncomfortable it will be travelling like that.

Same with some of the women, dressed as if they've just stepped out of Vogue magazine but wouldn't be seen anywhere in clothes that are comfortable.

Then there are always the kids running about. Screaming and shouting at their lovely parents. Seeing them covered in tattoos, wearing shirts that fitted them ten years ago that only get brought out for holidays. Spare flesh hanging over the sports trousers, with a command of language that was taught in the Chubby Brown school of English.

Colburn thought, "this is England though and it's great."

He wondered to himself if ever anyone noticed that whatever flight you're on, the plane is parked at the furthest gate away from the lounge. Always the longest walk.

The light on their flight was showing, "go to gate."

They picked up their papers and book and began the long stroll that takes you to that secret place called the Gate Lounge. Here you can sit and observe all the other passengers on your flight. Hoping that the largest ones are not sitting next to you.

If all goes to plan, a pleasant lady will announce over the loudspeaker system that the plane is ready for boarding. Calling first and business class travellers to come up now.

After them, it's usually those with walking difficulties and those with children.

Possibly if they are sensible, the staff will call up those with boarding cards for the rear rows first. Then the middle rows then the front.

Colburn usually asked for seats near the rear of the plane. Simply because you can observe the bulk of the plane and its passengers. You could get on sooner and get a space for carry-on bags in the overhead locker. The air quality at the rear of the plane was poor but it was quieter and you could get some sleep.

Once the staff had checked their boarding cards, they walked down the galley and onto the plane.

Two of the staff stood there greeting everyone, they were probably miming "good morning" as a record played.

Walking through the business class seats, Colburn mused to himself, "you don't get that much for your money in here. The bed is only useful on the return journey overnight. Anyway, their companies would be paying for that, not them."

It's always a fight to get up the aisle of a plane.

People trying to wedge cases into the overhead lockers that at first sight looked impossible.

Holding up the incoming passengers as they attempt to force the case in.

Eventually it goes, but why not check it in the hold? Obviously didn't want to wait at the carousel.

After several stops, waits and nearly blowing steam, they arrived at their row.

Two seats with a window, Jim next across the aisle.

Colburn and Jim put their small bags into the lockers. They all sat down and adjusted their seat belts.

"Thank God," thought Colburn, "even being tall, you have just enough room in here. This is the only time I wish I was five foot high."

Jim thought of the women in the check in queue, "she should be comfortable on this flight."

At least for most of the flights now, they put the safety instructions on the video.

You wonder if anyone really takes notice.

Val settled down to her book.

Colburn and Jim, who were both more used to the comforts of a Hercules transporter plane, put in earplugs, donned face masks and tried to sleep.

Only the nudging of the flight attendants woke them up, to serve up the tinfoil and plastic coated dinner.

At least they thought, it was something to eat, if not the best of nutrition.

The tea was just palatable but neither drank alcohol, certainly not on transatlantic flights.

Without waiting for the inevitable, "more tea Sir," they resumed their sleeping posture while Val was still engrossed with Clive Cussler.

Sometimes it can appear a lifetime but on awakening, Colburn checked the flight details on his video.

He leant across the aisle and nudged Jim, "only about forty minutes to landing, need to get up and walk about. We don't need DVT on this trip."

Jim got up and walked to the rear of the plane. Colburn followed.

They both stood around an emergency exit, stretching and swinging their legs to encourage better circulation.

After about ten minutes of easy aerobic exercise, Val joined them to stretch and massage a few leg muscles.

None of the passengers, who were dashing to or waiting for a toilet, really gave them a second look.

A few of the flight attendants, looked strangely at them.

"Just getting the circulation moving," Colburn joked with one of them.

He got the look as if he had just crawled out from under a stone.

He thought, "I wonder if their job requires the surgical removal of humour."

The captain announced over the speaker system, "twenty minutes to landing."

Val noted after checking the video screen, "we're circling around already, obviously we haven't got a landing spot yet. It'll be more than twenty minutes."

She was right, after three circles around the Washington area, the captain announced the final approach.

Seats upright, tray tables stashed, seat belts on.

Ten minutes later, a landing any kangaroo would have been proud of.

Finally the message, "Welcome to Washington. Please

stay seated until the plane has come to a complete stop and the seat belt signs are switched off."

Does anyone listen? Some of the passengers were already opening the overhead lockers, extracting their belongings from the misshapen heap inside.

It probably took another ten minutes for the plane to come to a stop at the gate.

Colburn, Jim and Val remained seated. They had seen this too many times before.

Eventually Colburn and Jim got up and took their packs from the lockers.

Everyone was standing in the aisles.

Jim thought, "after the first class has alighted, then business class, then any upgraded cattle class. It will take another ten minutes for this queue to move."

Eventually the queue did move and the three made their way to the front exit, smiling at the attendants and receiving, "thank you for travelling with British Airways, have a nice day."

They walked off up to the main corridor area, following the signs that said, "Immigration."

When you consider that there could be nearly three hundred people on any flight, you wonder why people rush. Maybe they get through immigration early but their luggage won't be off the carousel. Probably only have carry on baggage.

Just like any airport, the plane seemed to park the farthest away from where you want to be. Having a pleasant stroll through helps regain the blood circulation in the legs. Then finally you come to the queues, snaking around the plastic tapes again, into the area of Hades called Customs and Immigration.

They all waited their turn, maybe about 30 minutes. Eventually they were next.

They were travelling as a group, all three went to the customs official.

Val went first, handing over her passport and visa waiver form.

"Put your right index finger on there, now your left, stand in front of the camera.

Are you all travelling together?" said the official.

"Yes," replied Val, "my husband has the customs declaration form."

He ripped the bottom section of the visa waiver form, stapled it into her passport and stamped it.

Jim went next, going through the same routine and stood by Val.

Then Colburn went up to the desk.

After the fingerprints, the official stared at his computer screen and appeared to press a buzzer under his bench.

"Are you here on business or pleasure?" he asked.

"Purely pleasure. We're having a long weekend break," replied Colburn.

"Could your party go with those gentlemen." The official pointed over to two very large military looking men. Dark trousers and khaki shirts polished black shoes and carrying side arms.

"This way please, follow me," one spoke in a commanding voice.

All three trudged off to a side room of customs.

One of the men spoke, "please sit down."

Colburn spoke, "we'll stand and leave that door open."

"As you wish," replied the man, "we seem to have a problem."

"OK then, explain it to me," said Colburn.

"It's quite simple. There are instructions on your details, to contact our Intelligence Agency. So that's what is happening," said the man.

Colburn, Jim and Val huddled together.

"It's obvious someone doesn't want us here," said Jim, "but don't we know a few folks over here?"

Colburn knew what he meant. They had both worked in the past for some agencies over here and there were a few favours owed.

Colburn walked over to the man at the desk.

"I need to ring the CIA Headquarters now. I want to call Colonel Abrahams. Believe me pal, his department is a bit higher than your Homeland Security."

Looking stunned the military men stared at each other.

"Ring it now," demanded Lord, "or we just walk out of here and I wouldn't advise you try to stop us. You could create an international incident. After all our countries do have a special agreement."

The man nervously dialled a number.

"Is there a Colonel Abrahams there? This is Homeland Security at Washington Dulles."

Eventually a voice answered with "what's the problem?"

"Sir," the man stuttered, "I have a Colburn Lord and his party here. Instructions were to detain them."

"Put him on the phone," roared Abrahams.

The security man nervously handed the phone to Colburn, "he wants to speak to you."

Colburn took the phone, "are you still sitting behind that desk you old sod? You should be retired by now."

Laughter was heard from the phone.

"You haven't changed, still the ignorant pig," replied Abrahams. "What bother are you into now?"

"Nothing you couldn't sort out. Val, Jim and I are just here for a weekend break and the sheriff here wants to jail us. Sort it out can you?"

Colburn handed the phone back to the startled officer.

No one heard the words that came down the phone but the officer's face turned through purple back to white. His hand was shaking when he handed the phone back to Colburn.

Abrahams spoke, "that should have sorted it out for you. If you have time drop in, but on the quiet I'm telling you, watch your back. Someone will be on your tail."

Colburn replied, "thanks for the help, you know I'm retired. Just here for a break."

Abrahams replied, "you'll never retire and there's people around who think you don't do anything unless there's a problem."

"Might see you then, thanks again," replied Colburn as he put the phone down.

He looked across at the man behind the desk who was feverishly stamping his passport.

"Sorry to have inconvenienced you all," he mumbled appearing terrified of what he just heard.

They all picked up their passports and walked out.

As Colburn was leaving, he turned to the men, "if he threatened to see you in Cuba, don't believe him. He would just send you to Baghdad."

Both their faces went an ashen colour.

"Next time," Colburn said, "know your enemy and don't pick on the little people. They might just jump up and bite you."

With that they all headed to the baggage reclaim area.

"Well that passed the time away," said Val.

"I think that had to be anticipated but Abrahams warned me, to watch my back," said Colburn.

Jim interrupted, "then we can assume we're going to be followed. How nice, it'll be fun losing them."

"No, we don't want to lose them, just confuse them," said Colburn.

Val laughed, "that's easy to do and look, there are our bags.

Colburn and Jim hauled the bags off the carousel and they headed for the exit, first handing in the customs declaration form. Then outside to the taxi rank.

They all knew eyes would be on them watching every move.

One good thing about American taxis is the price is always stated on the cab door. At least the basic price is, whatever you pay still depends on the distance travelled.

The bags were loaded into the boot. Jim and Val sat in the rear seats, while Colburn got into the front with the driver. It's always cheaper to take a shuttle bus, if you know which one.

Colburn informed the driver, "Holiday Inn Downtown."

Drivers over there are usually talkative.

This one looked of African origin, probably Somali

thought Colburn. Come over here to find a better life and end up driving a taxi. At least he's paying taxes to the Government. He checked out the inside of the cab, looking for signs of eavesdropping. Even the driver looked like a driver.

Trousers that had seen better days, shiny seams where they had been repeatedly pressed. A white shirt that appeared to have seen the inside of a launderette too many times and wearing trainers that had been through a muddy field. At least the inside of the cab was clean and tidy. The usual no smoking and eating signs plastered all over.

"Been here before?" said the driver with a kind of pigeon English and Texan drawl.

That to Colburn was always a starter for a driver to take you on the scenic route, doubling the fare.

"Many times," replied Colburn, "just take the ninety five, swing South a little and pick up the number one, Rhode Island Avenue. We need to be at the hotel as soon as possible."

"No problem," the driver replied realising his passengers knew the area.

The roads from any airport onto a freeway always seemed the same.

Condos being built, even though they couldn't sell them. The American consumer was in too much debt, the banks wouldn't lend any more money.

Then there were the standard signs of Ambulance chasers, Insurance agents and whopping big burgers.

Seeing the more appetising places like Wendy's, Chick-fil-A, and Arby's, they all thought of their increasing waistlines, especially the food in an Outback Steakhouse.

Pity there's nothing like those in England, the mind telling the brain, you're hungry.

No wonder there's so much obesity. No one here ever cooks, straight from work to an eating house or if they're very posh, home first to change and then out to eat.

The choice is phenomenal.

Driving into Washington is unlike most American cities. In those you can observe the downtown area from afar usually with their sky-scraping blocks of mirror tiled insurance companies, rising from the ground like a volcanic landscape.

Here were generally low-rise buildings with the roadsides scattered with bars, shops and attractive flowerbeds.

This is the nation capital. Traffic lights holding up the flow at every block. All lanes teeming full of traffic.

Eventually they negotiated Logan Circle intersecting Thirteenth Street and travelling two more blocks to fifteenth.

The Holiday Inn straddled the corner of fifteenth and Rhode Island. The driver swung across the road and parked under the awning in front of the main entrance.

Colburn looked at the clock showing the dollars mounting up, it was only thirty eight.

He thought nineteen pounds for that drive. In England you would be ripped off for fifty.

The driver got out and unloaded the bags from the trunk.

Colburn slipped him a fifty note.

"Keep the change," he said.

The driver smiled half shocked that English people knew how to tip.

Tipping is a way of life in America.

It used to be ten per cent but nowadays fifteen per cent was the normal.

Colburn always tipped well. Even in Europe you get better service if you tip well.

The driver handed Colburn his card.

"If you need anything else on your stay just call me, I'll pick you up. Now have a good day."

He drove off leaving the three to negotiate the revolving doors with their cases and down the few steps to Reception.

The desk appeared to be staffed by three people, one male and two females.

The young ladies were dealing with a family, their two children already starting to run riot around the seating area.

The man came to the desk.

"May I help you Sir?" he enquired.

"Reservation, name of Lord," Colburn replied.

The man started scrolling through his computer screen. Both Colburn and Jim leaned on the desk, watching the eyes for any signs of recognition. Any flickering of the lashes would mean a warning had been given. He was of black American stock, only about five six and looked as if he belonged behind the desk.

He looked up without flinching, "two rooms, one double and one single," he said.

"That's correct," replied Lord, "clever how all this electronic booking works, makes life a lot simpler.

"Sure does," replied the desk clerk, swiping the

electronic key cards and handing them to Lord. "How will you be paying for this?"

Colburn handed over his credit card suddenly Val stopped him.

"Use the Marks and Spencers card. I might as well have the points."

Colburn smiled and exchanged the credit cards.

The clerk half laughed, "my wife sure does the same, builds up her credits for Christmas."

Colburn replied as he leaned into the clerk's private space, "you can never be right with a women. Just let them think they are."

The clerk handed the key cards over, "elevators are just around the corner. You're all on floor two. Do you need a reservation for dinner this evening?"

Val replied, "yes, for six thirty, three persons."

"Consider it done Ma'am, you have a nice day," said the clerk.

"You know," said Jim, "what I like about America is the politeness. When they say have a nice day, it actually sounds as if they mean it."

"That's because they do," said Val.

They took their own cases with them, Jim still slipped the Bellboy five dollars.

You never know if and when you need them, he thought. Forward planning, just in case.

No matter which hotel in any part of the world you book into, you always seem to get the room farthest away from the elevator. At least there is less noise.

Opening up their room Val said to Jim, "six thirty downstairs."

"I'll be at the bar," replied Jim.

When you first walk into any hotel room, normal people just look around. Check the wardrobe, drawers and bathroom. Not Colburn, he was checking the light fittings, telephone, looking under the beds and behind the drawers.

"I presume you're looking for listening devices," said Val, "or are you checking the maids' cleaning ability?"

"Everything seems OK," said Colburn.

"Is it safe to unpack now?" asked Val.

Colburn lay down on the bed, throwing a couple of the pillows up for a better headrest.

"You go ahead love, I'm just going to close my eyes for five minutes," said Colburn.

"Why not? Hate to think you strained anything," replied Val, seemingly indignant but knowing he would be planning ahead.

Having stretched out for ten minutes Colburn sat up. Val had unpacked everything and had the coffee machine on the boil.

"You never get enough sugars, do you? Remember to get some from the machines downstairs, there's free coffee twenty-four seven," said Val.

Colburn got up, stripped off and went for a shower.

He shouted from the bathroom, "you know the hardest thing you have to do when you're on holiday?"

"What's that?" replied Val.

"Figure out how the bloody shower works," Colburn shouted.

"Don't be too long," said Val, "coffee's nearly ready."

Val sat on one of the armchairs with her coffee, waiting for Colburn to finish.

She switched on the television, the only programmes

she ever watched was CNN News and the Weather Channel. The rest were just a jumble of useless information and re-runs of programmes seen too many times since the sixties.

Colburn emerged from the bathroom, towelling his hair dry.

"It's a great power shower, better than a Jacuzzi. You'd think someone was pebble-dashing your body."

"There's your coffee, I'm going in now. Check the local forecast for the next few days," said Val, with that she was throwing off her travelling clothes and disappearing slowly into the shower.

Washed and changed, Val donned a long denim skirt and white crinkle blouse.

She slipped on her "Hotter" shoes, "it's nearly six-thirty and I'm hungry," she said.

"I'm ready now," replied Colburn.

"You're not going out dressed like that," Val looked indignant.

Colburn was wearing a denim shirt sporting the Texas Longhorns logo and a pair of jeans that had never seen the wash for years.

"This is America Val, people don't dress for dinner over here," said Colburn.

"I know that," replied Val, "but that's not an excuse for you."

Colburn relented and put on a pair of blue slacks.

"Now isn't that better?" said Val.

Colburn glowered but he knew she was right.

They left their room, double-checking that it was locked and took the elevator to the ground floor.

They spied Jim already in the bar, half way through a glass of beer.

Val sat down at a nearby table. Colburn went to Jim.

"Take your drink over there, I'll get us another round," said Colburn.

He got the drinks, paid the barman over the odds with a tip and put the three glasses on the table. Walking down the bar area, he went to a woman sitting at the restaurant reception desk.

"Name's Lord. Have a table booked for three. We're sitting over in the bar area, can you let us now when you're ready?"

"Certainly Sir, would you like to take the menus with you and I'll get your waitress to take your order," she replied.

Colburn walked back to the table and handed Val and Jim a menu.

"God!" exclaimed Jim, "prices have shot up since we were last here."

"It's all relative," replied Val, "it's still half the price we pay back home."

After a few minutes a smart young lady dressed in the customary white shirt and black skirt hugging just above the knee, came over to them. She was definitely American.

Slightly tanned appearance about five feet eight and a perfect hour glass figure. Obviously a college student Jim thought.

"Hi, I'm Judy," she said, the accent seemed local, "are you ready to order or would you like a few more minutes?"

One thing you do in American restaurants when the

waitress comes to take your order, is be ready to order. If she goes away, she could get caught up with other customers and you will be down in the pecking order for getting your meal.

"I'll have the chicken with vegetables please," said Val always the figure conscious.

Colburn looked up, "and I'll have a prime rib steak and give my apologies to the chef, I want it well done, even cremated, with fries please."

She looked at Jim, he smiled, "make that two, same for me."

"Any more drinks?" she said, "any starters?"

"Val replied, "no thanks, we're fine but can we have water at the table?"

"Will do," the waitress replied and walked away.

Jim said, "back home we would wait at least three quarters of an hour after ordering, let's see how long this takes."

Val interrupted, "that's only because you two have your steaks carbonised and I've got to sit and wait."

They were all quietly drinking, looking around, observing.

"This is quite a nice place," said Val.

"It's a good tourist hotel, that's why I picked it. There's plenty of activity and tour bus companies use this as well. The more people around the better. We might get left alone," said Colburn.

"And pigs might fly," replied Jim.

Exactly twenty-two minutes after ordering, Judy returned. "Your table's ready, if you'd like to follow me."

Jim muttered under his breath, "to the ends of the earth darling."

Val heard him and dug into his ribs with her elbow.

Jim gasped out, "hell can't I even look these days?"

"She's young enough to be your daughter," said Val.

"I don't have a daughter," replied Jim, "you can just look in the shop window, you don't have to go in and buy anything."

They all sat down it was close to seven o' clock, midnight back home. Time to eat and sleep, catch up with the body's time clock.

Any displacement in local time causes the human body to react.

It usually works out that for every two hours of time displacement, the body needs one day to adapt.

Cortisol, a major steroid, has a diurnal variation. Unfortunately these variations do not come evenly spread every twelve hours. Cortisol peaks and dips at midnight and six in the morning. Even something simple like serum Iron peaks twice a day.

In the Army all this is taken into account, they usually called it acclimatisation.

Colburn and Jim always joked about English or British teams when they travelled abroad to compete. Nothing appeared to be done scientifically or medically. Other nations would physically test their people to see when the body adaptation was complete. The Army did this that was why they were the envy of fighting forces around the world, but not in sport. Of course the British Army is a professional outfit, sport is amateur and that's what they were, amateurs. You can't compete using guesswork, one day someone might realise that. Thank God for the training of the Army.

Judy dished out their meals, serving Val first.

"Please enjoy," said Judy, "I'll be back to check if all's OK."

Both steaks looked liked bread when it's overcooked in the toaster.

Colburn had often joked with Val telling her that making toast was just a way of altering protein structure. As various degrees of heat are applied, the protein structure alters and changes colour. Hence toasting. If you continue to the end destruction, all protein matter ends up as carbon. Hence the black appearance.

Jim and Colburn loved their steaks cooked like this. For them seeing no blood was a guarantee that any bacteria had been destroyed. To them this was healthy and logical. To eat meat dripping with blood was an open invitation for food poisoning and they took no chances.

"Chicken OK Val?" asked Colburn.

"Excellent," she replied.

"This is one of the best steaks I've had," said Jim, "this steak knife cuts through it like butter."

Judy came around, "everything OK?" she enquired.

"Everything's fine," replied Colburn.

Judy walked away, "she's a nice lass, I like to see them good at their job. You can leave the tip Jim," said Colburn.

Jim looked up from his plate, muttering OK through a mouthful of beef.

Val was just finishing her meal, taking a drink of the iced water when she observed a military figure.

"Looks like we've got company," she said.

Colburn looked around, spotted the man walking toward them and stopping at their table.

"I'm not going to ask you how you found us," said Colburn.

Colonel Abrahams replied, "you wrote it on your visa waiver form. The address of your first hotel is mandatory. May I have a quick word?"

"Sit down and join us, we're nearly finished," said Jim.

"Nice to see you again Jim," said Abrahams; "your manners never change."

Jim replied, "every time you asked us to do something for you, we felt like mushrooms. You know the saying. Keep them in the dark and every now and again pour some crap over them."

"I know we've had a few problems in the past," said Abrahams.

"A few!" exclaimed Jim.

"This time I'm here to help you," replied Abrahams.

Colburn was finishing his last few fries, "look we're here for a weekend break, that's all," he said chewing the fries.

Abrahams leaned a little towards him, "we both know you don't do holidays and I don't want to know why you're here. There are a couple of things you should know.

Since you checked in at the airport, the computer system has been going haywire informing every agency and agent we have that you're in the country."

Colburn joked, "so I'm a popular guy."

Abrahams continued, "I've tried to find out why you are so popular but this problem goes right up the ladder, to the top."

"That's OK," said Colburn, "if everyone is looking at what we're doing, the criminals will have a field day. Look, I don't mind being followed at all. I'll even give you an itinerary. We will be visiting as many of the tourist attractions that we have time for, that's all."

"Fine," said Abrahams, "you have it your way but I have found out that you will be followed and I don't know why."

Colburn replied, "obviously someone at the top doesn't want the little fish feeding in the pond. You also realise then that they know you're here now."

"But they don't know why," replied Abrahams, "they'll assume I'm here to warn you off."

"Point taken," said Colburn, "you'd better go now before they think you're our pal."

Abrahams stood up, reached for Val's hand and said, "lovely to meet you Mrs Lord, how the hell do you put up with him?"

"He just grows on you," replied Val.

"Yeah," said Abrahams, "like a parasitic fungus. Nice seeing you again Colburn, and you Jim."

With that he turned away and left. They observed from the table the military staff car pulling away outside.

"Well that was exciting," said Jim, "at least we know where we stand. What do we do now?"

Colburn thought for a moment, then moved into the chair Abrahams had been sitting in. Suddenly he put one finger to his lips, feeling under the table.

"The crafty bastard," he muttered extremely quietly, pulling up a small electrical devise and dropping it carefully into a filled glass of iced water. "Always expect the unexpected."

"And trust no one," said Jim, "that's a smart piece of equipment. Range on the microphone is at a least one mile. Could be listening in the State Department,

Capitol Building or sitting on the steps of the Lincoln Memorial. How the hell are we going to do this?"

Colburn was still smiling, "by just doing what the tourists do for the next two days, enjoy the sites."

"I get you," said Jim, "we just give them the run-around and break ever Federal Law they have."

Colburn nodded, "then we go home. Everyone fancy another round before bed?"

Val looked up, "I think I'll have a frozen margarita this time."

"Mines a Sam Adams," said Colburn, "and it's your round Jim."

Colburn beckoned Judy over, "could we have our bill please," he asked.

Judy scribbled a few notes on her pad, ripped out the paper and placed it in a leather folder and left it on the table.

Colburn checked the bill, signed for it to be put on his room account and left a twenty-dollar bill in the folder courtesy of Jim. He thought Judy deserved that, after all they must put up with some idiots at times.

Jim got the round in and put them down on a nearby table.

"Never noticed before, see what they've got in bottles."

"What's that then?" replied Colburn.

"Newcastle Brown Ale, in bottles and they have it on draught," replied Jim.

Colburn looked at Jim as if he was an idiot, "first thing, does it travel well? Next, it's only three hundred millilitres not five hundred and thirdly why put it on draught?

If you saw it on draught in England, would you buy it?"

"No bloody way," replied Jim; "it would ruin it."

"Precisely," said Colburn.

Val interrupted saying quietly, "well if they have a parabolic listener pointed at us, all they've heard is a discussion on the merits of Brown Ale. Now I'd like to take my drink up to the room, I'm getting tired."

"So what time in the morning?" asked Jim.

"Nine OK Val?" said Colburn.

"That's fine," she replied pressing the elevator button.

The phone buzzed in Jock Strane's pocket. He flipped it open. The caller ID said Stewart.

"What's up Boss?" Strane enquired.

"Where the hell are you?" asked Stewart.

"Lord's hotel in Manchester, he's returning Monday. Got everything covered."

"He's in bloody Washington," Stewart shouted down the phone line, "the Yanks are going ape shit wanting to know why he's there."

Strane replied, "that's their problem Boss. Let them worry about it and chase him around. The action will be over here, not there."

"You'd better be right," retorted Stewart, "or your carcass will be back in Angola."

Stewart cut the conversation.

Strane turned to Doug, sitting next on a couch at the bar area.

"Lord's in Washington."

"Nice for him, hope he enjoys the sights," replied Doug.

"What the hell is he doing over there?" said Strane.

"Obviously looking for something," replied Doug.

"In your Capital?" said Strane, "what's the connection?"

"It's not our job to worry over that, wait until they're back. It will all pan out," said Doug.

Jim stared down at his breakfast. Two eggs over easy, waffles with maple syrup. The smallest sausages you could imagine and bacon.

He looked over at Val tucking into croissants; "you can't get decent bacon over here can you?"

Colburn had the same, "just pour down the calories, we'll need it for the walking. Let them follow us on foot, give them some exercise. Then we'll hit the Metro and use cabs. That'll give them something to think about," he said.

Washington DC is a city made for walking. Some say the grid lines are made up like the Freemason's Square and Compass. Getting about is simple.

With bicycle-friendly streets, ample sidewalks and one of the safest, cleanest and efficient public transportation system in the country.

DC is easy to navigate around.

The city's most famous landmarks are centred in and on the National Mall and Memorial Parks. Spanning about two and a quarter mile from the Lincoln Memorial to the US Capitol.

Ample grassy spaces, Museums and Memorials flank it. The grass playing host to festivals and performances.

Beyond the familiar sights, the city is a rich network of colourful neighbourhoods, vibrant nightlife and cultural attractions. These areas delight visitors with walking tours, sidewalk cafes and quaint boutiques.

Most major hotels and attractions are located within minutes walking time of a Metrorail stop.

DC cabs run on a zone system instead of using meters. The basic rates are posted in each cab, by law, although now there is a gas surcharge. Even the Americans are complaining about the price of Gas.

After breakfast, Colburn and Jim picked up their backpacks. Stuffed two bottles of water each in the side pockets and with Val, headed by the swing doors.

It was a sunny Friday morning, the street thronging with traffic. Tour buses and people were milling around. Most of the workers were already at their desks. The rest walked briskly around, usually in flip-flops, shorts and T-shirts, carrying the mandatory Starbucks coffee with their mobile phone glued to their ear.

"Which way?" said Jim.

Colburn replied, "go right past the Doubletree to Scott Circle."

The three just strolled along, no need to rush. They had ample time.

Jim spotted the proverbial black sedan across the road, tinted windows and polished paintwork.

It started to move slowly from about seventy-five yards behind.

"Looks like we've company already," said Jim.

Colburn replied, "and a couple of walking pals."

Val and Jim slowly turned their heads seeing two white males in shiny grey suits carrying newspapers. They could have been ordinary businessmen had it not been for the obligatory earpiece and occasionally chatting into the sleeve of their coats.

At Scott Circle they walked onto 16th Street heading south, past the Courtyard Hotel and The National Geographic Society.

Another three blocks brought them into Lafayette Park with the imposing rear view of the White House and its lawns.

Val said, "if that car is on the far side on the White House when we get there. Then we know for certain there's eyes on us."

They forked left heading for 15th and down past the Treasury Building. Eventually turning back right, past the West Wing to the front elevation of the White House.

Sometimes in front of here, it's like a madhouse.

Everyone wants his or her photograph with the White House in the background.

Singles couples but mostly large groups jockeying for position, for the best shot.

Val simply leaned on the railings, pushed her camera through and took a shot.

She turned to see the sedan parked across the road, seemingly fighting for position between the pedestrians and the protestors.

"Hope they have a nice day," said Val.

They walked back to 15th and down to the White House Visitor Center.

All they wanted was a few brochures but the men following were fervently communicating.

Jim said, "wonder if they think we're going to rob the White House?"

Colburn replied, "the White House is basically living space. Yes, there's the Oval Office but most work is carried out in the West Wing. Anyway Jim, we've been there, done that and got the T-shirt."

Both of them, in their former occupations had been guests of the Americans.

Outside the Center, the three consulted the brochures, pointing toward the White House. The followers were unsure what this meant, just as Colburn had anticipated.

"They'll put extra guards on there now," said Colburn, "they dare not take any chances. Let's go for a bit of History now."

They walked via the Ellipse, crossing Constitutional Avenue, staying on the 15th.

Val started taking more pictures.

"You get a better shot of the Washington Monument from here," she said.

The obelisk of the monument is one of the major sights in DC.

Standing at one end of the Mall with the Capitol Building at the other.

Walking over the grass area taking more pictures, across 17th to the World War Two Memorial.

This is basically circular in shape with the names of the states circled within a wreath around a central water feature with fountains. Quite a moving and quiet area, considering the hundreds of people walking around, observing, taking pictures.

The memorial celebrates a generation of Americans who emerged from the Depression to fight and win the most devastating war in history.

Inscriptions at the base of the pavilion fountains mark key battles of the war. The twin Atlantic and Pacific pavilions symbolise a war fought across two oceans. The wreaths of oak and wheat on each of the pillars symbolise the nation's industrial and agricultural strength. Both of which were essential to the success of the global war effort. The four thousand gold stars on the Freedom Wall commemorate the more than four hundred thousand Americans who gave their lives in the war.

Placing the memorial between the Washington Monument and Lincoln Memorial reflected the importance of World War Two in preserving and internationalising democratic ideals won under George Washington and defended by Abraham Lincoln.

They headed on towards the reflecting pool.

Taking the left side of the pool, where most of the tour buses park, they walked through West Potomac Park. They passed the World War One Memorial and then the Korean Memorial. Here, a group of nineteen stainless steel statues depict a squad on patrol. Strips of granite and juniper bushes suggest the rugged Korean terrain, while windblown ponchos recall the harsh weather.

The images reflect the determination of U.S. forces and the countless ways in which Americans answered their country's call to duty.

On a granite wall is a message, inlaid with silver, "Freedom is Not Free."

"The reflecting pool makes a lovely picture," said Val.

"It's better at night," replied Jim.

Colburn glanced around, "see we still have our suited friends. If we have time, we could take a night tour around here."

They ambled on to the Lincoln Memorial.

Looking like a copy of the Parthenon on the Acropolis, stone steps lead up and into one of the most photographed areas in the World.

The massive statue of Lincoln sitting in his chair commanding the nation like Zeus on Olympus.

Nineteen feet tall and nineteen feet wide made from twenty-eight marble blocks. Murals adorn the walls depicting principal events in Lincoln's life. Below them on the north and south walls are the inscriptions of the Gettysburg Address and his second Inaugural address.

The whole building is constructed primarily of Colorado Yule marble and Indiana limestone. The thirty-six columns around the memorial represent the states in the union at the time of his death.

An area that had been in more movies than John Wayne.

After taking the statutory pictures, they sat among the crowds on the steps looking back over the pool towards the obelisk.

Val said, "you can't come here and not do this. It's been in loads of films."

Colburn replied, "also gives you an overview of our followers. Wonder what they're reporting in now."

Jim laughed, "if we start pointing at that statue and the chiselled scrolls on the walls, there will be extra guards here as well."

"Good point," said Colburn as he stood up with his camera making sure everyone could see him taking the shots, "now I think we'll lead them on."

The three got up, walked down the steps and round onto 23rd.

"Are we giving FDR a miss then?" asked Val.

Colburn replied, "for today, anyway."

Another thirty minutes took them past the State Department and George Washington University and into Foggy Bottom.

"Be ready now," said Colburn, "we're going underground."

Without hesitation, the three descended the steps of the Metro at Foggy Bottom.

Quickly grabbing day tickets, they headed down and onto the platform stating east.

The underground train soon arrived. The Blue Line.

They mingled with the tourists. Not packed like sardines as the London tubes normally are, but clean, airy and spacious carriages. As the doors were closing, Jim spotted the hounds frantically sending messages.

The train headed out stopping first at Dulles, then Arlington Cemetery past the Pentagon.

They got off at Pentagon City.

"Why here?" asked Val.

"Just for you," replied Colburn, "there's a big fashion center here."

"So we're going shopping?" asked Jim.

"Why not?" replied Colburn, "we're on holiday and there's food courts in there. I'm starving."

After a couple of hours of Val dragging them from shop to shop, Colburn and Jim were tiring.

They grabbed an Arby's beef sandwich and an everlasting Coke.

The only purchase they made was in Pay Less for Shoes. Buying trainers at half the price you pay in England.

Outside the Mall, they flagged down a taxi.

Loading up Val's carrier bags, Colburn instructed the driver to take Washington Boulevard. Stopping outside the Pentagon for photos, then up to Arlington cemetery to view the Kennedy graves.

Probably the best known of more than one hundred national cemeteries, Arlington's green slopes shelter veterans from every war than has involved the nation.

Over two hundred and ninety thousand service personnel and their family members rest on the 624 acres of Virginia land across the Potomac River from the Lincoln Memorial. The granite and marble markers and memorials reflect the tide of American history, beginning in the Civil War.

The grounds originally belonged to the famous confederate general, Robert E. Lee but the title to them was lost after the Civil War when the south was defeated.

About twenty-four burials are still conducted there, every weekday.

Cape cod stones frame the eternal flame of John F Kennedy, lying alongside his brother.

Then back over the Arlington Memorial Bridge, round the Lincoln Memorial, up 23rd to Washington Circle, taking New Hampshire Drive to the famous Dupont Circle.

Back down Massachusetts Avenue to Scott Circle and to the hotel.

Colburn tipped the driver an extra ten dollars.

Walking inside Jim said, "I wonder where they think we are going to strike?"

Colburm answered, "it's just like fishing, you bait the hook and wait for a response, then you strike. Dinner at six again OK?"

"See you downstairs," said Jim, "don't forget to sweep your room, you can bet there's been more in there than the cleaner. Put the radio on loud, drowns most of the sound."

"Will do," said Colburn.

Dinner was a repeat of Friday night.

None of them altered their eating habits. Chicken and burnt steaks were served again.

After checking the table and flower vase, Jim concluded that it was OK to talk freely.

From the window configuration and where they were seated, it would be impossible to eavesdrop. Even with a sophisticated device.

"So what's the plan for tomorrow?" asked Jim.

"I thought we should do the Mall," replied Colburn, "we can start at the Washington Monument and head towards the Capitol. Our shadows will enjoy the culture trip. They've probably never been in those galleries along there. I have in mind to split up eventually. Val wants to visit the National Gallery of Art, east and west. So I thought you and I could go and play in the Air and Space Museum. There are plenty of places to eat. Virtually all the galleries have eating places inside and there will be thousands of people knocking about. That OK with you Val?"

Val finishing off her meal replied, "it's OK but I would like to find a Wal-Mart before we go home."

Jim said, "I wouldn't mind that. I always get my shirts from the sales racks."

Colburn looked over at Jim, "yes you can tell."

Jim screwed his nose a little, "nothing wrong in looking for a bargain," he said.

"Of course not," said Val, "leave him alone," casting a sympathetic arm around Jim.

Colburn continued, "the way I see it is there will be thousands of folks around tomorrow. Saturday brings in all the school trips and tour buses but I don't want our suited friends to lose us totally. They can only report what they see and we are just seeing the sights of this wonderful city. The more we look at, the more confused they will be. If I had to conclude what we were up to, all I could say is they are sightseeing."

Jim stroked his chin, "I reckon there's someone somewhere who thinks we're up to something. They won't give up watching."

Colburn replied, "that's to our advantage. We need them to watch and be confused. I want them to follow us everywhere we go. I know that Sunday will be tricky but we'll have to find a way to give them the slip, without them realising it. So tomorrow that's why we'll split up for a while. Jim and I will separate in the afternoon. He can go to the Smithsonian and I'll go to the American Indian Museum. Divide and conquer is the order of the day. We just make sure there's a couple of occasions our followers lose us, maybe only for ten minutes. Say three times tomorrow. Let them get used to panic. Then they'll spot us again and they'll be fine with that. I suggest we lose them in the museum shops, nip into the restrooms for a while and let them find us later. This should make them think we've got bladder problems drinking so much bottled water and they will expect to miss us for a while on Sunday. We will have dinner out tomorrow. Maybe catch a cab to Georgetown. That area will be leaping, makes it more difficult to follow us."

Looking across at Val he continued, "we might just have time for the Shops at Georgetown Park and then hit Blues Alley."

"That sounds fine to me," said Val.

"Roger, Wilco," said Jim.

"I need to buy a phone card," said Colburn, getting up and headed for the Hotel shop.

"What's he want one of those for?" Jim asked Val.

"Haven't got a clue," answered Val, "but no doubt it's all part of forward planning."

Jim looked puzzled. He stood up as Val got up and they walked to the Hotel reception area. Colburn was already back there sporting a phone card.

"Just in case we need to make calls," he said.

"Like to whom?" asked Jim.

"Don't know yet but these things are mighty handy over here and cheap," replied Colburn, "anyway, time to hit the sack. As they say, tomorrow's another day."

Breakfast was the usual repeat of Val with the croissants and fruit and Colburn and Jim with cholesterol in every mouthful. Val wondered how they stayed so fit considering the rubbish they threw down their throats.

Saturday morning was another fine day. The local weather channel had predicted a twenty per cent chance of rain, nothing to worry about. The humidity was forecast to go higher and the pollen count would be increased. Pity for the asthmatics.

Val had put shorts on today, saying she could do with

a tan on her legs that comes from the ultra-violet rays of the sun and not a sun bed. Certainly not out of a bottle.

The shorts were fairly cut-away denims topped off with a broad belt of Native American Indian design. Her T- shirt was an off-white plain variety. After all, white reflects heat, and dark colours absorb it. Nothing is better than being comfortable. Today was going to be warm.

Jim sat in light blue Chino trousers and a short sleeved shirt that had a classic design that no one had ever seen. He said he got it from Marks but it looked more like a cross between Punk Rock and Hawaii-5-O. White socks and trainers adorned the rest of him.

Val had laid out Colburn's clothes.

Lightweight denim jeans and a blue Wrangler shirt but he still insisted on trainers.

He always maintained they were the best for walking as long as they were doused on the inside with Mycota Foot Powder.

Picking up their backpacks they headed out noting the black sedan and the mandatory followers across the street.

Jim looked at Colburn, "should we shout over Good Morning?" he joked.

This time they headed straight across the road down 15th Street to Massachusetts Avenue, turning left to Thomas Circle. Then straight down 14th Street.

They were just strolling along. You couldn't hurry there were too many people and a hell of a lot of traffic.

At each block they waited until the green hand showed "Walk." Even then traffic was still crossing their path. Walking was supposed to be easy in this town but only if you keep your eyes open for the traffic ignoring the signs. At least the drivers here are polite when they hit you.

Eventually they passed the Ronald Reagen Building and International Trade Center before emerging onto Constitution Avenue.

They strolled in the glorious sunshine along the avenue heading in the direction of the Capitol building.

Jim noticed a couple of dozen police cars, some parked, others tearing off toward the Capitol.

"Surely they're not here to greet us," he said jokingly.

Val replied, "seems something's going on. Look at their gear."

One transit type van was parked at the rear of the Natural History Museum.

About two dozens officers poured out.

Dressed in dark blue uniforms and bullet-proof vests. Helmets with visors, plastic shields and side arms. This was full riot gear.

Jim groaned, "that's all we need, getting blamed for a riot."

Colburn approached one of the officers.

"Good day," he said, "we're just visiting and I don't want my family here if there's going to be any trouble."

The officer replied, "from England?" speaking with a Southern Virginian drawl.

"Yes" answered Colburn, "just here for the weekend."

"There's no great problem," said the officer with strong assurance, "later on this morning there's a Neo-Nazi rally in the Mall, marching up to the Capitol."

"Good God," exclaimed Colburn, "didn't think there was anything like that over here."

"You'd be surprised if you knew what crap we have to deal with," said the officer, "but you lot will be OK, now have a nice day."

Colburn gratefully thanked the officer.

"You heard all that," he said, "seems like the lads will be busy today."

Val and Jim walked on smiling.

Anything that would distract the authorities could be helpful.

At the corner of Constitution and 9th they crossed the road in front of the National Archives.

Jim groaned, "just look at that queue."

Already several dozen people were waiting to get in. The line snaking along the ramp in front of the door, along Constitution and up 9th street.

"Colburn said, "there should be fewer tomorrow but we'll just have to wait and mix in with the tourists and school teachers with their classes."

Past the Archives, they walked down 7th onto the grassy area of the Mall.

"OK, here's the plan," said Colburn, "behind us are the two Art Galleries you want to visit Val and straight across is the Air and Space Museum. How about we give it two hours and meet up in the café of the American Indian Museum for some late lunch.

I expect our followers will split now. Two for you Val and two for us. Don't forget what I said about losing them. Let them worry a bit then reappear. Jim and I will have some time looking at the exhibits, then split and lose them. Look on it as fun and relax."

Val kissed Colburn on the cheeks, "see you in a couple of hours then," she said and off she saunted to view the Art.

Colburn and Jim crossed the grass over Jefferson Drive.

Already there were at least two dozen tour buses parked along the Drive.

Hundreds of people were thronging the steps of the Museum waiting to enter through their security.

This museum is full of old racing cars, aeroplanes old and new and some of the most amazing mock up spacecraft outside Houston.

They entered and checked their bags and bodies through security. They went straight to the escalators and up onto the first floor and walked back to the glass balcony overlooking the entrance.

Colburn said, "look out for the suits, then let them see us up here."

It was nearly five minutes of observing the crowds thronging in, when Jim noticed two large men, suited, apparently flashing some form of identification at one of the guards.

"There's our company," he said, nudging Colburn and nodding towards the main door. "They are really amateurs at this. They stick out like a sore thumb.

You couldn't miss them. Everyone in here is dressed like a slob and they come in looking like they're going to the Oscars."

Colburn smiled and said, "shorts and T-shirts are not standard dress. God knows what they would be like doing proper field work."

Jim laughed, "as long as they're as bad doing wet work, we're OK."

They walked away, Colburn mumbled under his breath, "this lot wouldn't get a job as a bouncer in Mothercare."

The men obviously spotted Jim and Colburn, they started up the escalator.

Colburn said, "they shouldn't miss you in that shirt Jim. Magnum would be proud of you. Now you go left and I'll swing right and we'll see how Noddy and Big Ears react. Use the restrooms, we'll cross back so it looks as if we're enjoying the exhibits and I'll meet you at the shop entrance in one hour."

Jim walked off, "have fun," he shouted.

The followers could do nothing but separate and follow one each.

Colburn walked to one end looking at the suspended aeroplanes and eventually sat on a seat outside a restroom. The noise from the visiting crowds was loud, in particular the young family members and schoolchildren. Colburn longed for the peace and quiet of his village. His follower stopped and leaned on a rail about fifty yards away. The crowds were obstructing his view. Colburn noticed him turning away possibly communicating with his partner. He smartly jumped up and turned straight into the restroom.

The follower turned back his head and not seeing Colburn, virtually ran to where Colburn had been sitting. Frantically he spoke on his communicator.

"I've lost him. You got eyes on the other?" he said.

"Sure do," came the reply.

At that moment of turning to speak so anyone in the crowds wouldn't notice, Jim veered off into a restroom.

"Shit," came a reply, "mine's a no-show now."

Just like bees around flowers, the two security men darted in and out of the crowds. Sprinting from one exhibit area to the next, peering up and under.

After about ten minutes of frantic searching, Noddy spoke in his microphone.

"Got Colburn again. Must have been the crowds. He's just looking at the exhibits."

"Roger that, just spotted his pal. Everything's OK," said Big Ears.

Eventually after a good look around, Colburn and Jim met up at the shop entrance.

"Good fun this," said Jim.

"Like taking candy off a baby," said Colburn, "there's a sign that says restrooms at the back of this store. We'll use those."

The racks of toys and assorted jumble in the shop were about shoulder height.

If you wanted something on the bottom shelf, you would be out of the line of sight.

The shop was large in floor area with an escalator to a lower ground floor.

Colburn said, "our friends are over there," nodding towards the entrance, "you go first and lose yourself for ten minutes."

Jim went straight to the restrooms, while Colburn browsed the tacky gifts.

The outside of the shop was glass, so you could walk all around and look in.

Colburn could already see one of the followers looking up and down the aisles from outside. Jim was missing.

After ten minutes Jim reappeared and as he crossed Colburn's path, went straight to an area of the window close to the door. At that time both followers were close together and taking that opportunity of being out of their line of sight, Colburn ducked into the restroom.

All of a sudden Jim noticed frantic waving of arms and communication exchanges.

He smiled to himself picking up a furry toy of a space shuttle. Wondering do people actually buy this crap?

After about ten minutes Colburn re-joined Jim. The followers appeared relieved still warily looking from the outside glass, in.

Colburn said to Jim, "now for the big act. You go down the escalator. One will have to follow, and I'll nip back in there and dodge the one up here. When you have him at the far side downstairs, get back up here fast and I'll meet you at the main door."

Jim wandered off down the escalator. Sure enough, one of the followers slid into the shop mingling with the dozens of people looking for bargains and followed Jim downstairs. Colburn noticed his man watching his partner and then disappeared.

Once again frantic communications were exchanged between the followers.

"I've lost him," said one voice.

"I've got the other," came the reply.

Jim ducked down appearing to look at some of the books on sale. His follower came warily to the rear of the racks, peering around each one. Reaching the back, he radioed in, "Christ, I've lost mine now."

Jim had stayed low, his presence not apparent from eye level and headed straight back up the escalator.

"I can see yours, he's coming back up," said one follower. His partner racing off up the escalator just in time to nearly bump into Colburn reading some of the History books on sale but kneeling down behind a rack.

Colburn didn't even look up. He put the book down and walked out to meet Jim at the entrance.

They both walked out into the bright sunshine, both putting on shades and turned right outside heading toward the Capitol.

Jim said, "I enjoyed that. They're still right behind."

Colburn replied, "now they will be expecting to lose us for a short while. As long as they find us, they will have no reason to suspect anything."

They crossed 4th street and walked up the ramp toward the American Indian Museum.

Young kids were playing in a nearby fountain, splashing water all over their friends.

The entrance to the Museum virtually faced the Capitol.

There were at least two dozen police wagons parked in front around the Grant Memorial and between the Peace and Garfield Memorials.

Jim mused as they turned to enter the Museum, "obviously the protestors aren't going to get anywhere near to the Capitol."

Colburn replied, "then neither can we. Val wanted some photos, looks like she'll have to make do with long shots."

This Museum was light and airy, well air-conditioned.

The amphitheatre downward ramps led around a fountain with native canoes exhibited.

They saw the sign that said restaurant and spotted Val already with her coffee.

They wandered over and sat down.

"Had a good day Val?" asked Jim.

"Couldn't be better," she replied.

"How did it go with your tail then?" asked Colburn.

"I lost them a couple of times. Then let them see me taking notes about some of the pictures," said Val, "they might even think we're here to steal some art."

"Good work, so now I expect they're all outside checking notes. They'll only send one in here. So what are we eating? Throw us a couple of menus Jim."

Colburn went to the desk and ordered lunch. A chicken salad for Val and two large hamburgers with fries for Jim and himself. He returned to the table saying, "we get our own coffee over there. The waitress will bring us our meals when they're ready."

The coffee in most of the States is wonderful. Especially Starbucks, where visitors usually buy a pint mug with the city landscape painted into the ceramics. Every Starbucks in every major city and town have their own mugs. Quite a collector's item.

Jim moaned as usual, "the only thing I don't like is having to use these creamers. Wouldn't you think in a place like this they'd have a milk delivery? No, everyone uses this crap. If I wanted cream in my coffee, I'd ask for it."

Colburn replied, "and you can't get a carton of curry sauce with your fish and chips."

Jim retorted again, "and have you seen what they do to Kebabs, or Gyros over here.

They fill them up with all that crappy Mayo and ruin the taste of good satisfying cholesterol."

They all laughed quietly.

The waitress approached with the salad and burgers. She was dressed in the attire of a proper waitress.

Val said afterwards, "it's really nice to see that. You only see that in Devon or Cornwall teashops. They used to dress like that to serve you in Robbs at Hexham.   A bit of old England."

Jim was devouring his burger, "I never eat burgers back home, the meat is awful. Just like Kentucky Fried Chicken. Once you have eaten it over here, you will never eat it in England. There's no comparison."

The restaurant had glass windows. Not only could you see out, others can see in.

It was apparent that their followers had decided to wait outside to observe their movement patterns.

"At least they're allowing us a bit of piece and quiet for lunch," said Val.

"Just take your time Jim. We have to work out our homecoming strategy back to the hotel. This is what I think we should do. Eventually we'll split up.

If we leave here and bear right up 3rd we will hit Independence Avenue.

Then if we bear left back toward the Monument, at the Smithsonian, Val will duck down the Metro on the Blue line heading to Franconia-Springfield. Get off at McPherson Square, then 15th takes you to Thomas Circle up Massachusetts to Scott Circle, and then you're back at the hotel.

We can have a look in the Smithsonian if you like but then you and I walk across the grass up 12th to the Federal Triangle. You take the same Blue Line but only to the next stop the Metro Center."

"Sounds just like home," said Jim.

Colburn continued, "take the Red Line to Shady Grove and get off at Dupont Circle.

Then walk back down Massachusetts to Scott.

I'll double back after Jim goes, down Pennsylvania to

Penn Quarter. I'll be passing the rear side of the Archives, the Public Vault area, just to check for any increase in Federal activity. Then I'll get the Metro there, the Green Line to China Town. I'll change to the Red Line and follow Jim back to the hotel. I reckon that should give them a good afternoon out. Once we're back, important things first, siesta time. We'll all meet up a seven at the bar. Any questions?"

"I may be doing a bit shopping on the way back," said Val.

"Anything you like," replied Colburn, "just keep the tail busy."

"No problem," said Val.

"Want me to lose mine?" asked Jim.

"A few times," said Colburn, "I might even detour to Ford's Theatre first, always wanted to see that."

Jim groaned some more as he drank his coffee, "that's all we need, these amateurs thinking we're out to duff a President."

Colburn smiled as he looked out of the window at the small band of followers, "now there's a thought."

After the late lunch, the plan was executed perfectly.

Colburn arrived back at the hotel ten minutes after Jim, hearing the screech of tires in the street and observing the black sedan.

"Hope they've had a good time," he thought, seeing four men feverishly communicating, perspiring and gesticulating with each other.

At least they would report to control nothing suspicious. They wouldn't say they had lost them a few times. That would look bad on their records.

He sat in the lobby after filling a cup of coffee, from the free table. They even had Earl Grey tea there. He picked up the local paper, only reading the sports section and the small piece on European sport. After all, nothing that happened in the World was important, or so it seemed in US papers.

Val arrived back about forty minutes later, carrying four plastic bags.

"Hope we're not overweight in our cases," said Colburn.

"Don't be silly," Val replied, "it's only lightweight things. Make me a cup of tea, will you?"

"Then can I have my siesta?" asked Colburn.

"You can have what you like," replied Val.

Colburn gave her a loving smile.

"Everything except that," she said, knowing what he was thinking.

Dinner that evening was a quiet affair in the hotel restaurant. Walking around for much of the day was tiring. So Georgetown was out.

It was easier to sit in peace and quiet and enjoy the steak dinners.

All that was spoken was Colburn's reminder to discuss Sunday over breakfast.

Bedtime was early.

Tomorrow would be a long day.

Plans had to be gone over in the mind until there was no room for error.

Colburn knew the idiom, constantly update, refresh and assess, what could go wrong?

SUNDAY.

The three met over breakfast at eight-thirty. There was no need for any hurry today.

The Archives Exhibition did not open until ten.

Val had her usual healthy option of croissants and jams but did concede by having a couple of waffles with maple syrup. Earl Grey tea was ordered.

For Colburn and Jim, the fry-up of high cholesterol ingredients and two eggs over easy. Coffee was amply available.

Jim had scoured the area earlier for microphones. It was all clear.

Colburn said, "we can't actually finalise our plans until we're inside the Archives. So just take your time over the food and let it settle. We'll have a sit down in the lobby and have a few cups of coffee before we set out. Our friends out there will just have to wait. I think when they see us at the Archives, they'll send two round to the Public Vaults side and keep two with us. This means that the two round the far side will be out of our view. They will have to stay there just in case we can go out that way. The other two will try to observe us themselves but there are three of us. This should give us an opportunity one of us at a time not to be noticed. That side is supposed to be closed to the public on Sundays, so they'll just have to flash their badges to security and wait in there, just in case. They can communicate anyway."

Jim butted in, "they could send for reinforcements."

Colburn continued, "that's always a possibility but today's Sunday. All the work rotas will have been worked out for the weekend. Hell, they'll not want to pay too much overtime. Most of the other agents will be away or at home. So by the time they realise that they might need some back up, our work will be long over. Hopefully."

Val sipped her tea, put down the cup and started spreading raspberry jam over a piece of croissant. " Something's been bugging me for a while about this Magna Carta. I know how it got here, via the Perot Foundation then a Sotheby's auction, but it's said they purchased it from the Brudenell family. These folks were the Earls of Cardigan. I can't quite fathom out a connection to our search."

Colburn leaned back in his chair and stretched his arms, "that's a valid point, if this is the piece of the puzzle we want, why has it remained in Welsh hands until 1984.

Jim, unusually, didn't look puzzled. Polishing off one of his eggs whole, he gulped and said, "how about when the Cathedral goods were raided by the Crown. It's possible this Charter was one of the stolen items, like the Gospels. Our old pal Cotton seemed to get his hands on most things, including the originals. He might have just given one of the 1297 ones to that Welsh family. I'm not saying that's right but it's possible."

Colburn grinned, "sometimes Jim, you amaze me. It is logical to assume that. This one could have been removed from Durham. There's no way of verifying it though."

"There is," replied Val.

It was Colburn's turn to look puzzled, "explain it then," he said.

"Quite simple," said Val, "we look for any code. If there isn't one, then we go to Lincoln or Salisbury, or both. What we do know is that someone in the fifteen or sixteen hundreds left a clue, so we find it. It just seems to me that the four that are claimed to be the originals would have been examined thoroughly. No doubt with all the sophisticated technology that has been around in the last twenty years, both the front and back of those manuscripts would have been searched. After all, it's only been in the last twenty years or so that DNA analysis has been possible. My guess is that this manuscript here was only authenticated on the front. Examining the paper, the writing and the inks was all that would have been necessary at the time. It is a genuine one anyway."

Colburn leaned back on the table, with a quiet voice said, "so what you are saying is the whole of the manuscript was probably not looked at."

Val replied, "yes, the Welsh family probably had to sell it to maintain the upkeep of castles or family homes. Otherwise they may have gone broke. You have to feel sorry for the aristocracy, having to let ordinary people into their homes so that they can keep them. Remember the Window Tax, a lot of stately homes had windows bricked over so the tax would be less."

"I know," said Colburn, "daylight robbery."

"So," said Jim, "are we spending another night out?"

"Probably," replied Colburn, "we'll work on the details later. Val gets to come back here in a comfortable bed."

"How are we going to make them think we've left as well?" asked Jim.

"I think Val and I will be overheard having a row about you and I going drinking tonight," said Colburn.

"We do that a lot though, she doesn't mind," replied Jim.

"Yes but if we go somewhere she thinks we shouldn't, then she'd complain," said Colburn.

"Where do you think you two are off to then?" asked Val.

"Thought we might argue about us going to Hooters," said Colburn.

"If there was one back home, I would," said Val.

"Goody, goody," said Jim, "just like the Cathedral door."

"What do you mean?" asked Val.

Jim replied with a gleam in his eyes, "big knockers."

"Well just dream about it Jim but it makes a good point for an argument," said Val.

"The place shuts up at five, latest five-thirty, so I reckon we'll argue about ten minutes before and you stomp out. Play mad with us, said Colburn.

The only thing we have left to do is order a packed lunch from the kitchen, any preferences?"

"Any meat with Monterrey Jack cheese is fine for me," said Jim.

"Pastrami on rye bread for me," said Val.

"Mines going to be a baguette of anything but we need them wrapped well in tinfoil," said Colburn.

"That won't keep them that fresh," said Val.

"No," replied Colburn, "but we have some gear we can wrap in the sandwiches and even when it goes through the x-ray machine, it will only show metal wrapping. When we open our bags up, all they'll see is a limp sandwich in the throws of bacterial contamination."

After breakfast and a thorough re-run of the tentative plan, Colburn ordered the packed lunches from Reception and asked them to be delivered to their rooms as soon as possible.

They arrived some twenty minutes later. Jim was with Colburn and Val.

"Before we go out today, Jim, I want you to pack your suitcase as if we were leaving now. We may not have time to get back here tomorrow. Val will make the necessary arrangements for transport," said Colburn.

"Another day of Cat and Mouse then," said Jim.

"Probably so," replied Colburn.

"You know they'll stop us before we get on our plane, don't you," said Jim.

"Of course they will. They have to but when they find nothing they'll have to let us board our flight. Or create a National incident. After all, nothing is being stolen. We're just borrowing it for a while and we won't even take it out of the Archives," said Colburn, "now pack your electrical bits in the tin foil, leave a bit of the sandwich sticking out of the top."

Jim carefully unwrapped all the sandwiches, placing the electronic components carefully at the base of bread. He placed the lenses in tissue paper, folded it neatly and put them inside. His laser pen was double wrapped in foil and the miniature drill placed along side of it. Nothing could be left to chance. Every combat soldier was taught the necessity of adaptation but that meant something had not gone to plan.

Batteries could be kept on his person. They would be needed for their cameras.

Everything was placed in the three backpacks, bottled water in the outside pockets and the mandatory Coke, inside.

Val had the television on, switched to the Weather Channel.

"Forecast's not so good for later today," she said, "they say eighty per cent chance of thunderstorms and they'll be right."

Colburn looked across at the screen, "seems the security folks in the Archives may be in for a storm tonight," he laughed, "anything that gives us an advantage. I take it the place won't open up until eight-forty five, maybe nine. Then we'll have to figure out how to get out. Once we are out we find a phone. I'll use the phone card and call up our friendly cab driver from the airport. He'll like another big tip and I reckon if we offer him fifty over the top, he'll drive like Lewis Hamilton.

If we can get down the Metro at Penn, take the Green Line to Chinatown, then the Red Line to Union Station. We can have him pick us up there and straight to the airport."

"What about our luggage?" asked Jim.

"When you get back here tonight Val, have dinner as usual. I guess someone will ask where we are. Just act annoyed and tell them we've gone drinking and you don't approve. That information may well get fed back to the agents. Then later, ask reception for a Bellboy to come for the luggage about ten in the morning. Pay the bill and get reception to call you a cab for the airport."

Val said, "the agents will see I'm alone."

Colburn replied, "I'm hoping they think they just missed us last night after our drinking or they may think we pulled. Then they have to follow you and all hell will break loose looking for us. If everything goes to plan, we meet up at the airport, about noon. Flight isn't until four

275

and they won't open the desk until three hours before take off. So we'll just have to wait. I've got the number of the British Embassy just in case."

Jim interrupted again, "we also have a direct number to a very important person, haven't we?"

"Only for emergencies, Jim," replied Colburn.

"Makes you wonder though, if anyone high up knows what's going on. Or are they keeping information from flowing?" said Jim.

"Nobody talks to each other over here," said Colburn, "everyone's out for themselves. Score a home run and you go up the ladder. Make a fool of the government and you're in the crapper."

Jim stretched and smiled, "well let's see who turns up then, someone will you know."

Colburn nodded his head, "whoever is pulling the strings will want to know what's going on and they can only do that at the airport, before we leave. Don't forget put plastic tags on your suitcase. It saves them cutting the steel one off. I think we can guarantee our cases will be searched after check in."

Val switched the television off, "so what do you think will happen when they find nothing, because there's nothing to find," she said.

"That's their dilemma," said Colburn, "we just act nice and show them all the digital photos we've took and smile. In the end we'll wave them goodbye."

"And pick up our tail again in England," said Jim, "surely now the Americans are involved they won't let it rest there."

Colburn replied, "I have a feeling the Americans have always been involved and yes, they won't let it rest, I wouldn't. Now if we're ready for today, let's go."

Down the elevator, into the lobby area and straight to the newspapers. Colburn sat in a chair, put his feet up and smiled. "I reckon if we get there about one, it should be enough time to have a good look around. Today is going to be a great history lesson."

Val said, "our friends are getting ready to move out there, must have spotted us."

Jim replied, making a coffee, "give it about thirty minutes, then we'll go. Should have got them edgy by then. Three sugars, Colburn?"

After thirty minutes, all three put on their backpacks and left the hotel. They strolled down Massachusetts Avenue to Thomas Circle circumnavigated the roundabout continuing on to Mount Vernon Place. The traffic was lighter this morning, crossing the roads was a little easier. Far to the East across the Potomac River they could see dark clouds beginning to mass. Their colour seemed more purple than grey but the wind was light so the cloud movement was slow. At the moment the sun burned down a glorious eighty degrees.

They turned down 9th street, passing the Washington Renaissance Hotel on the left. Hardly talking, occasionally stopping to peer into a shop window, not to check out the sales but to get a reverse reflection across the street. Their shadows were still there.

Passing the Reynolds Center and the American Art Museum, Jim jokingly remarked, "wonder if we would ever get a trade stand in there?" He pointed to the building on their left.

Colburn looked across, "only if we were found out," he replied.

It was the International Spy Center.

Continuing on past the FBI Building, Val said, "we should have asked for a visit there. It may have saved them some time and money."

"At least we can talk freely here. The chemicals plastered on those walls and windows block out anyone trying to listen in," said Colburn.

Walking on he noted, "as long as we don't end up in there."

Val and Jim looked over.

It was the Department of Justice.

Nearing Constitution Avenue Jim let out a quiet groan, "didn't think there would be a queue today, just look at that."

The side entrance of the National Archives already had dozens of people forming a line.

Colburn remarked, "it's not as bad as yesterday, got no choice, we wait."

The people in the line stretched down the concrete ramp leading to the door down onto the sidewalk and paralleling the avenue. Most seemed to be school children on an outing, dressed in jeans or shorts and T- shirts with the usual nametag hung around their necks. Not many appeared to be normal tourists. The teachers were trying to keep order during the boredom of waiting. Attempting to explain the history before they entered. At least the history from the American point of view.

The three of them joined the line, occasionally taking a swig of water from their bottles.

Suddenly the line moved.

People were entering the building.

The line decreased, they were no more than ten feet from the door when the movement stopped.

One of the teachers at the front of the line shouted over to those behind, "they're only letting about one hundred in at a time."

"Great," said Jim.

"We're in no hurry," said Colburn.

Val was observing the young kids running about, drinking Coke, checking their dollar bills and making an unholy noise.

A teacher standing next to her said, "sorry about the kids, they're just excited."

"That's OK," replied Val.

"You're from England?" said the teacher.

"Yes," replied Val, "just here for a long weekend, researching some history."

"That's what we're trying to teach the kids," said the teacher.

"That's good," replied Val, "but the history we're following goes back far more than the Independence War. Back at least to 1346, where a forerunner of Washington fought at a battle in Northern England and his family dates back to the year 1000 AD."

"Gee, I never realised that the family went back that far," said the teacher.

"Well, I suppose that's the difference between your history and ours. Yours seem to start when us English colonised this place. Ours starts back way before the Romans came over. If you ever come to Britain, don't stay in London, come up North. We have more castles and cathedrals than anyone else does over there," said Val.

After another forty minutes, the people at the front of the queue suddenly stood erect.

"Looks like we're on the move," said Jim.

The line filed through the doors and toward the security area.

Coats, belts, wallets and anything carried was placed on the conveyor belt of the x-ray machine. Body searches were continuing on the far side, before picking up belongings. This seemed more thorough than the airport.

All three packs and coats were placed on the belt. Walking through the search area and being patted down by security, one of the guards called them over.

"Could you open your bags please?" he said.

"That's no problem," replied Colburn as he reached to pick up his pack. The others did the same.

"Hey, you're English?" said the guard.

"We all are," replied Colburn, opening his bag and pulling out street maps, reading book and then his sandwiches.

The guard stared at the sandwich. Three-quarters covered in tin foil, with limp lettuce and meat hanging out the end.

"Hell, that's what they are," said the guard. He shouted over to his partner.

"It's their lunch."

Val and Jim took out their sandwiches and showed the guards.

Val said, "we got the hotel to put us up a packed lunch. We were not sure how many places would be open on a Sunday."

"That's fine," said the guard, "you all have a nice day now."

He waved all three through.

The layout of most attractions in America means that

you have no choice than to go into the shop prior to the exit. Val thought, at Dollywood by Pigeon Forge, the main shop is the exit. You have no other way out. This shop was central between the entrance stairs and the exit stairs on the far side, leading you out onto 7th street.

Colburn said, "we can shop later but for now I'm buying a copy of the Magna Carta."

The shop was the typical museum shop.

Countless copies of the Declaration of Independence, Constitutions, books galore and tacky reminders of you being there.

Colburn purchased a copy, stuck it in the side of his pack, paid twenty dollars plus tax for the privilege and walked out.

They were on the ground level.

The lower level comprised of the William McGowan Theater, the theater lobby and Charters Café.

The main exhibit level was the next floor up.

The stairs led straight into the Rotunda area that held the Charters of Freedom.

Off to the right was the Presidential Conference Center, comprising of the Washington, Jefferson, Madison and Adams Rooms.

To the left were the Boeing Learning Center where the resource room provided methods and materials for teaching and the Lawrence F. O'Brien Gallery where special exhibitions showcasing National Archive holdings and travelling exhibitions from Presidential Libraries were featured.

The rear of the building contained the Public Vaults. These were not open to the public on Sundays. That was a pity. In those stacks and vaults were the records of all three branches of the Federal Government. They also contained interactive vaults where you can learn, discover and create. In here were documents, recordings, maps and photos that revealed the stories that made history.

Val thought, "maybe some other time, if we're allowed back in the country."

They climbed the steps, following the crowds up to the Rotunda area.

Here the lighting appeared extremely dim, obviously to try and maintain the integrity of the old parchments.

Four steps led into this area and the crowds were already lining up again waiting to be allowed in. The female guard dressed in her grey uniform of jacket and trousers, was a coloured lady no more than five feet in height.

Jim noted that when she descended the steps, she was out of sight, the crowd masking her from view.

Eventually she stationed herself on the top step. She was directing the flow of the crowds into some form of queue. After waiting over one hour to get in, you had to queue again to obtain entrance into the Rotunda.

What the crowds had come to see was the original Declaration of Independence, the Constitution of the United States and the Bill of Rights.

These were exhibited around the semicircular Rotunda in glass cases, obviously electronically guarded.

The three of them waited patiently in the queue. They were allowing about forty people in at a time.

Eventually they climbed the four steps and entered the Rotunda, being allowed only to begin on the left and work around to the far exit in a clockwise manner.

The Rotunda was a large room but not massive. The

tall dome appearing to fly away into the Washington sky.

On the walls were two large murals created to animate the architecture and to convey to visitors the importance of the documents.

The left mural depicted the Declaration of Independence. Jefferson presenting a draft copy to John Hancock.

The mural on the right depicted James Madison offering the final draft of the Constitution of the United States to George Washington.

Val noted with reverence the enormity of the history they showed.

Jim had to make his usual comment, "if they had lost, all those would have been hung. What they did was high treason."

People moved slowly around each glass showcase, usually spending more time at the parchment of the declaration. It was surprisingly faded. They could hardly make out any words. Hancock's signature was still apparent but the others you could only make out with a leap of faith. The glass case appeared to have laser protection. One small schoolboy leaned on it and the telltale red laser lines appeared from the sides. The guard at that point quickly ushered the boy off the exhibit.

After spending some twenty minutes examining the parchments, all three wandered out of the right hand exit along past the Conference Center and back into the main dimly lit corridor of the rotunda.

There seemed to be a never-ending flow of visitors, coming in, waiting, and then going out.

Colburn said to Val, "something we need to check out from here."

The three descended the rear stairs to the lower level.

A couple of marble benches sat in the middle of the corridor outside the theater.

There were a few people milling around but only using the restrooms.

They walked to the side of the theater lobby.

Charters Café was in darkness.

Jim said, "just as well we've got sandwiches, this isn't open on Sundays."

There was the usual seating area at one side of the café with plastic tables and seats.

All were immaculately clean. At the other side were stainless steel worktops. The food was obviously prepared in this area and kept hot or cold.

Colburn leaned over the top of the worktop.

"There's sliding doors on the other side," he said, "Val keep watch at the entrance I need a look in."

Val moved to the entrance of the café, no one was in the corridor.

"All clear," she whispered.

Colburn and Jim walked round the benches. There seemed three rows of these all perfectly cleaned ready for Monday.

Jim said, "we could sleep under there," pointing to the storage area under the benches.

Colburn replied, "that's the idea, security wouldn't need to inspect these. They certainly would check the restrooms thoroughly."

They returned to where Val was standing.

Val said, "I was just wondering where our tails were. I haven't noticed them since we came in."

Colburn replied, "they'll be covering the exits, there's no other way out."

"Then how do we make it out then?" asked Jim.

"They'll not be there in the morning. They will assume they've missed us and check the hotel. When they see Val they will assume we're in or coming in," said Colburn.

"Or out for a drink?" said Jim.

"Precisely," said Colburn, "now let's go and have a look at our objective."

They climbed the stairs past the entrance level and back up to the main level.

As they re-entered the Rotunda corridor, sitting on their right in it's own alcove, was the exhibit of the Magna Carta.

In the West Rotunda Gallery alcove the exhibit was displayed in an all glass case on four free standing legs. It, like the other parchments was dimly lit.

Jim casually dropped his pack down and sat on the floor by the stand.

The crowds waiting to enter the Rotunda obscured the security staff's view. No cameras were seen pointing this way.

Jim leaned under the exhibit.

"Seems like it's glass all round, can't see any electrics though," said Jim.

Colburn put his hands on the glass and leaned to create a little pressure.

"Anything happening Jim?" he said.

No laser lights were seen.

"Jim said, "I'll check it later but I don't think it's wired."

Jim stood up and moved round the other side. Colburn and Val peered into the glass from above.

"You're the expert Jim, how do you reckon we can get it out," said Colburn.

"I can cut some of the glass from the bottom and slide my hand in. It will come out," said Jim.

"Fine," said Colburn, "can you get it back in?"

"No problem," said Jim, "I'll need some glue for the glass. It'll be ages before they notice."

Colburn smiled, "notice what, we're not stealing it. We're putting it back. You can buy glue in the shop. OK now, it's nearly four. Time to get to the shop and Val and I can perform our great finale."

Jim went downstairs first into the shop and bought the glue and a picture sticker book. He thought it might be noticed if someone bought just glue.

Passing Val and Colburn on the stairs he said, "meet you in the café."

Colburn nodded and carried on down past the shop to the exit area.

There were three security men in various positions guiding the crowds out.

As they approached the first guard, Colburn squeezed Val's hand.

"Now," he whispered.

Only a couple of feet from the first guard, Val whipped round quickly and faced Colburn.

"What did you just say?" she shouted indignantly.

"I said that we were going to have a boys night out," replied Colburn smugly.

"And just leave me sitting in," retorted Val.

"You can go where the hell you like," shouted Colburn.

"Yeah, you two go to Hooters all night and I sit in," said Val, "I don't think so."

The nearest security man stepped in, "could you keep your voices down," he said.

Val turned and glared at him, "you know what he wants to do tonight, go to Hooters and drink."

Colburn jumped in, "so what?" Val pushed Colburn away. He fended off her advances.

Val angrily replied, "so what, you go where you bloody like, I don't care, I'm going back to the hotel."

She stormed off past the security men and as she reached the exit door she turned, "don't wake me up when you come back, you're in enough trouble."

Not only did all the security hear but two of the surveillance team heard it also.

That was the intention.

Colburn turned to the security guard, "you know, someone once asked me how many happy years of marriage I'd had. I told them two but I've been married twenty."

The security man half smiled, "calm down now Sir, I'm sure all will end up OK," he said.

Colburn was still raging, "what's the problem about having a few beers in Hooters?" he said.

The guard laughed, "well nothing, it's more like an institution over here. Well worth having a look."

"That's what I was trying to tell her," said Colburn, "she thinks the place is full of shapely young girls."

"It is," replied the guard.

Colburn calming down now said, "I know that but I wasn't going to tell her."

The guards were laughing.

Scores of people were passing and staring.

"Look," said Colburn, "I'm just going back into the shop, maybe I can buy her something."

He turned and walked back, noticing all the guards were busy again ushering the crowds out. They had enough to concentrate on. He went straight to the stairs and down. Jim was sitting on a bench outside the restrooms.

"How did it go?" asked Jim.

Val and I had a row, she stormed off back to the hotel," said Colburn.

"Exactly as planned," said Jim.

"Exactly," replied Colburn, "she will lead them a dance back to the hotel. At least one will follow. With all these crowds the others will think they've missed us, just like before. It will be another set of guards here in the morning. When we leave the exit guards will think we've had a quick visit."

"OK," said Jim, "which stainless steel bed do you want?"

Jim and Colburn walked into the café, round behind the benches, picked the row farthest from the entrance and slid back the bench doors.

They unpacked their backpacks.

They climbed in. There was ample room for two of them. They laid down using their packs for headrests.

"Now can I eat my sandwiches?" said Jim.

"Just be careful you don't swallow any tools," said Colburn.

They both took out their sandwiches and an orange drink.

Colburn whispered, "eat heartily my friend, it's the last for a while. Got the tools ready?"

"Sure have," replied Jim.

He devoured the sandwich, polished off the drink and lying down closed his eyes.

Colburn pulled the doors shut and laid down.

"Time check for 0200 hours," he said.

Jim looked at his watch, set a buzzer alarm and slept.

Nothing was going to happen until then.

Security would thoroughly check every room in the place and they would certainly check the café but not the bench shelves.

It was lock down time until early morning.

Any security patrols could be timed.

It would take less than ten minutes to diamond cut the glass.

If any security did observe the exhibit, the copy would be in place.

Colburn and Jim had to examine the parchment then replace it.

The security cameras were looking into the rotunda and corridor so as long as they kept out of view, all would be OK.

What could go wrong?

EARLY HOURS MONDAY MORNING.

Jim nudged Colburn with his foot and whispered, "we've got company."

Footsteps were plainly heard. First coming down the steps, then along the corridor and into the café area.

Through minute cracks in the steel doors, they could see flashlights apparently checking the area.

No one had been down here before and this was nearly two in the morning.

The lights seemed to be searching up and down the aisles of the benches.

Colburn and Jim steeled themselves.

They both knew they would have to leap out and overpower the guards quickly.

That would present little problem but then a fast change in plan would be necessary and an escape now would alert the authorities too soon.

They heard one set of footsteps stop outside the bench they were hiding in.

Jim coiled himself ready to attack.

Another set of steps alerted Colburn.

He touched Jim on his leg twice, indicating two but held his hand there.

Jim knew that meant, not yet.

The flashlights were searching all over the café.

Suddenly one of the guards shouted out, "there it is, I knew it was down here."

Colburn and Jim waited, sweat started to appear on their brows. They were ready to spring out.

"I'll get it," answered another voice, "keep your light on there."

Colburn and Jim had to wait; any movement now would give the game away.

Were these guards still checking for unwanted visitors?

There was no way of knowing.

All they could do was to be ready to attack and silence the guards.

The sound of rubber suction was heard.

The creaking of hinges.

A bright light shone outward into the café.

Movement towards the light, footsteps slightly fading but voices still audible.

The guards were searching.

"Got it," one shouted, "it was here."

"Thank God for that," said the other guard, "let's get it upstairs."

The creaking of hinges was heard again and the light seemed to disappear.

Footsteps were leaving the café area.

"I hate having to use creamer in my coffee. I knew there would probably be cartons of milk in that Fridge. Now I can enjoy my drink," said one of the guards.

Colburn's grip on Jim eased.

Both wiped a little perspiration from their brows.

"Might as well start now," whispered Colburn, "while they are having a brew."

They both eased out from inside the bench.

Standing up they stretched a few times, picked up their kit and silently made their way out of the café.

There were no lights on downstairs, everything in total blackness.

Above they could hear the rumbling of the forecasted thunder followed by lightening flashes.

The storm seemed directly overhead.

Creeping to the stairs, they eased their way up the steps to the ground level.

They heard, between the thunder rumbling, guards obviously watching television and chatting.

They crept round the corner and up the steps to the main level.

There were restrooms to the right and restrooms directly behind the wall at the rear of the Magna Carta exhibit.

Colburn whispered, "we'll use those if necessary, one of us in each."

Jim nodded.

The main gallery floor was dimly lit as usual giving it more of a ghoulish feel in the air. Punctuated with lightening flashing down through the dome, it seemed reminiscent of an episode of the Adam's Family.

Colburn knelt down and shone his pen torch across the floor.

No red lights.

The floor area was clear, probably only laser technology in the Rotunda.

Crawling at floor level, they eased their way forward to the exhibit stand.

Jim placed himself underneath the stand and shone his pen torch at the glass bottom of the case.

Colburn crawled next to him.

Jim leant over and whispered, "I can see the underside of the parchment but this torch is just splitting into the spectrum through the glass. There's nothing apparent to read."

"To be expected," said Colburn, handing Jim the diamond edge cutter.

Jim took the cutter and slowly scribed a rectangle near the base of the glass exhibit.

"Shit," he said, "it's too thick to cut right through. Hand me my other pen torch."

Colburn handed Jim the torch.

Flicking a few switches on the side of the pen and turning the end as if extracting the graphite lining from a pencil, a bright red beam suddenly shot out of the end.

Pointing this beam over the area he had just cut, he re-traced the path of the rectangle.

This was a miniature laser beam, set just to the thickness of the glass.

He was nearing the end of the cut, when he stopped.

"Hand me the rubber suction pad," he asked Colburn.

Colburn found the pad in Jim's pack and handed it to him.

Jim placed the pad near the centre of the glass cut and fixed it there.

He continued the laser cut and at the last moment, grabbed at the rubber pad as the glass fell away.

He placed it behind him out of sight.

Reaching up with his right hand into the exhibit, he grasped the lower end of the parchment and slowly started to pull it down.

The parchment eased out.

He handed it to Colburn who took out the copy he'd bought at the shop, unrolled it in the opposite direction to flatten it and handed it to Jim.

Jim slowly eased the copy back into the glass case until it was in the exact position.

He picked up the cut glass piece and placed it in his pack.

"Let's get back down," he whispered.

They both crawled off to the stairs stood up and retraced their steps back to the café.

Once back in the dark of the café, Colburn unrolled the parchment on the bench and examining the reverse.

Shining only a pen torch, he could see no discernible writing on the back.

Whispering to Jim he said, "no obvious detection by white light."

Jim groaned quietly, "didn't think it would be that easy."

Colburn rummaged through his pack and brought out a small box.

It contained the coloured lenses.

These fitted into the side of his pen torch and measured the full range of the white light spectrum, from the infra red to the ultra violet.

By swapping each lens, small variations in wavelength could be made, just like the old laboratory spectrophotometers.

He whispered to Jim, "dependant on what ink was used, obviously old invisible types, they should be able to be read at one of these wavelengths.

The lenses could check wavelengths from 200 to 800 nanometers.

Starting with the red lens at the lowest wavelength, Colburn scanned the back of the parchment.

Nothing was observed.

It was on his third change of lens, about 540 nanometers, that Colburn nudged Jim.

"We've hit pay dirt."

Jim looked over his shoulder.

"Good God," he said, "isn't science wonderful. If you read it out, I'll write it down."

Colburn started at the top of the parchment.

The writing was quite large and descriptive.

The first line read; Dragon, Great and Grymme.

Second line; Full of Fire and Venymme.

Third line; Wide Throat and Tuskes Grete.

Colburn stretched up.

"That it then?" said Jim.

"I've checked all the back, that's it," replied Colburn.

"All this work for that," said Jim, "it's not even a rhyming clue."

"Suppose it must mean something," said Colburn, "let's get it back, we can think about it later."

As Colburn lifted one corner of the parchment, his pen fell and rolled a little.

A couple of the lenses fell out.

A faint violet colour shone out of the pen, nearing the ultraviolet range. It was closer to 700 nanometers. It shone on the bottom corner of the parchment.

"What the Hell," Colburn stopped in his tracks. He picked up the pen and scanned the parchment.

In the bottom right corner, new letters appeared.

"There's more writing here," exclaimed Colburn, "must have used different inks."

"Read on," said Jim.

Letters read; None but the Brave and Bould.

"Sure you've got it all," said Jim.

"That's all that's showing up" replied Colburn.

He quickly scanned the intermediary wavelengths but nothing else emerged.

"That's the lot," said Colburn, "now let's get it back."

Retracing their previous steps to the main level, they could hear television programmes coming from the entrance level, drowned by the occasional thunderclap.

Crawling back under the exhibit, Jim felt for the copy and pulled it out.

Colburn handed him the original and he slid it back into position, using angled forceps to hold up the top layer of a plastic cover.

Taking the tube of glue out of his pocket, he squeezed a little around the edge of the glass attached to the rubber sucker. Then he replaced the glass into the cut position and removed the sucker.

He whispered to Colburn, "unless they look underneath, no one will notice there's been a problem. By the time they do, we'll be long gone. No robbery though."

Colburn saw that all the kit and their copy of the Magna Carta, was packed away and they crept back to the café.

"All we have to do now is wait until morning and file out with the crowds," said Colburn.

"I'm getting some more sleep," said Jim, "I'll worry about that in the morning."

Colburn mused over a few thoughts; "this place will be open at ten. Café staff may be in before then. We'll probably have to relocate."

"I know," said Jim, "in the restrooms again."

"We'll go out with the first exit of visitors. There'll be a different shift of security staff on in the morning. No one will have seen us come in," said Colburn.

"Hopefully no one who heard your play acting with Val," replied Jim.

It was about eight-thirty when Jim heard the first footsteps coming down the stairs.

Shortly after that, they heard buckets being moved and the slop of water on the floor.

The cleaners were in.

Jim and Colburn waited at the entrance to the café until the cleaner had decided to work in the restroom.

Then they both headed for the opposite staircase and drew breath as they stopped for a moment.

"Change of plan then?" asked Jim, "we can't play hide and seek on the staircases for another hour."

Colburn thought it over. The different escape scenarios had been going through his mind all night but he knew there was only one exit. They had to stay hidden until after opening time.

"Let's get up to the main level but hug the corridor walls out of sight of the cameras and head for the Conference Center," said Colburn.

Jim never argued the point.

In the main level they made their way round the walls past Madison, Jefferson, Washington onto Adams. There were restrooms opposite if required.

Colburn tried the door on Adams.

It turned.

"Get in here," he said pulling Jim by the arm.

Inside was an amphitheatre for audience and speaker and plenty of cover behind the speaker's rostrum.

They headed straight over and sat on the floor behind the large lectern.

The heart rate reduces fast. In well-trained people, a couple of minutes brought it back to below 70 beats per minute. They soon recovered.

The adrenaline rush took a little longer. The rise in

adrenaline is mirrored by an increase in lactic acid. They stretched out their legs and massaged them for several minutes. The lactate would soon be back down in the aerobic range.

Closing their eyes, they waited.

Jim couldn't help his comment, "we're in the Adams Room aren't we?" he asked, "I've always wanted one of his fireplaces in my house."

Colburn looked at him, breathed deeply and closed his eyes, ignoring the inane comment.

Nothing was happening, time passed.

Over the silence came the sound of voices.

They both breathed a sigh of relief.

The sound was visitors, excited chatter, kids screaming, parents and teachers trying to restrain them. It was the sound of Heaven.

They both got up and walked to the door. Sliding it open a fraction, Colburn looked out into the corridor.

"Now, straight across into the restroom, Go," he said.

Jim only needed three paces and he was inside, Colburn followed.

"Let's give it at least twenty minutes. If someone comes in, we wash our hands and go," he said.

Only about twelve minutes had passed when a typical looking Virginian walked in. Built like a brick outhouse, six-six and at least 22 stone.

Colburn and Jim were washing up, splashing water on their faces and drying themselves with the paper towels.

They both smiled and nodded at the guy as they passed to go to the door.

Outside Jim commented, "see what he was carrying?"

"I noticed," replied Colburn.

"It's a takeaway from Wendys. The last thing he needs is something to eat. Candidate for a heart attack, I reckon," said Jim.

They ambled past Madison back into the main level corridor of the Rotunda.

Peering carefully around the corner, Colburn noticed dozens of people already forming a queue and plenty going out.

He turned to Jim, "when they start to leave we'll join them."

Jim nodded in approval.

They walked past the rear of the queue and glanced at the Magna Carta.

"It looks really peaceful sitting there," said Jim.

"Looks as if it hasn't moved for years," Colburn said and smiled.

A large party of schoolchildren was leaving the Rotunda area. One of their teachers was frantically trying to explain the reasons for the US Constitutions, while shepherding her group down the stairs.

Colburn and Jim tagged along. Before reaching the ground level, they found themselves in the middle of the group.

The first wave of children was exiting.

Jim was nearing the first guard who looked at him inquisitively.

Was he going to stop him?

Jim suddenly waved his hand as if to motion the kids through.

Several of them passed him and walked to the exit. Jim followed smiling at the guards but putting on a look of exasperation, as if fed up with the kids.

Colburn saw the acting and repeated it, without speaking, grumbling under his breath as if cursing the children.

Then they were outside.

They quickly scanned the area for their followers.

None seemed in evidence.

They hurried up 7th and down into the Metro at Penn.

Taking the Green Line as planned, they changed at the next stop, Chinatown to the Red Line and out to Union Station.

Coming out into the station area, they saw it festooned with elegant shops and cafes unlike most ex-rail stations you would see.

Colburn searched for the phone card and pulled out the taxi number.

"Now find a phone before the balloon goes up."

There were ample phone stations around. Colburn inserted all the code numbers on the phone card and eventually dialled the taxi.

The taxi driver certainly remembered him.

"We're at Union Station, can you pick us up. We need to go to the airport?" asked Colburn.

"Sure," came the reply, "wait out in front. I'll have to pull in where the other taxis are."

"What's your number, so I can spot you?" said Colburn.

The taxi driver replied and said "ten minutes, out front."

They made their way outside into the sunlight. All the storms had passed.

They looked over to 3rd street.

"Can't see any of our friends around," said Jim.

"How nice of them not to say Goodbye," replied Colburn.

"Wonder if they'll notice anything in the Archives," said Jim.

"In time," said Colburm.

Sure enough in about ten minutes, they saw their taxi pulling up.

They piled in.

"Had a good visit?" asked the driver.

"Absolutely fabulous," replied Jim.

"Where's your wife, not leaving her are you?" said the driver.

"No, of course not. She's doing some last minute shopping, meeting us at the airport," said Colburn.

With that the driver headed down 3rd, across D.Street, up North Capitol Street to New York Avenue and out to the airport.

At a similar timing, Val had tipped the bellboy taking the luggage to reception, instructing him to call her a cab.

Down in the lobby she paid the two room bills and when the taxi pulled up outside she thanked the staff, left 10 dollars on reception desk and went out.

The bellboy put the luggage into the trunk and said, "have a good trip home."

Inside the taxi, Val said, "Washington International please," and settled down.

She could see some frantic movement and communications from and between the surveillance across the road. One car started up and followed.

The play was coming to a climax, she thought.

It was a pleasant ride to the airport, especially on a sunny day.

Eventually the taxi pulled in to International Departures.

She had already spotted Jim and Colburn waiting outside the main door.

As she got out of the taxi, she waved them over.

The driver took the three cases out of the trunk and Val tipped a ten over the odds.

"Thank you ma'am," he said, "have a good flight."

Jim and Colburn got their cases.

"Successful trip then?" asked Val.

"Got some more writing," replied Colburn.

Suddenly they all turned hearing a screeching of tires and seeing smoke billow up from a now stationary sedan.

Four suited men got out and began making their way towards them.

"Here we go again Val, play time," said Colburn.

Just within earshot of the security men, Val started.

"Don't you honey me asshole. Left me in the hotel while you two go on the drink and you stop out all night. Don't you dare speak to me."

Quite a lot of travellers were passing, trying not to hear what was going on.

"I'm sorry but we just didn't notice the time and when it got too late, I didn't want to disturb you," said Colburn almost pleading.

Val shouted back, "disturb me, you're the one that's disturbed. Wait until you're home. You'll pay for this dick head."

A security man was seen on a microphone obviously reporting in.

He said, "he's in trouble with his wife. The men look like shit. They've been out drinking all night."

He seemed to get a reply, or an order.

He waved to the other men to return.

Val and Colburn were still shouting entering the airport automatic doors.

Then they closed behind them.

All seemed quiet now apart from the usual loud voices of an airport departure lounge.

"Now let's get booked in," said Colburn, "hope you remembered our tickets and passports Val?"

"You'd be in the proverbial if I had forgotten," replied Val.

They all joined the check-in queue, eventually handing over their passports and E-tickets and getting their boarding cards.

Their cases were tied with the plastic strips, so if anyone wanted to search them, they could.

There was a few pair of used mens socks placed strategically on the top of the clothes. They were welcome to them.

Eventually they joined the usual queue for the x-ray machine, snaking around the makeshift aisles. Without any problems they exited that area and into the large duty free area of the departure lounge. One of the staff had even looked at the copy of the Magna Carta Colburn had stuffed down the side of his backpack. Keeping everything in plain sight was the easiest way of hiding anything. Looking at the mark that said "Copy," he rolled it back up and had handed it back to Colburn.

Still with three hours to go to take off, they found some seats and flopped down.

Colburn said, "I'm shutting my eyes for an hour, then we might have a hot dog or burger, fancy it?"

"I'm with you," said Jim, settling down and closing his eyes.

"Are you going to tell me then?" asked Val.

"What?" replied Colburn.

"Whatever it was you found," Val whispered in his ear.

Colburn opened his eyes and looked at her, "the walls have ears, wait until we're in the air."

"OK," said Val, "I'll look forward to that but I intend to sleep. Remember this is an overnight flight, so I reckon it can wait until we're back in England."

"Probably for the best, just in case the Air Marshall has a listening device," said Jim without opening his eyes.

They all settled back, Val took out her book and read.

Colburn and Jim had their eyes closed but always attentive to the surroundings.

Time for some seems to drag at airports but if you plan your time, it goes quick.

They never bothered eating.

Val eventually nudged both of them.

"Gates been called," she said.

They stood up and stretched, then ambled off with the rest of the travellers to the designated gate.

There they sat another thirty minutes, when eventually the call came, Flight 207 is ready for boarding.

The three were nearly last to board, luckily the flight wasn't full.

Still ample room in the over head locker.

Jim flopped down into his aisle seat. "As soon as the Fasten Seat Belt sign is off, I'm sleeping," pulling the blanket out of the plastic bag already.

"Me too," said Colburn, "Val just tell the stewardesses not to disturb us until breakfast. Sorry about this love but I'm knackered."

Val smiled at him and pulled the blanket over his legs.

He found his facemask and earplugs and settled down.

It's hard to sleep with the seat in the upright position, so Colburn and Jim merely closed their eyes.

It wasn't long before they felt the plane taxi out, another twenty minutes on the runway, then with the forward momentum increasing and a backward movement with the body, Colburn thought, "Newton was right, every action has an equal and opposite reaction."

The take off was smooth and eventually the seat belt light went out.

Colburn and Jim put their seats back, pulled up their blankets and went to sleep.

Val thought, "I might as well travel on my own, so much for their company."

Eventually the time of day caught up with her and she slept.

The smiling faces of the girls with the trolleys woke everyone up with an hour to landing.

They served what appeared to be a croissant that had seen better days, a bottle of water, orange juice, butter and the complimentary plastic knife, fork and spoon.

A cup of tea after the so-called breakfast tasted like it had been made the day before but everyone was grateful for it.

Never mind deep-veined thrombosis because of lack of movement, the lack of good oxygen is just as bad with the side effect of dehydration.

That's why the three didn't take alcohol and used only bottled water.

With thirty minutes left, the breakfast was cleared away.

As soon as the trolleys had passed by, Val got up to use the toilets and spruce up.

Colburn and Jim just stood up and exercised for the circulation.

The captain's voice came over the loudspeaker system; "flight crew prepare for "landing."

Tray tables up, seats in upright position, no bags or shoes in the aisles and seat belts fastened.

Everyone on board begrudgingly obeys.

Eventually touchdown at Manchester.

The senior stewardess shouts into the PA system.

"Welcome to Manchester, England. Please stay seated until the aircraft has come to a complete stop at the gate."

As if people took notice of that.

The three just sat and waited until the line appeared to be moving, then got the bags from the over head locker and slowly ambled down toward the front of the plane.

Going through business class, Jim noted the blankets and newspapers strewn everywhere. He thought, "there's a lot of untidy folks flying today."

They exited the plane with the customary, "thanks for

flying with us," ringing in their ears and headed up the ramp towards immigration.

Colburn thought as he walked, "at least we're EU Passports, straight through to the carousel."

There wasn't much delay at customs, there never seems to be when you're coming home. The baggage handlers must have been working well, their luggage appeared quite quickly. They dragged their bags off the carousel and headed for the exit, green with nothing to declare.

Outside it was the usual throng of people waiting, ducking and diving all over to see who is coming through. Chauffeurs with names written on pieces of cardboard picking up the businessmen.

Colburn headed straight to the blue courtesy phone and dialled the number the hotel had given him.

A voice replied, "the minibus will be with you in five minutes. It's taking some folks for a drop off at departure."

"Thank you," replied Colburn. He turned to Val, who was still stretching and yawning, "five minutes outside they said."

Jim blinked as if the daylight hurt his eyes, "OK, let's go."

The minibus arrived on time, picked them up with their cases in the boot.

The drive back to the hotel parking was only ten minutes.

As they pulled into the parking area Colburn said, "just drop us off near reception."

They got out, tipped the driver, recovered their luggage and ambled up the car park to their car.

After loading up, they got in. Colburn drove and Jim sat next to him.

They left Val to sleep in the back.

As they pulled out onto the road and headed for the M56, Jim was the first to speak, "we've got company again."

"I spotted them," said Colburn, "hope they've had a nice break. Now let them follow us home. We need to see, at some time, who the hell they are."

"I'm game if you are," replied Jim.

The drive home was uneventful and tedious.

At least they were home and the Americans couldn't touch them.

When the glass at the bottom of that exhibit was eventually noticed, no one would be able to tell when it happened. So they were safe.

They let Val sleep until they were pulling into the Village, the drive only took two and a half-hours.

"We're home then?" she said.

"Right at your doorstep," replied Colburn.

He parked the car, unloaded the boot and the three of them headed into the house.

"Don't say it Jim," said Val.

"Say what?" replied Jim sounding astonished.

"I'll put the kettle on," said Val.

Colburn and Jim put the cases in the living room.

"When we sit down over tea, then I think its time to work out the latest piece of the puzzle," said Colburn, "are you feeling up to more trivia Val?"

Having had some sleep on the plane and in the car on the way home, Val was feeling reasonably awake. All of them knew that later that day, they would have to sleep to re-invert their body clocks. It may even be three days before their correct sleep patterns were resumed.

"OK," she said, "let me see what you discovered."

Jim took out a crumpled piece of paper from his top pocket, laid it on the table and flattened it out.

Val carefully mused over the words.

Colburn said, "the first few lines were apparent straightaway. Then I spotted the rest later, could be written by someone different or just another grade of ink."

Val was tracing out each line Jim had written with her finger.

"Now we know from past experience that each line usually is a clue itself," said Val.

"Well can you make anything from it?" asked Jim.

"At first glance, no," said Val, "but if you make another cup of tea. We'll try to fathom it out."

Jim plugged in the kettle, "shit," he shouted, "I've just had a belt of static."

"Now you know what I've been telling him for weeks, that's dangerous," said Val.

Jim dutifully made a pot of tea, three cups, plenty sugar for the boys and brought them out to the table.

Val was still musing, looking puzzled over the writing.

"Well, in my opinion, each line tells us nothing," she said.

"But it must lead us somewhere," replied Colburn.

"It is as it seems, merely stating in old English, a description of a dragon," she remained looking perplexed.

"It did come from Wales," said Jim, "the land of the dragon."

Colburn got up and ambled around the room apparently talking to himself.

"What we have is a description of a dragon. It can't be the St. George dragon. St. George was Roman soldier, can't have anything to do with this. There's nothing else in our history about a dragon.

This one was great and grim, full of fire and venom with a wide throat and great tusks.

That's how the old English is translated but it doesn't help at all."

"Is that all you saw in the writings on the parchment?" asked Val.

"Yes, apart from that notation near the bottom," replied Colburn.

"Well Jim's written None but the Brave and Bold," said Val.

"Let me see," said Colburn.

Colburn checked the paper carefully, "That's right, apart from Jim not spelling that word the same."

"Which word?" asked Val.

Colburn pointed to Jim's writing, "Jim's written the word Bold because that's how I pronounced it but on the parchment it was spelled Bould. Does it make any difference? In translation it means bold."

Val looked at him and smiled, "does the story of the Brave and the Bould, not ring a bell with either of you two?" she asked.

Colburn and Jim both had blank expressions on their faces.

"I'll give you another clue," said Val, "how about the Tale of the Brave and Bold, Sir John."

The boys still looked vacant.

"OK then try this, the Romance of Sir Dygore," said Val, "the story of an early fourteenth century knight returning from the Crusades."

Both Colburn and Jim broke into a smile.

"Well, Well, Well," said Jim.

"That's what's it's all about," said Colburn, "not a dragon as such, but a great big worm."

"Precisely," said Val, "what we have here is a description of the famous Lambton Worm.

And what did the brave and the bold do with the worm?

He threw it down a well."

"So," remarked Colburn, "I also think that this is a description of what we are looking for. It is great, grim, with venom full of fire. Rings a bell doesn't it?"

Jim said, "the fire of the Gods no less."

"Could well be," replied Colburn, "someone has known about this power, described it and hid it."

"OK," said Jim, "but where would it be hidden?"

Val stood up and stretched, "you two need to follow historical stories more. He threw it down a well. If any power had been seen from whatever we're looking for, in those days it would have been frightening to the point of magical. So you would want to dispose of it as soon as possible. You wouldn't take it far, too scary. Get rid of it fast, leave clues afterwards. So down the well it goes, just like young Lambton did. What we have to remember is the story would be well known by the Middle Ages. So anyone could use the story as clues."

"All we need now is to find a well," said Jim.

Colburn leaned over to a chest of drawers.

He took out an old map of the Cathedral and Castle at Durham.

Slapping the map on the table, he pointed to a part of the green inside the Castle compound, "X marks the spot," he said.

Jim and Val peered at the map at the place Colburn had indicated, it read;

"Site of Old Well."

Jim looked up from the table with an inquisitive look on his face.

"Over the last several days I've dug up an obelisk, robbed the Cathedral and Castle, borrowed the Lindisfarne Gospels and a Magna Carta, now you want me to find an old well and dig it up?"

"Sounds about right," said Colburn.

Jim smiled, "and all the time we've probably got British and American agents watching us."

"That's precisely the point," replied Colburn, "they're just watching, passive surveillance. They'll not make a move until they're ready."

"And when do you think that will be?" asked Jim.

"Not until we find something. Then they'll all want to know," said Colburn.

Val leaned back in the chair and stretched, "what plans have you got when they come calling?"

Colburn thought what the answer could be, then said, "haven't got a clue, make them a cup of tea and discuss it. Our priority is to locate the well and have a look down.

We have to get onto the Castle Green, locate a hole, dig down and see if we come up with anything."

Jim said, "and who do you think they'll let dig up the Castle Green?"

Colburn replied, "what I have in mind, is a workforce that digs up the ground, usually causing an inconvenience.

They have their working area covered by a little tent so no one can see what they are doing and people know they are there but take no notice."

Val said, "I know who you're thinking about and it just might work."

Jim was still looking puzzled, "OK," he said, "I give in, who are you thinking of impersonating now?"

Colburn and Val practically replied in unison, "BT."

"You know," replied Jim, "British Telecom dig all over and no one asks questions about what they are doing, it's brilliant. I can come up with their van and kit, no problem."

Colburn patted Jim on his shoulder, "I didn't think it would be a problem for you Jim."

Val got up from the table.

"I'll make us some bacon sandwiches. Then what I suggest is that we unpack and rest up, then you two can figure out the details of a BT incursion onto the Castle Green.

I don't know about you Jim but I'm getting tired, could do with a sleep in my own bed."

Jim said, "after bacon sandwiches, I'll go home, make a few phone calls and see you in the morning."

Colburn said, "don't use the BT landline, just in case, use your mobile. It takes longer to check those calls."

"Will do," said Jim.

The text message on the phone screen read, Lord home now? Continue watch. Americans confused.

Strane held the phone out and showed Doug the screen.

"Seems like you lot haven't got a clue, nothing changes does it?" he said.

Doug looked over his pint of beer, "over there no one talks to each other that's why they get confused."

"Just as well you and I have joined forces," said Strane, "what instructions are you getting?"

"Same as you," replied Doug, "watch and wait."

"Then what?" asked Strane.

Doug took a mouthful of beer, "the way I see this going is quite simple. If Lord finds anything, we take it away from him and report in."

Strane looked a little confused, squirming in his bar seat, "but whom do we report back to, your people, mine or both?"

Doug had a slight smile when he answered, "that's something you and I have to sort out but not yet."

CHAPTER TWENTY-SEVEN

Jim was back at his home making frantic phone calls, trying to borrow a BT van.

He wanted one of the newer ones, kind of cream white with a coloured world logo.

He knew that for a couple of hundred, he could have a loan of one that was already checked out to do repair work.

All that was required was that it had the full compliment of tools and equipment.

It would be delivered back, hopefully, in the same condition as he received it.

He needed the digging tools, the electrical sounding equipment for detecting cables but a pulley with nylon ropes was essential.

It wasn't too long before he received a call indicating that the van could be delivered to his home with all the equipment he had ordered.

He called Colburn in the morning to let him know.

"That was Jim Val, he's got the van and equipment," said Colburn replacing his phone on the charger.

"Now what?" asked Val.

"First we take the village bus into Durham with my

equipment," replied Colburn.

There were only four buses a day from the village and two of those were the school run. The others left at quarter to eleven and one.

Gathering up all the necessary tools, Colburn and Val locked the back door and ambled down their back lane and round onto the village green.

There was no bus stop as such in their village, you just waited in the middle and it stopped for you. That's idyllic village life.

Looking down the road they could see the bus coming along the road. Sure enough, it stopped and let them on.

Hardly anyone used the service. It was a wonder why it was still going.

They paid two adult fares of nearly three pounds each. It was no surprise that people used their cars, even with the cost of petrol rocketing.

The bus pulled away taking the twisting road towards Sunderland Bridge village and out onto the A167 heading north.

Just across the River Bridge, the bus pulled into a proper stop and three people got on.

Most of the people who got on at this stop were tourists staying at the hotel.

It was probably cheaper for them to leave their cars in the hotel car park.

Jock Strane looked up from his morning newspaper.

He was sitting with Doug in the hotel lounge area,

hoping their rooms would be cleaned first.

He saw the bus pulling in at the stop, people from the hotel were getting on.

"Jesus Christ," he shouted slamming the paper down.

"Just leave that coffee Doug, let's go."

"What's the problem?" asked Doug, seemingly reluctant to move.

"I've just seen Colburn Lord on that bus across the road, we need to follow it," said Strane.

Doug and Strane both made a beeline for the front exit and round to the right to their rooms. They had adjacent rooms, numbers four and five, their cars parked outside.

Taking Doug's hired car they reversed swiftly and then forward to the main road.

Pulling straight out, they headed after the local bus, which they spotted before the Cock of the North roundabout.

Then they slowly followed the bus through Durham.

At the Market Place stop, Colburn and Val got off.

Strane said, "let me off here and go and park up. Just follow the road round you'll see the car park signs. I'll follow them and phone you with directions."

He jumped out of the car and Doug drove off towards the Milburngate car park.

With plenty of people around, it was easy to follow without being noticed.

Colburn and Val walked up towards the Castle and Cathedral grounds.

Around the Palace Green, several couples were

enjoying the morning sunshine.

While it was frowned upon sitting on the grass, no one bothered you.

You just enjoy the atmosphere of one of the world's greatest heritage sites.

Strane dialled his cell phone, "get up to the Palace Green Doug, Colburn and his wife are nosing around up here."

He flipped his phone shut and quietly sat on one of the benches strewn around the green, observing Colburn and Val walking near to the Castle entrance.

Doug arrived about ten minutes later, Strane waving him over.

"They're just standing over there talking, must be up to something," said Strane.

"At least this time they're where we can see them," replied Doug.

Colburn seemed to ease his way over the grass below the castle wall near to the entrance. He sat down. Val quickly joined him.

He had noticed that the telephone cable to the entrance kiosk ran outside the wall and under the ground.

With nothing but a quick sleight of hand he gripped the cable close to the grass, hands behind his back.

Val deftly slipped him his Swiss Army Knife with the wire cutters open.

In one movement he cut through the wire. Both stood up and walked away to the road.

He took out his cell phone and dialled Jim.

"Whenever you're ready Jim, everything's set," he whispered into his phone.

"OK, Val would you like to have a look in the library

for a while? Jim will be about twenty minutes. You can stay in there, then go home on the next bus. Jim and I will be excavating."

A BT van pulled up outside the castle entrance.

Colburn walked over and Jim got out.

Doug nudged Strane, "there's something going on alright. What the hell is he doing with that van?"

Strane replied, "I guess they've decided to work another job, saves taking benefit."

"Let me do the talking," said Colburn, as they both strolled to the entrance kiosk.

The security guard was patiently directing visitors to various points of interest in the grounds.

"Good Morning," said Colburn, "we're here to check on the phone lines, there's been problems all over Durham."

"Nothing wrong with ours," replied the guard.

"Well, we were called from the Dean's office about intermittent breakdowns and we've traced the lines back up to here," said Colburn.

"I'll have to check for authority," replied the guard.

"By all means, we'll just bring up the van," Colburn smiled as he turned away.

The guard picked up his phone.

Nothing, it was dead.

"Funny," he said, "it was working a while ago."

"That's the problem," said Colburn, "it comes and goes. One of the hardest problems to locate the cause."

He took out his mobile.

"Have this call on BT," he said, "what number do you need?"

The guard looked on a checklist and shouted out a telephone number.

Colburn dialled the number and handed his phone to the guard.

"It's ringing," he said.

The guard took the phone, never looking at the screen and placed it to his ear.

A voice answered.

"Dean's Office."

"This is the Castle security. I have British Telecom here wanting to do work on phone lines. Is this OK?" asked the guard.

The voice replied, "unfortunately, yes. The Dean is furious that some of the lawn will have to be removed. We have been assured by BT that everything will be replaced as it was. Just tell them to go ahead."

"Thank you," said the guard and handed the phone back to Colburn, "just go ahead and do what you have to do."

"We're sorry for the inconvenience," said Colburn, "we just need to bring our van in."

Val Lord was sitting on a bench on the far side of the green.

She pressed the off button on her phone and flipped it shut, thinking, "I must have a polite telephone voice." She never even wondered who the Dean's secretary actually was.

Colburn and Jim got back in the BT van and drove it through the entrance and round the green. They parked opposite the Cosin's Staircase entrance, by the part of the green indicated on Colburn's old map.

Opening the back of the van, they unloaded most of the gear they expected to use.

First the ground surveying equipment.

Jim put on the earphones and started to survey the green in a grid system.

It had to look good, just as any BT worker would do.

This equipment included a type of ground sonar that would pick up solid objects deep underground.

Colburn used this type of sonar to locate shoals of fish in the rivers.

After surveying an area of about ten metres square, Jim stopped and examined the read out.

Colburn looked over his shoulder at the small screen.

"There's no doubt about it," said Jim, "it's showing a circular area about three feet across. Right where you would expect."

"Now," said Colburn, "we need to erect the tent over that area and start digging. How deep is it?"

"I reckon up to two feet of earth," replied Jim, "but I can't tell after that. It's probably pretty deep."

They took out the tent equipment and erected it over the area Jim had indicated.

Fastening it down with metal pegs. It looked like an elongated semicircle of red and white stripes.

Jim remarked, "At least it matches with Sunderland's colours."

"Let's hope there's no Newcastle supporters around then," answered Colburn.

Inside they started to remove the top turf and carefully

placed the sods outside the tent.

These would be going back into position on completion of the work.

That's if BT were doing the job.

Working on their knees, the topsoil came away easily and was piled up inside the tent.

Jim was working in the hole a couple of feet down, when his spade hit something solid.

Carefully excavating the rest of the soil, Jim exposed what appeared to be a metal lid covering a circular area.

"OK," said Jim, "now what?"

Colburn examined the lid.

"There's no obvious handles, so I can only assume the lid fits directly onto the well."

He started scraping around the circumference of the lid, revealing a small groove around the whole of the lid.

"Get the crowbars," said Colburn.

Jim went to the van and brought the crowbars back.

Colburn took one and placed one end into the groove and leaned on it.

There was a slight movement of the lid.

"Get a bar in the other side Jim and we'll lever together," said Colburn.

Jim placed his crowbar, opposite where Colburn had his.

"After three," said Colburn, "one, two, three."

The lid moved upwards.

Colburn grasped one side of the lid and pulled it away.

They both looked down.

Nothing but blackness.

"Now we need the flashlights," said Colburn.

Jim handed one to Colburn and they both shone the strong lights into the hole.

All that was apparent was dirty stones, overgrown with lichen and moss, spiralling down into blackness.

"How deep does it go?" asked Jim.

Colburn picked up a stone from the dug soil and dropped it down.

They listened intently.

Nothing.

"Well at least there's no water, however deep it is," said Jim.

"It must be at least two hundred feet above the river level," said Colburn, "there's no way it's that deep. The water must have been higher years ago and just receded over the years. Even when the river is in flood it barely reaches thirty feet higher than normal. It floods a few of the shops along the bank, even the supermarket car park. It never gets any higher. But that's not to say it didn't then."

"Fine," said Jim, "so we have to go down."

"Seems like it," answered Colburn, "we need the nylon rope and the pulley system in the van."

Jim went out to the van.

There were a few dozen visitors milling around.

Another tour was ongoing.

People looked at the van and tent but took no notice of the workmen.

Jim brought back the rope and pulley.

Colburn placed the pulley on some solid ground, dropped one end of the rope down the well and wound the other end around the two-pulley system.

Using this system would make it easier to support the

weight of a man's body for lowering and raising.

Colburn wrapped the nylon rope around him and fashioned a harness through his legs.

Jim checked the rope was moving freely through the pulleys.

All his pockets were loaded with gear that may be needed, small hammers, picks and especially lights, penlights and torches with extra batteries.

He started to lower himself into the void with Jim taking the strain.

"Just keep feeding the rope down, until I say stop," said Colburn.

He was lowered slowly examining the rotten stones of the well walls on the way down.

Jim shouted down, "this rope is only one hundred feet, be careful."

"No need," came the reply, "I'm standing on solid ground about forty feet down."

Colburn examined the walls with his flashlight.

All were covered in moss and lichen that had never seen the light of day for six hundred years. He wondered what kind of bacteria would be in there.

He shouted up to Jim, "we'll have to scrape these walls. You better tie the rope up and get down here."

"Will do," replied Jim.

Tying the middle of the rope around the pulley about the fifty feet mark, he dropped the free end down the well and started to climb down.

The floor was solid, covered with broken wood, stones and hard soil. Nothing to indicate anyone had been down there for years.

They began scraping the walls down to the bare stone

with their chisels.

The air down the well was stagnant to say the least.

Jim had already covered his nose with a handkerchief.

Working by the flashlight, slowly scraping clear years of anaerobic growth, something fell on their heads.

It was the remainder of the nylon rope.

The metal cover was closing the opening of the well above them.

Suddenly, apart from their torches, all was darkness.

"Jesus Christ," said Jim, "who the hell did that?"

Colburn grimaced, "obviously someone who wants whatever is down here, to stay down here. Now we have to get it out.

Jim flashed his torch at Colburn, "listen cousin, I don't care about getting out what's down here, we need to think about getting us out."

Doug and Jock Strane emerged from the tent.

"That'll give them something to think about," said Doug, " if they are after something, that's just concentrated their minds a little."

Strane wasn't so sure, "you don't piss off a bloke like Lord, if he comes after you, you run."

They both walked out of the castle grounds and returned to the carpark.

Colburn and Jim were entombed in the Castle well, air running out, time running out and no signal on the mobile. This time things did not look good for the duo. They had been through plenty of situations causing them concern before but this one had all the markings of an insurmountable problem.

Jim sank to the floor of the well, "this one is going to take a bit of thinking about. Can't climb back up, no holds and too steep."

Colburn was flashing his light around the walls, "if someone did come down here, they got out as well," he mumbled.

"They probably had a rope ladder," said Jim staring at the light on the wall from Colburn's torch, " at least there's no snakes down here."

"What makes you assume that?" asked Colburn.

Jim looked up from his sitting position and pointed to a place on the wall where the light from Colburn's torch was shining.

"Someone's drawn pictures on the wall. See where you've scraped it away, it looks like a snake being chased away. Maybe St. Patrick was here before he went to Ireland."

Colburn sat beside Jim and pointed the light at the wall.

"Looks like you're right," he said.

Colburn stood up and began to slowly scrape away more of the dirt around the picture area.

Suddenly he leaned on one hand against the wall and turned to Jim.

"I don't think this is a snake, it's the Lambton Worm being chased away."

They both frantically worked on clearing the area around the engraving and found it was only on one stone of the well.

"It has to be here," said Colburn, "we need to loosen the plaster around this stone."

Scraping with their hammer and chisels, the plaster around the stone began to break free. They seemed to have loosened the stone completely but there was no way of levering it out.

"OK," said Jim, "now what?"

Colburn thought for a moment, "if this stone was meant to be removed, let's say in the future, there would be a way of doing it. There's no lever mechanism for extracting it though."

"Like it said, only the brave and bold," said Jim.

"Sometimes Jim, you come up with miracles," said Colburn.

Jim looked puzzled, "do I?" he said but looking pleased with himself.

"Tell me Jim, how would the brave and bold go about this problem?" said Colburn

"Probably charge straight in head first," replied Jim.

"Exactly," replied Colburn.

"I'm not head butting that rock," cried Jim.

"No, we put our feet against it and push, instead of pulling," said Colburn.

It was too far across the well to push with their backs against the wall.

Turning around, they put their hands on one wall and one of their feet on the stone.

"After three," said Jim.

"OK," said Colburn, "three."

With the force of their feet pushing, the stone moved slowly inwards, then suddenly dropped out of sight.

They stood up and shone their torches into the hole.

"There has to be some kind of mechanism around," said Jim, "well, here goes."

He put his hand into the void and felt around.

Then he smiled.

"I knew it, there's a lever of some sorts in here."

"Then pull it Jim," said Colburn.

Jim pulled the lever. It moved slowly towards him. Suddenly Jim fell back into the well, as the lever moved back.

A grumbling sound was heard. Stone grinding on stone.

The section of well wall above and below where the picture stone was just fell away.

Looking into the dusty gloom, shining their lights, they could see a passage hewn out of the solid rock.

"I suppose we are meant to go this way," said Jim.

"Seems like it's the only way," replied Colburn, "so let's go."

Picking up their gear and the ropes, they stepped over the fallen masonry and into the passageway.

Taking one small step at a time, inching along the passage, using the torchlight to check the walls and floor for signs, clues, anything.

After about six feet of passageway, Colburn was leading when Jim cried out.

"Just gone into a pothole, felt like loose earth, nearly twisted my ankle."

He hardly got the words out of his mouth when they heard a thunderous roar behind them and a straight slab of solid rock fell down over the entrance and blocked where they had entered.

Jim lifted his foot and noticed a metal lever that he had stood on.

With the dust settling Colburn said, "so they made

booby traps did they? Clever sods. Looks like the only way is forward."

Jim, as usual, groaned "forward to where?"

Colburn was still smiling, "the thing is Jim, whoever built this got out. So there will be a way out, somewhere."

Jim retorted, "this could have been put in when the foundations of the Castle and Cathedral were built. How do we know they got out?"

Colburn replied, "we haven't seen any skeletons have we?"

"No," said Jim, "not yet."

"Right," said Colburn, "from now on we do the bomb disposal course. Check every step, before we put the foot down and follow this passage."

Jim pulled out his compass and flashed his light at it.

"From the angle of that hole in the well, this passage is practically due South, heading back under the Palace Green. We should only be thirty to forty feet underground, seems a bit much for foundations."

Colburn stopped and turned to Jim, "I think whoever built this was not intending anyone following them. This was built for a purpose."

There were no markings of any kind on the walls and they were not rough cut.

This passage had been made with first class masonry, smoothing the walls to a fine sheen.

Each step was carefully monitored, time was passing.

Oxygen debt was a possibility.

Jim used the nylon rope, making ten feet markers, to

monitor their progress.

"I reckon we should be just outside the Castle walls now," he said pulling through the rope to another marker.

Colburn turned to him, "and right under the moat outside, the one that Cosin filled in. Now we know why."

Jim looked past Colburn down the passage. There would have been an exit in former times, coming out in the side of the moat fortifications.

Not now, before them was an exit and carved on top of the exit was a figure.

Unmistakable from ancient history and mythology, a human with a bull's head, a Minotaur.

Colburn and Jim looked up at the carving.

There was only one way to go.

Inside they knew what they would find.

A Labyrinth.

They leaned against the rock face and looked at each other.

No words were spoken, it was never necessary between these two.

Just a collective sigh, a sound of resignation, a fact that these two had to play at being Theseus, only with booby traps.

"Have you ever been to Hampton Court, Jim?" asked Colburn.

"No," replied Jim, "have you?"

"I went there with Val a few years ago," said Colburn.

"And what happened?" asked Jim.

"We got lost," replied Colburn.

Jim just looked at him and groaned again, "great."

Colburn began to relate a story, "before we go any further, we need to remember the exact meaning of this situation. The name labyrinth is always associated with King Minos of Crete and the Palace at Knossus. Minos was only a title, like Caesar or Pharaoh. The rooms and passageways at that Palace are now thought to be the origin of the word labyrinth. There were over fifteen hundred of them, there can't be that many here."

Colburn inched into the next passage, while Jim waited.

Shining his torch all around he saw three exits carved into the stone.

"That's where it begins," said Colburn, "pick any one from three."

"At least there's only three. Surely there must be clues to the right one," said Jim.

"Doesn't look like it this time," replied Colburn, "its going to be a leap of faith. Better get roped up like mountaineers. I'll lead."

"You're welcome to it," replied Jim.

They checked their gear and supplies in their packs and tied the rope around themselves about three metres apart. Jim reeled up the other rope and draped most of it around his neck and shoulders.

The three entrances appeared to be hewn out of the solid rock but just before that the passage opened up into a larger area like a small courtyard.

Jim joked, "just like Dante's Inferno, abandon hope all ye who enter here."

Colburn was studying the floor, walls and ceiling.

Something seemed to be troubling him.

He thought if you go down one passage and you come to a dead end, you just turn round and come back. Then try another. Surely it can't be that easy.

He looked around the floor and walked over to pick up some large rocks, heavy ones.

"What do you need those for?" asked Jim.

"Something's not right here," replied Colburn.

Colburn placed the large rocks by his feet. Picking one he threw it hard onto the floor down one of the exits. The rock bounced away down the passage.

Suddenly an almighty clap like thunder occurred.

Not only did the whole floor of that passage collapse into a void, the roof caved in simultaneously filling the void. No one in there could have survived.

The dust was settling, Colburn seemed unmoved, "we'll not go that way then," he said, "looks like some of the moat filling has moved."

He flashed his torch along the passage.

Where the roof had caved in, there seemed to be a wooden structure for a secondary roof. He mused to himself, Cosin must have put in wooden flooring before filling in the moat. In dry soil the wood could have lasted another thousand years, clever man.

If this maze keeps going in this direction, not only will we go under the Palace Green but also we'll end up back at the Cathedral, any further and we'll be in the river.

"Right, Jim, that leaves us two entrances, any bets?" asked Colburn.

"Throw the stones down them both," said Jim.

Colburn heaved the stones down both tunnels, bouncing them heavily off the floor, nothing happened.

"Well it's anyone's guess now," said Colburn.

"Like it's how to confuse an Irishman," said Jim, "show him two shovels and say, take your pick."

"Jim your jokes get worse as you get older," said Colburn.

"The old ones are always the best," said Jim, "let's take the middle one."

Roped together they set off down the middle tunnel carefully examining every step, foothold, handhold and roof.

About thirty yards in, Colburn stopped. His flashlight was drawn to some obscure carvings on the wall.

Jim came up alongside him and peered at the pictures.

"It seems logical, before proceeding, that we have to make sense of those," said Colburn. "If you had an army of folks down here looking for treasure, you already had to split your troops into three parties. One would already be dead.

Logic dictates that something will befall the other searchers and it's not happening to us. So let's see what these are all about before we go on."

They both brushed away centuries of dust from the stone carvings.

As they examined the picture shining their torches, what appeared was a medieval knight in full armour, kneeling before another, having a sword on his shoulder.

Jim said, "it's looks like some bloke being knighted, that's all."

"That's probably what it is. It is the significance that's

important," said Colburn.

He thought on, "if continuing means knighthood then we have to kneel down, and crawl."

Jim picked a rock from the floor, "why don't we try the rock trick again?"

He threw the rock into the tunnel, bouncing it off the floor.

Suddenly, with a grating of metal, iron spikes appeared from both sides of the tunnel, intersecting each other.

Colburn turned and grabbed Jim's arm, "get back now."

Jim turned and ran, not stopping until he could see the tunnel exit where they had come in.

He felt the rope go tight, pulling him backwards. He dug his feet into the ground grasping the rope.

Turning round taking the strain, he couldn't see Colburn.

Keeping the strain on the rope, edging a few feet at a time, suddenly there appeared a vast chasm in the floor.

He looked over, a voice shouted.

"Don't just stand there, pull me up," Colburn was dangling in mid air over a gap in the ground. Jim couldn't see the bottom.

He pulled on the rope and eventually Colburn emerged over the edge of the precipice.

"That was a close one," he said.

"How did you guess that one?" asked Jim.

Colburn was sitting on the ground catching his breath.

"When I saw the spikes, I realised that even kneeling we could not get through. That trap would only take out one or two searchers. So it was reasonable to assume that it activated another one. One that would prevent anyone returning. You get knighted and you walk backwards, not forwards."

"Good call," said Jim, "at least we know which tunnel to start with now."

"We do indeed but remember, there has to be something to prevent people getting back. Going forward has to be the answer," said Colburn.

Slowly but surely, Colburn and Jim edged down the remaining passage.

The walls of rock were nearly black in colour, the flashlight dancing off the shadows eerily pointing them forward.

"This passage doesn't seem to have much cut away, its nearly all natural formation," said Jim.

Colburn replied, "I have a feeling that this is a natural tunnel. It's just like the side craters of a volcano. Makes you wonder if all those millions of years ago, this was a volcano, leaving all these underground passageways as vents. Over the millennia, the top eroded and was eventually levelled out with soil and the river did the rest. So the Castle and Cathedral were probably built on that volcanic rock. When foundations were being dug or any other excavations, these passages were found."

"It's a nice historical thought," said Jim, "but does it helps us now?"

"Not at all," replied Colburn.

"Thanks a bunch," said Jim, "anyway I thought this was some sort of maze, not a straight tunnel."

"Just count your blessings," replied Colburn, "it is different rooms just like Knossus."

He looked a few feet further into the torchlight.

"See, you couldn't keep your mouth shut, could you?"

Jim moved closer.

"What's the problem now?"

They both stared ahead to a blank wall of rock. All around them was solid, no way out except reverse.

Colburn began examining the walls with his light for any signs of help. Wiping dirt off with his hands.

After nearly completing a total grid search of the walls, he noticed some etchings on the rock facing them.

Brushing away the years of accumulated dirt, strange signs appeared.

The signs seemed to be four in a line down, with one either side of the central position.

Colburn groaned quietly, "God knows what these are."

Jim was smiling.

"Wish I had a camera to catch this moment," he said.

"Why?" replied Colburn.

"It seems for once, I know something that you don't. Got to note this day down in history," said Jim.

"OK then, you win, what is it?"

Jim shone his light onto the wall.

"What we have here cousin is a Celtic Cross made up of Runestone markings. Now what we have to figure out is what the runic markings mean."

Colburn questioned the scenario, "why would Celtic markings be down here?"

Jim replied, "Runes were used as a form of writing. The old Anglo-Saxon alphabet had twenty-eight runes, increasing to thirty-three over time. I remember, as late

336

as 1639, there was an edict in Iceland, banning the use of Runes. In the late nineteenth century, pastors in rural Scandinavia were required to read and write with Runes. This was despite the efforts of the Catholic Church to stamp out their use."

"Sometimes, you literally amaze me Jim," said Colburn.

"Just a bit of a hobby. I'll read your Runes back home, if we get there.

The thing is, this cross was one of the usual ways of rune casting.

Looking back, looking at the present and then the future," said Jim.

"Can you interpret it then?" asked Colburn.

"Let me see," said Jim.

"The sign on the right is ERHWAZ and indicates the past.

The four here, from the top are LAGUZ, meaning a new situation.

Next down is PERTH, meaning a challenge.

Then FEHU, meaning what's going on now.

Last is MANNAZ, which means foundation.

The sign on the left is DAGAZ, indicating the future."

"Wonderful," said Colburn, "what does it all mean then?"

"It means we have to solve this to progress," said Jim.

"Can you solve it?" asked Colburn.

Jim peered at the ERHWAZ sign, "we have to read

these in order, so that any prediction that is written here, can come true. Maybe."

"What do you mean, maybe?" asked Colburn.

Runes were like Oracles," said Jim, "often talking in riddles and comments that could be taken two ways. Hopefully this is straightforward. Here goes.

That sign in the past position is linked with death."

Colburn nearly laughed, "they got that one right."

Jim continued, "not always literal death. That can be avoided if you have endurance and the ability to foresee consequences."

Colburn muttered, "forward planning Jim."

Jim said, "second off bottom, in the "Now" position is FEHU. This indicates wealth of some kind. In the olden days it meant cattle, or how many you had but I think this time it is telling us we need energy and hard work. That seems a reasonable assumption of what we have done to get to this place.

The bottom rune, MANNAZ, is telling us the foundation we need before progressing.

This is the starting point and indicates that us as humans have to co-operate to progress.

Second down, PERTH. This is the mystery rune, meaning a game of chance and skill, needing good sense.

The top one, LAGUZ, is the new situation. Usually associated with water. It shows a time for cleansing and unseen powers are active here.

The one on the far left, DAGAZ is what is in store for us in the future. It does, however mean a breakthrough in life and light. It usually calls for a leap of faith into the void."

"That's it then?" said Colburn.

Jim replied, "you have to put them all together for a forecast. My interpretation is that we have travelled a dark and dangerous path, with a lot of hard work and energy. We have co-operated well together to make it this far.

From now on, we will need all our skill and good sense to overcome the situation we will find ourselves in. Probably to do with water but if we overcome this we will breakthrough and triumph but not before our faith is put to the test."

Colburn was musing, trying to put some logic into the meanings.

"OK, we've done some hard graft to get here. We've helped each other but where do we go from here. There must be something to tell us, something we've missed."

He began again, carefully examining the Celtic Cross rune symbols, running his fingers around the grooves of each sign. His hand drifted to the left-hand sign for the future.

"Jim, there's more grooving here," he said.

He was tracing out a groove travelling far to the left of the future rune.

His hand stopped.

Brushing away more dirt and dust, the flashlight showed another rune sign.

"What's this one Jim?" he said.

Jim shone his light and tracing over it with his fingers.

"Good God," he exclaimed, "this one is SOWELO, more commonly known as SIGEL. This is the sign that was totally misused by Hitler's Germans. It means spiritual warriors victory.

This is the victory symbol, the victory of light over darkness.

It also means the Power of the Sun."

Colburn smiled again, "so we're still on the right track then. Whatever it is, it's something to do with power. Surely can't be solar power, can it?

Now how does this help us go forward?"

He peered more closely at this runic symbol.

"Jim, shine your light here as well, I'm sure there's some writing around it."

Jim held his torch close, both concentrated on the sign.

Colburn spelled out the words from around the sign.

"Nothing in Excess."

"Now Jim, I know what this is this time," said Colburn, "this is the second phrase from the famous Oracle at Delphi. The most famous one being, Know Thyself."

"So," said Jim, "if we do nothing in excess, then surely it must mean we do something that takes little effort."

"Just like this," said Colburn as he gently pressed the victory sign.

Before them, the rock face groaned, throwing up a thick cloud of dust.

They both covered their eyes and noses as slabs of stone fell away.

As the dust settled, part of the wall had fallen,

allowing them to step over the rubble and down into another passage.

Colburn looked at Jim, "seems like we have to go this way pal."

Jim followed, "remember what the forecast said, be prepared."

"Just like our scouting days Jim, nothing changes," replied Colburn.

This passage was similar to the rest, more natural than hewn.

There was enough height for them to stand upright and they carefully examined each step before they took it.

Jim was checking the rope for distance.

"Colburn," he said, "I reckon we have to be practically underneath the Cathedral by now."

"That's what I was thinking Jim. I reckon these passages have been known since the foundations were laid," replied Colburn, "and the knowledge of their whereabouts would have been passed from Bishop to Bishop and the sacred Three. So people have been down here since the founding of the Cathedral."

"I was just thinking, the old Crusaders and their followers were great builders of war machines and fortifications," said Jim, "wouldn't have took too much effort to fortify and booby trap this place."

"Just keep your eyes open, we have to come across something soon," said Colburn thinking, "otherwise we'll be in the river.

Oh hell, I should have kept my mouth shut."

Jim moved up alongside Colburn who was shining his torch down a hole about three feet across.

"This it then?" said Jim flashing his light around.

This was not a room. It was a dead end. All there was there, was a hole in the floor.

Colburn picked up a small rock from the floor, put one ear to the hole and dropped the rock in. Counting three seconds, he heard a splash of water.

"OK," he said, " in theory it's probably a hundred feet down with water at the bottom."

Jim replied, " the runes were right, told us to expect water."

Colburn looked up and around, "we'll need to tie the rope somewhere and drop down the hole."

Jim looked around; "there's nothing that will hold the rope. Remember the runes, work together and overcome. I'll take your weight and lower you."

Colburn looked at Jim sorrowfully, "but once I'm down there, I can't get you down."

"I know that," said Jim, "we've worked together until now but the runes say continue the quest. I'll stay here."

"I'm not leaving you here Jim. Either we both go or we try to find our way back'" said Colburn. Jim shook his head, "get going," he said.

Colburn wrapped the nylon rope around his waist.

"Lower me down slowly and if the strain is getting too much, pull me back," he said.

Colburn climbed over the hole and Jim let out the rope.

He descended slowly, examining the area with the flashlight for any sign of escape.

There seemed nothing, he was just swinging on the

rope.

He couldn't leave Jim alone, they'd been through too much together.

Suddenly the rope went slack and a shout came from Jim.

"Are you OK Colburn?"

Colburn flashed his light around.

In the centre of this room was a pit.

The one that his stone had travelled down finding water eighty feet below.

He was standing on a wide ledge surrounding the pit, plenty of room to walk around.

Swinging on the rope had made it possible to land on solid ground.

He shouted back to Jim, "tie the rope around you Jim, drop the end down here."

"Will everything be OK?" replied Jim.

Colburn nearly laughed, "take a leap of faith Jim. Lower yourself down from the hole and just drop."

Jim always trusted Colburn.

He dropped the rope down, climbed over the hole, gripped the sides and let go.

Falling with acceleration due to gravity, it seemed like an eternity of blackness.

Suddenly he felt the rope pull him to one side.

Colburn's arms grabbed him.

He landed by Colburn, in his arms, both teetering near the edge of the hole. They stepped back.

The room was shaped like a bottle. He had just dropped down the neck. From the hole at the top you could only see straight down into blackness and eventually water. The sides around seemed like an illusion but they were back together again.

Jim looked up and stared around, "without taking that leap of faith you wouldn't know this was here. Thank God for the Runes."

"Thank the Norsemen Jim," said Colburn.

Looking around they could see the remnants of the masonry works. Bits of decomposed rope, old and broken wooden ladders and flashing the light across the room showed a passage. A passage out?

The walked slowly round to the passage of the other tunnel still carefully watching their steps. Masons digging out the sides of the bottleneck had created this ledge.

After only about ten feet Colburn looking through the beam of light remarked, "Jim, this must be it."

Jim came up from behind, both torches frantically surveying the area.

It was another room but not like any before.

This was indeed built by masons.

The walls still showed plaster and frescos, there were stone pillars and the ceiling was vaulted.

As the lights shone to the far end of this room, there it was, still in all its splendour,

a high altar but with what looked like a coffin on top of it.

The floor was solid with occasional mosaic patterns.

It was obviously a place of worship.

Jim remarked, "this looks more like the inside of an old Cathedral or Abbey."

Colburn was already making his way towards what appeared to be an altar.

In the light of his torch, he could make out various vestments.

Some looked like the coverings used by Knights, even the occasional Templar cross was seen.

The floor was strewn with wooden caskets.

He paused and opened one.

Inside were stones of differing colours.

He remarked to Jim, "these have to be some of the Cathedral treasures, these are worth a fortune."

Jim smiled and said, "I like the sound of that."

"No Jim, I mean these belong to the Cathedral," he let a few of the stones fall through his fingers, "this must be some of the treasure given by kings and the high ranking visitors that came here years ago.

When the dissolution came, it was reported that the supposed treasure of this Cathedral was a myth. They found hardly anything."

"So," said Jim, "they spirited all of this away so the Crown couldn't get their hands on it."

"That's the way it looks," replied Colburn going over to check another casket.

Opening the lid, he saw crystal glasses. The next one contained ivory carvings.

There were cups and crosses strewn around.

Jewels, gold and precious stones.

He looked at Jim in the light of his torch, he looked sad, "this is indeed the vast treasure hoard of this Cathedral. It's been lost for five hundred years."

"So, what now?" asked Jim.

"Now we find what we've come for," replied Colburn.

"Leave this lot lying here," said Jim sounding surprised.

"It's been here a long time, it's not going anywhere

soon," replied Colburn.

He shone his light toward the altar stone and moved towards it.

Examining the carvings around the altar his gaze took him to the coffin sitting on top.

"I'm reminded that there was an original Saxon church and monastery here, supposedly already containing famous relics.

In addition to the body of St. Cuthbert, there were thought to be the bones of the Venerable Bede as well. All that was supposed to have been destroyed prior to starting the building of the Cathedral."

Jim was just staring around in wonder, "I suppose where the original site is being shown now, was not necessarily the original site."

"Looks like that's extremely likely," replied Colburn, "there were all sorts of strange happenings reported in those days, before Cuthbert's remains were in place and settled."

The stone coffin on the altar had no markings.

Something that Colburn found strange and puzzling.

"If this was so important Jim, why are there no markings, insignia or any way of telling what it was for?" said Colburn.

Jim replied, "it seems to me that if something is left in plain view, with no apparent signs telling us what it is, then someone meant us to check it out."

"Just what I was thinking," said Colburn, "let's get the lid off."

Scraping around the seal area of the lid with chisels,

eventually the groove of the lid became clear.

They inserted the chisels in opposite sides and tapped lightly with the hammers.

Movement was noticed, the lid was loose.

Colburn levered up one side, while Jim gripped the lid close by.

He lifted and pushed at the same time.

The lid slowly ground against its rock case and moved.

At just past the halfway point, gravity took effect and the lid crashed over the side of the coffin onto the rock floor, sending up a large dust cloud.

Shielding their eyes and mouths from the dust, they both shone their torches into the coffin.

Nearly filling the inside of the stone area, was a box.

A box covered in various carvings.

About four feet long and eighteen inches wide, with two hinges along one side of the top and a metal bolt apparently keeping the lid shut.

Colburn looked over to Jim, "this is it Jim, what the chase was all about."

Jim was puzzled, "what is it?" he asked, "what about all this money lying about?"

"If we take any of that, we'd be stealing from the church," said Colburn, "like grave robbers. When we get out of here, we can let the church authorities know about this place. I've no doubt there'll be a reward."

"That's what I like to hear," replied Jim, "but just one question. How the hell do we get out of here?"

They carefully lifted the wooden casket out of the stone coffin and placed it on the ground.

"Open it up then," said Jim.

"Best not to do that here," said Colburn, "always remember the curse of the Pharaohs. You never know the future. We need to examine it properly, back home."

Jim flashed his torch around the walls and vaulted ceiling, "if someone brought all this down here, they must have had some device for carrying it. Most of this is too heavy to lift on its own."

They both wandered off, staring at the walls with their lights.

There didn't seem to be a straightforward answer to the question, "how did they get this treasure down here?"

There was no door, no staircase only solid rock walls and ceiling.

Colburn sat on the altar steps and thought.

He began his typical mumbling when pondering over a question.

Shining his torch up to the ceiling he said, "if this is down here, it probably was once used for worship."

Jim replied, "that seems logical."

Colburn continued, "so that ceiling as it is now, would be somewhere close to the floor area of the Cathedral. Therefore I can only assume that there has to be a blocked entrance up there, leading at one time, down here.

The way out has to be in that roof."

Jim shone his torch around. It was only maybe, twenty feet up to the roof but where in the roof?

Colburn was still musing over his thoughts, "surely any way down here wouldn't come down the middle, it would probably come down in the corner angles. Now two of those angles are on the walls in the direction we've just come from. So we need to examine the two corner angles on the Cathedral side."

Jim walked to the far corner, slowly examining the roof sections for signs of any disturbance that might indicate an entrance.

Colburn started on the angle behind the altar.

Shining the light upward, he stared at the ceiling, moving in inches around the dusty floor.

His foot kicked into something hard.

He looked down and in the light he saw wooden struts, definitely planks.

Bending over and picking one up, he looked at the others and shouted to Jim.

"Over here Jim."

Jim wandered over slowly, looking at the precious stones thinking, "what a shame."

Reaching Colburn he said, "another problem? I'm dirty, tired and hungry and getting annoyed at whoever put that cover on. I'm in no mood for more puzzles."

"No puzzles Jim, this has been a wooden staircase at one time. Looks like our answer is up there," said Colburn flashing his light up to the corner of the wall and ceiling, "somewhere up there has to be the entrance to these steps. We need to get up on that ledge and have a look."

Jim noticed that the walls were polished no place for hand or toe grips, impossible to climb.

The only protruding part of the wall was a three sided carving looking like a cherub with angel's wings, which probably was a hexagonal base for one of the columns.

"I could throw a rope over that," said Jim, "if you could climb up one side of the rope, I can hold the other flat against the wall and take your weight."

"See Jim, always working together," Colburn replied.

Jim threw the rope up and around the carving. It was unsteady but with Jim holding one end, Colburn began to climb up. It was reminiscent of the climbing ropes in a school gymnasium, hard to do but with practice and using the legs to push as well as the arms to pull, you reach the top.

Colburn gripped the carving with one hand, then let go of the rope and reached out for the ledge with the other.

Using his upper body strength, he hauled himself up and climbed onto the ledge.

The ledge consisted of about one foot of stonework all around the ceiling, interspersed with columns.

Colburn stood up and took his torch out of his jacket pocket, shining it around.

"Can you see anything?" shouted Jim.

"Nothing yet," came the reply, "I'll try to see what's solid stone first."

Colburn began tapping the stone around the ceiling with the base of his torch.

Nothing, everything seemed solid.

"There's just nothing here," shouted Colburn, "I'll try closer to the ledge."

Colburn carefully knelt down and started tapping around the bottom of the wall.

He was getting close to the projected carving he had used to climb up when, in slightly overreaching to tap the base of a column, some of the ledge gave way under his weight and he tumbled over.

The flashlight fell to the ground close to Jim but Colburn just managed to cling on to the carving.

It seemed as if he was looking directly into the carved face of an angel when his hold on the top slipped.

He just managed to grab the wing portions of the carving, hanging in mid air.

"Out of the way Jim, I'm just going to drop back down," he said.

The drop was only about ten feet, no problem for someone with parachute training.

Then the unexpected occurred.

The angel wings he was holding suddenly gave way and he crashed to the ground.

Picking himself up from the dust, he looked up at the carving. There was a noise of gears grinding and dust billowed out above the cherub.

The wings had not broken off, they had just both bent downward and the column behind the carving had moved.

Standing back a little they both shone the torches up.

The pillar seemed to have moved outwards, or at least half the pillar had.

"Well, there's a surprise now," said Jim, "you must have activated some mechanism for opening that column. That must be the way down."

"And our way out," smiled Colburn, "now I just have to get back up, sling the rope around again Jim."

Jim repeated the operation and Colburn climbed up.

Standing more carefully on the ledge, he eased his body around the column and looked inside.

There was a stone staircase, leading up.

"Tie the rope around that box and I'll haul it up here," said Colburn.

Jim took the rope and made a sling around the box.

Colburn took up the slack and the strain.

Eventually he hauled the box over the ledge and into the open base of the column.

He untied the box, threw one end of the rope down to Jim and took the strain.

Jim climbed up the rope, grasping Colburn's hand at the top and stood up.

Colburn noted, "must have had these steps down to here, then that wooden staircase to the bottom. The last person to use this place must have put these mechanisms in place and sealed everything off."

"Can we go home now?" asked Jim, looking weary.

"Onward and upward," replied Colburn, "I'll take this end of the box, you lift the other and we'll see where this takes us."

Taking one step at a time, they carried the box upwards.

It seemed an eternity but eventually they came to a wall.

Putting the box down, Colburn started tapping on the wall with the base of the torch.

The echoes sounded more like thin wood and plaster.

"I hate to say it Jim but I reckon we're inside the Cathedral," said Colburn.

He took his chisel and hammer, listened for any sound and began chipping plaster away.

He'd guessed right, behind a thin layer of plaster was a wooden wall structure.

Quickly and as quietly as possible he levered the plaster away until the area was large enough to slightly bend down and get through.

He turned to Jim, "I'll have to lever off some of these planks to see where we are," he said.

"What, and walk out into the Cathedral carrying that box, looking like a couple of tramps," said Jim.

Colburn chipped part of a plank away, enough to spy through a small hole, then looked in.

"If I've got my bearings right, we're in the central part of the Cathedral. I can make out the Light Infantry Chapel to the right."

Jim groaned again, "home sweet home."

Colburn continued, "so if I'm right, straight across is the North Transept, then the Central Tower. So we must be at the side of the South Transept."

"So what does that tell us then?" enquired Jim.

"It tells us that we're right under the clock," answered Colburn.

"Does that mean anything?" asked Jim.

Colburn thought for a while, "Val knows more about this than me but from what I can remember, it was at Bishop Cosin's insistence that this great clock was repaired."

"So," said Jim, "it's possible that the repair to this clock was the final act of sealing in a secret."

"Very likely," said Colburn.

"So now what do we do?" asked Jim, "surely we can't break through here, it would destroy the clock area."

"Time to think again," said Colburn as he started

wandering around the top of the staircase area.

"If we don't go forward into Cathedral, then we have to go in reverse. If you remember the Cathedral floor plan, behind us is the Chapter House but in that corner between the Memorial Chapel wall and us is open land. I reckon if we can remove a couple of the stones at the bottom, we can get out."

"You're talking about removing the foundations?" asked Jim.

"No, that wall's been repaired so many times over the years, it should come away easy," said Colburn.

He walked to the corner of the stairs area and bent down. Taking his hammer and chisel, he began to chip around the plaster of the stones.

It was soon falling out. Years of re-plastering had left a lot of the original repairs, soft.

"We only need about three stones out, then we crawl out with that box," said Colburn.

Eventually enough plaster from the first stone was removed. Colburn and Jim sat on the floor and pushed against it with their feet. The stone moved out more easily than they thought. Looking through the gap, they saw open green land and fresh air.

They both leaned back and drew in gulps of oxygen. It was nectar from the Gods.

Two more stones were easily removed, and then Colburn crawled through.

Jim passed through the box, pushing it out and crawled out himself.

They sat there, on the grass for a few minutes.

"Another successful enterprise Jim," said Colburn.

"I'll agree with you when I get home and have a

shower," he replied.

They put their jackets over the box and picked it up.

They walked around and outside the Nine Altars Wall and back out onto the Palace Green.

It had seemed like an eternity but the clock was only saying five. Practically six hours underground had flown by.

There were still several dozen visitors wandering around the green, some staring at two scruffy workmen.

They walked past the security gatehouse of the Castle and straight back to their BT van, still waiting for them next to the Sunderland camp.

They quickly loaded the box into the boot of the van.

"Now," said Colburn, "we need to leave as few clues as possible for the time being. Let's push the soil and turf back in there."

They re-entered their tent, shovelled the soil back onto the metal lid, firmed it all down and replaced the turf. You could still see the turf had been cut but it would self-mend in a few days, grass was like that.

Packing up the tent, gathering their equipment and stashing everything over the box in the boot, Colburn said, "let's get home."

Jim started the engine.

Colburn took his phone and dialled a number.

Jim listened intently to the conversation.

He rang the steward at Auckland Castle with an urgent message for the Bishop.

The message followed that there were stones fallen from the rear of the Cathedral near to the outside of the

Chapter House. Inside the wall was an old passageway that appeared to lead to a part of the Cathedral that had been unused for centuries. Inside there were the remnants of the Cathedral treasure that had been hidden from the King's Commissioners and asked that the Police and Fire Brigade be informed so that they could assist in their recovery.

The Steward obviously thought it was a hoax call but had to act, by informing the Bishop who then informed the appropriate authorities.

It wasn't long before all hell broke loose around the Palace Green.

Police cordoned off the area.

The Fire Brigade located the loosened stones and sent a man in roped up.

When he reported back, the Bishop was informed.

Eventually stones were removed to create a small doorway in that side of the Cathedral, with enough space to allow the Bishop and his retinue in.

Then the relocation of all the remaining artefacts began.

Jock Strane and Doug were in their usual positions each with a pint of John Smith's in front of them.

The staff in the motel had got used to the two of them drinking and eating in the place. Although it had been mentioned that, as visitors to the area, they hardly ever went out.

Jock glanced down at the map on the small television screen by his side.

"Seems like the tracker you put on that BT van is

working. Lord seems to be heading back home," said Strane.

Doug replied, "just make sure he does, otherwise it's another chase to nowhere."

"He passed here a couple of minutes ago and he's turning in at that pub up the road, he's going home alright," said Strane.

"So he got out of that drain, did he?" said Doug, "wonder why he was down there and how the hell did he find a way out?"

The television was on in the lounge area and Carol was reading the Northeast news.

A breaking story appeared.

She started to report that a significant find of Cathedral treasure, including precious metals and stones, had been located in a secret vault underneath Durham Cathedral.

It seemed that this vault had not been in use for centuries and the wealth it contained was immense.

"Shit," said Strane, "Lord must have had something to do with that and he's given it all back to the Church authorities. As if they haven't got enough."

Doug mused over his pint, "if it was you or I, what would we do? There's no way you could fence that sort of treasure trove. You have to go for a finder's fee or insurance pay-off. So why didn't Lord do that? Own up to finding it and get the glory.

So if he doesn't want that money or glory, I bet there's something else he found and he didn't leave it in there."

Strane's mobile buzzed, he looked at the text message.

"Looks like we'll find out soon," he said, "passive

surveillance is finished. Now we go for him."

"I can't make a move until I'm directed," said Doug.

Strane replied, "when this news filters through to the States, I reckon you'll get orders to move, so you're just pre-empting that."

"I suppose you're right," said Doug, "my superiors will still want to know what this is really all about."

"Mine do," said Strane, "and I'm authorised to find out."

"So what do we do know?" asked Doug.

Strane sat back and finished his pint.

"We need to formulate a plan of action. One that means we can secretly find out what Lord knows, steal it from him and take the glory and money for ourselves. If it happens that there is anything our governments should know, we can decide later whether to inform them.

For now the plan is extremely simple, we go to his house and kick his bloody door in."

Colburn and Jim had pulled up the BT van at his house.

Jim rang his associate to come and take it away, saying he owed him one.

They carefully took the wooden box out of the boot and carried it up the garden path.

Val was waiting at the back door.

"You two look like the proverbial bag of crap. What the hell have you got yourselves into this time," she said.

"This I think, is what all the fuss is over," Colburn remarked as he and Jim manoeuvred the box into the house.

Val stared at it, "wait until I put some plastic sheeting down on the bench, that looks filthy."

Jim replied, "it's been covered in dust and cobwebs for five hundred years. You would be dusty if someone left you that long."

Val continued, "I've been watching the news. I knew you must have had something to do with it. The Bishopric is overjoyed at the return of the treasures but why did you let them know about it. Is there nothing in this for us?"

Colburn replied, "they can have everything except this. This has to be what was described in the codes and messages left as clues."

Val placed a large sheet of plastic over the worktop.

Colburn and Jim lifted the box onto the surface.

All three began to examine the box.

Colburn began the pre-amble.

"What we have here seems to be a container, probably made of some sort of wood, about four feet long and eighteen inches wide."

Leaning around the box he continued, "the same at the back except for two metallic fittings that probably act as hinges. The lid seems only attached by a metallic bolt apparatus."

Jim was anxious to view all around, "if it has only got a bolt and hinges, surely that means it was meant to be opened?"

Colburn replied, wariness in his voice, "that would appear correct but let's not get too excited. This has been around a long time. I suppose there's been plenty of people who could have emptied this out.

We need to be extra careful."

"Why?" asked Jim.

"Remember Carter's opening of Tutenkamun's Tomb and the curse," said Colburn.

"You don't believe in curses," said Jim jokingly.

"Of course not," replied Colburn, "what killed them all was probably some ancient bacteria or fungus that had been lying dormant for centuries, maybe even a virus. So whatever this box contains could be contaminated with foreign protein and I don't feel like breathing it in."

"OK," said Jim, "time for the Noddy suits."

Noddy suits were the nickname for the clothing issued by the Army to combat Nuclear, Biological and Chemical warfare agents.

Colburn had always kept suits handy, he always used to say, "if we're attacked, by the time the government tells us what to do, we would be toast."

He was always prepared for the unexpected, his family and friends were important to him.

Val had a pastry brush in her hand and was carefully brushing away some of the accumulated dust and dirt from the box's surface.

She uncovered dozens of carvings all over the box.

Jim said, "does any of this mean anything to you Val?"

"Not yet," she replied, "but these carvings are really beautifully done."

Colburn was still standing back thinking, "we don't even know how old this box is, so we can't hazard a guess where it came from."

Val got a magnifying glass and began an examination of some of the carvings.

After a couple of minutes she stood back.

"I'm not an expert on things like hieroglyphics but I

am positive that these date well before that era. They look like some form of Cuneiform writing."

"You mean like old Phoenician writing?" asked Colburn.

"No," replied Val, "old Phoenician writing only stems from about one thousand years before Christ."

Jim said, "you mean this is about three thousand years old?"

"Sorry to disappoint you Jim, but no. This writing appears to come from a time well before that."

Jim gasped, "Whoa."

Val continued, "the oldest writings or alphabet were thought to be of Phoenician origin, then Aramaic, Hebrew, Syriac then Arabic.

These carved signs appear to be Canaanite in origin or even before, perhaps Proto-Canaanite. This could put it before fifteen hundred BC and perhaps a lot older."

Colburn was studying Val's words, listening intently, "so what you are saying is what we have here is a box with markings from four thousand years ago and probably a lot older?"

"Yes," replied Val, "I would need to check it out.

These markings could be an early alphabet. This could be original writing from the people that invented the wording.

Judging from the changes in time line of the Egyptian dynasties."

Jim interrupted, "what do you mean, change in time line?"

Val said, "recent discoveries have shown some of the Egyptian dynasties to have been incorrectly dated. I know the Egyptians aren't pleased about it and maybe the Church of Rome but a lot of what is now known is a lot older than previously thought.

So I reckon we're talking about at least fifteen thousand years BC."

Jim gasped, "surely there wasn't anyone around in those days who could craft this box, make those hinges so perfect and fit a bolt."

Colburn said, "well Jim, I think we have to accept that if this box is that old, whoever made it was damn good."

Jim replied, "it's so good it's creepy. Hang on a minute, is what you are saying, there was somebody alive then who could craft this box."

Colburn smiled at Jim, "that's exactly what I'm saying and if they could make this and the metal work, what else could they do?"

Val said, "let's go in and discuss this further. I don't want that opened until we've seen all the options."

All three went into the living room and sat down. Colburn and Jim knew as well as anyone, that any further action had to be planned before execution.

Jim leaned back in his chair and put his feet up on the recliner.

"My assessment of the current situation is this.

I've slept on a pew and broken into the Cathedral. Slept in a broom cupboard and robbed the British Library. Broken down a plastered wall in the Castle. Had a nice trip to America followed around by their security. Slept in a tin serving hatch and broken into the Magna Carta. Then I get back here and someone entombs me in a labyrinth. Then finally we break through the walls of the Cathedral with this box.

Have I missed anything?"

Val laughed, "poor dear, you've had a rough time then."

Colburn began his overview of the current situation.

"Whatever we have obviously came from a period in time many thousands of years ago. A time when no one was supposed to be able to write or communicate.

That leads me to believe that there was indeed, in those days, a superior class of humans who could do these things."

Jim interrupted, "you do mean humans, as like us, do you?"

Colburn continued, "I'm not talking ET here, I'm making a logical assumption that there was a class of ancient people who were obviously masters of their trades, possibly even having a social class and government, who knows?

These people apparently were extremely sophisticated and probably lived in societies and cities still unknown to us. They developed what is or is not, inside that box and if they could develop societies to construct that box, they may certainly have constructed some weapon, even for self-defence.

That's what other folks want to know about, they always want to know about armaments.

Seeing as we have no records of these people now, it would seem likely that they disappeared in a short space of time.

Now that could be fire, flood, earthquake or global warming. The construction of the continents as we know them now was still occurring in that time frame.

Rising sea levels or volcano lava could have forced them to flee their cities, probably separating into smaller groups. This would mean a dilution of knowledge. These groups may have eventually joined with others of lesser knowledge and became societies we know about now but not with the total knowledge. That would have to be learned again through time and evolution.

The original people were obviously artisans, metalworkers, scientists and mathematicians. Just look at those hinges, they are perfectly made. You can't get a workman nowadays to put hinges on your door that good.

So I believe one portion of these people carried with them this box and through time and death, it was passed on down the line. For what purpose, we'll attempt to found out.

Eventually it was hidden but I believe not at first in Durham.

I would anticipate that this was located, from Val's deciphering, somewhere in the Middle East area, exactly where may stay unknown.

It was used, or misused for centuries, until someone hid it supposedly forever.

There were plenty of traders coming to the British Isles, even before the Romans, so it could have come with them. There were also the Norsemen, who worked around that area. They could have brought it and given it as a treasure to the Cathedral people.

Only the Prince Bishop and his immediate loyal folks would have known about it, so I am assuming this is why they mention it. They seemed to be afraid or wary of it, which's why they called it the "Fire of the Gods" and probably why it was left underground all those years ago, with the instructions to find it, if and when someone could."

"And that's exactly what we did," said Jim.

"And that's why we should be extra careful," said Colburn, "something so precious, or dangerous could lie inside and we're taking no chances, let's get suited up."

Up in a back bedroom, Colburn pulled a suitcase from under the bed.

Typically a fawn colour with brown binding, well known in the Army.

Opening it up, he handed Jim a rolled up package, then trousers and respirator.

Jim unrolled the package.

Army combat jackets were made to turn inside out and be rolled up neatly.

Jim put on the trousers and jacket.

They both came downstairs looking like they did years ago when Val never knew where they were.

Both were carrying respirators, full facemasks and black rubber gloves.

You soon learn the effectiveness of your mask when you're in a CS gas chamber. Told to take off your mask and recite your Army number. If you have anything on your chest, the coughing brings it up but it's a feeling you have to experience.

Putting on their respirators, Colburn signalled for Val to stay put while they walked to inspect the box.

Colburn stood at one end, while Jim took the other. They looked apprehensive.

Colburn nodded to Jim.

With one hand they held the box still.

With the other, Jim pushed the bolt slowly as Colburn pulled it towards himself.

The bolt gave way and moved slowly.

Millimetres at a time.

Eventually the bolt passed through its holding pin and released, the lid was free.

Colburn indicated to Jim to lift the lid back, holding up three fingers.

Then two.

Then one.

They began to ease the lid open.

It had opened about half an inch, when Colburn motioned to Jim for a flashlight.

Jim handed Colburn the light, keeping the lid still.

Colburn looked inside but couldn't make out any shape or form.

The lid had to be opened wider.

Keeping the flashlight in one hand and bending to see inside through his respirator, the lid was eased open to about two inches.

Colburn instinctively knocked Jim's arm with the flashlight.

The end of the box lid fell.

Colburn retained his grip on his side of the lid and let it fall shut, slowly.

He stood back and pulled off his respirator.

Jim did the same.

"What's inside?" he said.

Colburn took a few quick breaths, looking frightened.

"All I saw was a small cloud looking like gas with white particulate matter."

"I'm pleased your reactions are still as quick," replied Jim.

"Don't know what it is but it could be toxic, we'll have to test it," said Colburn, "shout of Val to get me one of those sterile universal containers out of my medical kit."

Jim went in and asked Val to get him the container.

She returned with it and asked, "have we got a NBC alert?"

Jim replied, "don't know yet, I just hope it's not a weapon of mass destruction."

"Great," she groaned.

Jim handed the bottle to Colburn, "how do we get a sample inside there?" asked Jim.

Colburn replied, "I'll use an empty drinking bottle with a plastic straw. Put this container inside it, and use the straw to extract that white material. I'll squeeze the bottle, insert the straw inside the box and let go. The vacuum should pull the particles into the bottle. You just hold the box slightly open."

Colburn fixed up his makeshift apparatus and they both repositioned their respirators.

He tapped Jim on the shoulder and raised one thumb.

Jim slightly moved the lid and Colburn squeezed the bottle and inserted the straw inside the box.

He gently let go of the bottle, which appeared to re-fill with air.

Pulling back the straw, Jim carefully closed the lid.

Leaving on their respirators and gloves, Colburn loosened the plastic bottle top.

He felt inside for the container, withdrew it and quickly screwed the plastic lid down tightly.

Holding up the sterile container, they both observed white particulate matter circulating around and settling on the bottom.

They both removed their respirators and gloves.

"Now what?" said Jim.

"Now we get this stuff analysed," said Colburn, "I've got a pal of mine who owes me a favour. He's in charge of the Microbiology Department at the local hospital. Until we find out what this stuff is, we're not touching that again."

Colburn reached over and slid the bolt to seal the lid.

"It can stop right there, we'll just cover it up for now," said Colburn, "anyway I think it's time we had a good rest. Want to stay here tonight Jim?"

"As long as Val does me a fry up in the morning," said Jim.

"I'm sure that can be arranged," replied Colburn.

"When are we going to give the Lord's a surprise then?" asked Doug.

"Only mistakes are made in a hurry," replied Strane, "I can guarantee he'll be studying his next move and we'll be there watching. What we do, is be ready to act at the right time."

"And what might be the right time?" asked Doug.

"When he's figured it all out," replied Strane.

"Then can I kick his door in?" enquired Doug.

"No need for that," replied Strane, "I'm just going to knock on his door and say Hi, what have you found now?"

"And then?" asked Doug.

"This is England. He'll show us and then we'll all have a cup of tea," said Strane.

Doug never believed it would happen that way. That was not his agenda.

CHAPTER TWENTY-EIGHT

Jim opened the curtains the following morning. He had already dressed and washed.

The sun was shining. It was a beautiful day, clear blue skies.

He stood for a while admiring the view over the Wear Valley onto the far hills.

It seemed the sun always shone on those hills first but with the North-South alignment of the Lord's house, the sun would be shining in their front room.

Being well domesticated and Army trained, he made his bed first and went downstairs.

His olfactory senses were heightened, the nostrils dancing.

There was nothing like the smell of bacon frying.

As promised, Val was in the kitchen making breakfast.

Colburn was up and studying the box.

"Morning all," said Jim.

"Breakfast in a couple of minutes," shouted Val.

They all sat down around the table and ate the high cholesterol food, fried bread as well.

The sterile container had been sealed in a plastic bag and kept in the fridge overnight.

Val wasn't happy at that but she knew there would be no leakage of whatever was in there.

Colburn said, as he munched through waffles, "Jim and I will take that sample up to the Pathology Department of Dryburn Hospital."

Val jokingly said, "you mean the University Hospital at Durham."

"Yeah," replied Colburn, "I forgot it was remodelled and re-named."

After breakfast, Colburn and Jim went out with the sample, took Colburn's car and drove out of the village towards Nevilles Cross and down to the hospital at the Lanchester roundabout.

After pulling into the car park, luckily finding a place, Jim grudgingly went to the Pay and Display machine.

He returned with the ticket and stuck it onto the inside of the front screen.

"This is nothing more than a rip-off," he said, moaning at Colburn.

They entered the hospital, looking for the signs that said "Pathology" and followed the corridors around until they saw the sign for Microbiology.

At the reception desk, they asked for Dr. Goode.

Colburn and Jim had both known Dr. Goode in their Army days.

He was a brilliant fellow but the typical absent-minded professor.

The receptionist came off the phone and said, "Dr. Goode is coming out to meet you."

Of course, nowadays, you just can't walk into these places.

Security is tight, you have to be escorted.

David Goode appeared at reception.

"It's really good to see you two again, come on down to my office," said Goode.

Dr. Goode was a man in his early fifties, slightly built and nearly bald. His laboratory coat was always brilliant white and immaculately pressed.

Walking down the Pathology corridors Goode said, "tell me what you're after when we get into the office. These walls have ears and financial administrators."

"What makes you think we're after something?" asked Colburn.

Goode looked across at him, "my memory is OK, when did you two not want something done on the quiet?"

They all went into the office, Goode shut the door.

"Alright now, the finance people are in charge. You can't do anything any more unless it's been quoted for. Patients don't seem to matter, not like it used to be. I didn't train to be told what I can and can't do by pen pushers. All I'm doing now is shuffling files around and waiting for my pension to kick in. Anyway what's your problem?"

Colburn brought out the sealed plastic bag with the universal container and handed it across the desk to Goode.

"We need to know, fairly urgently, if that material in there is hazardous."

"Might have known you'd bring me something unusual," said Goode, "I'll put it through as possibly a biohazard and say we're doing tests for the Army. The pen pushers will want to create a bill, so I'll tell them it's to go to the Ministry of Defence. That'll confuse them."

"What can you do on it?" asked Jim.

"It would be easier to tell you what I can't do. I'll find out what it is," said Goode.

"Normal culture will only take overnight for aerobic and anaerobic bacteria, anything else will take a further twenty four hours. I'll let you know the primary results tomorrow morning."

"We'll leave it with you," said Colburn standing up, "thanks again for your help Dave, I really appreciate it. I owe you one."

"A pint will do," said Goode.

"You're on," replied Colburn.

Jim and Colburn left, returned to their car and went back to Lord's house.

Dr. Goode took the sample into the laboratory and placed it into the fume cupboard.

Taking several different agar plates, he carefully opened the container.

With a metal loop, sterilised in a Bunsen flame, he took samples of the contents and plated them out on the culture medium.

Carefully sealing the plates, he put them in the incubator.

He knew how to handle potential toxins, after all he used to be one of the top boffins at Porton Down.

Samples were on blood agar, chocolate agar, agar for non-lactose fermenters.

If there were any strange bacteria, he would find them.

White powder was no stranger to him but it was always dangerous delving into the unknown, extra precautions were always taken.

The next twenty-four hours would tell him nearly everything.

Taking a small sample of the powder, he mixed it with sterile saline on a microscope slide and placed a coverslip on top. This was for macroscopic analysis to see if there were bacteria present. Through the microscope on oil immersion, about eight hundred times magnification, he could observe the particulate matter and its motility.

Strangely enough no coccus, single or in chains, or rods were observed.

There didn't appear to be bacteria present, although that was never an indication of sterility.

He scanned the sample thoroughly before disposal in a yellow plastic bin that went for incineration.

More saline particle mixtures were put on slides and warmed for them to dry out.

Then various stain materials were applied and washed off after the appropriate time.

After drying these were scanned with the microscope.

Even with the common Giemsa stain, no bacteria were observed.

There was nothing more to do except wait until the bacterial incubation was over.

The following day, Goode examined all the agar plates.

There was no bacterial growth at all.

Knowing Colburn was suspecting something, he took a small portion of the sample into the Biochemistry laboratory and spoke to the Chief Biochemist.

"Jack, can you run these particles through the mass spectrometer. I have a feeling they may be metallic?" asked Goode.

"No problem Dave, I'll do it now," replied Jack.

Taking the particulate matter, he partially dissolved it in a solvent, then placed it in a test tube, put it on the turntable and pressed the start button.

Sample probes came out to aspirate the standards, quality control and test material.

The instrument whirred into action.

After only a few minutes, the chart recorder started printing out.

Jack looked at the results.

"We're doing this on the quiet I assume?" asked Jack.

"For a friend," replied Dave.

He checked the metallic controls then the quality controls and stared at the printout, giving valency, atomic weight and number and purity.

"Let me write on here what these results tell me and then I don't want to know anything else, ok?" said Jack.

He scribbled a few notes down on the chart printout and handed it to Dave.

Looking at the writing, Dave said, "are you certain of this?"

"Sure am, now get lost. I don't want to know about this," said Jack.

"Thanks Jack," said Dave and left to return to his department.

Dave sat down in his chair, pulled out his mobile and dialled Lord's number.

Colburn answered.

"Hi Dave, what have you got for me?"

"I don't know what crap you're dealing with now Colburn and I don't want to know, so here's the results and don't phone me back," said Goode.

"There's no bacteria at all in the sample, it appears absolutely sterile."

"Well that's good news," replied Colburn.

"I don't know what you're going to make of these other results though," said Goode.

"What tests did you do?" asked Colburn.

"I had a feeling that the particles may be metallic, so I had them tested in the Chemistry laboratory," said Goode.

"So, what was it then?" enquired Colburn.

"The results showed the white powder to be metallic, in fact it's Gold," said Goode.

"What!" exclaimed Colburn, "you're sure of that?"

"I'm sure but there's more. The particles are not just pure Gold, they are orbitally rearranged monatomic molecules. The purest you can ever find. The likes of Newton were striving for years to make this stuff," said Goode.

"My God," said Colburn, "you're talking about White Gold."

"Sure am" replied Goode, "now you have your results, forget you came here, ok,"

"I was never there," said Colburn, "thanks again Dave."

Colburn switched off his phone.

Val and Jim just stood.

Val said, "did I hear you correctly?"

Colburn looked at them both, "well, it's not bacteria, it's molecules of pure White Gold."

Jim butted in, "hang on a minute. You've determined this thing is thousands of years old and inside are molecules of Gold that have only been discovered in the last few years."

Colburn nodded his head, "that's exactly what we have. We can open the box now and see what's inside."

Val took hold of Colburn's hand, "listen, this is thousands of years old, so someone then knew how to distil and refine Gold. This is incredible, unbelievable.

I just want to say one thing more before you two proceed."

"What's that?" said Colburn.

"Remember Pandora, she opened the box and brought calamity on the World," said Val.

"Yes," replied Colburn "but she managed to keep Hope in."

Jim looked sorrowfully at them both, "let's just hope there's nothing in there that's going to create a calamity in here."

Colburn turned towards the kitchen, "come on Jim, there's only one way to find out."

Val walked behind them into the kitchen area, she seemed troubled.

"I don't like this. I've got a bad feeling about that box, it worries me," she said.

"I've been thinking about that powder, it's not just there on its own. It must be there for a purpose, so hang on a minute."

"We need to have a look," said Colburn.

"Listen," said Val, "the Chemistry and Physics of those elements show the electrons to be in a high spin orbit and low energy state which makes them superconductive.

They can remain stable in this form and one of their effects is Zero-Point Energy.

The initials of them, ORME are the same as the Hebrew word for "Tree of Life" and also associated with the word "Manna."

Some people believe that the Ark of the Covenant was merely a container for this powder. So as a superconducting electrical device, it would explain the incredible properties associated with the Ark, from levitation to blast of eternal fire.

What I am trying to say is that there are theories, that thousands of years ago, either extraterrestrials or a supreme society was on this earth.

Their purpose was to mine for gold and other precious metals.

They supposedly used mankind as miners or slaves but set up the rudiments of civilisation to control them. They gave knowledge of what they were doing to selected humans, those becoming the elite.

The Ancients knew all about the superconductivity of this metal in using it, they were supposed to be able to levitate and activate the bulk of our brain that we don't use.

It can supposedly transfer its own weightlessness to a block of stone and there is evidence that the Hathor Temple on Mount Horeb in Sinai was involved in the construction of the Pyramids, due to its furnaces there that have been excavated.

It certainly would give credence as to how they lifted those massive blocks of stone."

"So what you are deducing, is that this material is from an ancient society that is now extinct?" said Jim.

"Not quite," replied Val, "history tells us that certain things were passed down and sometimes got mis-translated in the process. This is obviously an extremely ancient artefact and this has been passed down through time.

Some of those carvings are ancient lettering and some I believe are others that tell a story but I'm not looking for spaceships. I do however, believe in an ancient civilisation that was superior at that time and has been wiped out or diluted down.

What you need to remember is that precious elements occur in some herbs and vegetables.

Grapes for example, their roots go deep into the earth where there is a greater concentration of these elements. The deepest mines on earth are gold mines and volcanoes are a source as well."

"So what's the main point then?" said Jim.

Val continued, "if the ancients controlled with these so-called precious metals, it surely follows that anyone who controls this supply could control mankind.

However, even if someone controls it all, it's possible they will never understand the implications of it."

"So do you really believe all that Val?" asked Jim.

"Prove me wrong," Val replied.

Colburn grinned and said, "that's maybe what the governments are playing at. They're not really bothered about an ancient weapon when they've got nuclear. They want to play at controlling other Nations. Not to attack them, just bend their minds to theirs.

So what have we in Pandora's Box, the Ark, the Philosopher's Stone or just nothing?

I think it's time Jim."

Colburn and Jim donned their respirators and rubber gloves.

They had heeded Val's words about superconductivity, placing plenty of inert paper material around the box on the workbench surface.

All doors were closed, Val was in the living room.

No wind or draught could be allowed.

The powder had to be kept still and inside the box.

Everything was now prepared.

Colburn took one end of the lid, Jim on the other.

His fingers showed three, then two, then one, open and lift.

Millimetres at a time.

The box lid moved slowly, not a creak from the hinges.

Finally it was just past the upright position, when the lid came to rest against the rear wall of the house.

Colburn and Jim tentatively peered into the container.

The white powder was gently settling all around the interior.

They waited a few minutes until the contents became clear.

Through his respirator, Jim groaned, "Oh My God."

Colburn stared inside.

Val was shouting from the door way, "are you all OK?"

Colburn and Jim stood up and took a pace backwards, they knew as long as the powder wasn't disturbed, everything would be all right.

Colburn signalled to Jim, safe to take respirators off.

Both removed them and their gloves.

They signalled for Val to come in.

She carefully opened the door as not to create any wind movement.

Colburn said, "you can look now but hold your breath, try not to disturb anything yet."

Val crept up to the workbench and leaned over to see into the box.

Jim spoke quietly, "looks like Pandora left a bit more in here this time."

All she said when she looked in were the words, "it's beautiful."

She gazed down, her eyes wandering all around the box and there inside, mostly covered with the white powder, artefacts that had never seen the light of day for at least five hundred years.

The bottom and sides of the box were covered in a silk-like material.

At both ends of the box, there appeared to be something solid covered by the material.

Lying, one at both sides and one down the middle were metallic rods.

Over the top of these at one end lay the largest red stone she had ever seen and lastly over the rods was a white golden figure in the shape of a bird's claw.

"It's magnificent," she said.

Jim looked at Colburn, "now what do we do?"

Colburn replied, "we at least extract that gold claw and the stone and brush them down. This lot must have a meaning. It must do something."

"And they must be worth something," said Jim with a smile.

"Get back in the lounge Val and close the door slowly, Jim and I will get these out," said Colburn.

Val slowly retreated to the lounge.

Colburn and Jim replaced their respirators, put on their gloves and slowly extracted the golden claw and stone.

Placing them on the paper, they proceeded to brush all the powder off them.

Then slowly tipped the brushed powder back into the box.

Leaving the rods inside, they closed the lid and bolted the box. None of the powder escaped.

They then opened the lounge door, took off their respirators and gloves and heaved a great sigh of relief.

They put the objects down on the lounge table.

"That golden claw must be made of that gold, the powder just comes off it over time," said Colburn.

"It has to be worth a bit," said Jim.

"Probably is," said Colburn, "but we just can't walk into the Northern Goldsmiths shop and say, can you value this. It will have to go back to the Cathedral."

Val spoke, "I think with what we've donated to the Cathedral funds already, a reward is not out of the question."

"I agree," said Jim.

Colburn was staring at the red stone, "I could be wrong but I think this is a ruby."

Jim interrupted, "if that's the case, it's worth a King's ransom and before you two say anything, I know it has to go back eventually. They'll have to give us something for that."

Val sat puzzling at the artefacts.

"I've just had a thought," she said, "there's no way these items would have just been stuffed in a box and handed down the centuries. I believe that the contents of that box all went together to mean or form something. We just have to figure out, what?

The shape of that claw fascinates me.

It looks like a skeletal hand but it seems as if the claw was meant to hold something and look at the wrist part. There seems to be a circular ring area, as if something fitted in there."

Colburn and Jim stared at the claw.

"I think she's right," said Jim.

"She usually is," replied Colburn.

"You're not leaving them there," said Val.

Colburn heaved some bubble wrap out of a nearby drawer and carefully packaged the claw and stone.

Then he placed them in a spare drawer of the unit.

"Right, now we can sit and consider our next move," he said.

The three sat around the table.

Colburn and Val were thinking about the find.

Val said, "I'd like to concentrate on the pictorial carvings. The ones around the outside of the box are really fascinating but now we have more on the inside of the lid and I believe there is more of a story with those."

"How do you mean?" asked Jim.

"When I first glanced at the carvings, I got the impression that it seemed more like a historical map. What we have to consider if I'm right, is the world centuries ago, did not have the coastlines we have today.

Through volcanic activity, global warming and

cooling and sea level changes, any shapes of areas would have substantially altered.

I could try and set up a computer model, say for ten and then twenty thousand years ago, to see if I can fathom out what the carvings mean and if there is any message in them."

Colburn leaned back in his chair, "if you concentrate on that Val, Jim and I will attempt to work out what all these pieces are for. I'm sure as well, that they do something."

Jim was just looking a bit down; "all this money's worth and we're giving it away."

"Not just yet," replied Colburn, "we may salvage something out of this, although we'll only get taxed more.

There's no hurry though. We will take that box to pieces in due course and then hopefully all will be revealed."

Val sat up, "you're not dismantling that in here. Find somewhere else to do it."

"OK," said Colburn, "we'll take it down Jim's. Couldn't mess his place up much more."

Loud knocks were heard on the back door.

Colburn sat upright, "not expecting anyone, are we?"

He suddenly thought of the box on the workbench.

"Christ, you can see the box through the window. Too late now."

He got up and walked slowly into the kitchen and through to the back door.

He observed two figures waiting outside.

Opening the door about one-third wide, he looked out.

"Well, well, now there's a face only a mother could love. I should have known you wouldn't be far away from trouble."

A voice replied, "and it's always nice to see you Colburn. We need to talk."

The figure of Jock Strane crossed the threshold, followed by Doug the Texan.

Colburn closed the door.

"And who have you got tailing you Jock?"

"Sorry Colburn, this is an associate from America. Just call him Doug," said Strane.

"So," said Colburn, "I had a feeling that the Yanks would be involved but I bet you never knew why.

Come on through."

Strane and Doug walked through the kitchen and into the lounge, of course they looked hard at the box on the bench.

Val looked up as they entered.

"My God, never thought you'd get out of Africa, Jock.

"It wasn't easy," he replied.

"Pity they didn't keep you there," said Jim.

"Good to see you as well Jim," said Strane.

"At least now," said Jim, "we can put faces to the bugs on the cars."

"You knew about them?" said Strane.

"If you'd asked nicely, we'd have let you follow us properly," said Jim laughing, "and who is this associate of yours?"

Doug held out his hand, "just call me Doug," he said in his Texan drawl, "and it's a pleasure to meet you Ma'am," shaking Val's hand.

"Well isn't it nice to meet someone that has manners," said Val.

"Manners," shouted Jim, "these two shut us in a tomb."

"Just an oversight," replied Strane, "I knew if I focussed your minds on the problem, you would work it out.

And, judging from that box out there, you worked it out."

Colburn sat back down, "so tell me, you're obviously not working on your own. Who's running you?"

Strane pulled up a chair. Doug stood by the kitchen door.

"Look Colburn, I've always been straight with you."

"Probably because I would have ripped your neck off," replied Colburn.

"Now, no need to be like that. I think we should discuss this like friends and see what we can work out," said Strane.

"OK," said Colburn, "tell me your story and then the Redneck can have a go."

Strane began, "all I can tell you is that I got hauled in to a particular department and was told to shadow you, to see what you were up to, that's all."

"No Jock, that's never all and what were you told to do at the end?" asked Colburn.

"OK, I was told to get whatever you found," said Strane, "and it looks to me as if you have found something."

"We sure did," said Colburn, "but not what you lot expected. Don't treat us as fools. I know your governments thought there was some kind of weapon involved but there's not."

"Surely," said Doug, "that's for us to decide."

"Not at all," replied Colburn, "it's for me to decide."

Val could see Strane and Doug grimacing at the thought of their next potential move.

She thought to diffuse the situation.

"Let me see if I've got this right. You two have instructions from your governments to get whatever we find and then what. Are you two going to fight it out and the winner takes all? Seems rather pathetic to me.

If we show you exactly what we found, can we go from there?"

Strane looked at Doug and nodded.

"Seems like a fair idea Val," said Strane.

"Right, so before all the macho stuff and testosterone kicks in again, how about a cup of tea?" said Val.

"Sounds like a real good idea Ma'am but may I have coffee?" said Doug.

Doug backed into the kitchen, only a couple of feet away from the box.

"Mind if I have a look at the box?" said Doug.

Colburn shouted, "look, don't touch."

Val filled the kettle and boiled the water.

She set out four cups for tea and one for coffee.

At nearly the boiling point, she knocked off the kettle and poured the water into the cups with the tea bags. Jim and Colburn took plenty of sugar.

"How many sugars Jock?" she shouted through.

"Three will be fine Val," he answered.

"Now Yank, how do you like your coffee? I'll just need to boil a little more water. It will be done in a minute," said Val.

"Two sugars are fine," Doug mumbled.

Val put two spoonfuls in a cup.

As she turned to put more water in the kettle, she looked across the serving bay into the extension and down the barrel of a nine-millimetre Brownie pistol.

"Now that's not very friendly," shouted Val.

Colburn jumped up and saw Doug standing next to the box holding the gun.

"How dare you bring that in here," said Colburn enraged.

Strane looked surprised and embarrassed, "sorry Colburn, I didn't know he was carrying."

Colburn looked at Strane, "I can guess which one of you was getting the prize then."

The reality of the situation hit Strane.

If everything had gone to plan, Doug would have used his weapon on him.

"Now just back out of the kitchen, Mrs. Lord," said Doug.

Val turned and walked into the lounge.

Doug while keeping his weapon trained used his other hand to slide the bolt open.

Then he lifted the lid.

All he saw was metallic rods.

He put his hand in and felt for anything present.

Nothing.

Pulling back his hand, the white powder blew up all over his arm.

He wiped it away on his jacket.

"OK," he said, "what's been removed?"

Val shouted through, "make your coffee and let's discuss it."

Seemed like a reasonable idea.

The coffee grounds were in the cup, so was the sugar, no chance of poisoning then.

His hand moved to the kettle on its electrical pad.

He flicked down the "ON" switch on the kettle.

Quickly turning to glimpse the electrical socket switch, he placed his finger on it.

Turning back, keeping his gun levelled and to check everyone was still.

He pressed the switch down.

Immediately, a blue flame shot up his arm and then covered his whole body.

He gasped for breath, dropping his gun.

Colburn moved like lightening to pick it up.

The blue flame lit up his whole body and he grasped at his heart.

Suddenly the flame extinguished.

Doug dropped to the floor.

"Jesus Christ," shouted Strane, "what the hell was that?"

Colburn stuffed the weapon in his belt and went to Doug's aid.

Jim already was pressing the carotid artery.

"No pulse," he shouted.

Colburn looked up and back at Val.

"His heart's stopped, he's gone."

"What happened?" asked Strane.

Val replied, "well Jock, I've told Colburn countless times to fix that plug. I said it would cause problems."

"Problems," said Jock, "we've a dead Yank on the floor."

"He shouldn't have been greedy," said Colburn.

Jim and Val quietly smiled to each other.

Both realised that the superconductivity of the white powder would easily take electricity.

The static from the electrical plug was the conduit needed to transfer the electrical charge to the powder.

Unfortunately for Doug, the electrical charge stopped his heart, permanently.

They were not going to elaborate why.

Jock Strane was on a need to know basis and he didn't need to know.

Col burn looked at Strane's shocked face, "before we do anything else, we need to extract this body. Where were you two staying?"

Strane was still shaking, "the motel down the road, by the river."

Colburn said, "when it's dark we'll remove the body back to his room. It will just appear he died of a heart attack."

Strane shouted back, "he bloody well did. Housekeeping's in for a shock and he hasn't paid his bill."

Val interrupted, "have some sympathy Jock."

Colburn looked at Strane, "now you're on your own, tell me who you report to, or would you like me to guess. How about Stewart?"

Strane nodded.

"It stands to reason that rat would get involved. His department has been tied up with the Americans for years. He feeds the government with information but only the information he wants them to know. I think I might have to curtail his career."

Jim smiled and said, "it would be nice to get one over on him, instead of him leaving us in the crap, as usual."

"In time Jim, might just phone him and give him an offer he can't refuse," said Colburn, "but for now let's get rid of the Yank."

Darkness hit about eight-thirty.

The body was carefully lifted in Strane's car and covered in the boot.

Colburn and Strane drove back to the motel.

Pulling up in front of number five, they checked for any human movement.

Quickly opening the boot, Strane extracted the key card from Doug's pocket and they carried the body inside. Removing the clothes, they placed the body in the bed and tucked it in. Goodnight and Goodbye, Doug.

Strane went outside and next door, number four, his room.

"I'll pack up, be about five minutes," said Strane.

His suitcase was thrown into the boot and he went to reception to check out.

The staff thought it strange to be checking out on a night but they charged for the full day anyway.

Strane returned to his car and got in.

"Any problems?" asked Colburn.

"They asked me if my American friend was leaving as well. So I told them he wasn't a colleague, just someone I met at the bar. Had a few drinks together. That'll keep them quiet until the morning," said Strane.

"OK Jock, take me back home. You can stay at the Croxdale Inn up the road," said Colburn

"You've got plenty room at your house, haven't you?" said Strane.

"Not where you're concerned Jock," said Colburn, "after all, I don't trust you. Drop me off at home, go and check in and you can come up in the morning, OK."

"Suits me fine," said Strane.

"It'll have to," replied Colburn.

Strane drove into the village and dropped Colburn off at his house. Then he left.

Colburn went inside.

"Everything go OK?" asked Jim.

"Fine," replied Colburn, "Jock will be up in the morning but I think we need another chat on future planning, what to do about Jock, Stewart and those artefacts.

I'll send a message to Stewart and get him up here.

He'll come alone because he won't want anyone to know what's going on.

He probably thinks he's controlling the situation.

Now, Jim and I will take Jock down Jim's house in the morning with the artefacts.

Jock doesn't know what we have and we'll be ready for him when he does.

Then we'll try and fathom out what these things do."

Val said, "I want to study the carvings more. I'm sure there's a message somewhere."

Jim jumped in, "if you fathom out the message, give us a ring, it might be assembly instructions, we could use those."

Colburn was walking about, thinking, "need to look at those metal rods Jim, get your gloves on."

They both put on their rubber gloves, Colburn slid open the bolt and both grasped the lid and slowly opened the box.

The powder had settled.

Colburn took out the three rods, examining each in turn.

"See how this one bends at the top in a right angle. I'm sure that fits the ring area of the gold claw and these other two fit together with ferrules, like my fishing rods."

He assembled the three together. They stood about eight feet high all together.

He continued, "if the claw fits on the top here, then what?" he mused.

"The claw would have to go in this upright position, palm up, so to speak.

That would appear to be where that red stone might fit."

Jim was carefully feeling around the box, pressing and pulling anything that looked loose.

"I think there's something else in the ends of the box. If I can pull back that material cover, we can get at it."

Jim carefully started pulling at the material covering one end of the box.

As it came away, Jim saw a white solid structure.

"This looks like a lump of granite or something like it. Let me check the other end."

Pulling away the material cover revealed a similar rock at the other end.

He lifted them out onto the workbench, one at a time.

The rock structures were practically square at their base with solid rock up to about four inches. Then machined out of the other side of the rock was a geometric design looking like small rock pyramids.

The other rock, Jim noticed appeared to be a mirror image of the former.

He laid them side by side on the bench and slowly brought them together.

"These fit together perfectly," he muttered, "I wonder why?"

"That, we'll do tomorrow. We have to put these somewhere, I don't want Strane seeing them," said Colburn, "and just to make things interesting Jim, there's a bored hole in the end of one of the rocks and it looks like those rods fit it."

"OK," said Jim, "put those rocks away, I could do with a good sleep.

Fry up in the morning Val?"

"What else would there be Jim?" she replied.

Colburn closed the box, checked that everything was in place, put the stones in a cupboard and locked the doors.

"We'll just see what tomorrow brings, goodnight Jim," he said.

Jim replied, "goodnight all, tomorrow could be an interesting day."

The morning broke with Jim again enjoying the view of the patchwork quilt of greens and browns on the horizon. The sun was dancing off the fields of wheat and rapeseed,

The wild field poppies were swaying in the gentle breeze, looking like little red hands waving in the bright daylight.

He could smell the usual frying. Val was a precious delight.

He came downstairs, his plate was just being put down on the table, with the customary brown sauce.

"Morning Val," he said, "where's Colburn?"

"I'm in here," came a reply from inside the extension, "just getting a perspective on these carvings. Val's told me she's worked a bit out."

Jim sat down and tucked in.

"Can't it wait until after breakfast?" said Jim.

Val came in from the kitchen and put a cup of tea down. Then she got her tea and Colburn joined them round the table.

They were just about to start the conversation when the crunching of pebbles was heard from outside.

Colburn turned his head to look down the garden.

He saw Strane's car on his driveway.

"We've got company," he said.

"I'll make him a cup," said Val.

Strane tapped on the door and opened it.

"Come on through," shouted Colburn.

Strane came in and sat down, Val brought him a cup of tea.

"OK," he said, "what do we do now?"

Colburn put his cup on the table and leaned over, invading Strane's space; "we don't do anything. You have no rights and your job is finished. Report in to Stewart and go home."

"Now you know I can't do that," replied Strane, "I have a little matter with Immigration that needs sorting out and Stewart is holding the cards."

Jim looked up, "that's what I like about the European Union, free and unhindered travel and access to all. It's just that you took the decision to make money with your

Army knowledge and then you moan when it doesn't work out. Never mind Jock, you know the old saying, God works in Strangeways."

Colburn spoke up, "all the treasures of the Cathedral have been returned and that's what this investigation was all about. I've no doubt the university archaeology department will be kept busy for years. It all belonged to them anyway."

Strane replied, "are you expecting me to believe that. If I report that in, I'll be a laughing stock. I know you too well, you've kept something back."

"Only that box," grunted Jim.

"Maybe so, but what was really inside it. What killed Doug?" said Strane.

Just as he said those words, they heard from across the field at the rear of the house, sirens blaring on Police cars and Ambulances, going towards Durham.

Colburn smiled, "looks like housekeeping was a bit early this morning. We really should inform the Americans."

He was grinning about the situation and stood up to go upstairs.

After four steps, the stairway turned at right angles.

He turned around and put his hands above him on the landing floor railings.

Standing there he said, "Jock, if you behave, you can come with us while we try and sort out a puzzle. There is a little more to the story but it's not important."

Strane stood up from the table and moved a little behind Val.

"You know I have to take it all to Stewart," he said,

"and I know you lot won't let me. So I have to take action."

With lightening speed, Strane put his arm on Val's shoulder, just as a stiletto knife came out of his sleeve, pressing against Val's carotid.

Colburn erupted, "throw that down Jock and go. This is the only chance I'll give you. No-one harms my family."

"Seems to me I hold the cards. I want the rest of the treasure and you'll give me it because I'm holding the knife," said Strane.

Colburn's face turned from anger to amusement, "you calling that little thing a knife, now this is a knife."

Along the landing floor at the side of the stairs, Val had pinned up several photographs but there was one souvenir hanging up, facing the wall, out of sight to anyone in the house.

Colburn's hands, by leaning on the lintel across the room, were out of sight as well.

His right hand lifted the pouch, as his left hand withdrew one of his favourite souvenirs.

"Now this is what I call a knife Jock," Colburn said as the rapid speed of his hand movement showed Strane what he was holding.

The fifteen-inch, precision made, curved blade of a Gurka Kukri.

One of the most feared weapons in hand to hand combat.

Colburn walked down the four steps holding the weapon.

Strane knew his gamble had failed.

He dropped the knife on the floor.

Jim immediately grabbed it, stood up and frisked Strane for other weapons.

Colburn approached Strane with the curve of the blade pointing right at his throat.

"That wasn't very nice Jock after all the hospitality we've shown you. I'll tell you what you do now. Get on your phone to Stewart and tell him mission accomplished but his presence is required to determine what to do with what you've got. Now that's not difficult is it?" said Colburn.

Val stood up, a little shaken and turned to look Strane straight between the eyes.

Without saying a word she brought her knee up to say hello to his groin.

"That's for wasting a good cup of tea," she said.

Strane crumpled on the floor clutching his manhood.

Jim said, "told you not to piss her off."

Eventually recovering to a sitting position on the floor, Strane reached inside his coat pocket and took out his phone.

He speed dialled a number.

"You need to get up here, right away. This is big and I don't know what to do with what I've got. I need extraction fast."

Strane listened for a moment, then shut off the phone.

"Hand that over, I might need to send our friend some grid reference," said Colburn.

Strane handed him the phone.

"Now what to do with you," Colburn mused, "I

suppose you could go the same way as that Yank, if you want. It's quick."

"So is that the weapon then?" asked Strane.

"Nope," answered Colburn, "there isn't any weapon, only the treasure we found for the Cathedral. You just wouldn't believe it. For the sake of old times you can go wherever you like. You owe me now. I suggest you get in your car and get as far away from England as you can. I've heard Panama City is nice, no extradition."

Strane slowly arose hobbling out to the kitchen and to the back door.

He turned, "I told that Yank not to mess with you but he wouldn't listen. Just charged in, like in the movies but I don't know who he was reporting to. Honestly."

"It's OK Jock, I do," replied Colburn, "we all met him on our trip to Washington. The likes of him and Stewart swim in the same cesspool."

Jock was trembling a little, "sorry it had to turn out this way. I took this job just to watch you all. It wasn't supposed to get heavy."

He walked out the door and down the path to his car.

Val walked out after him.

"Jock," she shouted.

Strane stopped and turned round.

"Just tell me one thing, whatever made you think you'd get the better of those two?

Strane thought for a moment, "I had the drop on you all, thought it was easy then."

"Listen Jock," said Val, "Both you and Colburn have carried out some strange work for the system. Don't you think it's time to retire? He really is retired you know."

"Val you're a gracious lady. He doesn't deserve you but I think you're right this time.

I hear Cuba is nice. I'll send you a Christmas Card," said Strane.

Val returned to the house.

Strane pulled away.

Jim spoke up, "think that's the last of him?"

Colburn replied, "not at all but not for quite a while, we'll see him again sometime.

Now where were we?

They all sat back down at the table, all a little relieved.

"Right," said Colburn, "Jim and I will take the artefacts down his place and try to sort it out, OK?"

Jim replied, "Roger that, after another cup of tea, OK Val?"

Colburn and Jim loaded the wrapped artefacts into the car and drove off, leaving Val to study the box.

Jim's house, like Colburn's, had a garage at the bottom of the garden.

They pulled up outside the garage.

It was fitted with a Henderson, up and over door.

Jim turned the handle and lifted up the door.

Unlike most garages, Jim's was an Aladdin's cave of cast-offs but everything was neatly stacked and labelled.

All his electrical kit carefully wrapped in waterproof paper.

They unloaded the artefacts. Jim closed the door and switched on the garage light.

Colburn unwrapped the stones, they appeared to be some form of quartz.

Placing the solid stone on the garage floor, he picked up the second stone carefully twisting and turning it around so the geometric protrusions fitted perfectly.

The top stone showed a perfectly bored hole.

Taking the metallic rods, Colburn examined them closely.

"I'd love to know what metal this is. I've seen nothing like it before."

"We could get it tested at the university," said Jim, "but if it is something strange, they'll want to know where it came from."

"If I had to hazard a guess," said Colburn, "I'd say it was meteorite material."

Jim looked across at him, "don't start about ET again," he said.

"Well, if I'm right, I'm thinking who could have made these perfect rods from a meteor and what sort of tools would it take to do it. The mind boggles," said Colburn.

He placed the first rod into the hole, the second fitted into the first and then the third one with the right-angled bend went on top.

They both stood back and looked.

Jim bent down on his knees to examine the base further. That was when Colburn noted some of Jim's hair was being drawn toward the structure.

"Hang on a bit Jim, there's static coming from that base," said Colburn.

"I'll soon find out," said Jim.

From one of his benches he picked up an Avometer.

"Clip that earth wire to the water down pipe," said Jim.

Colburn clipped it on.

Jim turned the dials to show voltage and took the positive lead in his hand.

He placed the lead on the base.

The meter flickered.

"Christ," he said, "there's an electrical current running through it."

He put the positive probe on the metal rods and took reading at the different sections.

Looking at Colburn with surprise he said, "there's an increase in current from the base and through each section. It's as if there was a step-up transformer in the rods.

With a small voltage at the base, there's no great danger of a shock but you could get a jolt from the top.

If a larger voltage was applied to the base, the result would be astronomical."

Colburn mused again, "thinking back through some of the history, what if a voltage like a lightening bolt was applied?"

Jim looked surprised, "with that sort of starting power, the result would be off the scale, an electrical discharge of immense proportions. It could destroy anything around it."

"So," said Colburn, "how could you control it?"

"Surely you couldn't," replied Jim.

"Well I think whoever created this, did control it," said Colburn.

"How?" asked Jim.

"I think we're about to find out," replied Colburn.

He unwrapped the gold claw.

This circular ring at the rear of the claw appeared to fit onto the right-angled bend of the top metallic rod.

The claw fitted just like an upturned hand, palms up.

"What I'm thinking is if there is an increasing electrical current flowing through these rods, this white gold, being a superconductor must only enhance it. It has to increase the strength of the current."

"So what is the red rock for?" said Jim.

"I think it sits in that clawed hand," said Colburn.

Colburn unwrapped the red stone. It was blood red and looked as if it had been cut in the best diamond houses of Europe. Each of the multiple facets shone brilliantly.

He began to place the stone carefully into the gold claw.

Pushing it into place, they both noticed that the fit was absolutely perfect.

"That's it, is it?" said Jim.

"As far as I can tell, that's it," replied Colburn.

They both walked all around the equipment staring at the base, the rods and the claw containing the stone.

"So much for that," said Jim, "are we wasting our time or what? Let's go in and put the kettle on and have a re-think."

Colburn was standing to one side, hands on hips trying to work out what it was.

Jim was at the front of the claw, looking over at the stone.

He noticed his electrical meter on the ground, thinking, "I'll put that away."

Bending down to pick it up, his body had just moved from the front of the claw when a whirring sound was

403

heard. A bolt of red light shot straight out of the stone through the claw.

The red beam hit the garage door faster than light speed and burned a hole through it.

"What the bloody hell was that?" shouted Jim.

Colburn had seen it all happen.

"Just as well you got out of the way of that," said Colburn.

"What was it then?" asked Jim.

"See what it did to the metal of the garage door, pretty good," said Colburn.

"So, what the hell is it?" said Jim.

Colburn smiled at Jim.

"I think we've found the weapon Jim. What came out of there was a primitive but a really effective Laser."

Jim was hauling himself off the garage floor.

He looked with amazement at the artefacts and what they had created.

"It's bloody amazing," said Jim, "all those centuries ago and they invented a laser machine."

"That red stone has to be a ruby Jim," said Colburn, "that's the only stone that would make this work."

"A ruby," said Jim, "that size of stone must be worth millions."

"Probably is," replied Colburn.

"The thing is, the early forms of ruby lasers used an artificial ruby, usually cylindrical, lying along the axis of a helical discharge tube containing Xenon. When a electrical charge was passed through, sometimes the ends of the ruby were silvered, the red light beam shot out of the end in the direction of the electrical flow.

The atoms are in an excited state and using an

appropriate wavelength of light, this stimulated emission produces photons, which stimulate further emissions.

The light produced is by all the photons being in step with one another and you get a continuous beam of light."

"There isn't a continuous beam, it stopped," said Jim.

"Possibly only because the electrical source was low," replied Colburn; "it may have to recharge itself."

Colburn's hearing was excellent.

Suddenly he grabbed Jim and pulled him towards the rear of the garage.

No sooner had Jim got his breath back, the laser made the whirring sound and another beam of red light shot out.

This time as the light was being emitted, Jim accidentally kicked the base.

The beam cut through the garage door across several inches of the metal.

Then it ceased again.

"OK," said Jim, "I've seen enough, let's dismantle it."

Colburn had no hesitation.

Jim grabbed the rods from the quartz, Colburn removed the ruby and everything was re-packed in the bubble wrap and paper.

After re-examining the ruby stone before packing, Colburn noted, "the beam shot straight out of this shaped point here but there are several shaped facets on this end. One wonders what the effect would be if more electrical power was applied.

I think there would be multi-beams coming out."

"That would be awesome power," remarked Jim, "but what would this lot ever be used for?"

"That's the question Jim," answered Colburn, "that beam would cut through just about anything. God knows what it would do to humans."

"So you reckon someone used this as a weapon?" asked Jim.

"I do," replied Colburn, "and I think the story of its use, somehow was written down and eventually got back to America.

Going back ages to something Val said. One of Washington's ancestors was there when the Cathedral Bell tower was destroyed. Makes you wonder if he'd rigged this lot up and it went haywire and it was this that destroyed it. Stands to reason he would have made some note about it. Later on, all Washington's papers would go the America and when he became President, he possibly noted it down in the President's Book."

"Passed down the line and then you have the drawing of the obelisk," said Jim.

"That's a fascinating scenario Jim and there's nothing to say you're wrong," said Colburn.

"I believe that this was originally designed as a working tool, probably for cutting metal and stone. Makes you wonder if the stones of the Pyramids were cut by laser. They're accurate enough for that to have happened.

Someone realised that this tool could give them an advantage in warfare. Times never change do they?

There's nothing to say that assumption isn't correct."

"But then it was lost and hidden," said Jim.

"Could be there's some in-built safety mechanism preventing it being used for aggression," said Colburn.

"That's a bit far fetched," replied Jim.

"I don't necessarily mean some mechanism that would turn itself off. I have some thoughts about that but I need to talk it over with Val first," said Colburn."

"Then we need to work out what to do about Colonel Stewart.

I hope that Val can come up with some reasonable explanation of all this but what I will say Jim, I think we deserve that stone at least. The British Museum will pay a fee for all this. You can buy a new garage door.

Let's get this lot back to my place."

Colburn and Jim packed up the car and returned to Colburn's house.

Val was in the extension still musing over the carvings with a magnifying glass.

"Found out anything?" she asked Colburn.

"You are not going to believe it," said Jim.

"After years with him, I'll believe most things are possible," said Val, "what have you two come up with now?"

Colburn and Jim went into the lounge and sat down, Val followed.

"We assembled all the pieces as we presumed they went together and when they were all together, there was an electrical current produced from the base, through the rods.

Then the stone, which incidentally is a ruby, was placed in the claw and fitted to the top rod and we waited," said Colburn.

"Then what?" said Val.

"A bloody laser beam shot out and straight through Jim's garage door," answered Colburn.

"Well, that puts a different light on the matter," said Val.

"Yes," said Jim, "a bloody big red light."

"So that's your weapon found," said Val.

Colburn looked up and stretched again in his chair.

"I think it was originally made as a tool and later on someone realised it's potential as a weapon, possibly of mass destruction.

I also believe that there has to be some safety device, whatever it is, that stopped it being used."

"Now, I think I may be able to help there," said Val.

"Some of those carvings appear to be just faces or images of Gods, or whoever was worshipped at that time. Some of the symbols, I've managed to decipher using the old alphabet but it's not entirely perfect.

Those on the top of the lid appear to be saying that oracles or seers would keep mankind in check."

Colburn interrupted, "therefore we can deduce from that, if this tool had been misused, an oracle or seer would have somehow managed to stop the misuse.

Fascinating theory."

"It's not theory," said Val, "basically that's what is says."

"Now I know history isn't my strong point," said Jim, " but if you two are right, you're saying that some oracle managed to get this back, not to be destroyed but hidden forever."

"You're right Jim," said Val, "it would have been hidden away but probably centuries later it was found and transported here."

Colburn said, "it didn't take rocket science to put it together and I believe on occasions it was assembled. But whoever did it didn't know what it was.

However, someone must have written about it."

Val interrupted, "and there's your American connection."

"That's exactly what we thought," replied Colburn.

"I still think it was used as a cutting tool, perhaps the stones of the pyramids or the Hanging Gardens. Can you imagine what a place those people lived in with all this technical knowledge."

"I've just had a thought," said Jim, " what if, inside the box, the top rod was inserted into the base with the claw and ruby fitted. What would happen to someone outside the box who carried something metallic about his person?"

Colburn replied, "I imagine there would be a hell of a jolt of static electricity."

"That's what I was thinking," said Jim, "would make a hell of an Ark, the Rod of Moses inside. Laser writing of the Ten Commandments, who knows?"

Colburn and Val looked at each other. Jim's comments were not laughable. They had some valid points. The surprise was showing on their faces.

Jim continued, "don't worry. I'm not saying this is the Ark but it could be something similar. From what's described in the Bible, if you're a believer, it could have been bolts of electricity coming from the Ark. That's reasonable to assume."

Val sighed, "it is reasonable Jim but let's not go down that avenue just yet. This box appears to be just a receptacle for carrying those artefacts around and nothing more. There still are more letters to decipher. Maybe they will tell us about its origin."

Colburn was agitated, "The Americans think they

are on the trail of an ancient weapon and perhaps that's partly true. So we'll have to throw them off the scent because this is of immense historical value."

"And expensive," said Jim.

"Val," said Colburn, "Jim and I decided that the artefacts would be safer in the British Museum so eventually we're going to make them an offer."

"But surely they should go back to the Cathedral," said Val.

"I think they've had enough out of us. These we have can add to our Pension Funds quite nicely," replied Colburn, "it's only fair."

Val said, "at least we now know what was meant by the Fire of the Gods. Can you imagine, centuries ago, laser beams shooting out at invading Armies."

Colburn replied, "the trouble is, I think it was used by invaders and not for defence. That's what caused all this to begin."

"Surely you don't believe in Oracles Colburn?" said Jim.

"It really doesn't matter what we believe nowadays, people believed in them then.

After all, some still go to fortune tellers, you use rune stones, Val has tarot cards, and they are all methods of hopefully looking into the future. So people do believe and they certainly did centuries ago.

So what we have is just a simple laser and nothing else.

Governments have sophisticated laser apparatus now, they're used in all sorts of activities, especially medical. No one should want what we have and at this present time no one really knows that we have anything at all.

I just need to work out a way of fixing Stewart for good."

"Any thoughts about that yet?" asked Jim.

Colburn smiled and said, "We need an accurate weather forecast for the next few days. I'm sure that somewhere on the hills we'll find Thor throwing his thunderbolts."

Jim laughed, "use the high ground and see him coming."

"Not just that," replied Colburn, "we'll ruin his reputation and credibility. So we need a place that fits the bill historically and military."

"We know just the place," said Jim, looking at Val.

"And where pray, might that be?" she asked.

Colburn looked at her lovingly, "The Roman Wall."

CHAPTER TWENTY-NINE

Colburn took out Jock Strane's mobile phone.

He pressed on the word names and scrolled through them.

Colonel Stewart's personal number was there.

He hit the button for text messaging.

"55 Degrees North, 2 Degrees West.
IMP. CAES. TRAIAN. HADRIANO. AUG. p.p.

Personal immediate attention required.

Thurs. 23rd   22.00 Hours. Housesteads.

All answers there.

He hit the send button.

"What did you write there?" asked Jim.

"Just gave him the co-ordinates and a time, he can work out the Latin," said Colburn, "I've already checked the weather forecast, in two days there will be thunder in the air."

Val had seen it, "what it said Jim is; To the Emperor Hadrian, father of his country.

I love that area," she said, "possibly the most beautiful scenery in Britain.

The thing is, it was lucky to ever be built.

Initially the Romans never gave a thought to a permanent frontier in Britain.

It was almost a hundred years after Julius Caesar, that Claudius needing an easy victory invaded Britain and this time the Romans stayed put.

Britain at that time was a community of several tribes but the expansionist policies of Nero, Claudius's successor, were halted by the Boudicca rebellion and it was only under the Flavians that expansion got under way.

The northern governor Agricola, built many roads for his Army but when he and his legion were recalled for other duties, the Romans withdrew from Southern Scotland.

Nearly eighty years after the Claudian invasion, they probably decided that Roman Britain had no effective northern frontier. They were probably comparing things to the frontiers of the Rhine, Danube, Euphrates and the sea.

Now when Hadrian came to power, he found trouble in Britain. So he selected a line running along the Tyne to the Solway, about 76 Roman Miles, seventy of ours.

Hadrian's instincts were for peace, so the wall went up.

From Wallsend at the North Sea end to Carlisle, through to Bowness on the Solway.

The thing is, contrary to popular belief, the wall was not a closed frontier.

At one Roman mile intervals were fortified gateways or Milecastles.

These were not just for military use, they controlled the passage of local tribesmen and traders. Affording security to those in the South, while not cutting them off completely from the North.

Of course, just like nowadays, money began to run out, so some of the wall was just earth works and some of the stone work got narrower to save money.

Perhaps had they put more thought into it, it wouldn't have taken them nearly one hundred years of fighting and building before the finished product marked the frontier of the Roman Empire.

Just as a matter of interest, anybody north of the wall were considered savages."

Jim laughed, "nothing's changed much then," he said.

Val retorted, "that's not fair Jim."

Jim looked at her, "Val," he said, "you haven't been to an old firm derby match, have you?"

Val glared back at Jim, she knew he was probably right.

Jim said, "Colburn, remember the Fairs Cup second leg semi-final at St. James against Rangers?"

"I certainly do," answered Colburn, "when Newcastle scored their second goal, one side of the ground went eerily silent, while the other three sides erupted.

After the match we had to run the gauntlet of bottles and stones, to get back to our transport. They were savages alright and not a lot has changed."

"Well that's football for you," said Val, "but I was talking about another World Heritage site and Housesteads is the most magnificent example of Roman building.

With the wall following the majority of the Whin Sill, these forts were built on the Southern side with just a deep ditch to the North.

Housesteads is the prime example of a military fort, barracks and major trading post."

Colburn said, "what I've got planned will not harm or interfere with heritage."

Val replied, "you've said that before."

"What we will do Jim, is go up there tomorrow and book into a Bed and Breakfast place, probably in Corbridge and see the lay of the land. I would expect Stewart to get there early so he would think he had the advantage. So we'll tour the site tomorrow and set up the following day when visiting time is over," said Colburn.

"Possibly a couple of beers on the night?" asked Jim.

"Only a couple," replied Colburn, "we'll both need all our faculties to outwit him but I've got a few thoughts on the matter that we can discuss on the travel up there."

Colburn and Jim checked the packing of the artefacts making sure there was no possibility of any short circuits.

They used slightly larger backpacks, so that all the equipment and overnight clothes would fit.

They changed into walking gear.

Waterproof anoraks, trousers and boots. They looked the typical hikers.

Ponchos were rolled and carried in a side pocket, Tilley hats on their heads.

Rain was on its way.

They expected storms.

Val had scanned the Internet and booked them in a small hotel in Corbridge.

The good thing about a tourist area, especially in the North East, was an ample supply of hotel rooms.

"You all set then?" asked Colburn.

"Ready when you are," replied Jim.

They said their goodbyes and walked towards Colburn's car.

"We'll take mine this time, Stewart will be expecting to see it," said Colburn.

"OK," replied Jim, "you drive."

Driving out of the village eastwards took them onto the road leading to the AI M Motorway.

While it would be a much more scenic drive, past Lanchester, Consett and over the moors, it was quicker by motorway.

After a few minutes they passed the Durham exit and headed North.

After Washington services, the road forks north or to the Coast.

Following the North road, they passed the "rust bucket" otherwise known as "The Angel of the North." A magnificent structure that has become a World famous landmark.

Driving on past the Team Valley trading estate and avoiding all the traffic trying to cut them up joining the road, they drove past one of their favourite views, the Federation Brewery.

A little further along they passed Val's favourite place, the Metro Centre, Europe's largest shopping mall and a Mecca for tourists and locals alike. Headed by a flagship Marks and Spencers.

The road swung to the right and crossed the Tyne, and then Colburn took the left slip road for the A69.

This road continued all across the country to Carlisle and while the early part of the road from Newcastle is dual carriageway, the bulk of the road after Hexham, is one lane and for many drivers, a death trap.

On this section of the road, Colburn kept his speed to the required fifty.

A few miles outside Hexham, Jim pointed out the brown information signs for the Roman Wall. They turned off the road and headed for Housesteads Fort.

Eventually after driving the country roads for a while, they pulled in at the Visitor Centre and parked up.

Colburn switched off the engine, "let's get a cup of tea first and then go up to the site."

They got out and walked to the centre.

The car park was nearly full, even though bad weather was expected.

Not many hikers were in evidence, they would be walking the wall.

The Centre thronged with parents and children.

"Why do we have to work on school holidays?" said Jim.

The noise from an assorted amount of five to ten year olds could have competed with the roar of a football crowd.

It wouldn't be so bad if they would all walk but they seemed to be competing in several races zigzagging across and around the shop.

Why kids want to be dressed like Roman soldiers with plastic helmets and swords, can never be answered. Like the reason for the parents buying them, it couldn't be to keep them quiet, the noise just echoed around. It was loud enough to call up the souls of departed soldiers.

Colburn and Jim went to the small kiosk and ordered two teas.

They sat outside on the wooden tables and benches.

The small children seemed to follow them, charging around using their plastic swords like air guitars.

Jim leaned on the table and groaned, "it was easier going to war," he said, "at least you knew where the noise was coming from."

"Most of the time Jim," replied Colburn.

They drank their tea, picked up their backpacks and headed out of the rear of the shop to the stile that begins the walk over the hills.

Just as the walk begins, on the far hill the Roman Fort came into sight.

"That's a good trek from the road," said Jim.

"Remember Jim, picture the area without a road, just cart tracks. That's what it would have been like back then," said Colburn.

The track descended into a valley before turning upward towards the fort.

Before starting to ascend the hill, Colburn noted, "this is an excellent position to defend."

Close to the side entrance of the fort was an old farmhouse that doubled as a small museum and where you paid for your entrance tickets.

They got their tickets and walked back up to the fort.

To the ignorant eye, the area might appear to be just a few rocks, some in the semblance of a building, some just stuck in the ground appearing to be nothing at all.

Then at the highest point of the fort, the rocks appear to be in some form of regular structure that was obviously a building.

Most visitors hardly notice the officer's quarters and barrack area, they just head for the far wall. THE WALL.

Visiting historic sites takes imagination. If you can perceive the finished product, imagining the elaborate preparations of surveying, organising work details and transport, all before any start was made.

This wall was a visible and physically controlled frontier of the province of Britannia.

Much of it built in stone, turf being used to finish it in the west.

Working parties from three legions laboured on it, supposedly as a solution to the problems of the northern frontier.

The place would have been a hive of constant activity from building it, to its garrison.

Supplies would be brought daily for the troops and traders would try to make money from the soldiers along its length.

Looking over the far side, a vast ditch was evident at the base of the wall, to deter any Scots from attacking.

Colburn and Jim wandered around the remnants of this great fort, not just admiring the view for miles over the countryside but marvelling at the engineering feat of construction and fortification.

This certainly could be defended and you could observe any unwanted visitors.

The site was perfect for Colburn's plan.

Below the main barracks area on the south-facing

wall close to the South Gate, was an area of a deep pit enclosed by high walls.

It was dug as a latrine area next to the baths.

The Romans even had designed running water for their toilets.

This part of the wall was high and overlooked the path visitors had to follow.

Colburn scanned the surrounding area for other ways to enter.

Only the West Gate area seemed appropriate but the actual entrance was to small for attack.

He decided that the South face had to be the most reasonable choice, after all, Stewart had no reason to suspect anything but Colburn knew that he would.

Following the line of the Wall in an easterly direction, it meandered down a deep gully and up over the next hill. On top of that hill was a dense mound of trees.

Colburn recognised the advantage of a perfect overview of the fort.

"When we get back tomorrow, I want you to use that copse as cover. You should be able to follow anything that occurs. You'll need your night vision lenses and the camouflage poncho. The weather should be abysmal, just perfect," said Colburn.

Jim was taking note of the surroundings.

"Unless he wants to walk miles in the bad weather, he'll park up nearby, might just use the car park. I'll spot his car first and deal with it. Then I'll see that everything goes to plan," said Jim.

"Have you still got that farmer friend of yours around here?" asked Colburn.

"Sure have, you need some equipment?" replied Jim.

"Find out what his farm stock is, can you?" said Colburn.

"I'll ring now and find out," replied Jim.

Jim rang the farmer and said he would get back to him.

"Get back on to him and make him an offer he won't refuse. I just want to borrow something for a few hours," said Colburn.

Jim rang again and fixed a time for a pick up.

A couple of hundred notes sweetened the labour.

"I need to go back to the shop and I think that's all we can do today," said Colburn.

They walked off back down the slope and up to the car park.

Colburn wove his way through the children's brigade and made his purchase.

He met Jim outside and they walked to their car.

Colburn was carrying a cardboard cut out of a Roman soldier. It had to be put together in sections.

"This will give him a target in the dark. Then we'll know what his exact intentions are," said Colburn.

"I would have thought his intentions were quite obvious, steal whatever we have and take care of you," said Jim.

"Nice to know someone cares, isn't it?" replied Colburn.

They drove back to the A69 junction and turned east bypassing Hexham. They headed towards Corbridge and their hotel.

After parking up, booking in, checking their room and showering, they headed for the dining room and their usual peppered steaks, carbonised.

Sitting in the small bar lounge area afterwards, with pints of John Smiths' free flow, Colburn was musing over the area in his head.

"You know Jim, I could never fathom out why so many people who come to visit the Roman Wall and it's forts, never spend some of their time exploring this place. When I was young, I used to come to this area to explore the Roman sites.

This place was called Corstopitvm, it has the Stanegate Fort and settlement. The most striking thing about this site aside from the remains is the undulating ground, probably caused by subsidence after the Roman departure. It looks now as if the town had been built on the waves of a turf sea. It's very strategically placed near to the lowest fordable place of the Tyne.

Dere Street crosses the river here, from York and continues to Barbaricum.

The Antonine name Corstopitum is probably a Romanisation from the original Celtic name. The Roman-British name is interpreted as "The Valley of the Resounding Noise." The name seems to reflect its importance as a busy garrison town, close to the Scottish border.

The garrison here was composed of cohorts taken from several of the legions who were stationed around Britain. The first to be here was the Legio 11 Augusta from Caerleon in Wales, then the Legio V1 Victrix from York and these were added to by the Legio XX Valeria from Chester.

There are plenty of Latin inscriptions on the stones found around here."

"Like second and third century graffiti," said Jim.

"Precisely," answered Colburn, "they were proud of their units."

"So were we," said Jim.

Colburn continued, "there's at least a dozen stones with markings from the Sixth Legion.

They found a Trajan coin beneath the Fort with a date of AD 103. As Emperor Trajan began withdrawing troops from here, and elsewhere, for his second Dacian campaign, it appears they burned down the first fort, levelled the ground and built another one. There's even evidence of a further rebuild in the early times of Hadrian.

No doubt then that this place was a major garrison town and supply route for the Wall. All sorts of animal bones have been discovered, showing the town not only bred them but the folk hunted them.

Also over twenty altar stones have been found to various Roman Gods, although the greatest number were dedicated to Apollo Maponus, who was Romano-Celtic and Veterus, who was Germanic. So there was obviously a good European content of the forces. The German God's altars have been found in several places in the forts along the Wall and in forts along the supply route from York.

All the temples discovered so far, were built in a classical style but seeing as the population were predominantly Roman citizens, it's not surprising the temples looked like the Pantheon.

There's something like seven different temples around this town.

People should really take the time to come here and see the history. This place is one of the greatest treasures in the North east."

"Well after that, do you want another drink, then we'll hit the sack?" asked Jim.

"Fine with me," replied Colburn.

The next morning began with the usual full English breakfast after which they checked their gear, packed the bags, paid the bill and loaded up the car.

"What are we going to do all day. Its going to be a long day until ten tonight?" asked Jim.

"Thought we might park up in Hexham, have some dinner in Robbs' tea rooms, wander round the Sele and enjoy the day," said Colburn.

"Sounds OK with me, apart from those black clouds on the horizon," said Jim.

Colburn looked to the South East. Far down the country it was apparent the storm clouds were brewing.

"Looks like the forecasters might have got it right," said Colburn.

"Thank God for small mercies," replied Jim.

They got in the car and drove the three miles into Hexham.

It was easier to park in the Supermarket Car Park and leave it there.

They only needed about two hours so parking there would be OK.

Any longer than that would get them a fine.

Dressed in hiking gear they fitted in well walking up the hill of the main street.

The Sele is a grassy hill near the town centre, laid out as a park being open to the public since 1753.

They walked to the summit of the hill, called the Priest's Seat and sat on the grass.

The day was humid, darker clouds were looming fast from the South East.

"This is a remarkable place," said Colburn, "it always seemed strange that numerous Roman stones have been found here but they all appeared to originate from Corbridge. The Romans must have thought that it was not the ideal place to defend.

It's protected on one side by the Tyne and that is only fordable when the river is low but even then it's dangerous because of its bed of quicksand.

It flourished more in Saxon times. After the victory of Latin over Celtic Christianity at the synod of Whitby in AD 664, Wilfred was the supremo in the northern church.

Ten years later, Queen Etheldid of Northumbria gave him a large stretch of land in Hexhamshire and he built a Roman type church on a basilica style.

The area got ravaged by the Danes for a couple of hundred years and the church was burnt to the ground but about AD 1050, Eilaf started the reconstruction and his son completed it in the Norman style.

No one really knows about the shape or size of the original church.

The Scots burned the town a few times but everything eventually was rebuilt.

The remains of the castle and gaol are worth seeing as well.

Many of the castles and large houses around here have Roman Wall stones in them.

I suppose it was looked on as cheap building material.

Rain's coming soon," said Colburn.

They picked up their packs and wandered off down the hill to the Market Place and wandered round to Robbs for lunch.

After lunch they strolled back down the Main Street and round to the car park.

They put their packs onto the rear seat and set off back over the river to the A69, heading West.

The rain was falling lightly. The wipers were on speed three.

They saw more ominous cloud formations to the South, they appeared to be more purple in colour than grey. Faint rumblings of thunder could be heard far off.

The wind speed was less than five miles an hour, which meant the worst of the weather was still hours away.

If the calculation were correct, it would be directly overhead by ten tonight.

The drive back to Housesteads Visitor Centre, only took twenty-five minutes.

Pulling in off the road and parking, they went for their usual cup of tea from the small kiosk. Jim carried a large golf-type umbrella.

Colburn was looking at him, questioning why the umbrella was needed.

"We've got plenty of wet weather protection on, why do you need that?"

Jim replied, "if I've got to spend hours driving to the farm and back here up in that knoll of trees, I'm keeping as dry as possible, for as long as possible."

"Fair comment" said Colburn; "you pay for the teas then. We've been wetter around Brecon."

"And in a few jungles," replied Jim.

They sat down on the wooden benches.

Colburn was re-checking the plan in his mind.

"We need to go up a check out the area for our exact positions.

Then we can come back down for a burger and you can nip off to your farmer pal and meet me back here. I'll tell the wardens that we're walking the wall, maybe camping and are leaving our car here. Then it won't get towed away.

If we wait until most of the activity up in the fort has ceased, then settle down until dark, I'll set things up in the fort and we'll keep in touch by text, ok."

After their tea, they set off up the long incline towards the fort.

Quite amazingly, there were ample visitors walking the area, even in the bad conditions. Some were walking the Wall.

Instead of using the West Gate, they skirted around the base of the fort wall to the South and then East and clambered onto the Wall.

Walking towards the knoll of trees, they were observing the surroundings.

"You can get a good view of the car from up there," said Jim.

"I expect Stewart will pull in next to ours, there's no need to pull off the road and head overland. He knows he needs to talk with me," said Colburn.

They jumped down from the Wall just as they lost sight of the fort.

Wandering through the trees and shrubbery, they found their perfect observation point.

They could see the fort area again and down to the car park area.

"This is perfect," said Colburn, "if you observe from here, you'll see everything but don't interfere unless I call."

"Roger that," answered Jim.

The spot chosen was a small undulation in the ground. Jim could lie there and cover himself with a camouflaged poncho. He had chosen ordinary binoculars. In bad weather he could see just as much as using infra-red lenses.

Colburn would be down in the fort area waiting.

The rain was becoming a little more persistent now.

Many of the visitors started heading back towards the Centre.

"Time for Burgers and Chips, I think," said Jim.

"Everything seems in order, let's go," replied Colburn.

They walked back down the grass and up to the Visitors Centre.

Jim ordered the Burgers.

Colburn went inside the Centre to find the Head Ranger.

There's no problem of walking in bad weather, as long as someone in authority knows what you're doing and where you're headed.

Colburn knew that as long as they were back for their car, there would be no problems.

He told the Ranger that if conditions did worsen, they might abandon the walk.

This put the thought in the Ranger's mind that if the car was gone in the morning, the hikers had given up. Therefore there would be no need to alert any rescue teams.

Colburn returned to his Burger.

"Everything set for leaving the car," said Colburn, "after this you go to the farm and I'll stay here."

"I should be back in about one hour," said Jim.

"No later," said Colburn, "it will be pretty dark by then and the storms clouds are gathering pace."

"I'll be back in time," said Jim.

Finishing his Burger, Jim left in the car for his friend's farm.

Colburn had another cup of tea and bought a couple of fruit drinks for later.

After another browse around the shop, he noticed Jim pulling back into the car park.

This time the car was parked at the spot farthest away from the Centre but directly in line with the knoll of trees on the far hill.

Colburn walked out and to the car.

Getting in he handed Jim one of the fruit drinks.

"Plenty of carbohydrates in that for later," he said.

Jim looked at the plastic bottle, carefully examining the ingredients.

"You know I don't like to drink these. They taste alright but they have Dimethyl Dicarbonate in them as a preservative," he said.

"What's the problem with that?" asked Colburn.

"That chemical produces Methanol, they even measure the Methanol content during and after manufacture. You can imagine all those men sitting around at night in doorways with these drinks wrapped in brown paper bags. It's frightening what's in some food and drinks these days," said Jim, "but I'll drink it later, no crisps though, they make too much noise."

"This should be all over by eleven," said Colburn, "one way or another."

"Are you expecting Stewart to come armed?" asked Jim.

"I think he will," said Colburn, "its all part of the plan. He'll expect to get the drop on me and I'll let him."

"Or he'll just think he's done it," said Jim.

"Precisely," answered Colburn, "you got the goods in the boot?"

"All present and correct," said Jim.

"So while I'm busy with Stewart, you deal with the rest and then keep watch."

"No problem," replied Jim, "we are expecting him on time, even early aren't we?"

"He'll be a little early knowing him," said Colburn, "he's got no reason to assume there's a problem. Let's get all the gear out and get set up."

"As long as it's over by eleven, the sedative will be wearing off and I wouldn't want to be around then," said Jim.

Colburn smiled as he assembled his kit.

The rain was sheeting across the hills.

Clouds had turned a blacker shade of purple and the distant thunder was increasing in intensity.

They walked together until they reached the southern wall of the fort.

Jim took off towards the knoll of trees.

Colburn went through the South Gate, up onto the top of the wall at the Baths area.

Jim found his small ditch, dropped off his kit and donned his camouflage poncho.

Lying down on the ground, he checked his watch. One hour maximum, to go.

Pulling his Tilley hat hard down onto his head, he checked the car park area with binoculars. Only their car was left.

He settled down to keep watch, checked his mobile and sent a text to Colburn.

"All set up and watching."

Colburn's phone was on vibrate, he checked the message from Jim and replied.

"All OK here."

He assembled the cardboard cut out of the Roman soldier and placed it on its stand so that it was hanging half way down into the baths area and covered over with his poncho. He placed his hat on top of the cardboard helmet and tied it down. From afar it looked as if someone was sitting on the edge of the baths.

Colburn slipped down about six feet onto the grass floor of the baths.

With the poncho extending over the edge, Colburn could fit underneath it in the corner of the wall. He was high and dry.

He sat on the grass and unpacked the relics.

By his feet he placed the two stones, fitted together.

He assembled the three parts of the rod and leaned them against the wall, undercover.

The ruby was inserted into the gold claw but he kept it separate from the rod.

All seemed to be set.

He sent a text to Jim.

"Ready and waiting."

The thunder was closing in fast, crashing around the hills.

Then Colburn saw for the first time, what he'd been hoping for.

There in the distance was the first of the lightening bolts.

He thought to himself, light travels faster than sound, this should be overhead soon. I should have at least a half-hour time zone for the display.

Settling down, he closed his eyes and waited for Jim's message.

It was about twenty minutes later, with the rain lashing down and the thunder and lightening erupting all around the hills, he felt his buzzer vibrate on the phone.

He checked the message.

"Stewart here, coming straight on."

Jim followed his movements through the binoculars, coming from the parking area and up through the Visitor Centre area, onto the gravel path to the fort.

Stewart paused several times and seemed to be observing and checking through his own binoculars, night vision.

Jim knew that in pouring rain, the image would be more blurred than usual.

Stewart began the upward climb to the fort.

He appeared to be following the usual visitor's path, entering on the West Side.

Halfway up, he seemed to catch sight of a figure sitting on the wall, just waiting.

There was no way of making out who it was.

Colburn's phone buzzed, he checked the message.

"Entering West Gate, Off to check on the cars."

Jim got up and left his position, walking through the trees and down into the valley before coming up into the car park. No one would notice him in this weather.

The only light in the sky was the incessant lightening, practically overhead now.

Stewart was dressed in a poncho and combat hat. No doubt the combat fatigues were underneath. The rain just flowed away from his body.

He crept silently towards the figure on the mound.

Colburn couldn't hear any footsteps.

Then Stewart stepped on the only part of the path in the fort that was gravel.

Colburn had chosen well.

The scraping of DMS boots was heard.

The rain was virtually blinding Stewart.

He was within six feet of the figure when Colburn heard him shout out.

"Strane, is that you?"

It was reasonable to assume it was Strane, after all the message was sent from his phone.

There was no reply.

Stewart wasn't taking any chances.

He lifted up his flashlight and brought it down as hard as he could onto the head of the figure.

The hat and cardboard buckled under the attack.

Stewart's right arm holding the light continued onward and down, just like the perfect follow through of a golf stroke.

Being on the edge on the baths area, the cardboard figure shot into the air and down onto the ground below.

The follow through couldn't be avoided.

As his right arm flew over the place where the figure had sat, he tried to adjust his balance.

The force of the blow had left Colburn exposed underneath.

With lightening reflexes, he reached up and grabbed Stewart's arm and pulled.

Stewart tumbled headlong over the edge of the wall, somersaulting in the air and landing hard on the grass in the bottom of the baths.

It took him several seconds to focus and regain his breath.

During this time Colburn was forcing him down, checking for weapons.

"Good evening Colonel, nice night for a stroll," said Colburn.

Stewart looked up and snarled, "Lord."

Colburn got up and retreated to his corner.

"Thought you might be carrying," he said.

"Left it all in the car, didn't think I'd need it," said Stewart clambering to his feet and backing against the far wall about twenty feet away.

The rain was dripping down Colburn's face.

"So are you going to tell me what the hell you want?" he said.

Stewart virtually had to shout over another thunderclap that had been preceded by a bolt of lightening.

Colburn realised that the time between the lightening and the sound of thunder meant that the storm was nearly directly overhead.

"All I can tell you is that my counterpart in the States contacted me to put passive surveillance on you, just to see what was going on.

I could tell by the television reports, you found the Cathedral treasure but I knew you'd keep something back."

"So do the Yanks want the treasure or the power?" asked Colburn.

"They don't want any treasure but they do want to know what the power is supposed to be," said Stewart.

"Well if you're going to be good, I'll tell you and I'll show you," said Colburn.

Stewart smiled through the rain, "it's a deal," he said.

"Stay exactly where you are and I'll show you," said Colburn, "any other movement and I'll snap your neck. After all the Yanks sent one like Strane you know. Unfortunately he had a heart attack in bed."

"And I really believe that happened," said Stewart.

"Believe what you want, when the Yanks get him back they'll find his heart give out and that's the truth. If I'd wanted to knock him off, I could have done it anytime with any method but his heart wasn't in the job," said Colburn.

Colburn reached for the metal rod leaning against the wall.

"What I kept back is all here," said Colburn.

He lifted the gold claw with the ruby onto the top of the rod and placed the other end in the stones.

"What the hell is that lot?" exclaimed Stewart.

"It's the power of the Gods," replied Colburn, "just stay there and watch."

Stewart knew better than to move.

Colburn fished a plastic glove out of his jacket, just like those that surgeons wear.

Knowing that they would not conduct electricity.

It seemed like an eternity to Stewart, nothing was happening.

Colburn knew it would take a few moments to charge, then he recognised the buzzing sound.

"You might want to sit on the grass Colonel," he shouted.

Stewart slid down the wall into a sitting position.

No sooner had Stewart hit the grassy floor, when a beam of red light shot out of one of the points on the ruby and across towards where Stewart had been standing. Colburn moved the rods to alter the position of the beam.

After a while, Colburn lifted the rod out of the stone. The beam ceased.

"That's the power you were all looking for," said Colburn.

"It's nothing but a small laser," said Stewart, looking amazed, standing up and looking at the wall behind him.

There, inscribed on the wall where he would have stood, were the letters;

"S P Q R"

"I thought it was appropriate for here," said Colburn.

Senatus Populusque Romanus

The famous sign carried by the Roman Legions, meaning a partnership between the Senate and the People and probably the first logo in the World.

Colburn walked forward and retrieved his hat and poncho from the cardboard cut out and retreated back to the opposite corner to Stewart.

He lifted the quartz base from the grass floor to the top of the wall.

Grabbing the metal rod with the claw and ruby, he turned and walked up the stone steps at the side of the baths area.

Standing on the wall, he looked down at the Colonel.

"What happens now?" asked Stewart.

Colburn replied, "the way I see it is quite simple. History and Science belongs to everyone and not just a select few. You and your associates thought they might be onto some fabulous weapon when all you have is a simple laser.

This may well have been invented before we were out of our caves but that doesn't matter. The World has sophisticated lasers, for industry, medical and weaponry, so you don't need this simple artefact.

What I am going to do with this, is use it for scrap value. It will pay for my time and trouble. You can report back whatever you like but leave me out of it, or I might change my mind about you."

"What do you mean, change your mind?" asked Stewart.

"You are of no use to me, you can go home now," said Colburn

"How do I get out of here then?" said Stewart.

"Crawl out of that hole on the South side. That's how all the sewerage from these baths got out and you're no different," Colburn said laughing, the rain pouring down from his hat over his poncho, "go on get out and don't let me hear from you again at any time in the future."

Stewart turned and fell onto his knees.

He crawled through the open space that once carried the toilet sewerage and used bath water to the outside of the fort.

Colburn looked up at the dark night sky.

The once purple hue had turned into sheer blackness, only interrupted with the white forks of lightening.

He assembled the rod in the stone and with his gloved hand shielded even more with his poncho, he grasped the top of the rod.

Stewart was half running, sliding, slipping down the South grass area of the fort.

He reached the dip the ground where the path began to rise up to the Visitors Centre.

Looking back, he could see Colburn standing on the wall like Moses at the edge of the Red Sea.

As he hesitated, listening to the last clap of thunder, an almighty lightening fork lit up the whole area.

Colburn knew that the metal was not just a conductor but a magnet for electricity.

The lightening appeared to strike the ground of the fort and suddenly creep like Spanish moss, over the grass.

The white light reached the bottom of the metal and shot up the rods.

Colburn had positioned the claw so that it faced over the dip in the ground.

Light illuminated the rear of the claw and travelled straight into the ruby.

Out of the facets of the ruby, then came a roar that matched the very thunder that created it.

Colburn had stepped back from the rods at the final moment.

Between the four fingers of the claw and from around the sides, exploded not just a small single beam but streams of fire, like a circus flame-thrower.

The fire erupted from the facets and streamed out over the hillside.

Stewart saw the streams of fire heading towards him and threw himself to the ground crawling into a ball.

The ground around him, soaked with incessant rain, was scorched dry.

The flames seemed to continue for twenty seconds, perhaps more, then ceased.

Colburn took the rod out of its base, not wanting it to recharge.

He shouted across the grass to Stewart, "behold the Power of the Gods."

Stewart picked himself up and sprinted off towards his car.

Colburn was still standing on the wall, wondering with amazement how such a masterpiece could have been created.

His phone buzzed and he answered, his hands still shaking.

"What was that?" the voice asked.

"That's the real power Jim," Colburn replied.

"It was better than the Chinese Olympics," said Jim.

"Sure was, and this wasn't computer generated," replied Colburn, "you managed to finish your job then?"

"I reckon we have about thirty minutes before take off," said Jim.

"Time enough, where's Stewart now?" asked Colburn.

Jim whispered down his phone, "starting the car right now. He looks as if he's seen a ghost, that'll teach him a lesson."

"Not quite all the lesson yet," Colburn said as he started to dismantle the relics and put them into his backpack.

Colburn started to descend from the wall out of the South Gate and down the valley.

Ten minutes later he met Jim by their car.

"I reckon it's just about the right time, Stewart should be on the main road by now," said Colburn.

Using Strane's phone he dialled a number and waited for an answer.

"Which service do you require?" said the voice.

"Police please," Colburn replied.

"And what is the nature of your call?" asked the voice.

"I'm from the farm by Riding Mill and I was woken up by noise and a red light flashing. I saw a man and he was holding a gun, robbing my farm. When I switched the lights on he jumped into his car and drove off."

"Did you see the car or its registration," asked the voice.

Jim held out a piece of paper with a registration number on.

"Yes I did, I don't know the make but it was dark probably black, I got most of the number.

Colburn reeled off the number leaving the last two digits out.

"I'm sure he was headed back to the main road," said Colburn.

"Leave it with us," said the voice.

Colburn hung up.

They put their gear into the car, started it up and drove slowly out of the car park and back to the A69.

Once off the back roads, Colburn could see the occasional car and lorry on the main road, after all it was the major route up here for crossing the country.

Just as they were pulling up to the road, Colburn stopped.

"Hear that Jim?"

Through the dark and rain, they could hear the whirring of rotors.

Passing only a hundred-foot above them was a Police Helicopter, probably full of the armed response team.

"Nice one," murmured Colburn, then he turned on to road heading back toward Newcastle.

It was a quiet drive through Haydon Bridge, which took them onto the Hexham dual carriageway after another four miles.

Keeping well within the speed limits, they by-passed Hexham and eventually came down onto the last roundabout before the long stretch into Newcastle.

Up ahead they could see the sky lit up with red, orange and blue lights.

As they approached the roundabout, several policemen were holding up the main road traffic and diverting them onto the A69 Consett road.

Colburn slowed and dropped his window.

"Any problems officer?" he asked.

"We have an incident up ahead, you'll have to divert," said the policeman.

"Hope it's not too serious," said Colburn.

"No, we have everything under control," said the cop.

Colburn drove round the roundabout following the A69.

After two miles the road winds up a steep bank.

At the top Colburn pulled the car into a lay-by and they got out.

Clouds were starting to form as the thunderous weather headed north.

In the dark grey of the night, the occasional star could now be seen.

Away in the distance on the Newcastle road, blinking lights raced around the sky.

More than a dozen cars were there, with the helicopter manoeuvring around, its main beam staying centred on its victim.

"Looks like Stewart was speeding," Jim joked.

"I can just imagine the scenario. The helicopter picked up Stewart's car following the Newcastle road. The roadblock was set up with armed police.

His car was forced to stop with the helicopter landing behind him and the armed response team jumping out. All seasoned officers with fire power.

Stewart dragged out and handcuffed. They'd find his weapon in the glove compartment and best of all, when they opened the boot, two sheep lying in there drugged. How sad."

Colburn smiled, "it's a serious crime round here, stealing sheep and armed robbery.

He'll have some questions to answer. Can you imagine, a senior Civil Servant being an armed robber and cattle rustler."

He looked at Jim, both broke out laughing.

"Something tells me his superiors won't take kindly to him being arrested. I think we can safely say his career may well be over. Hope he's paid enough into his pension fund," said Colburn, "now let's get home."

The early morning drive via Castleside, Consett, Lanchester then home, was uninteresting but pleasant.

Pulling up at Colburn's house, they picked up their kit and the artefacts and went inside.

"Think it's bedtime Jim," said Colburn, "take your usual room, see you later in the morning."

Jim noticed a note on the dining room table, signed Val.

Picking up the note he read, "will talk in the morning, have deciphered the engravings on the box. Have found an interesting story."

Colburn looked at Jim, "might have known she'd find something. No doubt all will be revealed in the morning. Good night Jim."

Colburn had slipped quietly into bed, only slightly disturbing Val.

Through a sleepy haze she mumbled, "everything go OK?"

"Fine, tell you about it in the morning," Colburn yawned.

Val turned on her side; "I've got a story for you as well, goodnight love."

The morning began with the aroma of bacon slowly being fried.

Val knew it was healthier to grill it but Jim and Colburn liked their bacon well done and crisp.

Two full English breakfasts waited as their noses led them downstairs, to the sumptuous meal of saturated fats and high cholesterol.

The sun was breaking through the few light clouds, its rays dancing off the monbretia and dahlias in the back garden. It may turn out to be a glorious day.

Val sat at the table with Colburn and Jim.

"I've just heard some local news on the radio," she said, "looks like there was a major incident just outside Newcastle last night. Sounds like there was a major criminal arrested, for armed robbery and sheep stealing."

Jim looked up, "every time the cost of living goes up, someone will always want to turn to stealing. Could fancy a couple of lamb chops myself."

Colburn laughed.

"I believe it was Colonel Stewart Val, he got caught by an armed response squad."

"I suppose you two had nothing to do with it?" she replied.

"Now what makes you say that," replied Colburn.

"Just that the report said, a senior Civil Servant had been caught with two sheep and was armed," said Val.

Jim and Colburn just burst out laughing.

Colburn put his knife and fork down, "imagine what Stewart must have thought, being stopped by armed officers, hauled out of his car, spread-eagled and handcuffed with a hairy SWAT policeman kneeling on his back."

Jim was reeling with laughter, "and imagine the surprise when they opened the boot and found two sheep drugged. I'd love to hear him explain that away."

Even Val had to break into a grin, "I don't know how you did it, and I really don't want to know."

Colburn sat up; "at least that's the end of him."

Val interrupted, "but not the end of this saga."

CHAPTER THIRTY

Jim looked across at Colburn, then at Val, "what do you mean, not the end?"

Val leaned back in her chair, "while you two were off enjoying yourselves, I was here trying to make sense of that box.

I realised that the carvings or etchings around the outside depicted some form of worship to whatever Gods they had.

That's fine I thought, there's many civilisations since, left drawings, paintings and statues to the Gods they worshipped.

Then I turned my attention to the inside.

Remember that pump we have for blowing up balloons, I used the suction part to extract all the white powder and it's there in that plastic bottle.

There's about twenty grams in weight."

"That'll be worth something then?" asked Jim.

"Not as much as the rest of the story." Val continued, "after getting out all the powder, I worked on the inside of the lid. It was covered in more carvings.

I brushed it all down and cleaned it up. It took me hours mind you.

Then I used a small needle to clean up the dirt from

the whole lid.

When I'd finished, I noticed several parts that appeared to stand out, protruding.

They're in the form of carvings on square pieces of wood.

I'll show you."

Val went into the extension.

Colburn and Jim left their breakfasts and followed.

She lifted the lid and started to describe what she had found.

"After I'd cleaned it up, these were what I noticed."

She moved her finger, pointing out the carvings one at a time.

"See what I mean, these ones seem to be sitting proud of the others."

Jim leaned over and examined the carvings.

Colburn looked over his shoulder.

"OK," said Jim, "I see what you mean, but what do they mean?"

"That's where the story starts," said Val.

"I thought that this may be the language the civilisation used and if it was, does it tell a story? So I checked all the ancient texts we have and I think this was a language from more than fifteen thousand years ago.

All we have is the most ancient Canaanite alphabet, perhaps even Proto-Canaanite or even before.

So I took those letters and tried to figure out what they would be in the present day alphabet.

I deciphered it through Phoenician, Aramaic, Syriac, through Greek and Latin to the present day."

Jim was becoming excitable, "do you mean there's another clue."

"If you look closely at these letters, I'll show you."

Val took a piece of paper and carefully copied the figures.

When she finished she put the paper in front of Colburn.

He stared at the paper.

"Fine, I can see your scribbling, can you decipher it?" asked Colburn.

"I'm sure I have," replied Val.

"The left hand one, looking like an omega sign is actually derived from the letter "S"

Next is the derivation of the letter "I"

The third and seventh, as crosses, are the letter "T"

The fourth, looking like a bird, is the letter "N"

The fifth and last letters, looking like cow's heads, are the letter "A"

The sixth one, like a big comma, is the letter "L"

"As far as I can tell, I've got the lettering right."

Jim again was looking puzzled, "OK, I can see there's lettering there but the question is, do they mean anything?"

Colburn was staring intently at the square areas of the lettering.

He went upstairs and returned with a small pointed steel needle that he used for pulling body hair from his artificial flies.

Starting at the first letter, looking like an Omega sign, he scraped a little more away from the edges. He soon realised that the square was protruding from the surface of the box. He continued with every letter, each one protruded from the surface.

"It certainly seems as if someone is trying to send us a message," said Colburn.

Val suddenly stood upright, her face beamed both with shock and surprise.

"Good God, I've just realised what this is."

"Are you going to let me in on it then?" asked Jim.

"Now take your time," said Colburn.

"Think about it you two, even to this day, some writings are done this way and certainly hundreds and thousands of years ago, it was done that way," Val said.

"What way?" asked Jim.

Val took a deep breath, "in those days, they wrote from Right to Left, just read the lettering that way."

Colburn pointed to the right-hand letter.

It was an "A"

The next was "T"

Then "L" "A" "N"

Another "T"

"Hell, am I seeing this right?" send Jim.

The last two letters were an "I" then an "S"

Colburn's lips quivered as he mouthed the word silently.

"Have we got this right?" he asked more in disbelief.

"I'm certain we have," Val replied.

The word spelt; ATLANTIS.

The three stood back, silent for a moment, trying to take in the enormity of the situation.

Val walked away back into the kitchen.

"I think we all need another cup of tea," she said, "and I wouldn't mind if sometime you'll fix that plug."

She made three cups with ample sugar and they all sat down around the table.

There was hardly a word spoken.

Jim started, "I always thought the stories about that place were myths and legends."

"The trouble is," said Val, "the legends have to start somewhere and sometimes you find they have their roots in truth. Words get distorted over the years and eventually the tales, which were only told by mouth, never written, only appear to be from the mists of time. Therefore in modern times, they could never be believed."

"So what do we do now?" asked Jim.

Colburn took a sip of tea, "we think harder than we've ever done before. If this originated from where we think, we have to ask the question, what do we do now?"

Jim piped up, "what do we do now? We have a box carved with an address, full of artefacts that made up a weapon or working tool. Have I got that bit right? It seems to me that whoever first made this lot, meant for people to know where it came from and if that is the case, in those early days someone knew where that was. So it's not legend any more, it's the truth. That place did exist."

Val was quietly musing over thoughts in her mind.

"Let's start with what is commonly known, or thought to be known, because there are no records or archaeology to verify its existence," she said.

"That's until now," replied Colburn.

"That's correct for now," said Val, "but you have to wonder a thousand years ago, if the secret was the artefacts or where they came from. I believe the Prince Bishops had some idea what they were guarding and only left those clues for a future generation.

A generation that would know how to use and control the power for the benefit of mankind and possibly the box and its artefacts were meant to be returned."

Jim sat up surprised, "returned where, to the Cathedral?" he said.

"No," replied Val, "returned to the place they came from, Atlantis."

Colburn gave a gasp, "no one knows where it is,"

Val looked at him, "I believe there's still more to find."

Jim groaned, "No there can't be."

Val continued with her appraisal of the history, "I think it's fair to assume that some form of knowledge was passed from Bishop to Bishop but eventually the original text was lost in translation, so to speak.

Therefore, we have to weigh up the "Fors" and "Againsts" of this situation.

Atlantis can be considered as one of the World's first mysteries.

Of course we know that it could have been the home to a fantastic civilisation, living in some sort of paradise, then demolished by a catastrophe and now it's who knows where.

However, there is the other point of view, that it is a figment of Plato's imagination, using it as a backdrop for his plays, Timaeus and Critias."

Jim interrupted, "but how can all this help us with our problem?"

Colburn replied, "to evaluate any problem, the correct facts and that means historical facts if there are any, need to be presented. Only when we have all the facts available, can we determine the next course of action."

Val was looking at them both, grimacing, "I'm trying to give you the background, so listen in.

According to the Greek, Plato, Atlantis was a sort of Paradise, an Eden.

The place was made up of mountains and plains, rivers, swamps and lakes, with a thriving population. It had mining operations for precious minerals, especially Orichalc, which to them was only second to Gold. They built temples, palaces, harbours and docks.

This could indicate they traded with other colonies.

It seemed the people had a leader structure and obeyed laws, living the good life.

There was supposed to be ample timber and elephants."

"Surely with elephants it would narrow the search area down a bit," said Jim.

"Unfortunately Jim, elephant fossil bones or the precursors of elephants have been found in many places around the world, not just where you expect elephants now," said Val.

"The thing is, it's alright having this supposed Utopia, if no one knows where it was," replied Jim.

Val said, "one of the first things to consider is the time line. The ancient Athenians thought it was only a thousand or so years before Plato. Then, according to him, they were supposed to govern the Egyptian area and that doesn't add up.

Egypt, as we know, existed for thousands of years before Christ. There have been no references to Atlantis in Egyptian folklore.

Now that tells me that if Atlantis existed, at least in that area, it must have been thousands of years before the Dynasties of Egypt began.

I'm sure if any Egyptian priest had known about Atlantis, he would have written or mentioned it somewhere.

In fact there is a Hopi Indian myth that describes Atlantis as a place of great cities, which was destroyed by a flood.

I found that quite interesting because some of the carvings on the box are extremely similar to Native Indian signs."

Jim sat bolt upright, "you're not saying Atlantis is in America are you?"

"Not at all," replied Val, "there's a lot of myths and legends from around the world that describe a great flood."

Colburn said, "what we do know for certain, we may at this point in time be the only ones who know that Atlantis is real, it did exist."

Val continued, "it certainly did exist and we have to sort out where. Some of the best brains in the world have tried to fathom it out, even psychics and supposed telepaths have had a go. All have up to this present time, failed. We have proved its existence and that is a better starting point than anyone else had."

"So can you summarise where it's supposed to be?" asked Jim.

"Well," started Val, "there are several different places thought to be the location of Atlantis. Most people think like Plato, that it is a sunken island somewhere in the Atlantic Ocean.

Others believe it's near the Greek islands of Crete or Santorini.

The earthquake there in 1956, disturbed quarry

workings and archaeologists found human remains, bones, teeth and pottery, that have been carbon-dated with the results supposedly pointing to thousands of years earlier, but who actually knows?

The Atlantic islands, Azores, Canaries or Madeira, have the appearance of sunken islands with mountain peaks rising straight out of the ocean."

"What's so special about that geography?" asked Jim.

Val continued, " in general the land of Atlantis was supposed to be open to the sea to the South, surrounded by mountains to the North.

They even had military establishments and wide canals.

Rings of land and water surrounded great walls, the outer one being eleven miles in diameter. This, of course, was all speculation on Plato's part.

An interesting development was a suggestion that part of the Caribbean area could be the location and it's probably worth pursuing."

"Why do you think that?" asked Colburn.

"Well, do you remember the stories of the psychic Edgar Cayce?" asked Val.

"They're pretty vague, but yes," replied Colburn.

"He predicted in the 1920's that Atlantis would rise again in 1968," said Val, "of course it didn't but there's an interesting tail to that story. Scuba divers have located flights of steps and monolithic stones suggesting underwater pyramids.

However, these finds are in the famous "Bermuda Triangle".

That's the area from Puerto Rico, Eastern Florida and

Bermuda, where we've all heard tales of disappearance. These seem to have a common link with malfunction of instrumentation, radio and radar not working and compasses spinning around.

This would verify the idea at the time that the people from Atlantis possessed laser power worked by large crystals and they would interfere with electronics."

Jim started laughing; "you're joking surely."

Val replied, "not at all. The theory that they had laser power was postulated decades before lasers become part of our technology.

You two have just verified that theory, they did indeed posses laser power."

Colburn and Jim looked at each other, their faces with an expression of near disbelief.

"Let me tie this up," said Val, "even though you've proved one theory, it still doesn't help with the location. Some have suggested Tiahuanaco in Peru, even though it's up in the mountains over thirteen thousand feet.

There are large buildings with walls ten-foot thick and two hundred-ton foundation stones. All constructed with the accuracy of the Egyptian pyramids.

Many people are convinced that the ones who built it were not from this planet."

Jim laughed again, "here we go, ET built it."

"Well," continued Val, "if you consider that it was built with such precision and discoveries from around the area seem to suggest it was at one time near sea level.

They've found lines of salt in the mountains and what may have been cornfields under the present snow line and to cap it all, seashells from the shoreline of Lake Titicaca.

All this evidence would suggest that that place was once a port on the Pacific, which was elevated into it's present location by volcanic activity and the melting glaciers, all in the region of fifteen thousand or more, years ago."

"That's fantastic," said Jim.

Colburn stroked his chin, an indication of thought preceding an evaluation of the situation.

He started to speak, "technology has advanced a hell of a lot recently. We can send men to the moon."

Jim interrupted, "allegedly."

"Point taken," replied Colburn, "probes into outer space and other planets but we really know very little about what's under the ocean or for that matter, above it."

Jim said, "We obviously have verified one theory but how about a sailing vessel that just goes missing, no way it's due to Atlantis."

Colburn looked at him, a little sadness on his face, "you saw the power of the laser we have. If that was trained on a ship, it would soon go under the waves."

Jim looked puzzled, "are you saying that someone is under there destroying ships and aircraft?"

"No," replied Colburn, "but I could believe that at some time, for whatever reason, the laser activates and causes havoc."

Val interjected, "let loose the dogs of war."

"Let's hope not," said Colburn.

"I really need to study the other markings on that box, perhaps try some assimilation with Indian signs," said Val.

"What has always been postulated is that humans migrated over the Ice Bridge from Russia to Canada and down into America.

Consider the reverse. Could there have been a population movement from America to Russia and then onwards into Asia and the Middle East?

What I really need is to check on is what is said to be the shape of the continents before ice ages and global warming.

I need to get an accurate as possible map of the earth, so we can see what the landmasses were or are, from about fifteen to twenty thousand years ago.

This should tell us where the possibilities are."

Jim leaned back again, "where this place is, possibly? Surely we'll only get the possibilities that we already know."

"Perhaps," replied Val, "but we have to start somewhere and I'm going back to that box. I'm sure that wasn't just created to hold those artefacts."

The three got up and slowly wandered into the extension, the box was lying on the bench.

Colburn leaned towards it, "come on darling, let me into your secret."

As he stared at the box lid, Val was busy making drawings of the signs.

Jim leaned on the bench at the other end of the box.

"I just think it's strange to have all these intricate carvings for those letters and have them protruding out of the base of the lid. Seems to me as if they've become displaced over the years."

He slowly traced out the rectangular shape around the first letter on the right with his forefinger. Then he repeated it with both forefingers. The area had been thoroughly cleaned by Val.

Without thinking he gently placed both his thumbs on the picture of the letter, apparently stroking it.

His rubber soled shoes slipped on the tiled floor as he leaned, resulting in a push on the letter.

It moved inward and all heard a faint click.

Val looked up, "what did you do Jim?" she asked.

Jim looked terrified.

"Nothing, I just pushed the letter a bit, I slipped."

Colburn stared at the letter. It had relocated itself flush with the box inner surface.

He wondered.

"Try it with the next letter Jim," he said.

Jim with shaking hands placed his thumbs over the second letter and pushed.

It moved in.

"Do it with them all," said Colburn.

Jim pushed each in turn spelling out the name.

Each time a faint click was heard.

The last letter, Jim was apprehensive.

"You do this one will you?" he asked Colburn.

He took up a position behind Colburn, watching his movement.

Colburn gently pushed on the last letter.

It moved inwards, a faint click was heard. Then a section of the inner lid, about four feet by one, popped out.

Val, Colburn and Jim stood back and stared.

"Get me a plastic spatula," Colburn asked and Val obtained one from a kitchen drawer.

"I'm going to see if this section levers right out," he said.

He inserted the sharp end of the spatula into the crevice that had appeared and levered downwards.

The section began to move.

Inserting the spatula into the opposite side, he levered there.

Suddenly the whole section moved and fell out into Colburn's hands.

Reacting swiftly, he caught the wooden section and gently placed it to one side.

Val and Jim were staring at the space in the lid.

Colburn at first just glanced, then he saw what the others were looking at, and he gasped, "it's a triptych."

What he was seeing was a three-part picture.

From the right was a conglomeration of symbols, the centrepiece contained symbols with several pictorial views but the last picture on the left, was definitely a geographical map.

Val stood back and went for her Olympus FE 120 camera.

She took photos of the whole section and then the three sections separately.

Colburn and Jim still looked in amazement.

He shouted through to the room to Val, "what have we got here, or is it what I think it is?"

Jim started to become excited, "what do you think it is?" he said.

"I don't know what those symbols mean, perhaps Val can decipher those but I'm pretty sure that is a map of Atlantis."

He was pointing to the left-hand picture.

"You mean that could tell us exactly where it was?" asked Jim.

"Nothing's as simple as it looks Jim. That may well be the actual area of Atlantis in the days when this box was crafted. Geography has changed the continents since then."

Jim asked with a slightly puzzled look, "does this mean we still don't know where it was?"

"Val might come up with something if she can decipher those symbols," said Colburn "but for now I'm putting this wood section back in and covering this up. Don't want anyone seeing this, not just yet anyway."

Val had downloaded the pictures onto her computer and began to examine them.

"I can only do one at a time but I think we need to decipher the symbols first.

What is confusing me, is the central part contains old lettering and symbols that seem more akin to Native American. So before we look at the alleged map, I need to try and work out what this says. You never know it just might tell us where it is.

So for now, you two make the tea."

Colburn and Jim went into the kitchen to make tea and toast. They both knew when Val was working, not to disturb her line of thought.

Colburn said to Jim, "we need to work out something for the future. Obviously we can't keep all this, it will have to be returned, somewhere."

Jim looked a little sheepish, "you mean we have to give back the gold claw and the ruby?"

"I'm afraid so Jim, I'm sure we'll get some finders fee," said Colburn, "but not that box. We'll keep that, after all, if someone gets the treasure that should keep them happy. I think that box will be useful to us in the future."

Val was studying the photos intensively on her laptop. Scribbling frantically, making notes and checking them with her text books.

She relaxed a little, attempting to assimilate the script into some form of order.

Starting the right hand picture symbols, she started to describe the scenario.

"What I think we have here is three historical sections. The one I'm working on seems to be a history of the area, the centre piece was the present time when the box was made and the third picture is a pictorial map."

Jim perked up, "you're saying we have a map of where Atlantis was?"

"It's not as simple as that Jim," replied Val.

"Never is," said Jim.

"From what I can make out, the history begins with these symbols, which are similar to Native American," Val continued pointing out the separate lettering.

Those eagle type feathers indicate the chief or headman, the next are morning stars followed by an arrow, remembering right to left.

This could translate as the chief or head of the civilisation came from the skies to give guidance and protection."

"I knew it," said Jim excitedly, "the ancients were extra-terrestrial."

"Maybe yes, maybe no," said Val, "there's nothing here to prove that point.

The letters continue with the Hogan sign, then

461

running water followed by deer tracks and raindrops. This should mean the permanent home and happiness gave constant life with ample crops and game, or words to that effect.

However it continues, with the symbol of night and day, then running water followed by lightening and a lightening arrow, then this symbol of a man and an arrow with a cross.

I can only deduce that this meant, at some time running water, swiftly left man with no protection. There may be other ways to interpret it, but that is one."

Colburn sat thinking, "that could fall into place with the suggestion of a catastrophic event."

No," said Val, "I don't think it was a flood. I think it was definitely rising water but over a period of time. They were losing their homeland to water."

Colburn said, "so it could have been just global warming of the ice cap, making sea levels rise. In those days, ice sheets locked up much of the world's water, lowering the oceans leaving vast coastal plains. Then the ice melted."

"You're probably right," said Val, "but if you look at the second picture graphics, it is seemingly telling us about their present day. Or how it seemed to them.

The first is this oak twig followed by the morning skies and those two arrows pointing toward each other. This means they summoned the holy ones for guidance hoping to ward off evil spirits.

Now there's an arrow, running water and what looks like a tepee.

This means that for protection and constant life they needed a temporary home.

The bags and the horse, indicate a journey, this is followed by a man, eagle and band of sky. That could indicate that a journey is needed to find life, freedom and happiness.

The next line shows a mountain range, a fence and a house of water.

The first means destination or it could say our destination must be guarded from the increase in water.

Interestingly enough the last line tells us where they went."

"This is the bit I've been waiting for," said Jim, rubbing his hands together.

"Don't get your hopes up Jim," said Val, "that first cross, then mountain range, cactus and day and night sign, does not say where they went. This means that many paths were crossed over mountains and desert, taking an immeasurable amount of time.

The last symbol of this sequence tells us, what I believe to be the important fact of all these symbols, the one of a circle with those two wavy lines across the diameter. This indicates the four ages of man, from birth to death. Infant, youth, middle and old age.

It is trying to tell us that their journey will take many paths, probably different directions. It's likely they split up and went in different directions looking for a new homeland and they knew it would take several lifetimes."

Val actually wiped a tear from her eye, "this story is sad and beautiful, an advanced society living happy and content for generations. Then the ice melts and they have to move, not knowing where to go, they split up and wandered."

Colburn leaned over and gave her a hug; "it is a beautiful story. What we have here is probably the first intelligent humanoids, wherever they came from originally. Living an idyllic lifestyle in a land of plenty."

Jim butted in, "do we still not know where that land was?"

"Not yet," replied Val, "global warming is not a new feature, it's happened many times during the existence of this planet. What I would like to check on, is the migration that took place. There's plenty of DNA evidence from thousands of years ago, about migratory patterns.

If we consider the third picture, that may give us a clue."

The three stared intently at the third picture Val brought up on the computer screen.

Jim pointed to a central feature; "this surely is common to a lot of societies."

He was pointing to a pyramid shape that seemed to have an eye on the apex and from this was radiating light or heat.

Colburn smiled, "maybe they were the first Freemasons but I think that designates laser light from the pyramid. They could have used it for street lighting or more likely warming up the area."

Jim said, "so in fact, with warming the area, they could have artificially created atmospheric conditions that eventually melted snow. They could have brought about their own downfall."

"Anything's possible," said Val, "but the rest of the drawing certainly fits in with what was thought to be true.

There are mountains on the far horizon with a

shoreline up front, possibly good arable and grazing land in between.

I can't make out the land shape from this picture. Obviously time and tide has taken its toll, so the borders that are showing there are not the borders we have now.

I'll have to try and find some global map from thousands of years ago, even those are partly guesswork."

Val stood up and went to her stock of reference books.

Colburn was musing over the map.

"It's always been postulated that humans migrated out of Central Africa to Europe, Asia, even Australia and America.

In fact DNA lineage found in Europe, supposed people reached the Great Lakes area around fourteen or fifteen thousand years ago. Why not the reverse?

There is not one shred of evidence to say that these Atlantean people ever existed, apart from now.

So with water levels rising, flooding into their homelands, they migrated in all directions.

Therefore using reverse logic, the groups split up and migrated. Some probably over the ice bridges, others along the permafrost line, others just followed the sun.

Most of the continents' landmass was passable by foot or simple boats.

So what I am postulating is that these people went in different directions all over the passable world at that time and settled.

Wherever they settled, over the following thousands of years, they became integrated with the humanoid population.

Then at some time, the migration from Africa began, that started off the human population as we know it."

"That's one hell of a theory," said Jim.

"These people were technically advanced, the only reason for that technical ability to be lost, is that there were no raw materials or the wrong raw materials," said Colburn.

"Eventually if things don't get made, they get forgotten, lost, and in time they become myths and legends. The original lands forgotten in the mists of time, surviving only in the minds and words of Oracles.

Val came over to the table with her books.

She printed out a copy of the photograph she took of the third picture, sizing it down to the same dimensions as a global map she had in her book.

Taking a pair of scissors, she cut out the section of the land and started to try and place it on the global map.

It was turned in all directions.

Colburn and Jim leaned over her shoulder.

She was constantly shaking her head.

Then she turned back a page.

This map seemed to indicate the world's shape about sixty thousand years ago.

She tried the picture in all directions on that map.

Suddenly she stopped and leaned back in her chair.

Jim and Colburn could see why.

"It's nearly a perfect fit," gasped Jim.

"Need to double check," said Val.

She opened another textbook, this one was defining just one geographical area.

Re-sizing a print of the map, she began placing the cut out on the new map.

After a few, twists and turns, re-orientating the cut out, she stopped.

The drawing from the box fit with over 95% accuracy to the area of her map.

Within standard deviation limits, she had just located the origin of the box and Atlantis.

Colburn gave her a hug, then hugged Jim.

"Between us we've just figured out one of the world's mysteries," he said, "and I can see now why it was appropriate for the Prince Bishops to have this secret."

Jim looked in amazement at the positioning of the map. Mountains to the North, sea to the South, plenty of good land in between.

"Jesus Christ," he said, "they were all Geordies."

Val started to check the salient point on the map.

The landmass was certainly connected to the now mainland of Europe.

No North Sea, just arable and probably fertile lands.

The mountains in the far distance stretched from South Norway connecting through Scotland and Most of England. The ice cap was from the mountains and beyond and this was what caused the migration with its melting.

Ample seashore to the South, for trading and fishing.

This area stretched from the British shore to Scandinavia and well into the European countries.

She stopped over the pyramid, trying to decide where that was in context.

"When the ice melted and the sea levels increased, all this area was flooded," she said, drawing a line around with her finger. "Everyone living there had to move.

Some would travel into Europe and beyond, others would trace the edge of the ice pack and travel west.

This exact place here is where the pyramid would be."

She took a pencil and marked the spot through the paper.

Taking away the paper, they all looked at the mark on the map underneath.

"So that's where the centre of their intelligence was situated," said Colburn, "we've always been on the right track."

"Told you," said Jim, "I always knew we were special."

EPILOGUE.

Four Months later.

Colburn yawned as he sat in his reclining chair.

Outside the sun was shining through a few fluffy white clouds, perfect conditions for fly-fishing. The trout would be moving for the fly although the big sea trout would only be coaxed in the evening or during the night.

He picked up the local newspaper and began to read the article about the Carol Service in the Cathedral.

It seemed that the Bishop had arrived and was just taking his stance in the pulpit, when he saw a large object wrapped in brown paper.

Waiting until the service was over, he had called the police in, just in case it turned out suspicious. They called in the Ordnance Corps from Catterick and when it was finally decided it looked safe, they opened it to find a rectangular plastic case and inside was a golden claw.

The accompanying note said, "this is part of the Cathedral treasure, please accept my apologies for not returning it sooner.

P.S. the case is vacuum-sealed. I strongly suggest you keep this under vacuum."

It was placed as an exhibit in the Cathedral along with other artefacts from the original church.

The article continued by saying the police would like to get in touch with the unknown benefactor.

"I bet they would," thought Colburn.

They had decided not to give the British Museum anything. What was found in Durham, would stay in Durham.

"Want a bacon sandwich?" shouted Val from the kitchen.

"Better make a few, Jim's coming up soon," he replied.

Jim had got back to riding his mower around the golf course.

The new fairway was up and running and the members were duly hacking it to bits every round.

Colburn had been in touch, via his contacts, with certain jewel experts in Amsterdam.

The ruby was worth a few pounds, several million in fact.

No one really needed it for a laser and its original use was best kept quiet.

In fact where it came from, no one knew, except it wasn't stolen.

The jewellery industry had asked a few questions about who had cut the facets but as they were going to make a profit, answers were not essential.

So the money was eventually paid into the Lord's bank account, which was left to accumulate interest. Apart from Jim's share.

Val put half a dozen crisp bacon sandwiches on the table just as Jim walked in.

"Your timing's immaculate Jim," said Val.

"I could taste these down home," replied Jim.

"How's the new car going?" asked Val.

"Like a dream," said Jim.

Some of his money had gone towards exchanging his old car for a brand new Ford.

He was never extravagant with money, apart from the fact he'd bought the land the golf course was on, so he could keep the membership private.

Eating into the sandwiches, Colburn and Jim were munching away, talking as if they were baboons in the trees.

"Can't you two eat first, instead of talking with your mouth full?" shouted Val.

Colburn nodded, "you got those old maps on you?"

Jim replied, "in my pocket."

"Need to see if they match up," said Colburn.

"After brunch," replied Jim.

Val brought out the tea and sat with them.

"Well, where do we go from here?" asked Val, "it's been a hell of a few months."

Jim smiled and looked up from his sandwich, picking up his mug of tea he said, "I've got some information that appears interesting," as he pulled a few folded papers from his pocket.

"It seems during the surveys for North Sea oil and gas, these maps were made.

They show quite conclusively sections of undersea land that could be buildings but what is certain, they show waterways or rivers."

Val and Colburn scanned the maps intensely.

She pointed out the suspected rivers and said, "you

need to overlay them with the current geography and see if you can match them up.

We know exactly where the centre was, let's see if we can determine the area."

"I don't know," said Colburn.

"We've been through a lot to get this far and we've done OK.

The Cathedral has its treasure back, plus the archaeology still ongoing.

It's made the Castle and Cathedral even more famous and tourists are flocking in, helping the local economy. What more could they ask for?

When you think that it was probably through ancient Oracles that the box and its contents were kept from humans. Carried away from here when that group of Atlanteans migrated in the European direction, then used as a building tool. You never know maybe for the Egyptian pyramids and no doubt for warfare.

Those wandering people, God knows where they settled. Obviously some perhaps around Santorini, others in Mesopotamia and far beyond that. They might even have made it across the pond and down into South America, in time. Perhaps the civilisations that we know about today sprang up from these wanderers. They knew how to build canals and pyramids, maybe they taught the locals. Perhaps they built some of the strange buildings we still have above ground and under the sea. During the passage of time, their knowledge became diluted and was eventually lost. Whatever remained was never meant to be misused, so someone was instructed to locate it and hide those artefacts. Possibly through the Norsemen, it ends up in Durham as part of the Cathedral treasure. It's hidden away, the secret passed from Bishop to Bishop, then eventually hidden and forgotten.

Then we have all the clues leading through history and across the pond, which we found and solved. I think we did quite well.

A bit of money for the ruby, the Griffin claw's back in the Cathedral and the box safely tucked away in the loft."

"That's something I meant to ask about," said Val, "whatever happened to those rods and the stones?"

"Easy," replied Colburn, "the stones are in the greenhouse supporting a couple of large plant pots. They shouldn't cause any problems there."

"And the rods?" asked Val.

Colburn leaned up and smiled, "I welded a ring of metal to the top."

"What for?" asked Val.

"I've made it into a new landing net. Every time I go fishing, it reminds me of the fun we had getting it."

Jim laughed, "you've got the Rod of Moses as a landing net?"

"If it was good enough for him to part the waters, it's good enough for me to land the trout," replied Colburn.

"Then you better not go fishing in a thunderstorm," said Val.

"I suppose that's one way of catching trout, electrify the water," joked Colburn.

"I wonder if the Atlanteans went fishing?" asked Jim.

"Even the Romans tied flies," replied Colburn, "with their expertise, I reckon they shot laser light at them."

"Straight out of the water, already cooked," said Jim.

Even Val started laughing.

I'll get the maps up on the computer," she said.

Bringing up a large map of the North Sea area, they overlaid the maps Jim had brought.

Using a pencil, Colburn traced the alleged waterways at the bottom of the sea, backward towards land.

It soon became apparent that it may have to be guesswork or logical deduction, as to where they may have originated.

The difference was, they had a drawing of the original area of Atlantis, some appearing to show land and waterways.

Val got her drawing of the Atlantis area.

It wasn't long before they could match up a few waterways with the geological survey map and then track back to the present landfall.

Val added all the detail to her computer map.

Then they stood back and looked with amazement at what appeared on the screen.

"Can you insert the placement of that pyramid?" asked Colburn.

Val ran the mouse over the screen and clicked.

"I reckon it was right there, plus or minus a few feet," she joked.

Jim looked and said, "what is that placement now?"

Val clicked the mouse a few times and the present geography appeared with the placement of the pyramid.

Colburn started to stroke his chin, thinking.

"That's a sign of trouble when he does that," remarked Jim.

"What we need now, are the old maps from the

National Coal Board, or whatever it is now. If we overlay the mine workings, we should see if they follow a logical pattern."

Jim said, "surely they just followed the coal seams."

"That's what you would expect but we need to follow the deep sea coal workings.

They should follow the seams of coal but I think they'll be either side of those riverbeds. That's where the forested areas would be and therefore the coal.

That coal would have been there in the time of Atlantis, if the miners never found any artefacts, it gives us a negative area in the search. The more we can rule out, the quicker it will be."

"The quicker what will be?" asked Val.

Colburn turned his head and smiled, "the quicker we'll find Atlantis."

"No way," said Val, "I'm not going underground or undersea, you can forget it.

Those coal seams will be flooded by now."

"We might not have to," said Jim, pointing at the map on the screen, "now we have the centre, everything else emanates from there. We have the central point of Atlantis. The seams will only be partly flooded, should be able to navigate them by dinghy.

"I agree," said Colburn, "how about we start in the spring?

No one would ever think of looking there."

AUTHOR'S COMMENTS.

First of all I would like to apologise to the Bishop of Durham for, in a literal sense,

"damaging some of his property."

While this story is entirely a work of fiction, it is based on several factual events, great buildings and works of art.

Alexander the Great did eventually defeat the Persian Army and a provincial governor had King Darius murdered. Ptolomy took charge in Egypt, beginning that long family dynasty. Alexander died in Babylon under mysterious circumstances at a young age.

Whether the power, or firepower of the Persians was hidden for eternity, remains questionable.

The Varangian Guard of Norsemen served around the Byzantium area for many years, becoming well known as fierce warriors. When their service was completed, they were allowed to take Palace plunder away with them.

Eric Bloodaxe did become Viking King at York and also died under mysterious circumstances on Stainmoor.

The wandering monks of Chester-Le-Street, were the guardians of any treasure and the Lindisfarne Gospels saved from there when the Vikings attacked.

They wandered all around the North of England for

a couple of centuries before settling on the Dun Holme or Durham, the site of the now world famous Castle and Cathedral.

In 1346, the Battle of Nevilles Cross took place.

The Scots camped near to Bear Park and the English around Hett Village.

The previous day, some of the forward battalions of the Scots were routed at the Battle of Butcher's Race. The family De Hertburn and then Wessington of the Old Hall, were ancestors of George Washington.

It is probable that any treasure would have been removed from the Cathedral at that time.

The Prince Bishops were formidable people, ruling over the area by the King's command. Many of them built great monuments and additions to the Castle and Cathedral.

The description of the Cathedral interior is as exact as I could be. The Bell Tower of the Cathedral was said to have been destroyed by lightening, perhaps!

The Mason Dixon line is as famous in England as it is in America. Dixon was a local lad and the description of his work around the world is historically accurate. As to whether he ever met Jefferson and Washington is unknown.

The Lindisfarne Gospels are held in the British library and that is a sore point in Durham, as they would like them to be returned. The pages described are factual but as to whether any code was written on then, is a figment of my imagination. Or is it?

The Royal Army Medical College sadly does not teach junior doctors and laboratory technicians any more. It appears that Tri-Service learning is cheaper these days. I do believe, however, the layout and workings of the original college are precise. Today it is part of the University of London and an Arts College.

In my personal opinion, a sad demise to an excellent centre of medical and scientific learning and research. I wonder what Porton Down does without this place?

I personally, have never been into the Durham Castle wine cellar but I live in hope.

The copy of the Magna Carta held in the National Archives in Washington did originally come from nobility in Wales. How they first came to own it, is unclear.

At the time of the Dissolution of the Monasteries, the King's Commissioners found no treasure in Durham Cathedral. The charter could have been removed then and given to the Welsh nobility at a later date. It would have been possible to write on its reverse at the time it was in Durham. The actual treasure has never been found, or has it?

Washington is a fantastic city. You can literally walk and visit most of the major attractions. I would certainly encourage anyone to visit this city.

The directions given in this book are accurate and the attractions along the Mall are numerous. I certainly recommend visiting the National Archives, even if you have to queue for a while. Their copy of the Magna Carta is still there, apparently undisturbed.

The description of Durham Castle follows fairly

precisely, the route which any guide would take. I hope that the details I have inserted will give you the urge to visit here.

Both the Castle and Cathedral as World Heritage Sites, have no equal in all of Britain.

There does appear to be an old Well at the side of the Castle Green.

Whether excavations under the Green would reveal a labyrinth of tunnels and an ancient place of worship is unknown.

Once again, my apologies to the Bishopric for digging up their property.

Crude lasers were made from light passing through a ruby.

Housesteads Roman Fort on Hadrian's Wall is another site well worth visiting.

My description of the immediate area is accurate and with Army training you can hide or attack on any terrain.

So I ask myself, could there have been such an advanced race of humanoids on this Earth, many thousands of years before the races of people we know now?

The answer is, yes. It may have been possible to sustain these life forms with their advanced technical knowledge. Those people could have split from their main centre of society due to adverse conditions and settled in other parts of the globe. Without the raw materials they required, their form of existence would have died out, to be replaced with a more simple form of life over the centuries. These people eventually became the Human Race. However, it is possible that the migrations of species we know could have been in any direction. From Africa to Europe and its fertile lands is definitely conceivable but what if the migration in the West was from America to Asia and not the other way?

Whether the fabled Atlantis ever existed is of course debatable. Or did my heroes actually find the evidence.

Watch Colburn Lord fly-fishing, you might just see a lightening rod.

Lightning Source UK Ltd.
Milton Keynes UK
08 October 2009

144699UK00001B/3/P